WILLIAM FAULKNER

THE
REIVERS

William Faulkner, one of the greatest writers of the twentieth century, was born in New Albany, Mississippi, on September 25, 1897. He published his first book, *The Marble Faun*, a collection of poems, in 1924, but it is as a literary chronicler of life in the Deep South —particularly in the fictional Yoknapatawpha County, the setting for several of his novels—that he is most highly regarded. In such novels as *Sanctuary* (1931), *The Hamlet* (1940), *The Town* (1957), and *The Mansion* (1959), he explored the full range of post–Civil War Southern life, focusing both on the personal histories of his characters (especially members of the Snopes family) and on the moral uncertainties of an increasingly dissolute society. His other novels include *The Sound and the Fury* (1929), *As I Lay Dying* (1930), *Light in August* (1932), *Absalom, Absalom!* (1936), *The Unvanquished* (1938), *Intruder in the Dust* (1948), *Requiem for a Nun* (1951), *A Fable* (1954), and *The Reivers* (1962). For the latter two books, he was awarded the Pulitzer Prize. He also wrote several volumes of short stories as well as collections of poems and essays.

In combining the use of symbolism with a stream-of-consciousness technique, he created a new approach to the writing of fiction. In 1949 he was awarded the Nobel Prize for Literature.

William Faulkner died in Byhalia, Mississippi, on July 6, 1962.

VINTAGE

INTERNATIONAL

BOOKS BY *William Faulkner*
AVAILABLE FROM VINTAGE

Absalom, Absalom!
As I Lay Dying
Collected Stories
A Fable
Flags in the Dust
Go Down, Moses
The Hamlet
Intruder in the Dust
Knight's Gambit
Light in August
The Mansion
Pylon
The Reivers
Requiem for a Nun
Sanctuary
Selected Letters of William Faulkner
The Sound and the Fury
Three Famous Short Novels:
Spotted Horses, Old Man, The Bear
The Town
The Uncollected Stories of William Faulkner
The Unvanquished
The Wild Palms

THE
REIVERS

◆◆◆◆

THE
REIVERS

A Reminiscence

◆◆◆◆

WILLIAM FAULKNER

VINTAGE INTERNATIONAL • VINTAGE BOOKS

A DIVISION OF RANDOM HOUSE, INC. • NEW YORK

FIRST VINTAGE INTERNATIONAL EDITION, SEPTEMBER 1992

Library of Congress Cataloging-in-Publication Data
Faulkner, William, 1897-1962.
The reivers: a reminiscence / William Faulkner. — 1st Vintage
International ed.
p.   cm.
ISBN 0-679-74192-5
I. Title.
[PS3511.A86R388   1992]
813'.52—dc20   92-50095
CIP

Manufactured in the United States of America
79B8

THE
REIVERS

◆◆◆◆

1

◆◆◆◆

GRANDFATHER SAID:

This is the kind of a man Boon Hogganbeck was. Hung on the wall, it could have been his epitaph, like a Bertillon chart or a police poster; any cop in north Mississippi would have arrested him out of any crowd after merely reading the date.

It was Saturday morning, about ten oclock. We—your great-grandfather and I—were in the office, Father sitting at the desk totting up the money from the canvas sack and matching it against the list of freight bills which I had just collected around the Square; and I sitting in the chair against the wall waiting for noon when I would be paid my Saturday's (week's) wage of ten cents and we would go home and eat dinner and I would be free at last to overtake (it was May) the baseball game which had been running since breakfast without me: the idea (not mine: your great-grandfather's) being that even at eleven a man should already have behind him one year of paying for, assuming responsibility for, the space he occupied, the room he took up, in the world's (Jefferson, Mississippi's, anyway) economy. I would leave home with Father immediately after breakfast each Saturday morning, when all the other boys on the street were merely arming themselves with balls and bats and gloves —not to mention my three brothers, who, being younger and therefore smaller than I, were more fortunate, assuming this was Father's logic or premise: that since any adult man worth his salt could balance or stand off four children in economic occupancy, any one of the children, the largest certainly, would suffice to carry the burden of the requisite economic motions: in this case, making the rounds each Saturday morning with the bills for the boxes and cases of freight which our Negro drivers had picked up at the depot during the week and delivered to the back doors of the grocery and hardware and farmers' supply stores, and bring the canvas sack back to the livery stable for Father to count and balance it, then sit in the office for the rest of the morning ostensibly to answer the telephone—this for the sum of ten cents a week, which it was assumed I would live inside of.

That's what we were doing when Boon came jumping through the door. That's right. Jumping. It was not really a high step up from the hallway, even for a boy of eleven (though John Powell, the head hostler, had had Son Thomas, the youngest driver, find, borrow, take— anyway, snaffle—from somewhere a wooden block as an intermediate step for me), and Boon could have taken it as he always did in his own six-foot-four stride. But not this time: jumping into the room. In its normal state his face never looked especially gentle or composed; at

this moment it looked like it was about to explode right
out from between his shoulders with excitement, urgency,
whatever it was, jumping on across the office toward the
desk and already hollering at Father: "Look out, Mr
Maury, get out of the way," reaching, lunging across
Father toward the lower drawer where the livery-stable
pistol lived; I couldn't tell whether it was Boon lunging
for the drawer who knocked the chair (it was a swivel
chair on casters) back or whether it was Father who flung
the chair back to make himself room to kick at Boon's
reaching hand, the neat stacks of coins scattering in all
directions across the desk and Father hollering too now,
still stomping either at the drawer or Boon's hand or
maybe both:

"God damn it, stop it!"

"I'm going to shoot Ludus!" Boon hollered. "He's probably clean across the Square by now! Look out, Mr
Maury!"

"No!" Father said. "Get away!"

"You won't let me have it?" Boon said.

"No, God damn it," Father said.

"All right," Boon said, already jumping again, back
toward the door and out of it. But Father just sat there.
I'm sure you have often noticed how ignorant people
beyond thirty or forty are. I dont mean forgetful. That's
specious and easy, too easy to say *Oh papa* (or grandpa)
or *mama* (or grandma), *they're just old; they have forgotten.* Because there are some things, some of the hard
facts of life, that you dont forget, no matter how old you
are. There is a ditch, a chasm; as a boy you crossed it
on a footlog. You come creeping and doddering back
at thirty-five or forty and the footlog is gone; you may
not even remember the footlog but at least you dont step
out onto that empty gravity that footlog once spanned.
That was Father then. Boon came jumping without warn-

ing into the office and almost knocked Father chair and all over, grabbling at the drawer where the pistol was, until Father managed to kick or stomp or whatever it was his hand away, then Boon turned and went jumping back out of the office and apparently, obviously, Father thought that was all of it, that it was finished. He even finished cursing, just on principle, as though there were no urgency anywhere, heeling the chair back to the desk and seeing the scattered money which would have to be counted all over now, and then he started to curse at Boon again, not even about the pistol but simply at Boon for being Boon Hogganbeck, until I told him.

"He's gone to try to borrow John Powell's," I said.

"What?" Father said. Then he jumped too, both of us, across the office and down into the hallway and down the hallway toward the lot behind the stable where John Powell and Luster were helping Gabe, the blacksmith, shoe three of the mules and one of the harness horses, Father not even taking time to curse now, just hollering "John! Boon! John! Boon!" every three steps.

But he was too late this time too. Because Boon fooled him—us. Because John Powell's pistol was not just a moral problem in the stable, it was an emotional one too. It was a .41 caliber snub-nosed revolver, quite old but in excellent condition because John had kept it that way ever since he bought it from his father the day he was twenty-one years old. Only, he was not supposed to have it. I mean, officially it did not exist. The decree, as old as the stable itself, was that the only pistol connected with it would be the one which stayed in the bottom right-hand drawer of the desk in the office, and the mutual gentlemen's assumption was that no one on the staff of the establishment even owned a firearm from the time he came on duty until he went back home, let alone brought one to work with him. Yet—and John had explained it to all of us and had our confederated sympathy and understanding, a unified and impregnable front to the world and even to Father himself if that unimaginable crisis had ever arisen, which it would not have except for Boon Hogganbeck—telling us (John) how he had earned the price of the pistol by doing outside work on his own time, on time apart from helping his father on the farm, time which was his own to spend eating or sleeping, until on his twenty-first birthday he had paid the final coin into his father's hand and received the pistol; telling us how the pistol was the living symbol of his manhood, the ineffaceable proof that he was now twenty-one and a man; that he never intended to, declined even to imagine the circumstance in which he would ever, pull its trigger against a human being, yet he must have it with him; he would no more have left the pistol at home when he came away than he would have left his manhood in a distant closet or drawer when he came to work; he told us (and we believed him) that if the moment ever came when he would have to choose between leaving the pistol at home, or not coming to work himself, there would have been but one possible choice for him.

So at first his wife had stitched a neat strong pocket exactly fitting the pistol on the inside of the bib of his overalls. But John himself realised at once that this wouldn't do. Not that the pistol might fall out at some irretrievable moment, but that the shape of it was obvious through the cloth; it couldn't have been anything else but a pistol. Obvious not to us: we all knew it was there, from Mr Ballott, the white stable foreman, and Boon, his assistant (whose duty was night duty and so he should have been at home in bed at this moment), on down through all the Negro drivers and hostlers, down to the last lowly stall cleaner and even to me, who only collected the Saturday accumulation of freight bills and answered

the telephone. On even to old Dan Grinnup, a dirty man
with a tobacco-stained beard, who was never quite completely drunk, who had no official position in the stable,
partly because of the whiskey maybe but mostly because
of his name, which was not Grinnup at all but Grenier:
one of the oldest names in the county until the family
went to seed—the Huguenot Louis Grenier who crossed
the mountains from Virginia and Carolina after the Revo-
lution and came down into Mississippi in the seventeen
nineties and established Jefferson and named it—who
(old Dan) lived nowhere (and had no family save an
idiot nephew or cousin or something still living in a tent
in the river jungle beyond Frenchman's Bend which had
once been a part of the Grenier plantation) until he
(old Dan) would appear, never too drunk to drive it, at
the stable in time to take the hack to the depot and meet
the 9:30 P.M. and the 4:12 A.M. trains and deliver the
drummers to the hotel, or on duty all night sometimes
when there were balls or minstrel or drama shows at
the opera house (at times, at some cold and scornful
pitch of drink, he would say that once Greniers led
Yoknapatawpha society; now Grinnups drove it), holding
his job, some said, because Mr Ballott's first wife had
been his daughter, though we in the stable all believed
it was because when Father was a boy he used to fox
hunt with old Dan's father out at Frenchman's Bend.

Obvious (the pistol) not only to us but to Father himself. Because Father knew about it too. He had to know
about it; our establishment was too small, too intricate,
too closely knit. So Father's moral problem was exactly
the same as John Powell's, and both of them knew it
and handled it as mutual gentlemen must and should: if
Father were ever compelled to acknowledge the pistol
was there, he would have to tell John either to leave it at
home tomorrow, or not come back himself. And John

knew this and, a gentlemen too, he himself would never be the one to compel Father to acknowledge the pistol existed. So, instead of in the overall bib, John's wife stitched the pocket just under the left armpit of the jumper itself, invisible (anyway unobtrusive) when John was wearing the jumper or when in warm weather (like now) the jumper hung on John's private nail in the harness room. That was the situation of the pistol when Boon, who was being paid to be and who in a sense had given his word that he would be at home in bed at this hour instead of hanging around the Square, where he would be vulnerable to what had sent him rushing back to the stable, came jumping through the office door a minute ago and made Father and John Powell both liars.

Only Father was too late again. Boon fooled him—us. Because Boon knew about that nail in the harness room too. And smart too, too smart to come back up the hallway where he would have to pass the office; when we reached the lot John and Luster and Gabe (the three mules and the horse too) were still watching the still-swinging side gate through which Boon had just vanished, carrying the pistol in his hand. John and Father looked at each other for about ten seconds while the whole edifice of *entendre-de-noblesse* collapsed into dust. Though the *noblesse,* the *oblige,* still remained.

"It was mine," John said.

"Yes," Father said. "He saw Ludus on the Square."

"I'll catch him," John said. "Take it away from him too. Say the word."

"Catch Ludus, somebody," Gabe said. Though short, he was a tremendously big man, bigger than Boon, with a terrifically twisted leg from an old injury in his trade; he would pick up the hind foot of a horse or mule and lock it behind the warped knee and (if there was something—a post—anything—for him to hold to) the horse or mule might throw itself but no more: neither snatch that foot free nor get enough balance to kick him with the other one. "Here, Luster, you jump and catch—"

"Aint nobody studying Ludus," John said. "Ludus the safest man there. I seen Boon Hogganbeck"—he didn't say Mister and he knew Father heard him: something he would never have failed to do in the hearing of any white man he considered his equal, because John was a gentleman. But Father was competent for *noblesse* too: it was that pistol which was unforgivable, and Father knew it—"shoot before. Say the word, Mr Maury."

"No," Father said. "You run to the office and telephone Mr Hampton." (That's right. A Hampton was sheriff then too.) "Tell him I said to grab Mr Boon as quick as he can." Father went toward the gate.

"Go with him," Gabe told Luster. "He might need somebody to run for him. And latch that gate."

So the three of us went up the alley toward the Square, me trotting now to keep up, not really trying to overtake Boon so much as to stay between Boon and the pistol and John Powell. Because, as John himself had said, nobody needed to study Ludus. Because we all knew Boon's marksmanship, and with Boon shooting at Ludus, Ludus himself was safe. He (Ludus) had been one of our drivers too until last Tuesday morning. This is what happened, as reconstructed from Boon and Mr Ballott and John Powell and a little from Ludus himself. A week or two before, Ludus had found a new girl, daughter (or wife: we didn't know which) of a tenant on a farm six miles from town. On Monday evening, when Boon came in to relieve Mr Ballott for the night shift, all the teams and wagons and drivers were in except Ludus. Mr Ballott told Boon to telephone him when Ludus came in, and went home. That was Mr Ballott's testimony. This was Boon's, corroborated in part by John Powell (Father himself had gone home some time before): Mr Ballott was barely out the front door when Ludus came in the back way, on foot. Ludus told Boon that the tire on one of his wheels had loosened and he had stopped at our house and seen Father, who had told him to drive the wagon into the pond in the pasture where the wood of the wheel would swell back to the tire, and stable and feed the mules in our lot and come and get them in the morning. Which you could have expected even Boon to believe, as John Powell immediately did not, since anyone who knew either would have known that, whatever disposition he made of the wagon for the night, Father would have sent Ludus to lead the team back to their stalls in the livery stable where they could be cleaned and fed properly. But that's what Boon said he was told, which he said was why he didn't interrupt Mr Ballott's evening meal to notify him, since Father knew where the mules and wagon were, and it was Father, not Mr Ballott, who owned them.

Now John Powell telling it: but reluctantly; he would likely never have told it at all if Boon had not made his (John's) silence about the truth a larger moral issue than his loyalty to his race. Once he saw Ludus walk empty-handed into the back door of the stable at the next coincident moment to Mr Ballott's departure by the front one, leaving only Boon in charge, John didn't even bother to listen to what tale Ludus would tell. He simply went back through the hallway and across the lot into the alley and on to the end of the alley and was actually standing beside the wagon when Ludus returned to it. It now contained a sack of flour, a gallon jug of coal oil and (John said) a nickel sack of peppermint candy. This is about what happened, because although John's word about any horse or mule while inside the stable was law, inviolable, even beyond Boon, right up to Mr Ballott or

Father himself, out here in no man's land he was just another wage hand in Maury Priest's livery stable and he and Ludus both knew it. Maybe Ludus even reminded him of this, but I doubt it. Because all Ludus needed to say was something like: "If word gets back to Maury Priest about how I borried this wagon and team tonight, maybe the same word gonter get back to him about what's sewed up in that jumper you wears."

And I dont think he said that either because he and John both knew that too, just as they both knew that if Ludus waited for John to report to Father what Ludus called the "borrying" of the wagon and team, Father would never know it, and if John waited for Ludus (or any other Negro in the stable or Jefferson either) to tell Father about that pistol, Father would never know that either. So Ludus probably said nothing at all, and John only said, "All right. But if them mules aint back in their stalls, without one sweat or whip mark on them and not even looking sleepy, a good solid hour before Mr Ballott gets here tomorrow morning" (you will have already noticed how both of them had completely dismissed Boon from the affair: neither Ludus to say, "Mr Boon knows these mules wont be in tonight; aint he the boss until Mr Ballott comes back in the morning?" nor John to say, "Anybody that would believe the tale you brought in here tonight in place of them mules, aint competent to be the boss of nothing. And I aint even good convinced yet that his name is Boon Hogganbeck") "Mr Maury aint just gonter know where that team and wagon wasn't last night, he's gonter know where they was."

But John didn't say it. And sure enough, although Ludus's mules had been back in their stalls a good hour before daylight, fifteen minutes after Mr Ballott reached the stable at six the next morning, he sent for Ludus and told him he was fired. "Mr Boon knowed my team was out," Ludus said. "He sent me himself to get him a jug of whiskey. I brung it back to him about four this morning."

"I didn't send you anywhere," Boon said. "When he come in here last night with that cock-and-bull story about them mules being in Mr Maury's lot, I never even listened. I didn't even bother to ask him where that wagon actually was, let alone why he was in such a sweating need of a wagon and team last night. What I told him was, before he brought that wagon back this morning I would expect him to go by Mack Winbush's and bring me back a gallon of Uncle Cal Bookwright's whiskey. I give him the money for it—two dollars."

"And I brung you the whiskey," Ludus said. "I dont know what you done with it."

"You brought me a half a jug of rotgut, mainly lye and red pepper," Boon said. "I dont know what Mr Maury's going to do to you about keeping them mules out all night but it aint a circumstance to what Calvin Bookwright will do to you when I show him that whiskey and tell him you claim he made it."

"Mr Winbush stays a solid eight miles from town," Ludus said. "It would a been midnight before I could get back to—" and stopped.

"So that's why you needed a wagon," Boon said. "You finally tomcatted yourself clean out of Jefferson and now you got to ramshack the country to locate another back window you can crawl in. Well, you'll have plenty of time now; the only trouble is, you'll have to walk—"

"You tole me a jug of whiskey," Ludus said sullenly. "I brung you a jug—"

"It wasn't even half full," Boon said. Then to Mr Ballott: "Hell fire, you wont even have to give him a week's pay now." (The weekly pay of drivers was two dollars; this was 1905, remember.) "He already owes me that for that whiskey. What you waiting for? for Mr Maury to come in his-self and fire him?"

Though if Mr Ballott (and Father) had really intended to fire Ludus for good, they would have given him his week's pay. The very fact that they didn't indicated (and Ludus knew it) that he was merely being docked a week's pay (with vacation) for keeping a team out all night without proper authority; next Monday morning Ludus would appear with the other drivers at the regular time and John Powell would have his team ready for him as if nothing had happened. Only, Fate—Rumor—gossip, had to intervene.

So Father, Luster and I hurried up the alley toward the Square, me trotting now, and still too late. We hadn't even reached the end of the alley when we heard the shots, all five of them: WHOW WHOW WHOW WHOW WHOW like that, then we were in the Square and (it wasn't far: right at the corner in front of Cousin Isaac McCaslin's hardware store) we could see it. There were plenty of them; Boon sure picked his day for witnesses; First Saturdays were trade days even then, even in May when you would think people would be too busy getting land planted. But not in Yoknapatawpha County. They were all there, black and white: one crowd where Mr Hampton (the grandfather of this same Little Hub who is sheriff now, or will be again next year) and two or three bystanders were wrestling with Boon, and another crowd where another deputy was holding Ludus about twenty feet away and still in the frozen attitude of running or frozen in the attitude of running or in the attitude of frozen running, whichever is right, and another crowd around the window of Cousin Ike's store which one of Boon's bullets (they never did find where the other four went) had shattered after creasing the buttock of a Negro girl who was now lying on the pavement screaming until Cousin Ike himself came jumping out of the store and drowned her voice with his, roaring with rage at Boon not for ruining his window but (Cousin Ike was young then but already the best woodsman and hunter this county ever had) for being unable to hit with five shots an object only twenty feet away.

It continued to go fast. Doctor Peabody's office was just across the street, above Christian's drugstore; with Mr Hampton carrying John Powell's pistol and leading, Luster and another Negro man carried the girl, still screaming and bleeding like a stuck pig, up the stairs, Father following with Boon, then me and the deputy with Ludus, and as many more as could crowd onto the stairs until Mr Hampton stopped and turned and bellowed at them. Judge Stevens's office was just down the gallery from Doctor Peabody's; he was standing at the top of the steps as we came up. So we—I mean Father and me and Boon and Ludus and the deputy—went in there to wait for Mr Hampton to come back from Doctor Peabody's office. It wasn't long.

"All right," Mr Hampton said. "It barely creased her. Buy her a new dress" (there wasn't anything under it) "and a bag of candy and give her father ten dollars, and that'll settle Boon with her. I aint quite decided yet what'll settle him with me." He breathed hard at Boon a moment: a big man with hard little gray eyes, as big as Boon in fact, though not as tall. "All right," he told Boon.

"He insulted me," Boon said. "He told Son Thomas I was a narrow-asted son of a bitch."

Now Mr Hampton looked at Ludus. "All right," he said.

"I never said he was norrer-asted," Ludus said. "I said he was norrer-headed."

"What?" Boon said.

"That's worse," Judge Stevens said.

"Of course it's worse," Boon said, cried. "Cant you see? And I aint even got any choice. Me, a white man, have got to stand here and let a damn mule-wrestling nigger either criticise my private tail, or state before five public witnesses that I aint got any sense. Cant you see? Because you cant take nothing back, not nothing. You cant even correct it because there aint nothing to correct neither one of them to." He was almost crying now, his big ugly florid walnut-tough walnut-hard face wrung and twisted like a child's. "Even if I managed to get another pistol somewhere to shoot Son Thomas with, I'd likely miss him too."

Father got up, quickly and briskly. He was the only one sitting down; even Judge Stevens was standing spraddled on the hearth before the cold fireplace with his hands under his coattails exactly like it was winter and there was a fire burning. "I must get back to work," Father said. "What does the old saw say about idle hands?" He said, not to anybody: "I want both of them, Boon and this boy, put under bond to keep the peace: say, a hundred dollars each; I will make the bond. Only, I want two mutual double-action bonds. I want two bonds, both of which will be abrogated, fall due, at the same moment that either one of them does anything that—that I—"

"That dont suit you," Judge Stevens said.

"Much obliged," Father said. "—the same second that either one of them breaks the peace. I dont know if that is legal or not."

"I dont either," Judge Stevens said. "We can try. If such a bond is not legal, it ought to be."

"Much obliged," Father said. We—Father and I and Boon—went toward the door.

"I could come back now, without waiting to Monday," Ludus said. "Iffen you needs me."

"No," Father said. We—Father and I and Boon—went on down the stairs, to the street. It was still First Saturday and trade day, but that's all it was now—that is, until somebody else named Boon Hogganbeck got hold of another pistol. We went on back along the street toward the stable, Father and I and Boon; he spoke now across the top of my head toward the back of Father's:

"A dollar a week for two hundred dollars is a year and forty-eight weeks. That window of Ike's will be another ten or fifteen I reckon, besides that girl that got in the way. Say two years and three months. I've got about forty dollars in money. If I gave you that as a cash down payment, I still dont reckon you'd put me and Ludus and Son Thomas in one of the empty stalls and lock the door for ten minutes. Would you?"

"No," Father said.

2

That was Saturday. Ludus was back at work Monday morning. On the next Friday my grandfather—the other one, Mother's father, your great-grandfather's father— died in Bay St. Louis.

Boon didn't actually belong to us. I mean, not solely to us, the Priests. Or rather I mean the McCaslins and Edmondses, of whom we Priests are what might be called the cadet branch. Boon had three proprietors: not only us, as represented by Grandfather and Father and Cousin Ike McCaslin and our other cousin, Zachary Edmonds, to whose father, McCaslin Edmonds, Cousin Ike on his twenty-first birthday had abdicated the Mc-Caslin plantation—he belonged not just to us but to Major de Spain and General Compson too until he died. Boon was a corporation, a holding company in which the three of us—McCaslins, De Spain, and General Compson—had mutually equal but completely undefined shares of responsibility, the one and only corporation rule being that whoever was nearest at the crises would leap immediately into whatever breach Boon had this time created or committed or simply fallen heir to; he (Boon) was a mutual benevolent protective benefit association, of which the benefits were all Boon's and the mutuality and the benevolence and the protecting all ours.

His grandmother had been the daughter of one of old Issetibbeha's Chickasaws who married a white whiskey trader; at times, depending on the depth of his cups, Boon would declare himself to be at least ninety-nine one-hundredths Chickasaw and in fact a lineal royal descendant of old Issetibbeha himself; the next time he would offer to fight any man who dared even intimate that he had one drop of Indian blood in his veins.

He was tough, faithful, brave and completely unreliable; he was six feet four inches tall and weighed two hundred and forty pounds and had the mentality of a child; over a year ago Father had already begun to say that at any moment now I would outgrow him.

In fact, although he was obviously a perfectly normal flesh-and-blood biological result (vide the moments in his cups when he was not merely ready and willing but even eager to fight any man or men either pro or con, depending on how the drink had taken him, for the right to ancestry) and hence he had to have been somewhere during those first nine or ten or eleven years, it was as if Boon had been created whole and already nine or ten or eleven years old, by the three of us, McCaslin–De Spain–Compson, as a solution to a dilemma one day at Major de Spain's hunting camp.

That's right, the same camp which you will probably continue to call McCaslin's camp for a few years after your Cousin Ike is gone, just as we—your fathers—continued to call it De Spain's camp for years after Major de Spain was gone. But in the time of my fathers, when Major de Spain bought or borrowed or leased the land (however men managed to acquire valid titles in Mississippi between 1865 and '70) and built the lodge and stables and kennels, it was his camp: who culled and selected the men he considered worthy to hunt the game he decreed to be hunted, and so in that sense not only owned who hunted it but where they hunted and even what: the bear and deer, and wolves and panthers also ranged it then, less than twenty miles from Jefferson— the four or five sections of river-bottom jungle which had been a portion of old Thomas Sutpen's vast kingly dream which in the end had destroyed not only itself but Sutpen too, which in those days was a sort of eastern gateway to the still almost virgin wilderness of swamp and jungle which stretched westward from the hills to the towns and plantations along the Mississippi.

It was only twenty miles then; our fathers could leave Jefferson at midnight in buggies and wagons (a man on a horse did it even quicker) on the fifteenth of November and be on a deer- or bear-stand by daybreak. Even in 1905 the wilderness had retreated only twenty more miles; the wagons bearing the guns and food and bedding had merely to start at sundown; and now a northern lumber company had built a narrow-gauge railroad for hauling logs, which connected with the main line, passing within a mile of Major de Spain's new camp, with a courtesy stop to let Major de Spain and his guests off, to be met by the wagons which had gone in the day before. Though by 1925 we could already see the doom. Major de Spain and the rest of that old group, save your Cousin Ike and Boon, were gone now and (there was gravel now all the way from Jefferson to De Spain's

flag stop) their inheritors switched off their automobile
engines to the sound of axes and saws where a year ago
there had been only the voices of the running hounds.
Because Manfred de Spain was a banker, not a hunter
like his father; he sold lease, land and timber and by
1940 (it was McCaslin's camp now) they—we—would
load everything into pickup trucks and drive two hundred
miles over paved highways to find enough wilderness
to pitch tents in; though by 1980 the automobile will be
as obsolete to reach wilderness with as the automobile
will have made the wilderness it seeks. But perhaps
they—you—will find wilderness on the back side of Mars
or the moon, with maybe even bear and deer to run
it.

But then, when Boon materialized at the camp one day,
full panoplied and already ten or eleven or twelve years
old, there were only twenty miles for Major de Spain
and General Compson and McCaslin Edmonds and
Walter Ewell and old Bob Legate and the half-dozen
others who would come and go, to travel. But General
Compson, although he had commanded troops not too unsuccessfully as a colonel at Shiloh, and again not too
unsuccessfully as a brigadier during Johnston's retreat
on Atlanta, was a little short in terrain, topography, and
would promptly get lost ten minutes after he left camp
(the mule he preferred to ride would have brought him
back at any time but, not only a paroled Confederate
general but a Compson too, he declined to accept counsel
or advice from a mule), so as soon as the last hunter was
in from the morning's drive, everyone would take turns
blowing a horn until General Compson at last got in.
Which was satisfactory, anyway served, until General
Compson's hearing began to fail too. Until finally one
afternoon Walter Ewell and Sam Fathers, who was half
Negro and half Chickasaw Indian, had to track him down

and camp in the woods with him all night, facing Major
de Spain with the alternative of either forbidding him to
leave the tent or expelling him from the club, when
lo, there was Boon Hogganbeck, already a giant, even at
ten or eleven already bigger than General Compson,
whose nurse he became—a waif, who seemed to have
nothing and know nothing but his name; even Cousin
Ike is not sure whether it was McCaslin Edmonds or
Major de Spain who found Boon first where whoever
bore him had abandoned him. All Ike knows—remembers
—is that Boon was already there, about twelve years old,
out at old Carothers McCaslin's place, where McCaslin
Edmonds was already raising Ike as if he was his father
and now and without breaking stride took over Boon
too as though he had been Boon's father also, though at
that time McCaslin Edmonds himself was only thirty.

Anyway, as soon as Major de Spain realised that he
must either expel General Compson from the club, which
would be difficult, or forbid him to leave the camp,
which would be impossible, and hence he must equip
General Compson with something resembling a Boon
Hogganbeck, there was the Boon Hogganbeck, produced
either by McCaslin Edmonds or perhaps by both of
them—Edmonds and De Spain himself—in simultaneous
crisis. Ike could remember that: the loading of the
bedding and guns and food into the wagon on the
fourteenth of November, with Tennie's Jim (grandfather of this Bobo Beauchamp of whom you will hear
presently) and Sam Fathers and Boon (he, Ike, was
only five or six then; another four or five years before he
would be ten and could make one also) and McCaslin
himself riding ahead on the horse, to the camp where
each morning Boon would follow General Compson
on a second mule until by simple force probably, since
at twelve Boon was already bigger than his charge,

Boon would compel him to the right direction in time to reach camp before dark.

Thus General Compson made a woodsman of Boon despite himself, you might say, in simple self-defense. But even eating at the same table and ranging the same woods and sleeping in the same rain even with Walter Ewell never made a marksman of him; one of the camp's favorite stories was about Boon's shooting, told by Walter Ewell: of being on a stand where he had left Boon (old General Compson had gone to his fathers at last—or to whatever bivouac old soldiers of that war, blue or gray either, probably insisted on going to since probably no place would suit them for anything resembling a permanent stay—and now Boon was a regular hunter like anybody else) and of hearing the hounds and realising that the deer was going to cross at Boon's stand, then of hearing the five shots from Boon's ramshackle pump gun (General Compson had bequeathed it to him; it had never been in the best condition while Compson owned it and Walter said his real surprise was that the gun had fired even twice without jamming, let alone five times) and then Boon's voice across the woods between them: "God damn! Yonder he goes! Head him! Head him!" And how he—Walter—hurried across to Boon's stand and found the five exploded shells on the ground and not ten paces away the prints of the running buck which Boon had not even touched.

Then Grandfather bought that automobile and Boon found his soul's mate. By this time he was officially (by mutual McCaslin-Edmonds-Priest consent, even McCaslin Edmonds having given up or seen the light at last when Boon failed the third grade for the second time too—or maybe the real light McCaslin saw was that Boon would never stay on any farm long enough to learn to be a farmer) a member of the livery stable staff. At first the jobs were mostly still the odd ones—feeding, cleaning harness and buggies. But I told you he had a way with horses and mules, and soon he was a regular driver of hired vehicles—hacks and cabs which met the daytime trains, and the buggies and surreys and light wagons in which the drummers made the rounds of the country stores. He lived in town now, except when McCaslin and Zachary both were away at night and Boon would sleep in the house to protect the women and children. I mean, he lived in Jefferson. I mean, he actually had a home—a single rented room in what in my grandfather's time was the Commercial Hotel, established in hopeful rivalry of the Holston House but never making the grade in that rivalry. But solid enough: where juries were lodged and fed during court terms and where country litigants and horse- and mule-traders felt more at ease than among the carpets and brass cuspidors and leather chairs and linen tablecloths across town; then in my time the Snopes Hotel with both hand-painted esses upside down when Mr Flem Snopes (the banker, murdered ten or twelve years ago by the mad kinsman who perhaps didn't believe his cousin had actually sent him to the penitentiary but at least could have kept him out or anyway tried to) began to lead his tribe out of the wilderness behind Frenchman's Bend, into town; then for a brief time in the mid-thirties leased by a brassy-haired gentlewoman who came briefly from nowhere and went briefly back, known to your father and the police as Little Chicago; and which you know, those glories but memories now, as Mrs Rouncewell's boarding house. But in Boon's time it was still the Commercial Hotel; in the intervals between sleeping on the floor of some Compson or Edmonds or Priest kitchen, he was living there when my grandfather bought the automobile.

My grandfather didn't want an automobile at all; he

was forced to buy one. A banker, president of the older Bank of Jefferson, the first bank in Yoknapatawpha County, he believed then and right on to his death many years afterward, by which time everybody else even in Yoknapatawpha County had realised that the automobile had come to stay, that the motor vehicle was an insolvent phenomenon like last night's toadstool and, like the fungus, would vanish with tomorrow's sun. But Colonel Sartoris, president of the newer, the mushroom Merchants and Farmers Bank, forced him to buy one. Or rather, another insolvent, a dreamy myopic gentian-eyed mechanical wizard named Buffaloe, compelled him to. Because my grandfather's car wasn't even the first one in Jefferson. (I dont count Manfred de Spain's red E.M.F. racer. Although De Spain owned it and drove it daily through Jefferson streets for several years, it had no more place in the decorous uxorious pattern of a community than Manfred himself did, both of them being incorrigible and bachelor, not in the town but on it and up to no good like one prolonged unbroken Saturday night even while Manfred was actually mayor, its very scarlet color being not even a scornful defiance of the town but rather a kind of almost inattentive disavowal.)

Grandfather's was not even the first automobile to see Jefferson or vice versa. It was not even the first one to inhabit Jefferson. Two years before, one had driven all the way down from Memphis, making the eighty-mile trip in less than three days. Then it rained, and the car stayed in Jefferson two weeks, during which time we almost had no electric lights at all; nor, if the livery stable had depended solely on Boon, no public transportation either. Because Mr Buffaloe was the man—the one man, the sole human being nearer than Memphis who knew how to—who kept the steam-driven electric plant running; and from the moment the automobile indicated that it was not going any further, at least today, Mr Buffaloe and Boon were inseparable from it like two shadows, a big one and a little one—the hulking giant smelling of ammonia and harness oil, and the little grease-covered soot-colored man with eyes like two bluebird feathers moulted onto a small lump of coal, who would barely have tipped a hundred pounds with all his (the city's too) tools in his pockets—the one motionless, staring at the car with a kind of incredulous yearning, like a fixed bull; the other dreaming at it, gentle, tender, his grimed hand gentle as a woman's as he touched it, stroked it, caressed it, then the next moment plunged to the hips under the raised bonnet.

Then it rained all that night and was still raining the next morning. The owner of the car was told, assured—by Mr Buffaloe, it appeared; a little strange since nobody had ever known him to be far enough away from the light plant or the little shop in his back yard, to have ever used roads enough to prophesy their condition—that the roads would be impassable for at least a week, maybe ten days. So the owner went back to Memphis by train, leaving the automobile to be stored in what, in anybody else's back yard but Mr Buffaloe's, would have been a horse- or cow-barn. Nor could we figure this: how Mr. Buffaloe, a meek mild almost inarticulate little man in a constant condition of unworldly grease-coated dreamlike somnambulism—how, by what means, what mesmeric and hypnotic gifts which until now even he could not have known he possessed, he had persuaded the complete stranger to abandon his expensive toy into Mr Buffaloe's charge.

But he did, and went back to Memphis; and now when electric trouble occurred in Jefferson, someone had to go by foot or horse or bicycle out to Mr Buffaloe's home

on the edge of town, whereupon Mr Buffaloe would
appear, vague and dreaming and without haste and
still wiping his hands, around the corner of his house from
his back yard; and by the third day Father finally found
out where Boon would be (had been) during the time
when he—Boon—should have been in the livery stable.
Because on that day Boon himself revealed the secret,
spilled the beans, with frantic and raging urgency. He
and Mr Buffaloe had come to what would have been
physical battle, had not Mr Buffaloe—that apparently
inexhaustible reservoir of surprises and capabilities—
drawn a greasy and soot-grimed but perfectly efficient
pistol on Boon.

That was how Boon told it. He and Mr Buffaloe had been
not merely in complete, but instantaneous, accord and
understanding in the whole process of getting the automobile into Mr Buffaloe's hands and the owner of it
out of town; so that, Boon naturally thought, Mr Buffaloe
would quickly solve the mystery of how to operate it
and they would slip it out after dark and ride in it. But
to Boon's shocked and outraged amazement, all Mr
Buffaloe wanted was to find out why it ran. "He's ruined
it!" Boon said. "He's done took it all to pieces just to
see what was inside! He wont never get it all back
together again!"

But Buffaloe did. He stood, mild and grease-stained
and gently dreaming, when two weeks later the owner
returned and cranked it up and drove away; and a year
later Buffaloe had made one of his own, engine, gears
and all, into a rubber-tired buggy; that afternoon, stinking noisily and sedately and not at all fast across the
Square, he frightened Colonel Sartoris's matched carriage
horses into bolting with the luckily empty surrey and
more or less destroying it; by the next night there was
formally recorded into the archives of Jefferson a city

ordinance against the operation of any mechanically propelled vehicle inside the corporate limits. So, as president of the older, the senior bank in Yoknapatawpha County, my grandfather was forced to buy one or else be dictated to by the president of the junior one. You see what I mean? not senior and junior in the social hierarchy of the town, least of all rivals in it, but bankers, dedicated priests in the impenetrable and ineluctable mysteries of Finance; it was as though, despite his life-long ramrod-stiff and unyielding opposition to, refusal even to acknowledge, the machine age, Grandfather had been vouchsafed somewhere in the beginning a sort of—to him—nightmare vision of our nation's vast and boundless future in which the basic unit of its economy and prosperity would be a small mass-produced cubicle containing four wheels and an engine.

So he bought the automobile, and Boon found his soul's lily maid, the virgin's love of his rough and innocent heart. It was a Winton Flyer. (This was the first one he—we—owned, before the White Steamer which Grandfather traded it for when Grandmother finally decided two years later that she couldn't bear the smell of gasoline at all.) You cranked it by hand while standing in front of it, with no more risk (provided you had remembered to take it out of gear) than a bone or two in your forearm; it had kerosene lamps for night driving and when rain threatened five or six people could readily put up the top and curtains in ten or fifteen minutes, and Grandfather himself equipped it with a kerosene lantern, a new axe and a small coil of barbed wire attached to a light block and tackle for driving beyond the town limits. With which equipment it could—and did once, of which I shall speak presently—go as far as Memphis. Also, all of us, grandparents, parents, aunts, cousins and children, had special costumes for riding in it, consisting of veils, caps, goggles, gauntlet gloves and long shapeless throat-close neutral-colored garments called dusters, of which I shall also speak later.

By this time Mr Buffaloe had long since taught Boon to operate his homemade one. They couldn't use the streets of Jefferson of course—in fact never again did it cross the line of Mr Buffaloe's front fence—but there was an area of open land behind his house which in time Mr Buffaloe and Boon had beaten down and (relatively) smoothed into a fair motordrome. So by the time Boon and Mr Wordwin, the cashier in Grandfather's bank (he was a bachelor, one of our most prominent clubmen or men about town; in ten years he had been a groomsman in thirteen weddings), went to Memphis by train and brought the automobile back (in less than two days this time; a record), Boon was already destined to be the dean of Jefferson motor-car drivers.

Then, as far as Boon's dream was concerned, my grandfather abolished that automobile. He merely bought it, paid what Boon called a sizable chunk of hard valuable cash for it, looked at it thoroughly and inscrutably once and then eliminated it from circulation. He—Grandfather —couldn't do that completely of course; there was that arrogant decree of Colonel Sartoris's which he—Grandfather—being the senior, could not permit himself to allow to stand, no matter what his own opinion of motor vehicles was. In fact, in this opinion he and Colonel Sartoris were absolutely eye-to-eye; until their deaths (by which time all Yoknapatawpha County's daytime air was odorous with gasoline fumes and its nights, Saturdays especially, filled with the clash of colliding fenders and the squeal of brakes) neither of them would lend a penny to any man they merely suspected was going to buy an automobile with it. Colonel Sartoris's crime was simply in having taken the *pas* of his senior in a move which they both approved—officially banning automobiles from Jefferson even before they got there. You see? Grandfather bought the automobile not as a defiance of Colonel Sartoris's decree. It was simply a calm and deliberately considered abrogation of it, even if only by weekly token.

Even before Colonel Sartoris's decree, Grandfather had had his carriage and horses moved from his back yard to the livery stable, where they were actually more accessible to Grandmother's telephone call than to her shout from an upstairs back window, because somebody always answered the telephone at the livery stable. Which Ned, in the kitchen or stable or wherever he happened to be (or was supposed to happen to be when Grandmother wanted him), didn't always. In fact, he was more often nowhere in range of any voice from Grandmother's house since one of them was his wife's. So now we come to Ned. He was Grandfather's coachman. His wife (the one he had then; he had four) was Delphine, Grandmother's cook. At that time he was "Uncle" Ned only to Mother. I mean, she was the one who insisted that all us children—three of us, that is, because Alexander couldn't call anybody anything yet— call him Uncle Ned. Nobody else cared whether we did or not, not even Grandmother, who was a McCaslin too, and certainly not Ned himself, who hadn't earned it even by just living long enough for the fringe of hair embracing his bald skull to begin to turn gray, let alone white (it never did. I mean, his hair: turn white nor even gray. When he died at seventy-four, except for having run through four wives he hadn't changed at all), and who indeed may not have wanted to be called Uncle; none of these but only Mother, who in the McCaslin sense was not even kin to us, insisted on it. Because he— Ned—was a McCaslin, born in the McCaslin back yard in 1860. He was our family skeleton; we inherited him in turn, with his legend (which had no firmer supporter than Ned himself) that his mother had been the natural daughter of old Lucius Quintus Carothers himself and a Negro slave; never did Ned let any of us forget that he, along with Cousin Isaac, was an actual grandson to old time-honored Lancaster where we moiling Edmondses and Priests, even though three of us—you, me and my grandfather—were named for him, were mere diminishing connections and hangers-on.

So when Boon and Mr Wordwin arrived with the car, the carriage house was all ready for it: new-floored and -doored, with a brand-new padlock already in Grandfather's hand while he walked slowly around the car, looking at it exactly as he would have examined the plow or reaper or wagon (the client too for that matter) on which a would-be patron of the bank was offering to borrow money. Then he motioned Boon to drive it on into the garage (oh yes, we already knew that was the name of an automobile shed, even in 1904, even in Mississippi).

"What?" Boon said.

"Drive it in," Grandfather said.

"You aint even going to try it?" Boon said.

"No," Grandfather said. Boon drove it into the garage and (just Boon) came out again. There had been astonishment in his face; now there was shock, divination, something like terror. "Has it got a key?" Grandfather said.

"What?" Boon said.

"A catch. A pin. A hook. Something you start it with." Slowly Boon took something from his pocket and put it into Grandfather's hand. "Shut the doors," Grandfather said, and himself walked up and snapped the new padlock through the hasp and put that key into his pocket also. Now Boon was fighting a battle with himself. He was in crisis; the matter was desperate. I—we, Mr Word-

win, Grandmother, Ned, Delphine and everybody else
white and black who had happened along the street when
the automobile came up—watched him win it, or that
initial engagement of pickets anyway.

"I'll come back after dinner, so Miss Sarah" (that was
Grandmother) "can try it. About one oclock. I can come
sooner if that'll be too late."

"I'll send word to the stable," Grandfather said. Because
it was a full-scale action: no mere squabbling of outposts.
It was all out, win or lose; logistics came into it, and
terrain; feint thrust and parry, deception; but most of
all, patience, the long view. It lasted the remaining three
days until Saturday. Boon returned to the livery stable;
all that afternoon he was never very far from the telephone, though not ostensibly, obviously so, revealing
nothing; he even did his work—or so they thought, until
Father discovered that Boon on his own authority had
deputised Luster to meet with the hack the afternoon
train whose arrival (unless it was late) always coincided
with the time, moment when Grandfather left the bank
for the day. But although the battle was still a holding
action requiring—nay, demanding—constant alertness
and vigilance instead of a drive capable of carrying
itself with its own momentum, Boon was still confident,
still on top: "Sure. I sent Luster. The way this town is
growing, we will need two hacks at them trains any day
now, and I been had my eye on Luster for the second
driver a good while now. Don't worry; I'm going to
watch him."

But no telephone. By six oclock, even Boon admitted
that today there would be none. But it was a holding
action; nothing was lost yet, and in the dark he could
even shift his forces a little. The next morning about
ten he—we—entered the bank as though by passing
afterthought. "Lemme have the keys," he told Grandfather. "All that Missippi dust and mud, let alone the

Tennessee mud and dust already under it. I'll take the hose with me from the stable in case Ned has mislaid yours out of sight somewhere."

Grandfather was looking at Boon, just looking at him with no hurry, like Boon really was the one with the wagon or hay baler offering to borrow fifteen dollars. "I dont want the inside of the carriage house wet," Grandfather said. But Boon matched him, as detached and even more indifferent, with even more time to spare, use.

"Sure, sure. Remember, the man said the engine ought to be run every day. Not to go nowhere: just to keep the spark plugs and magneto from rusting and costing you twenty, twenty-five dollars for a new one all the way from Memphis or somewhere, maybe all the way back to the factory. I dont blame you; all I know is what he told you; I'd just have to take his word too. But then you can afford it. You own the automobile; if you want to rust it up, it aint nobody else's business. A horse would a been different. Even if you hadn't even paid a hundred dollars for a horse you'd a had me out there at daylight lunging him on a rope just to keep his guts working." Because Grandfather was a good banker and Boon knew it: that Grandfather not only knew when to foreclose, but when to compound and cancel too. He reached into his pocket and handed Boon the two keys—the one to the padlock and the thing that turned the automobile on. "Come on," Boon told me, already turning.

While we were still up the street we could already hear Grandmother hollering for Ned from the upstairs back window, though by the time we reached the gate she had quit. As we crossed the back yard to get the hose, Delphine came out the kitchen door. "Where is Ned?" she said. "We been hollering for him all morning. Is he up there at the livery stable?"

"Sure," Boon said. "I'll tell him too. Just dont expect

him neither." Ned was there. He and two of my brothers were like a row of stairsteps trying to see through the cracks in the garage door. I reckon Alexander would have been there too except he couldn't walk yet; I dont know why Aunt Callie hadn't thought of it yet. Then Alexander was there; Mother came across the street from our house carrying him. So maybe Aunt Callie was still washing diapers. "Morning, Miss Alison," Boon said. "Morning, Miss Sarah," he said, because now Grandmother was there too, with Delphine behind her. And now there were two more ladies, neighbors, still in their boudoir caps. Because maybe Boon wasn't a banker nor even a very good trader either. But he was proving to be a pretty damned good guerrilla fighter. He went and unlocked the garage door and opened it. Ned was the first one inside.

"Well," Boon said to him, "you been here ever since daylight to peep at it through that crack. What do you think about it?"

"I dont think nothing about it," Ned said. "Boss Priest could a bought the best two-hundred-dollar horse in Yoknapatawpha County for this money."

"There aint any two-hundred-dollar horse in Yoknapatawpha County," Boon said. "If there was, this automobile would buy ten of them. Go be hooking up that hose."

"Go be hooking up that hose, Lucius," Ned said to me; he didn't even look around. He went to the automobile door and opened it. It was the back seat. Front seats didn't have doors in those days; you just walked up and got in. "Come on, Miss Sarah, you and Miss Alison," Ned said. "Delphine can wait with the children for the next trip."

"You go hook up that hose like I told you," Boon said. "I got to get it out of here before I can do anything to it."

"You aint gonter tote it out in your hand, is you?"

Ned said. "I reckon we can ride that far. I reckon I'm gonter have to drive it so the sooner I starts, the quicker it will be." He said: "Hee hee hee." He said: "Come on, Miss Sarah."

"Will it be all right, Boon?" Grandmother said.

"Yessum, Miss Sarah," Boon said. Grandmother and Mother got in. Before Boon could close the door, Ned was already in the front seat.

"Get out of there," Boon said.

"Go ahead and tend to your business, if you knows how to," Ned said. "I aint gonter touch nothing until I learns how, and just setting here aint gonter learn me. Go on and hook up, or whatever you does to it."

Boon went around to the driver's side and set the switches and levers, and went to the front and jerked the crank. On the third pull, the engine roared.

"Boon!" Grandmother cried.

"It's all right, Miss Sarah!" Boon hollered above the noise, running back to the guiding wheel.

"I don't care!" Grandmother said. "Get in quick! I'm nervous!" Boon got in and quieted the engine and shifted the levers; a moment, then the automobile moved quietly and slowly backward out of the shed, into the lot, the sunshine, and stopped.

"Hee hee hee," Ned said.

"Be careful, Boon," Grandmother said. I could see her hand gripping the stanchion of the top.

"Yessum," Boon said. The automobile moved again, backward, beginning to turn. Then it moved forward, still turning; Grandmother's hand still gripped the stanchion. Mother's face looked like a girl's. The car went slowly and quietly across the lot until it was facing the gate to the lane, to the outside, to the world, and stopped. And Boon didn't say anything: he just sat there behind the wheel, the engine running smooth and quiet, his head turned just enough for Grandmother to see his face. Oh yes, maybe he wasn't a negotiable-paper wizard like Grandfather, and there were folks in Jefferson that would say he wasn't much of anything else either, but for this skirmish anyway he was a skirmish fighter of consummate skill and grace. Grandmother sat for maybe a half a minute. Then she drew a long breath and expelled it.

"No," she said. "We must wait for Mister Priest." Maybe it wasn't a victory, but anyway our side—Boon—had not only discovered the weak point in the enemy's (Grandfather's) front, by suppertime that night the enemy himself would discover it too.

Discover in fact that his flank had been turned. The next afternoon (Saturday) after the bank closed, and each succeeding Saturday afternoon, and then when summer came, every afternoon except when rain was actually falling, Grandfather in front beside Boon and the rest of us in rotation—Grandmother, Mother, me and my three brothers and Aunt Callie that nursed us in turn, including Father, and Delphine and our various connections and neighbors and Grandmother's close friends in their ordered rote—in the linen dusters and goggles, would drive through Jefferson and the adjacent countryside; Aunt Callie and Delphine in their turns, but not Ned. He rode in it once: that one minute while it backed slowly out of the garage, and the two minutes while it turned and moved slowly forward across the lot until Grandmother lost her nerve and said No to the open gate and the public world, but not again. By the second Saturday he had realised, accepted—anyway become convinced—that even if Grandfather had ever intended to make him the official operator and custodian of the automobile, he could have approached it only over Boon's dead body. But although he declined to recognise that the automobile existed on the place, he and Grandfather had met on some unspoken gentlemen's ground regarding it: Ned never to speak in scorn or derogation of its ownership and presence, Grandfather never to order Ned to wash and polish it as he used to do the carriage—which Grandfather and Ned both knew Ned would have refused to do, even if Boon had let him: by which Grandfather visited on Ned his only punishment for his apostasy: he refused to give Ned the public chance to refuse to wash the automobile before Boon might have had a public chance to refuse to let him do it.

Because that was when Boon transferred—was transferred by mutual and instantaneous consent—from the day shift at the stable to the night shift. Otherwise, the livery business would have known him no more. That part of our Jefferson leisure class, friends or acquaintances of Father's or maybe just friends of horses, who could have used the stable as a permanent business address—if they had had any business or expected any mail —were less strangers there than Boon. If—when—you, meaning Father, wanted Boon now, you sent me to Grandfather's lot, where he would be washing and polishing the automobile—this, even during those first weeks when it had not left the lot since last Saturday and would not leave it again until the next one, backing it out of the shed and washing it again each morning, with tender absorption, right down to the last spoke and nut, then sitting guard over it while it dried.

"He's going to soak all the paint off of it," Mr Ballott said. "Does Boss know he's running the hose on that automobile four or five hours every day?"

"What if he did?" Father said. "Boon would still sit there in the lot all day looking at it."

"Put him on the night shift," Mr Ballott said. "Then he could do whatever he wants to with his daylight and John

Powell could go home and sleep in a bed every night for a change."

"I already have," Father said. "As soon as I can find somebody to go to that lot and tell him."

There was a shuck mattress in the harness room on which until now John Powell or one of the other drivers or hostlers under his command always spent the night, mainly as night watchmen against fire. Now Father installed a cot and mattress in the office itself, where Boon could get some sleep, which he needed, since now he could spend all day with complete immunity in Grandfather's lot either washing the automobile or just looking at it.

So now every afternoon, as many of us as the back seat would hold in our ordered turns would drive through the Square and into the country; Grandfather had already installed the extraneous emergency gear to be as much and inseparable a part of the automobile's equipment as the engine which moved it.

But always through the Square first. You would have thought that as soon as he bought the automobile, Grandfather would have done what you would have done, having bought the automobile for that end: lain in wait for Colonel Sartoris and his carriage and ambushed, bushwhacked him and really taught him how to pass ordinances restricting others' rights and privileges without consulting his betters first. But Grandfather didn't do this. We finally realised that he wasn't interested in Colonel Sartoris: he was interested in teams, vehicles. Because I told you he was a far-sighted man, a man capable of vision: Grandmother sitting tense and rigid and gripping the top stanchion and not even calling Grandfather Mister Priest now, as she had done as long as we had known her, but calling him by his given name as though she were no kin to him, the horse or team we

were approaching reined back and braced to shy and
sometimes even rearing and Grandmother saying, "Lucius! Lucius!" and Grandfather (if a man was driving
and there were no women or children in the buggy or
wagon) saying quietly to Boon:

"Dont stop. Keep going. But slow now." Or, when a
woman had the lines, telling Boon to stop and himself
getting out, talking quietly and steadily to the spooked
horse until he could get hold of the bit and lead the
vehicle past and remove his hat to the ladies in the buggy
and come back and get back into the front seat and only
then answer Grandmother: "We must get them used to it.
Who knows? there may be another automobile in Jefferson in the next ten or fifteen years."

In fact, that homemade dream which Mr Buffaloe
had created single-handed in his back yard two years ago
came within an ace of curing Grandfather of a habit
which he had had since he was nineteen years old. He
chewed tobacco. The first time he turned his head to
spit out of the moving automobile, we in the back seat
didn't know what was going to happen until it was already too late. Because how could we? None of us had
ever ridden in an automobile before farther than (this
was the first trip) from the carriage house to the lot
gate, let alone one going fifteen miles an hour (and this
was something else: when we were going ten miles an
hour Boon always said we were doing twenty; at twenty,
he always said forty; we discovered a straight stretch
about a half a mile long a few miles out of town where
the automobile would get up to twenty-five, where I
heard him tell a group of men on the Square that the
automobile made sixty miles an hour; this was before
he knew that we knew that the thing on the dashboard
which looked like a steam gauge was a speedometer),
so how could we be expected to? Besides, it didn't make

any difference to the rest of us; we all had our goggles and dusters and veils and even if the dusters were new, the spots and splashes were just brown spots and splashes and just because they were called dusters was no reason why they should not be called on to face anything else but dust. Maybe it was because Grandmother was sitting on the left side (in those days automobiles operated from the right side, like buggies; even Henry Ford, a man as long-visioned as Grandfather, had not yet divined that the steering wheel would be on the left) directly behind Grandfather. She said at once to Boon: "Stop the automobile," and sat there, not mad so much as coldly and implacably outraged and shocked. She was just past fifty then (she was fifteen when she and Grandfather married) and in all those fifty years she had no more believed that a man, let alone her husband, would spit in her face than she could have believed that Boon for instance would approach a curve in the road without tooting the horn. She said, to nobody; she didn't even raise her hand to wipe the spit away:

"Take me home."

"Now, Sarah," Grandfather said. "Now, Sarah." He threw the chew away and took out the clean handkerchief from his other pocket, but Grandmother wouldn't even take it. Boon had already started to get out and go to a house we could see and get a pan of water and soap and a towel, but Grandmother wouldn't have that either.

"Dont touch me," she said. "Drive on." So we went on, Grandmother with the long drying brown splash across one of her goggles and down her cheek even though Mother kept on offering to spit on her handkerchief and wipe it off. "Let me alone, Alison," Grandmother said.

But not Mother. She didn't mind tobacco, not in the car. Maybe that was why. But more and more that sum-

mer it would be just Mother and us and Aunt Callie and
one or two neighbor children in the back seat, Mother's
face flushed and bright and eager, like a girl's. Because
she had invented a kind of shield on a handle like a big
fan, light enough for her to raise in front of us almost as
fast as Grandfather could turn his head. So he could
chew now, Mother always alert and ready with the
screen; all of us were quick now in fact, so that almost
before the instant when Grandfather knew he was going
to turn his head to the left to spit, the screen had already
come up and all of us in the back seat had leaned to the
right like we were on the same wire, actually doing
twenty and twenty-five miles an hour now because there
were already two more automobiles in Jefferson that
summer; it was as though the automobiles themselves
were beating the roads smooth long before the money
they represented would begin to compel smoother roads.

"Twenty-five years from now there wont be a road in
the county you cant drive an automobile on in any
weather," Grandfather said.

"Wont that cost a lot of money, Papa?" Mother said.

"It will cost a great deal of money," Grandfather said.
"The road builders will issue bonds. The bank will buy
them."

"Our bank?" Mother said. "Buy bonds for automobiles?"

"Yes," Grandfather said. "We will buy them."

"But what about us?—I mean, Maury."

"He will still be in the livery business," Grandfather
said. "He will just have a new name for it. Priest's Garage
maybe, or the Priest Motor Company. People will pay
any price for motion. They will even work for it. Look at
bicycles. Look at Boon. We dont know why."

Then the next May came and my other grandfather,
Mother's father, died in Bay St Louis.

3

◆◆◆◆

It was Saturday again. The next one in fact; Ludus was
going to start getting paid again every Saturday night;
maybe he had even stopped borrowing mules. It was
barely eight oclock; I wasn't even halfway around the
Square with the freight bills and my canvas sack to carry
the money in, just finishing in the Farmers Supply when
Boon came in, fast, too quick for him. I should have
suspected at once. No, I should have known at once,
having known Boon all my life, let alone having watched
him for a year now with that automobile. He was already
reaching for the money sack, taking it right out of my
hand before I could even close my fist. "Leave it," he
said. "Come on."

"Here," I said. "I've barely started."

"I said leave it. Shake it up. Hurry. They've got to

make Twenty-three," he said, already turning. He had completely ignored the unpaid freight bills themselves. They were just paper; the railroad company had plenty more of them. But the sack contained money.

"Who's got to make Twenty-three?" I said. Number Twenty-three was the southbound morning train. Oh yes, Jefferson had passenger trains then, enough of them so they had to number them to keep them separate.

"Goddammit," Boon said, "how can I break it gentle to you when you wont even listen? Your grandpa died last night. We got to hurry."

"He didn't!" I said, cried. "He was on the front gallery this morning when we passed." He was. Father and I both saw him, either reading the paper or just standing or sitting there like he was every morning, waiting for time to go to the bank.

"Who the hell's talking about Boss?" Boon said. "I said your other grandpa, your ma's papa down there at Jackson or Mobile or wherever it is."

"Oh," I said. "Dont you even know the difference between Bay St. Louis and Mobile?" Because it was all right now. This was different. Bay St. Louis was three hundred miles; I hardly knew Grandfather Lessep except twice at Christmas in Jefferson and three times we went down there in the summer. Also, he had been sick a long time; we—Mother and us—had been there last summer actually to see him enter what was to be his last bed even if we didn't know it then (Mother and Aunt Callie, because your Great-uncle Alexander had arrived a month before, had been down last winter when they thought he was going to die). I say "if," meaning Mother; to a child, when an old person becomes sick he or she has already quitted living; the actual death merely clears the atmosphere so to speak, incapable of removing anything which was already gone.

"All right, all right," Boon said. "Just come on. Jackson, Mobile, New Orleans—all I know is, it's down that way somewhere, and wherever it is, they still got to catch that train." And that—the name *New Orleans*, not dropped so much as escaped into that context—should have told me all, revealed the whole of Boon's outrageous dream, intent, determination; his later elaborate machinations to seduce me to it should merely have corroborated. But maybe I was still recovering from shock; also, at that moment I didn't have as many facts as Boon did. So we just went on, fast, I trotting to keep up, the shortest way across the Square, until we reached home.

Where was much commotion. It was barely two hours until the train and Mother was far too busy to take time to mourn or grieve: merely pale-faced, intent, efficient. Because I now learned what Boon had already told me twice: that Grandfather and Grandmother were going to bury Grandfather Lessep also. He and Grandfather had been roommates, in the same class at the University; they had been groomsmen in each other's wedding, which possibly had a little something to do with why Mother and Father chose one another out of all the earth to look into her eyes forever more (I understand you call it going steady), and Grandmother and Grandmother Lessep lived far enough apart to continue to be civil and even pleasant to the other mother of an only child. Besides that, people took funerals seriously in those days. Not death: death was our constant familiar: no family but whose annals were dotted with headstones whose memorialees had been too brief in tenure to bear a name even—unless of course the mother slept there too in that one grave, which happened more often than you would like to think. Not to mention the husbands and uncles and aunts in the twenties and thirties and forties, and the grandparents and childless great-uncles and -aunts who died at home then, in the same rooms and beds they were born in, instead of in cubicled euphemisms with names pertaining to sunset. But the funerals, the ritual ceremonial of interment, with tenuous yet steel-strong threads capable of extending even further and bearing even more weight than the distance between Jefferson and the Gulf of Mexico.

So Grandfather and Grandmother were also going to the funeral. Which meant only incidentally that, lacking any other close kinfolks in town, we—me and my three brothers and Aunt Callie—would have to be sent out to Cousin Zachary Edmonds's farm seventeen miles away to stay until Father and Mother got back; it meant only incidentally that Father and Mother would be gone four days. What it actually meant was that Grandfather and Grandmother would not even come back after four days. Because Grandfather never left Jefferson at all, even to go only to Memphis, without spending two or three days in New Orleans, which he loved, either going or coming; and this time they might quite possibly take Mother and Father with them. It meant in fact what Boon had already told me twice by exuberant and still unbelieving inadvertence: that the owner of that automobile, and everyone else having or even assuming authority over it, would be three hundred miles from it for anywhere from four days to a week. So all his clumsy machinations to seduce and corrupt me were only corroboration. They were not even cumshaw, lagniappe. He could have taken the car alone, and doubtless would if I had been incorruptible, even knowing that someday he must bring it back or come back himself in order to face lesser music than he would if—when—Grandfather's police caught up with him. Because come back he must. Where else could he go, who knew nowhere else, to whom the words, names—Jefferson, McCaslin, De Spain,

Compson—were not just home but father and mother both? But some frayed ragtag judgment, some embryo gleam of simple yet-virgin discretion and common sense, persuaded him at least to try me first, to have me by as a kind of hostage. And he didn't need to try, test me first. When grown people speak of the innocence of children, they dont really know what they mean. Pressed, they will go a step further and say, Well, ignorance then. The child is neither. There is no crime which a boy of eleven had not envisaged long ago. His only innocence is, he may not yet be old enough to desire the fruits of it, which is not innocence but appetite; his ignorance is, he does not know how to commit it, which is not ignorance but size.

But Boon didn't know this. He must seduce me. And he had so little time: only from the time the train left until dark. He could have started cold, from scratch, tomorrow or next day or any day up to and including Wednesday. But today, now, was his best, with the car visible to all Jefferson, already in motion, already involved in the condition of departure; it was as if the gods themselves had offered him these scot-free hours between eleven-two and sunset, he to scorn, ignore them at his peril. The car came up, Grandfather and Grandmother already in it, with the shoebox of fried chicken and devilled eggs and cake for dinner since there wouldn't be a dining car until they changed to the Limited at the junction at one oclock and Grandmother and Mother both knew Grandfather and Father well enough by this time to know they were not going to wait until one oclock to eat dinner, no matter who was dead. No: Grandmother too, if the bereaved had been anybody but Mother. No, that's wrong too; Grandmother had a wider range than her son's wife; maybe all Mother would have needed was to be a female. It's not men who cope with death; they resist, try to fight back and get their brains trampled out in consequence; where women just flank it, envelop it in one soft and instantaneous confederation of unresistance like cotton batting or cobwebs, already de-stingered and harmless, not merely reduced to size and usable but even useful like a penniless bachelor or spinster connection always available to fill an empty space or conduct an extra guest down to dinner. Their grips were already tied onto the fenders and Son Thomas had already brought Mother's and Father's out to the street and now we all followed, Mother in her black veil and Father with his black arm band, us following with Aunt Callie carrying Alexander. "Goodbye," Mother said, "good-bye," kissing us veil and all, smelling like she always did but with something black in the smell too, like the thin black veil which really hid nothing, as if more than just a mechanical electric message over the copper wire had come that three hundred miles up from Bay St Louis; oh yes, I could smell it when she kissed me, saying, "You're the big boy, the man now. You must help Aunt Callie with the others, so they wont worry Cousin Louisa," already getting quick into the automobile beside Grandmother, when Boon said,

"I'll have to fill the tank for the trip out to McCaslin after dinner. I thought Lucius could come along now and help me on the way back from the depot." You see, how easy it was going to be. It was too easy, making you a little ashamed. It was as if the very cards of virtue and rectitude were stacked against Grandfather and Grandmother and Mother and Father. All right then: against me too. Even the fact that automobiles were only two or three years old in Jefferson abetted Boon—all right, us. Mr Rouncewell, the oil company agent who supplied all the stores in Yoknapatawpha County from his tanks on the side track at the depot, for the last two years had also had a special tank of gasoline, with a pump and a Negro to pump it; all Boon or anyone else who wanted gasoline had to do was, simply drive up and stop and get out and the Negro would lift off the front seat and measure the tank with his special notched stick and fill the tank and collect the money or (if Mr Rouncewell himself wasn't there) let you yourself write down your name and how many gallons in a greasy ledger. But, although Grandfather had owned the car almost a year now, not one of them—Grandfather or Grandmother or Father or Mother—had either the knowledge about how cars operated or the temerity (or maybe it was just the curiosity) to question or challenge Boon.

So he and I stood on the platform; Mother waved to us through the window as the train drew away. Now it was his move. He would have to say something, have to begin. He had managed to get the decks cleared and me in his power, at least until Aunt Callie began to wonder where I was to eat my dinner. I mean, Boon didn't know he didn't have to say anything, other than perhaps to tell me where we were going, and even that—the destination— didn't matter. He had learned nothing since about human beings, and apparently had even forgot what he once must have known about boys.

And now Boon himself didn't know how to begin. He had prayed for luck, and immediately, by return post you might say, had been vouchsafed more than he knew what to do with. They have told you before this probably that Fortune is a fickle jade, who never withholds but gives, either good or bad: more of the former than you ever believe (perhaps with justice) that you deserve; more of the latter than you can handle. So with Boon. So all he said was, "Well."

Nor did I help him; I took that revenge. All right,

revenge on whom? Not on Boon of course: on me, my shame; perhaps on Father and Mother, who had abandoned me to the shame; perhaps on Grandfather, whose automobile had made the shame available; who knows? perhaps on Mr Buffaloe himself—that rapt and divinely stricken somnambulist who had started the whole thing two innocent years ago. But I did feel sorry for Boon because he had so little time. It was after eleven now; Aunt Callie would be expecting me back in a matter of minutes, not because she knew it couldn't take more than ten minutes to get back home after she heard Twenty-three whistle for the lower crossing, but because she would already be in a driving impatience to get us all fed and on the way to McCaslin; she had been born in the country and still preferred it. Boon wasn't looking at me. He very carefully wasn't looking at me. "Three hundred miles," he said. "Good thing somebody invented trains. If they'd a had to go by mule wagon like folks used to, they couldn't even get there in ten days, let alone back in ten days too."

"Father said four days," I said.

"That's right," Boon said. "So he did. Maybe we got four days to get back to the house in, but that still dont give us forever." We went back to the car and got in it. But he didn't start it. "Maybe when Boss gets back in te— four days he'll let me learn you to run this thing. You're big enough. Besides, you already know how. Have you ever thought about that?"

"No," I said. "Because he aint going to let me."

"Well, you dont need to rush at it. You got four days for him to change his mind in. Though my guess is nearer ten." Still he didn't move to start the car. "Ten days," he said. "How far do you reckon this automobile could travel in ten days?"

"Father said four," I said.

"All right," he said. "How far in four days?"

"I aint going to know that either," I said. "Because aint anybody around here going to find out to tell me."

"All right," he said. He started the car suddenly and backed and turned it, already going fast, neither toward the Square nor toward Mr Rouncewell's gasoline pump.

"I thought we had to get gasoline," I said.

We were going fast. "I changed my mind," Boon said. "I'll tend to that just before we leave for McCaslin after dinner. Then so much of it wont evaporate away just standing around." We were in a lane now, going fast between Negro cabins and vegetable patches and chicken yards, with chickens and mongrel dogs leaping frantically from the dust just in time, out of the lane and into a vacant field, a waste place marked faintly with tire tracks but no hooves; and now I recognised it: Mr Buffaloe's homemade motordrome where Colonel Sartoris's law had driven him two years ago and where he had taught Boon to operate an automobile. And still I didn't understand until Boon wrenched the car to a stop and said, "Move over here."

So I was late for dinner after all; Aunt Callie was already standing on the front gallery, carrying Alexander and already yelling at Boon and me even before he stopped the car to let me out. Because Boon licked me in fair battle after all; evidently he hadn't quite forgot all he remembered from his own youth about boys. I know better now of course, and I even knew better then: that Boon's fall and mine were not only instantaneous but simultaneous too: back at the identical instant when Mother got the message that Grandfather Lessep was dead. But that's what I would have liked to believe: that Boon simply licked me. Anyway, that's what I told myself at the time: that, secure behind that inviolable and inescapable rectitude concomitant with the name I bore,

patterned on the knightly shapes of my male ancestors
as bequeathed—nay, compelled—to me by my father's
word-of-mouth, further bolstered and made vulnerable
to shame by my mother's doting conviction, I had been
merely testing Boon; not trying my own virtue but
simply testing Boon's capacity to undermine it; and, in
my innocence, trusting too much in the armor and shield
of innocence; expected, demanded, assumed more than
that frail Milanese was capable of withstanding. I say
"frail Milanese" not advisedly but explicitly: having
noticed in my time how quite often the advocates and
even the practitioners of virtue evidently have grave
doubts of their own regarding the impregnability of virtue as a shield, putting their faith and trust not in virtue
but rather in the god or goddess whose charge virtue is;
by-passing virtue as it were in allegiance to the Over-
goddess herself, in return for which the goddess will
either divert temptation away or anyhow intercede between them. Which explains a lot, having likewise noticed
in my time that the goddess in charge of virtue seems
to be the same one in charge of luck, if not of folly also.

So Boon beat me in fair battle, using, as a gentleman
should and would, gloves. When he stopped the car and
said, "Move over," I thought I knew what he intended.
We had done this before at four or five convenient and
discreet times in Grandfather's lot, me sitting on Boon's
lap holding the wheel and steering while he let the
automobile move slowly in low gear across the lot. So
I was ready for him. I was already *en garde* and had
even begun the counterthrust, opening my mouth to
say *It's too hot to sit on anybody today. Besides we better
get on back on home* when I saw that he was already out
of the car on his side while he was still speaking, standing
there with one hand on the wheel and the engine still
running. For another second or two I still couldn't be-

lieve it. "Hurry up," he said. "Any minute now Callie will come running out of that lane toting that baby under one arm and already yelling."

So I moved under the wheel, and with Boon beside me, over me, across me, one hand on mine to shift the gears, one hand on mine to regulate the throttle, we moved back and forth across that vacant sun-glared waste, forward a while, backward a while, intent, timeless, Boon as much as I, immersed, rapt, steadying me (he was playing for such stakes, you see), out of time, beyond it, invulnerable to time until the courthouse clock striking noon a half-mile away restored us, hurled us back into the impending hard world of finagle and deception.

"All right," Boon said, "quick," not even waiting but lifting me bodily across him as he slid under the wheel, the car already rushing back across the field toward home, we talking man-to-man now, mutual in crime, confederate of course but not coeval yet because of my innocence; I already beginning to say *What do I do now? You'll have to tell me* when once again Boon spoke first and made us equal too: "Have you figgered how to do it? We aint got much time."

"All right," I said. "Go on. Get on back to the house before Aunt Callie starts hollering." So you see what I mean about Virtue? You have heard—or anyway you will —people talk about evil times or an evil generation. There are no such things. No epoch of history nor generation of human beings either ever was or is or will be big enough to hold the un-virtue of any given moment, any more than they could contain all the air of any given moment; all they can do is hope to be as little soiled as possible during their passage through it. Because what pity that Virtue does not—possibly cannot—take care of its own as Non-virtue does. Probably it cannot: who to the dedicated to Virtue, offer in reward only cold and

odorless and tasteless virtue: as compared not only to
the bright rewards of sin and pleasure but to the ever
watchful unflagging omniprescient skill—that incredible
matchless capacity for invention and imagination—with
which even the tottering footsteps of infancy are steadily
and firmly guided into the primrose path. Because oh
yes, I had matured terrifyingly since that clock struck
two minutes ago. It has been my observation that, except in a few scattered cases of what might be called
malevolent hyper-prematurity, children, like poets, lie
rather for pleasure than profit. Or so I thought I had
until then, with a few negligible exceptions involving
simple self-defense against creatures (my parents) bigger
and stronger than me. But not any more. Or anyway,
not now. I was as bent as Boon, and—during the next
step anyway—even more culpable. Because (I realised;
no: knew; it was obvious; Boon himself admitted it in
so many words) I was smarter than Boon. I realised,
felt suddenly that same exultant fever-flash which Faustus himself must have experienced: that of we two
doomed and irrevocable, I was the leader, I was the
boss, the master.

Aunt Callie was already standing on the front gallery,
carrying Alexander and yelling.

"Dry up," I said. "Aint dinner ready? The automobile
broke down. Boon fixed it. We never had time to get the
gasoline and now I have to eat in a hurry and go back
and help him fill the tank." I went back to the dining
room. Dinner was already on the table. Lessep and
Maury were already eating. Aunt Callie had already
dressed them (she had dressed them to go seventeen
miles out to Cousin Zack's to spend four days as if they
were going to Memphis; I dont know why, unless it
was because she didn't have anything else to do between
the time Mother and Father left and dinner. Because

Maury and Alexander would both have to take a nap before we could leave) but by the front of his blouse, she would have to wash Maury off and dress him again.

Even then, I finished before they did and went back (Aunt Callie was still yelling, not loud in the house of course. But what could she do, single-handed—and a Negro—against Non-virtue?) across the street to Grandfather's. Ned had probably left for town as soon as the automobile drove off. But he would probably come back for his dinner. He had. We stood in the back yard. He blinked at me. Quite often, most of the time in fact, his eyes had a reddish look, like a fox's. "Why dont you aim to stay out there?" he said.

"I promised some fellows we would slip off tomorrow and try a new fishing hole one of them knows about."

Ned blinked at me. "So you aims to ride out to McCaslin with Boon Hogganbeck and then turn right around and come back with him. Only you got to have something to tell Miss Louisa so she'll let you come back and so you needs me to front for you."

"No," I said. "I dont need anything from you. I'm just telling you so you'll know where I am and they wont blame you. I aint even going to bother you. I'm going to stay with Cousin Ike." Before the rest of them came, I mean my brothers, when Mother and Father were out late at night and Grandfather and Grandmother were gone too, I used to stay with Ned and Delphine. Sometimes I would sleep in their house all night, just for fun. I could have done that now, if it would have worked. But Cousin Ike lived alone in a single room over his hardware store. Even if Ned (or somebody else concerned) asked him point-blank if I was with him Saturday night, it would be at least Monday by then, and I had already decided quick and hard not to think about Monday. You see, if only people didn't refuse quick and hard to think about next Monday, Virtue wouldn't have such a hard and thankless time of it.

"I see," Ned said. "You aint needing nothing from me. You just being big-hearted to save me bother and worry over you. Save everybody bother and worry that comes around wanting to know why you aint out at McCaslin where your paw told you to be." He blinked at me. "Hee hee hee," he said.

"All right," I said. "Tell Father I went fishing on Sunday while they were gone. See if I care."

"I aint fixing to tell nobody nothing about you," he said. "You aint none of my business. You's Callie's business unto your maw gets back. Unlessen you gonter transfer to Mr Ike's business for tonight, like you said." He blinked at me. "When is Boon Hogganbeck coming for yawl?"

"Pretty soon now," I said. "And you better not let Father or Boss hear you calling him Boon Hogganbeck."

"I calls him Mister in plenty of time for him to earn it," Ned said. "Let alone deserve it." He said, "Hee hee hee."

You see? I was doing the best I could. My trouble was, the tools I had to use. The innocence and the ignorance: I not only didn't have strength and knowledge, I didn't even have time enough. When the fates, gods—all right, Non-virtue—give you opportunities, the least they can do is give you room. But at least Cousin Ike was easy to find on Saturday. "You bet," he said. "Come and stay with me tonight. Maybe we'll go fishing tomorrow—just dont tell your father."

"No sir," I said. "Not stay with you tonight. I'm going to stay with Ned and Delphine, like I always do. I just wanted you to know, since Mother's not here where I can tell her. I mean, ask her." You see: doing the best I could with what I had, knew. Not that I was losing faith in ultimate success: it simply seemed to me that Non-virtue was wasting in merely testing me that time which was urgent and even desperate for greater ends. I went back home, not running: Jefferson must not see me running; but as fast as I could without it. You see, I did not dare trust Boon unbacked in Aunt Callie's hands.

I was in time. In fact, it was Boon and the automobile who were late. Aunt Callie even had Maury and Alexander re-dressed again; if they had had naps since dinner, it was the shortest fastest sleep on record in our house. Also, Ned was there, where he had no business being. No, that's not right. I mean, his being there was completely wrong: not being at our house, he was often there, but being anywhere where he could be doing something useful with Grandfather and Grandmother out of town. Because he was carrying the baggage out— the wicker basket of Alexander's diapers and other personal odds and ends, the grips containing mine and Lessep's and Maury's clothes for four days, and Aunt Callie's cloth-wrapped bundle, lumping them without order at the gate and telling Aunt Callie: "You might just as well set down and rest your feet. Boon Hogganbeck's done broke that thing and is somewhere trying to fix it. If you really wants to get out to McCaslin before suppertime, telefoam Mr Ballott at the stable to send Son Thomas with the carriage and I'll drive you out there like folks ought to travel."

And after a while it began to look like Ned was right. Half past one came (which time Alexander and Maury could have spent sleeping) and no Boon; then Maury and Alexander could have slept another half an hour on top of that; Ned had said "I tole you so" so many times by now that Aunt Callie had quit yelling about Boon and yelled at Ned himself until he went and sat in the scuppernong arbor; she was just about to send me to look

for Boon and the automobile when he drove up. When
I saw him, I was terrified. He had changed his clothes. I
mean, he had shaved and he had on not merely a white
shirt but a clean one, with a collar and necktie; without
doubt when he got out of the car to load us in he would
have a coat over his arm and the first thing Aunt Callie
would see when she reached the car would be his grip
on the floor. Horror, but rage too (not at Boon: I discovered, realised that at once) at myself, who should
have known, anticipated this, having known (I realised
this too now) all my life that who dealt with Boon dealt
with a child and had not merely to cope with but even
anticipate its unpredictable vagaries; not the folly of
Boon's lack of the simplest rudiments of common sense,
but the shame of my failure to anticipate, assume he
would lack them, saying, crying to Whoever it is you
indict in such crises *Don't You realise I aint but eleven
years old? How do You expect me to do all this at just
eleven years old? Dont You see You are putting on me
more than I can handle?* But in the next second, rage at
Boon too: not that his stupidity had now wrecked for
good our motor trip to Memphis (that's right, Memphis
as our destination has never been mentioned, either to
you or between Boon and me. Why should it have been?
Where else did we have to go? Indeed, where else could
anyone in north Mississippi want to go? Some aged and
finished creature on his or her deathbed might contem-
plate or fear a more distant destination, but they were
not Boon and me). In fact, at this moment I wished I
had never heard of Memphis or Boon or automobiles
either; I was on Colonel Sartoris's side now, to have
abolished Mr Buffaloe and his dream both from the face
of the earth at the instant of its inception. My rage at
Boon was for having destroyed, cast down with that one
childish blow like the blind kick of an infant's foot, the

precarious and frantic ramshackle of my lies and false promises and false swearing; revealing the clay-footed sham for which I had bartered—nay, damned—my soul; that, or maybe the exposing of the true shoddy worthlessness of the soul I had been vain enough to assume the devil would pay anything for: like losing your maidenhead through some shabby inattentive mischance, such as not watching where you were going, innocent even of pleasure, let alone of sin. Then even the rage was gone. Nothing remained, nothing. I didn't want to go anywhere, be anywhere. I mean, I didn't want to be *is* anywhere. If I had to be something, I wanted it to be *was*. I said, and I believed it (I know I believed it because I have said it a thousand times since and I still believe it and I hope to say it a thousand times more in my life and I defy anyone to say I will not believe it) *I will never lie again. It's too much trouble. It's too much like trying to prop a feather upright in a saucer of sand. There's never any end to it. You never get any rest. You're never finished. You never even use up the sand so that you can quit trying.*

Only, nothing happened. Boon got out, without any coat. Ned was already loading our grips and baskets and bundles into the car. He said grimly: "Hee hee hee." He said, "Come on, get started so you can break down and still have time to fix it and get back to town before dark." So he was talking to Boon now. He said, "Are you coming back to town before you leaves?"

Then Boon said: "Leave for where?"

"Leave to eat supper," Ned said. "Where does anybody with good sense leave to do at sundown?"

"Oh," Boon said. "You worry about your supper. That's the only supper you got to worry about eating."

We got in and started, me in front with Boon and the rest of them in the back. We crossed the Square

crowded with Saturday afternoon, and then we were
out of town. But there we were. I mean, we were no
forrader. We would come presently to the fork of the
road which led to Cousin Zack's, and we would even be
going in the wrong direction. And even if it had been the
right direction, we still would not be free; as long as we
still had Aunt Callie and Lessep and Maury and Alexander in the back seat, we were only free of Ned being
where nobody in the world had expected him to be,
saying Hee hee hee and Are you coming back to town
before. Boon had never once looked at me, nor I at him.
Nor had he spoken to me either; possibly he sensed that
he had frightened me with his clean shirt and collar and
necktie and the shave in the middle of the day and all
the rest of the give-away aura of travel, departure, sepa-
ration, severance; sensed that I was not only frightened
but angry that I had been vulnerable to fright; going
on, the sunny early afternoon road stretching on ahead
for the seventeen miles during which something would
have to be decided, agreed upon; on across the bright
May land, our dust spurting and coiling behind us unless
we had to slow down for a bridge or a sandy stretch
which required the low gears; the seventeen miles which
would not last forever even though there were seventeen
of them, the mileposts diminishing much too rapidly
while something had to be done, decided sooner and
sooner and nearer and nearer and I didn't know what
yet; or maybe just something said, a voice, noise, a
human sound, since no matter what bitter forfeit Non-
virtue may afterward wrench and wring from you, lone-
liness, solitude, silence should not be part of it. But at
least Boon tried. Or maybe with him it was just the silence
too and any un-silence were better, no matter how
foolish nor long-ago pre-doomed. No, it was more than

that; we had less than half the distance left now and something had to be done, started, fused-off:

"The roads are sure fine now, everywhere, even further than Yoknapatawpha County. A man couldn't want better roads for a long trip like a automobile funeral or something than they are now. How far do you reckon this car could go between now and sundown?" You see? addressed to nobody, like the drowning man thrusting one desperate hand above the surface hoping there might be a straw there. He found none:

"I dont know," Aunt Callie said from the back seat, holding Alexander, who had been asleep since we left town and didn't deserve a car ride of one mile, let alone seventeen. "And you aint gonter know neither, unlessen you studies it out setting in that front seat locked up in that shed in Boss's back yard tonight."

Now we were almost there. "So you want—" Boon said, out of the side of his mouth, just exactly loud enough for me to hear, aimed exactly at my right ear like a gun or an arrow or maybe a handful of sand at a closed window.

"Shut up," I said, exactly like him. The simple and cowardly thing would be to tell him suddenly to stop and as he did so, leap from the car, already running, presenting to Aunt Callie the split-second alternative either to abandon Alexander to Boon and try to run me down in the bushes, or stick with Alexander and pursue me with simple yelling. I mean, have Boon drive on and leave them at the house and I to spring out from the roadside and leap back aboard as he passed going back to town or any direction opposite from all who would miss me and have authority over me; the cowardly way, so why didn't I take it, who was already a lost liar, already damned by deceit; why didn't I go the whole hog and be a coward too; be irrevocable and irremediable like Faustus became? glory in baseness, make, compel my new Master to respect me for my completeness even if he did scorn my size? Only I didn't. It wouldn't have worked, one of us anyway had to be practical; granted that Boon and I would be well on our way before Cousin Louisa could send someone to the field where Cousin Zack would be at three oclock in the afternoon during planting time, and granted that Cousin Zack couldn't possibly have overtaken us on his saddle horse: he wouldn't have tried to: he would have ridden straight to town and after one minute each with Ned and Cousin Ike, he would have known exactly what to do and would have done it, using the telephone and the police.

We were there. I got out and opened the gate (the same posts of old Lucius Quintus Carothers's time; your present Cousin Carothers has a cattle guard in it now so automobiles can cross, not owning hooves) and we went on up the locust drive toward the house (it is still there: the two-room mud-chinked log half domicile and half fort which old Lucius came with his slaves and foxhounds across the mountains from Carolina in 1813 and built; it is still there somewhere, hidden beneath the clapboards and Greek Revival and steamboat scroll-work which the women the successive Edmondses marry have added to it).

Cousin Louisa and everybody else on the place had already heard us approaching and (except probably the ones Cousin Zack could actually see from his horse) were all on the front gallery and steps and the yard when we drove up and stopped.

"All right," Boon said, again out of the side of his mouth, "do you want." Because, as you say nowadays, this was it; no time any more, let alone privacy, to get some—any—inkling of what he now must desperately know. Because we—he and I—were so new at this, you

see. We were worse than amateurs: innocents, complete
innocents at stealing automobiles even though neither
of us would have called it stealing since we intended to
return it unharmed; and even, if people, the world (Jefferson anyway) had just let us alone, unmissed. Even if
I could have answered him if he had asked. Because it
was even worse for me than for him; both of us were
desperate but mine was the more urgent desperation
since I had to do something, and quick, in a matter of
seconds now, while all he had to do was sit in the car with
at most his fingers crossed. I didn't know what to do
now; I had already told more lies than I had believed
myself capable of inventing, and had had them believed
or at least accepted with a consistency which had left
me spellbound if not already appalled; I was in the
position of the old Negro who said, "Here I is, Lord.
If You wants me saved, You got the best chance You
ever seen standing right here looking at You." I had
shot my bow, Boon's too. If Non-virtue still wanted either
of us, it was now her move.

Which she did. She was dressed as Cousin Zachary
Edmonds. He came out the front door at that moment
and at the same moment I saw that a Negro boy in the
yard was holding the reins of his saddle horse. You see
what I mean? Zachary Edmonds, whom Jefferson never
saw on a weekday between the first ground-breaking in
March and laying-by in July, had been in town this
morning (something urgent about the grist mill) and
had stopped in Cousin Ike's store barely minutes after
I had done so myself; which, dovetailed neatly and
exactly with the hour and more Non-virtue had required
to shave Boon and change his shirt, had given Cousin
Zack the exact time necessary to ride home and be getting
off his horse at his doorstep when they heard us coming.
He said—to me: "What are you doing out here? Ike told

me you were going to stay in town tonight and he is
going to take you fishing tomorrow."

So of course Aunt Callie began yelling then so I didn't
need to say anything at all even if I had known anything
to say. "Fishing?" she hollered. "On Sunday? If his paw
could hear that, he would jump off that train this minute
without even waiting to telegraph! His maw too! Miss
Alison aint told him to stay in town with no Mister Ike
nor nobody else! She told him to come on out here with
me and these other chillen and if he dont behave his-self,
Mister Zack would make him!"

"All right, all right," Cousin Zack said. "Stop yelling
a minute; I cant hear him. Maybe he's changed his mind.
Have you?"

"Sir?" I said. "Yes sir. I mean, no sir."

"Well, which? Are you going to stay out here, or are
you going back with Boon?"

"Yes sir," I said. "I'm going back. Cousin Ike told me
to ask you if I could." And Aunt Callie yelled again (she
had never really stopped except for maybe that one long
breath when Cousin Zack told her to) but that was all: she
still yelling and Cousin Zack saying,

"Stop it, stop it, stop it. I cant hear my ears. If Ike
dont bring him out tomorrow, I'll send in for him Monday." I went back to the car: Boon had the engine already
running.

"Well I'll be damned," he said, not loud but with complete respect, even awe a little.

"Come on," I said. "Get away from here." We went
on, smoothly but quick, faster, back down the drive
toward the gate.

"Maybe we're wasting something, just spending it on
a automobile trip," he said. "Maybe I ought to use you
for something that's got money in it."

"Just get on," I said. Because how could I tell him,

how say it to him? *I'm sick and tired of lying, of having to lie.* Because I knew, realised now that it had only begun; there would be no end to it, not only no end to the lies I would continue to have to tell merely to protect the ones I had already told, but that I would never be free of the old worn-out ones I had already used and exhausted.

We went back to town. We went fast this time; if there was scenery now, nobody in that automobile used any of it. It was going on five oclock now. Boon spoke, tense and urgent but quite composed: "We got to let it cool awhile. They saw me drive out of town taking you folks out to McCaslin; they'll see me come back with just you and me alone; they'll expect to see me put the car back in Boss's carriage house. Then they got to see me and you, but separate, just walking around like wasn't nothing going on." But how could I say that either? *No. Let's go now. If I've got to tell more lies, at least let it be to strangers.* He was still talking: "—car. What was that he said about were we coming back through town before we left?"

"What? Who said?"

"Ned. Back there just before we left town."

"I dont remember," I said. "What about the car?"

"Where to leave it. While I take a santer around the Square and you go home and get a clean shirt or whatever you'll need. I had to unload all the stuff out at McCaslin, remember. Yours too. I mean, just in case some meddling busybody is hanging around just on the happen-chance." We both knew who he meant.

"Why cant you lock it in the carriage house?"

"I aint got the key," he said. "All I got is the lock. Boss took the key away from me this morning and unlocked the lock and give the key to Mr Ballott to keep until he gets back. I'm supposed to run the car in as soon as I get back from McCaslin and lock the lock shut and Boss will telegraph Mr Ballott what train to unlock the door so I can meet them."

"Then we'll just have to risk it," I said.

"Yes, we'll have to risk it. Maybe with Boss and Miss Sarah gone, even Delphine aint going to see him again until Monday morning." So we risked it. Boon drove into the carriage house and got his grip and coat down from where he had hidden them in the loft and reached up again and dragged down a folded tarpaulin and put his grip and coat in on the floor of the back seat. The gasoline can was all ready: a brand-new five-gallon can which Grandfather had had the tinsmith who made the toolbox more or less rebuild until it was smell-tight, since Grandmother already didn't like the smell of gasoline, which we had never used yet because the automobile had never been this far before; the funnel and the chamois strainer were already in the toolbox with the tire tools and jack and wrenches that came with the car, and the lantern and axe and shovel and coil of barbed wire and the block and tackle which Grandfather had added, along with the tin bucket to fill the radiator when we passed creeks or barrow pits. He put the can (it was full; maybe that was what took him the extra time before he came for us) in the back and opened the tarpaulin, not spreading it but tumbling it into the back until everything was concealed to just look like a jumbled mass of tarpaulin. "We'll shove yours under the same way," he said. "Then it wont look like nothing but a wad of tarpollyon somebody was too lazy to fold up. What you better do is go home and get your clean shirt and come straight back here and wait. I wont be long: just santer around the Square in case Ike wants to start asking questions too. Then we'll be gone."

We closed the door. Boon started to hang the open padlock back in the staple. "No," I said; I couldn't even have said why, so fast I had progressed in evil. "Put it in your pocket."

But he knew why; he told me. "You damn right," he said. "We done gone through too much to have somebody happen-chance by and snap it shut because they thought I forgot to."

I went home. It was just across the street. A filling station is there now, and what was Grandfather's house is now chopped into apartments, precarious of tenure. The house was empty, unlocked of course, since nobody in Jefferson locked mere homes in those innocent days. It was only a little after five, nowhere near sundown, yet the day was finished, done for; the empty silent house was not vacant at all but filled with presences like held breath; and suddenly I wanted my mother; I wanted no more of this, no more of free will; I wanted to return, relinquish, be secure, safe from the sort of decisions and deciding whose foster twin was this having to steal an automobile. But it was too late now; I had already chosen, elected; if I had sold my soul to Satan for a mess of pottage, at least I would damn well collect the pottage and eat it too: hadn't Boon himself just reminded me, almost as if he had foreseen this moment of weakness and vacillation in the empty house, and forewarned me: "We done gone through too much to let nothing stop us now."

My clothes—fresh blouses, pants, stockings, my toothbrush—were out at McCaslin now. I had more in my drawer of course, except the toothbrush, which in Mother's absence it was a fair gamble that neither Aunt Callie nor Cousin Louisa would remember about. But I took no clothes, nothing; not that I forgot to but probably because I had never intended to. I just entered the house and stood inside the door long enough to prove to myself that of Boon and me it wouldn't be me who failed us, and went back across the street and across Grandfather's

back yard to the lot. Nor was Boon the one who would
fail us; I heard the engine running quietly before I
reached the carriage house. Boon was already behind the
wheel; I think the automobile was even already in gear.
"Where's your clean shirt?" he said. "Never mind. I'll buy
you one in Memphis. Come on. We can move now." He
backed the car out. The open lock was once more hanging in the staple. "Come on," he said. "Dont stop to lock
it. It's too late now."

"No," I said. I couldn't have said then why either:
with the padlock snapped through the staple and hasp
of the closed door, it would look like the automobile was
safely inside. And so it would be: the whole thing no
more than a dream from which I could wake tomorrow,
perhaps now, the next moment, and be safe, saved. So
I closed the door and locked the padlock and opened
the lot gate for Boon to drive out and closed that too and
got in, the car already in motion—if in fact it had ever
completely stopped. "If we go the back way, we can
dodge the Square," I said. And again he said:

"It's too late now. All they can do now is holler." But
none hollered. But even with the Square behind, it still
was not too late. That irrevocable decision was still a mile
ahead, where the road to McCaslin forked away from
the Memphis road, where I could say *Stop. Let me out*
and he would do it. More: I could say *I've changed my
mind. Take me back to McCaslin* and I knew he would
do that too. Then suddenly I knew that if I said *Turn
around. I will get that key from Mr Ballott·and we will
lock this automobile up in the carriage house where
Boss believes it already is at this moment* and he would
do that. And more: that he wanted me to do that, was
silently begging me to do that; he and I both aghast
not at his individual temerity but at our mutual, our
confederated recklessness, and that Boon knew he had

not the strength to resist his and so must cast himself on my strength and rectitude. You see? What I told you about Non-virtue? If things had been reversed and I had silently pled with Boon to turn back, I could have depended on his virtue and pity, where he to whom Boon pled had neither.

So I said nothing; the fork, the last frail impotent hand reached down to save me, flew up and passed and fled, was gone, irrevocable; I said *All right then. Here I come.* Maybe Boon heard it, since I was still boss. Anyway, he put Jefferson behind us; Satan would at least defend his faithful from the first one or two tomorrows; he said: "We aint really got anything to worry about but Hell Creek bottom tomorrow. Harrykin Creek aint anything."

"Who said it was?" I said. Hurricane Creek is four miles from town; you have passed over it so fast all your life you probably dont even know its name. But people who crossed it then knew it. There was a wooden bridge over the creek itself, but even in the top of summer the approaches to it were a series of mudholes.

"That's what I'm telling you," Boon said. "It aint anything. Me and Mr Wordwin got through it that day last year without even using the block and tackle: just a shovel and axe Mr Wordwin borrowed from a house about a half a mile away, that now you mention it I dont believe he took back. Likely though the fellow come and got them the next day."

He was almost right. We got through the first mudhole and even across the bridge. But the other mudhole stopped us. The automobile lurched once, twice, tilted and hung spinning. Boon didn't waste any time, already removing his shoes (I forgot to say he had had them shined too), and rolled up his pants legs and stepped out into the mud. "Move over," he said. "Put it in low gear and start when I tell you. Come on. You know how to

do it; you learned how this morning." I got under the
wheel. He didn't even stop for the block and tackle. "I
dont need it. It'll take too much time getting it out and
putting it back and we aint got time." He didn't need it.
There was a snake fence beside the road; he had already
wrenched the top rail off and, himself knee-deep in mud
and water, wedged the end under the back axle and said,
"Now. Pour the coal to her," and lifted the automobile
bodily and shot it forward lurching and heaving, by main
strength up onto dry ground again, shouting at me: "Shut
it off! Shut it off!" which I did, managed to, and he came
and shoved me over and got in under the wheel; he didn't
even stop to roll his muddy pants down.

Because the sun was almost down now; it would be
nearly dark by the time we reached Ballenbaugh's, where
we would spend the night; we went as fast as we dared
now and soon we were passing Mr Wyott's—a family
friend of ours; Father took me bird hunting there that
Christmas—which was eight miles from Jefferson and
still four miles from the river, with the sun just setting
behind the house. We went on; there would be a moon
after a while, because our oil headlights were better to
show someone else you were coming rather than to light
you where you were going; when suddenly Boon said,
"What's that smell? Was it you?" But before I could deny
it he had jerked the automobile to a stop, sat for an instant,
then turned and reached back and flung back the lumped
and jumbled mass of the tarpaulin which had filled the
back of the car. Ned sat up from the floor. He had on the
black suit and hat and the white shirt with the gold collar
stud without either collar or tie, which he wore on Sunday; he even had the small battered hand grip (you
would call it a brief or attaché case now) which had belonged to old Lucius McCaslin before even Father was
born; I dont know what else he might have carried in it

at other times. All I ever saw in it was the Bible (likewise from Great-great-grandmother McCaslin), which he couldn't read, and a pint flask containing maybe a good double tablespoonful of whiskey. "I'll be a son of a bitch," Boon said.

"I wants a trip too," Ned said. "Hee hee hee."

4

◆◆◆◆

"I got just as much right to a trip as you and Lucius," Ned said. "I got more. This automobile belongs to Boss and Lucius aint nothing but his grandboy and you aint no kin to him a-tall."

"All right, all right," Boon said. "What I'm talking about, you laid there under that tarpollyon all the time and let me get out in the mud and lift this whole car out single-handed by main strength."

"And hot under there too, mon," Ned said. "I dont see how I stood it. Not to mention having to hold off this here sheet-iron churn from knocking my brains out every time you bounced, let alone waiting for that gasoline or whatever you calls it to get all joogled up to where it would decide to blow up too. What did you aim for me to do? That was just four miles from town. You'd make me walk back home."

"This is ten miles now," Boon said. "What makes you think you aint going to walk them back home?"

I said, rapidly, quickly: "Have you forgot? That was Wyott's about two miles back. We might just as well be two miles from Bay St. Louis."

"That's right," Ned said pleasantly. "The walking aint near so fur from here." Boon didn't look at him long.

"Get out and fold up that tarpollyon where it wont take up no more room than it has to," he told Ned. "And air it off some too if we got to ride with it."

"It was all that bumping and jolting you done," Ned said. "You talk like I broke my manners just on purpose to get caught."

Also, Boon lit the headlights while we were stopped, and now he wiped his feet and legs off on a corner of the tarpaulin and put his socks and shoes on and rolled his pants back down; they were already drying. The sun was gone now; already you could see the moonlight. It would be full night when we reached Ballenbaugh's.

I understand that Ballenbaugh's is now a fishing camp run by an off-and-on Italian bootlegger—off I mean during the one or two weeks it takes each new sheriff every four years to discover the true will of the people he thought voted for him; all that stretch of river bottom which was a part of Thomas Sutpen's doomed baronial dream and the site of Major de Spain's hunting camp is now a drainage district; the wilderness where Boon himself in his youth hunted (or anyway was present while his betters did) bear and deer and panther, is tame with cotton and corn now and even Wyott's Crossing is only a name.

Even in 1905 there was still vestigial wilderness, though most of the deer and all the bears and panthers (also

Major de Spain and his hunters) were gone; the ferry
also; and now we called Wyott's Crossing the Iron Bridge,
THE Iron Bridge since it was the first iron bridge and for
several years yet the only one we in Yoknapatawpha
County had or knew of. But back in the old days, in the
time of our own petty Chickasaw kings, Issetibbeha and
Moketubbe and the regicide-usurper who called himself
Doom, and the first Wyott came along and the Indians
showed him the crossing and he built his store and ferryboat and named it after himself, this was not only the only
crossing within miles but the head of navigation too;
boats (in the high water of winter, even a small steamboat) came as it were right to Wyott's front door, bringing the whiskey and plows and coal oil and peppermint
candy up from Vicksburg and carrying the cotton and
furs back.

But Memphis was nearer than Vicksburg even by
mule team, so they built a road as straight from Jefferson
to the south bend of Wyott's ferryboat as they could
run it, and as straight from the north end of the ferryboat to Memphis as they could run that. So the cotton
and freight began to come and go that way, mule- or
ox-drawn; whereupon there appeared immediately from
nowhere an ancestryless giant calling himself Ballenbaugh; some said he actually bought from Wyott the
small dim heretofore peaceful one-room combined resi-
dence and store, including whatever claim he (Wyott)
considered he had in the old Chickasaw crossing; others
said that Ballenbaugh simply suggested to Wyott that he
(Wyott) had been there long enough now and the time
had come for him to move four miles back from the river
and become a farmer.

Anyway, that's what Wyott did. And then his little
wilderness-cradled hermitage became a roaring place
indeed: it became dormitory, grubbing station and saloon

for the transient freighters and the fixed crews of hard-mouthed hard-souled mule skinners who met the wagons at both edges of the bottom, with two and three and (when necessary) four span of already geared-up mules, to curse the heavy wagons in to the ferry on one side of the river, and from the ferry to high ground once more on the other. A roaring place; who faced it were anyway men. But just tough men then, no more, until Colonel Sartoris (I dont mean the banker with his courtesy title acquired partly by inheritance and partly by propinquity, who was responsible for Boon and me being where we at this moment were; I mean his father, the actual colonel, C.S.A.—soldier, statesman, politician, duelist; the collateral descending nephews and cousins of one twenty-year-old Yoknapatawpha County youth say, murderer) built his railroad in the mid-seventies and destroyed it.

But not Ballenbaugh's, let alone Ballenbaugh. The wagon trains came and drove the boats from the river and changed the name of Wyott's Crossing to Ballenbaugh's Ferry; the railroads came and removed the cotton bales from the wagons and therefore the ferry from Ballenbaugh's, but that was all; forty years before, in the modest case of the trader, Wyott, Ballenbaugh showed himself perfectly capable of anticipating the wave of the future and riding it; now, in the person of his son, another giant who in 1865 returned with (it was said) his coat lined with uncut United States bank notes, from (he said) Arkansas, where (he said) he had served and been honorably discharged from a troop of partisan rangers, the name of whose commander he was never subsequently able to recall, he showed that he had lost none of his old deftness and skill and omniscience. Formerly, people passed through Ballenbaugh's, pausing for the night; now they travelled to Ballenbaugh's, always at night and often rapidly, to give Ballenbaugh as much time as pos-

sible to get the horse or cow concealed in the swamp
before the law or the owner arrived. Because, in addition
to gangs of angry farmers following the nonreturning
prints of horses and cattle, and sheriffs following those of
actual murderers into Ballenbaugh's, at least one federal
revenue agent left a set of nonreturning footprints. Because where Ballenbaugh senior merely sold whiskey,
this one made it too; he was now the patron of what is
covered by the euphemistic blanket-term of dance hall,
and by the mid-eighties Ballenbaugh's was a byword
miles around for horror and indignation; ministers and
old ladies tried to nominate sheriffs whose entire platform would be running Ballenbaugh and his drunks and
fiddlers and gamblers and girls out of Yoknapatawpha
County and Mississippi too if possible. But Ballenbaugh
and his entourage—stable, pleasure-dome, whatever you
want to call it—never bothered us outsiders: they never
came out of their fastness and there was no law compel-
ling anyone to go there; also, seemingly his new avocation
(avatar) was so rewarding that word went round that
anyone with sights and ambition no higher than one
spavined horse or dry heifer was no longer welcome there.
So sensible people simply let Ballenbaugh's alone. Which
certainly included sheriffs, who were not only sensible
but family men too, and who had the example of the
federal revenuer who had vanished in that direction not
so long ago.

That is, until the summer of 1886, when a Baptist
minister named Hiram Hightower—also a giant of a
man, as tall and almost as big as Ballenbaugh himself,
who on Sunday from 1861 to 1865 had been one of
Forrest's company chaplains and on the other six days
one of his hardest and most outrageous troopers—rode
into Ballenbaugh's armed with a Bible and his bare hands
and converted the entire settlement with his fists, one

at a time when he could, two or three at a time when he had to. So when Boon and Ned and I approached it in this May dusk of 1905, Ballenbaugh was accomplishing his third avatar in the person of a fifty-year-old maiden: his only child: a prim fleshless severe iron-gray woman who farmed a quarter section of good bottom cotton- and corn-land and conducted a small store with a loft above it containing a row of shuck mattresses each with its neat perfectly clean sheets and pillow cases and blankets for the accommodation of fox- and coon-hunters and fishermen, who (it was said) returned the second time not for the hunting and fishing but for the table Miss Ballenbaugh set.

She heard us too. Nor were we the first; she told us that we were the thirteenth automobile to pass there in the last two years, five of them in the last forty days; she had already lost two hens and would probably have to begin keeping everything penned up, even the hounds. She and the cook and a Negro man were already on the front gallery, shading their eyes against the ghostly flicker of our headlights as we drove up. She not only knew Boon of old, she recognised the automobile first; already, even after only thirteen of them, her eye for individual cars was that good.

"So you really did make it to Jefferson, after all," she said.

"In a year?" Boon said. "Lord, Miss Ballenbaugh, this automobile has been a hundred times farther than Jefferson since then. A thousand times. You might as well give up: you got to get used to automobiles like everybody else." That was when she told us about the thirteen cars in two years, and the two hens.

"At least they got a ride on an automobile for a little piece anyway," she said. "Which is more than I can say."

"You mean to say you aint never rode in one?" Boon

said. "Here, Ned," he said, "jump out of there and get them grips out too. Loosh, let Miss Ballenbaugh set up in front where she can see out."

"Wait," Miss Ballenbaugh said. "I must tell Alice about supper."

"Supper can wait," Boon said. "I bet Alice aint never had a car ride neither. Come on, Alice. Who's that with you? Your husband?"

"I aint studying no husband," the cook said. "And I wouldn't be studying Ephum even if I was."

"Bring him on anyway," Boon said. The cook and the man came and got in too, into the back seat with the gasoline can and the folded tarpaulin. Ned and I stood in the lamplight from the open door and watched the automobile, the red tail lamp, move on up the road, then stop and back and turn and come back past us, Boon blowing the horn now, Miss Ballenbaugh sitting erect and a little tense in the front seat, Alice and Ephum in the back seat waving to us as they passed.

"Whooee, boy," Ephum shouted at Ned. "Git a horse!"

"Showing off," Ned said; he meant Boon. "He better be sho proud Boss Priest aint standing here too. He'd show him off." The car stopped and backed and turned again and came back to us and stopped. After a moment Miss Ballenbaugh said,

"Well." Then she moved; she said briskly: "All right, Alice." So we had supper. And I knew why the hunters and fishermen came back. Then Ned went off with Ephum and I made my manners to Miss Ballenbaugh and, Boon carrying the lamp, we went upstairs to the loft above the store.

"Didn't you bring nothing?" Boon said. "Not even a clean handkerchief?"

"I wont need anything," I said.

"Well, you cant sleep like that. Look at them clean

sheets. At least take off your shoes and pants. And your maw would make you brush your teeth too."

"No she wouldn't," I said. "She couldn't. I aint got anything to brush them with."

"That wouldn't stop her, and you know it. If you couldn't find something, you'd make something to do it with or know the reason why."

"All right," I said. I was already on my mattress. "Good night." He stood with his hand up to blow out the lamp.

"You all right?" he said.

"Shut up," I said.

"Say the word. We'll go back home. Not now but in the morning."

"Did you wait this long to get scared?" I said.

"Good night," he said. He blew out the lamp and got on his mattress. Then there was all the spring darkness: the big bass-talking frogs from the sloughs, the sound that the woods makes, the big woods, the wilderness with the wild things: coons and rabbits and mink and mushrats and the big owls and the big snakes—moccasins and rattlers—and maybe even the trees breathing and the river itself breathing, not to mention the ghosts—the old Chickasaws who named the land before the white men ever saw it, and the white men afterward—Wyott and old Sutpen and Major de Spain's hunters and the flatboats full of cotton and then the wagon trains and the brawling teamsters and the line of brigands and murderers which produced Miss Ballenbaugh; suddenly I realised what the noise was that Boon was making.

"What are you laughing at?" I said.

"I'm thinking about Hell Creek bottom. We'll hit it about eleven oclock tomorrow morning."

"I thought you said we'll have trouble there."

"You damn right we will," Boon said. "It'll take that axe and shovel and bob wire and block and tackle and all the fence rails and me and you and Ned all three. That's who I'm laughing at: Ned. By the time we are through Hell Creek tomorrow, he's going to wish he hadn't busted what he calls his manners nor et nor done nothing else under that tarpollyon until he felt Memphis itself under them wheels."

Then he waked me early. And everybody else within a half mile, though it still took some time to get Ned up from where he had slept in Ephum's house, to the kitchen to eat his breakfast (and even longer than that to get him out of the kitchen again with a woman in it). We ate breakfast—and after that breakfast if I had been a hunter or a fisherman I wouldn't have felt like walking anywhere for a while—and Boon gave Miss Ballenbaugh another ride in the automobile, but without Alice and Ephum this time, though Ephum was on hand. Then we—Boon— filled the gasoline tank and the radiator, not because they needed it but I think because Miss Ballenbaugh and Ephum were there watching, and started. The sun was just rising as we crossed the Iron Bridge over the river (and the ghost of that steamboat too; I had forgot that last night) into foreign country, another county; by night it would even be another state, and Memphis.

"Providing we get through Hell Creek," Boon said.

"Maybe if you'd just stop talking about it," I said.

"Sure," Boon said. "Hell Creek bottom dont care whether you talk about it or not. It dont have to give a durn. You'll see." Then he said, "Well, there it is." It was only a little after ten; we had made excellent time following the ridges, the roads dry and dusty between the sprouting fields, the land vacant and peaceful with Sunday, the people already in their Sunday clothes idle on the front galleries, the children and dogs already running toward the fence or road to watch us pass; then in the surreys and buggies and wagons and horse- and mule-back, anywhere from one to three on the horse but not on the mule (a little after nine we passed another automobile; Boon said it was a Ford; he had an eye for automobiles like Miss Ballenbaugh's), on the way to the small white churches in the spring groves.

A wide valley lay before us, the road descending from the plateau toward a band of willow and cypress which marked the creek. It didn't look very bad to me, nowhere near as wide as the river bottom we had already crossed, and we could even see the dusty gash of the road mounting to the opposite plateau beyond it. But Boon had already started to curse, driving even faster down the hill almost as if he were eager, anxious to reach and join battle with it, as if it were something sentient, not merely inimical but unredeemable, like a human enemy, another man. "Look at it," he said. "Innocent as a new-laid egg. You can even see the road beyond it like it was laughing at us, like it was saying If you could just get here you could durn near see Memphis; except just see if you can get here."

"If it's all that bad, why dont we go around it?" Ned said. "That's what I would do if it was me setting there where you is."

"Because Hell Creek bottom aint got no around," Boon said violently. "Go one way and you'd wind up in Alabama; go the other way and you'll fall off in the Missippi River."

"I seen the Missippi River at Memphis once," Ned said. "Now you mention it, I done already seen Memphis too. But I aint never seen Alabama. Maybe I'd like a trip there."

"You aint never visited Hell Creek bottom before neither," Boon said. "Providing what you hid under that tarpollyon for yesterday is education. Why do you reckon the only two automobiles we have seen between now and

Jefferson was this one and that Ford? Because there aint no other automobiles in Missippi below Hell Creek, that's why."

"Miss Ballenbaugh counted thirteen passed her house in the last two years," I said.

"Two of them was this one," Boon said. "And even them other eleven she never counted crossing Hell Creek, did she?"

"Maybe it depends on who's doing the driving," Ned said. "Hee hee hee."

Boon stopped the car, quickly. He turned his head. "All right. Jump out. You want to visit Alabama. You done already made yourself fifteen minutes late running your mouth."

"Why you got to snatch a man up just for passing the day with you?" Ned said. But Boon wasn't listening to him. I dont think he was really speaking to Ned. He was already out of the car; he opened the toolbox Grandfather had had made on the running board to hold the block and tackle and axe and spade and the lantern, taking everything out but the lantern and tumbling them into the back seat with Ned.

"So we wont waste any time," he said, speaking rapidly, but quite composed, calm, without hysteria or even urgency, closing the box and getting back under the wheel. "Let's hit it. What're we waiting for?"

Still it didn't look bad to me—just another country road crossing another swampy creek, the road no longer dry but not really wet yet, the holes and boggy places already filled for our convenience by previous pioneers with brush tops and limbs, and sections of it even corduroyed with poles laid crossways in the mud (oh yes, I realised suddenly that the road—for lack of any closer term—had stopped being not really wet yet too) so perhaps Boon himself was responsible; he himself had populated the stagnant cypress- and willow-arched mosquito-whined gloom with the wraiths of stuck automobiles and sweating and cursing people. Then I thought we had struck it, except for that fact that I not only couldn't see any rise of drier ground which would indicate we were reaching, approaching the other side of the swamp, I couldn't even see the creek itself ahead yet, let alone a bridge. Again the automobile lurched, canted, and hung as it did yesterday at Hurricane Creek; again Boon was already removing his shoes and socks and rolling up his pants. "All right," he said to Ned over his shoulder, "get out."

"I dont know how," Ned said, not moving. "I aint learned about automobiles yet. I'll just be in your way. I'll set here with Lucius so you can have plenty of room."

"Hee hee hee," Boon said in savage and vicious mimicry. "You wanted a trip. Now you got one. Get out."

"I got my Sunday clothes on," Ned said.

"So have I," Boon said. "If I aint scared of a pair of britches, you needn't be."

"You can talk," Ned said. "You got Mr Maury. I has to work for my money. When my clothes gets ruint or wore out, I has to buy new ones myself."

"You never bought a garment of clothes or shoes or a hat neither in your life," Boon said. "You got one pigeon-tailed coat I know of that old Lucius McCaslin himself wore, let alone General Compson's and Major de Spain's and Boss's too. You can roll your britches up and take off your shoes or not, that's your business. But you're going to get out of this automobile."

"Let Lucius get out," Ned said. "He's younger than me and stouter too for his size."

"He's got to steer it," Boon said.

"I'll steer it, if that's all you needs," Ned said. "I been what you calls steering horses and mules and oxen all my life and I reckon gee and haw with that steering wheel aint no different from gee and haw with a pair of lines or a goad." Then to me: "Jump out, boy, and help Mr Boon. Better take your shoes and stockings—"

"Are you going to get out, or do I pick you up with one hand and snatch this automobile out from under you with the other?" Boon said. Ned moved then, fast enough when he finally accepted the fact that he had to, only grunting a little as he took off his shoes and rolled up his pants and removed his coat. When I looked back at Boon, he was already dragging two poles, sapling-sized tree trunks, out of the weeds and briers.

"Aint you going to use the block and tackle yet?" I said.

"Hell no," Boon said. "When the time comes for that, you wont need to ask nobody's permission about it. You'll already know it." *So it's the bridge* I thought. *Maybe there's not even a bridge at all and that's what's wrong.* And Boon read my mind there too. "Don't worry about the bridge. We aint even come to the bridge yet."

I would learn what he meant by that too, but not now. Ned lowered one foot gingerly into the water. "This water got dirt in it," he said. "If there's one thing I hates, it's dirt betwixt my nekkid toes."

"That's because your circulation aint warmed up yet," Boon said. "Take a-holt of this pole. You said you aint acquainted with automobiles yet. That's one complaint you wont never have to make again for the rest of your life. All right"—to me—"ease her ahead now and whenever she bites, keep her going." Which we did, Boon and Ned levering their poles forward under the back axle, pinching us forward for another lurch of two or three or sometimes five feet, until the car hung spinning again, the whirling back wheels coating them both from knee to crown as if they had been swung at with one of the spray nozzles which house painters use now. "See what I mean?" Boon said, spitting, giving another terrific wrench and heave which sent us lurching forward, "about getting acquainted with automobiles? Exactly like horses and mules: dont never stand directly behind one that's got one hind foot already lifted."

Then I saw the bridge. We had come up onto a patch of earth so (comparatively) dry that Boon and Ned, almost indistinguishable now with mud, had to trot with their poles and even then couldn't keep up, Boon hollering, panting, "Go on! Keep going!" until I saw the bridge a hundred yards ahead and then saw what was still between us and the bridge and I knew what he meant. I stopped the car. The road (the passage, whatever you would call it now) in front of us had not altered so much as it had transmogrified, exchanged mediums, elements. It now resembled a big receptacle of milk-infused coffee from which protruded here and there a few forlorn impotent hopeless odds and ends of sticks and brush and logs and an occasional hump of actual earth which looked startlingly like it had been deliberately thrown up by a plow. Then I saw something else, and understood what Boon had been telling me by indirection about Hell Creek bottom for over a year now, and what he had been reiterating with a kind of haunted bemused obsession ever since we left Jefferson yesterday. Standing hitched to a tree just off the road (canal) were two mules in plow gear—that is, in bridles and collars and hames, the trace chains looped over the hames and the plowlines coiled into neat hanks and hanging from the hames also; leaning against another tree nearby was a heavy double-winged plow—a middlebuster—caked, wings shank and the beam itself, with more of the same mud which was rapidly encasing Boon and Ned, a doubletree, likewise mudcaked, leaning against the plow; and in the immediate background a new two-room paintless shotgun cabin on the gallery of which a man sat tilted in a splint chair, barefoot, his galluses down about his waist and his (likewise muddy) brogan shoes against the wall beside the chair. And I knew that this, and not Hurricane Creek, was where (Boon said) he and Mr Wordwin had had to borrow the shovel last year, which (Boon said) Mr Wordwin had forgot to return, and which (the shovel) Mr Wordwin might as well have forgot to borrow also for all the good it did them.

Ned had seen it too. He had already had one hard look at the mudhole. Now he looked at the already geared-up mules standing there swishing and slapping at mosquitoes while they waited for us. "Now, that's what I calls convenient—" he said.

"Shut up," Boon said in a fierce murmur. "Not a word. Dont make a sound." He spoke in a tense controlled fury, propping his muddy pole against the car and hauling out the block and tackle and the barbed wire and the axe and spade. He said Son of a bitch three times. Then he said to me: "You too."

"Me?" I said.

"But look at them mules," Ned said. "He even got a log chain already hooked to that doubletree—"

"Didn't you hear me say shut up?" Boon said in that fierce, quite courteous murmur. "If I didn't speak plain enough, excuse me. What I'm trying to say is, shut up."

"Only, what in the world do he want with the middle-buster?" Ned said. "And it muddy clean up to the handles too. Like he been— You mean to say he gets in here with that team and works this place like a patch just to keep it boggy?" Boon had the spade, axe and block and tackle all three in his hands. For a second I thought he would strike Ned with any one or maybe all three of them. I said quickly:

"What do you want me—"

"Yes," Boon said. "It will take all of us. I—me and

Mr Wordwin had a little trouble with him here last year; we got to get through this time—"

"How much did you have to pay him last year to get drug out?" Ned said.

"Two dollars," Boon said. "—so you better take off your whole pants, take off your shirt too; it'll be all right here—"

"Two dollars?" Ned said. "This sho beats cotton. He can farm right here setting in the shade without even moving. What I wants Boss to get me is a well-travelled mudhole."

"Fine," Boon said. "You can learn how on this one." He gave Ned the block and tackle and the piece of barbed wire. "Take it yonder to that willow, the big one, and get a good holt with it." Ned payed out the rope and carried the head block to the tree. I took off my pants and shoes and stepped down into the mud. It felt good, cool. Maybe it felt that way to Boon too. Or maybe his—Ned's too— was just release, freedom from having to waste any time now trying not to get muddy. Anyway, from now on he simply ignored the mud, squatting in it, saying Son of a bitch quietly and steadily while he fumbled the other piece of barbed wire into a loop on the front of the car to hook the block in. "Here," he told me, "you be dragging up some of that brush over yonder," reading my mind again too: "I dont know where it came from neither. Maybe he stacks it up there himself to keep handy for folks so they can find out good how bad they owe him two dollars."

So I dragged up the brush—branches, tops—into the mud in front of the car, while Boon and Ned took up the slack in the tackle and got ready, Ned and I on the take-up rope of the tackle, Boon at the back of the car with his prize pole again. "You got the easy job," he told us. "All you got to do is grab and hold when I heave. All right," he said, "Let's go."

There was something dreamlike about it. Not nightmarish: just dreamlike—the peaceful, quiet, remote, sylvan, almost primeval setting of ooze and slime and jungle growth and heat in which the very mules themselves, peacefully swishing and stamping at the teeming infinitesimal invisible myriad life which was the actual air we moved and breathed in, were not only unalien but in fact curiously appropriate, being themselves biological dead ends and hence already obsolete before they were born; the automobile: the expensive useless mechanical toy rated in power and strength by the dozens of horses, yet held helpless and impotent in the almost infantile clutch of a few inches of the temporary confederation of two mild and pacific elements—earth and water—which the frailest integers and units of motion as produced by the ancient unmechanical methods, had coped with for countless generations without really having noticed it; the three of us, three forked identical and now unrecognisable mud-colored creatures engaged in a life-and-death struggle with it, the progress—if any—of which had to be computed in dreadful and glacier-like inches. And all the while, the man sat in his tilted chair on the gallery watching us while Ned and I strained for every inch we could get on the rope which by now was too slippery with mud to grip with the hands, and at the rear of the car Boon strove like a demon, titanic, ramming his pole beneath the automobile and lifting and heaving it forward; at one time he dropped, flung away the pole and, stooping, grasped the car with his hands and actually ran it forward for a foot or two as though it were a wheelbarrow. No man could stand it. No man should ever have to. I said so at last. I stopped pulling, I said, panted: "No. We cant do it. We just cant." And Boon, in an expiring voice as faint and gentle as the whisper of love:

"Then get out of the way or I'll run it over you."

"No," I said. I stumbled, slipping and plunging, back to him. "No," I said. "You'll kill yourself."

"I aint tired," Boon said in that light dry voice. "I'm just getting started good. But you and Ned can take a rest. While you're getting your breath, suppose you drag up some more of that brush—"

"No," I said, "no! Here he comes! Do you want him to see it?" Because we could see him as well as hear—the suck and plop of the mules' feet as they picked their delicate way along the edge of the mudhole, the almost musical jangle of the looped chains, the man riding one and leading the other, his shoes tied together by the laces looped over one of the hames, the doubletree balanced in front of him as the old buffalo hunters in the pictures carried their guns—a gaunt man, older than we—I any-way—had assumed.

"Morning, boys," he said. "Looks like you're about ready for me now. Howdy, Jefferson," he said to Boon. "Looks like you did get through last summer, after all."

"Looks like it," Boon said. He had changed, instantane-ous and complete, like a turned page: the poker player who has just seen the second deuce fall to a hand across the table. "We might a got through this time too if you folks didn't raise such heavy mud up here."

"Dont hold that against us," the man said. "Mud's one of our best crops up thisaway."

"At two dollars a mudhole, it ought to be your best," Ned said. The man blinked at Ned a moment.

"I dont know but what you're right," he said. "Here. You take this doubletree; you look like a boy that knows which end of a mule to hook to."

"Get down and do it yourself," Boon said. "Why else are we paying you two dollars to be the hired expert? You done it last year."

"That was last year," the man said. "Dabbling around

in this water hooking log chains to them things under-
mined my system to where I come down with rheumatism
if I so much as spit on myself." So he didn't stir. He just
brought the mules up and turned them side by side while
Boon and Ned hooked the trace chains to the singletrees
and then Boon squatted in the mud to make the log chain
fast to the car.

"What do you want me to hook it to?" he said.

"I dont care myself," the man said. "Hook up to any
part of it you want out of this mudhole. If you want all
of it to come out at the same time, I'd say hook to the
axle. But first I'd put all them spades and ropes back
in the automobile. You wont need them no more, at least
here." So Ned and I did that, and Boon hooked up and
we all three stood clear and watched. He was an expert
of course, but by now the mules were experts too, breaking the automobile free of the mud, keeping the strain
balanced on the doubletree as delicately as wire walkers,
getting the automobile into motion and keeping it there
with no more guidance than a word now and then from
the man who rode the near mule, and an occasional touch
from the peeled switch he carried; on to where the
ground was more earth than water.

"All right, Ned," Boon said. "Unhook him."

"Not yet," the man said. "There's another hole just this
side of the bridge that I'm throwing in free. You aint
been acquainted here for a year now." He said to Ned:
"What we call the reserve patch up thisaway."

"You means the Christmas middle," Ned said.

"Maybe I do," the man said. "What is it?"

Ned told him. "It's how we done at McCaslin back
before the Surrender when old L.Q.C. was alive, and
how the Edmonds boy still does. Every spring a middle
is streaked off in the best ground on the place, and every
stalk of cotton betwixt that middle and the edge of the

field belongs to the Christmas fund, not for the boss but for every McCaslin nigger to have a Christmas share of it. That's what a Christmas middle is. Likely you mud-farming folks up here never heard of it." The man looked at Ned awhile. After a while Ned said, "Hee hee hee."

"That's better," the man said. "I thought for a minute me and you was about to misunderstand one another." He said to Boon: "Maybe somebody better guide it."

"Yes," Boon said. "All right," he told me. So I got under the wheel, mud and all. But we didn't move yet. The man said, "I forgot to mention it, so maybe I better. Prices have doubled around here since last year."

"Why?" Boon said. "It's the same car, the same mud-hole; be damned if I dont believe it's even the same mud."

"That was last year. There's more business now. So much more that I cant afford not to go up."

"All right, goddammit," Boon said. "Go on." So we moved, ignominious, at the pace of the mules, on, into the next mudhole without stopping, on and out again. The bridge was just ahead now; beyond it, we could see the road all the way to the edge of the bottom and safety.

"You're all right now," the man said. "Until you come back." Boon was unhooking the log chain while Ned freed the traces and handed the doubletree back up to the man on the mule.

"We aint coming back this way," Boon said.

"I wouldn't neither," the man said. Boon went back to the last puddle and washed some of the mud from his hands and came back and took four dollars from his wallet. The man didn't move.

"It's six dollars," he said.

"Last year it was two dollars," Boon said. "You said it's double now. Double two is four. All right. Here's four dollars."

"I charge a dollar a passenger," the man said. "There was two of you last year. That was two dollars. The price is doubled now. There's three of you. That's six dollars. Maybe you'd rather walk back to Jefferson than pay two dollars, but maybe that boy and that nigger wouldn't."

"And maybe I aint gone up neither," Boon said. "Suppose I dont pay you six dollars. Suppose in fact I dont pay you nothing."

"You can do that too," the man said. "These mules has had a hard day, but I reckon there's still enough git in them to drag that thing back where they got it from."

But Boon had already quit, given up, surrendered. "God damn it," he said, "this boy aint nothing but a child! Sholy for just a little child—"

"Walking back to Jefferson might be lighter for him," the man said, "but it wont be no shorter."

"All right," Boon said, "but look at the other one! When he gets that mud washed off, he aint even white!"

The man looked at distance awhile. Then he looked at Boon. "Son," he said, "both these mules is color-blind."

5

◆◆◆◆

Boon had told Ned and me that, once we had conquered Hell Creek bottom, we would be in civilisation; he drew a picture of all the roads from there on cluttered thick as fleas with automobiles. Though maybe it was necessary first to put Hell Creek as far behind us as limbo, or forgetfulness, or at least out of sight; maybe we would not be worthy of civilisation until we had got the Hell Creek mud off. Anyway, nothing happened yet. The man took his six dollars and went away with his mules and double-tree; I noticed in fact that he didn't return to his little house but went on back through the swamp and vanished, as if the day were over; so did Ned notice it. "He aint a hog," Ned said. "He dont need to be. He's done already made six dollars and it aint even dinnertime yet."

"It is as far as I'm concerned," Boon said. "Bring the

lunch too." So we took the lunch box Miss Ballenbaugh had packed for us and the block and tackle and axe and shovel and our shoes and stockings and my pants (we couldn't do anything about the automobile, besides being a waste of work until we could reach Memphis, where surely—at least we hoped—there wouldn't be any more mudholes) and went back down to the creek and washed the tools off and coiled down the block and tackle. And there wasn't much to be done about Boon's and Ned's clothes either, though Boon got bodily into the water, clothes and all, and washed himself off and tried to persuade Ned to follow suit since he—Boon—had a change of clothes in his grip. But all Ned would do was to remove his shirt and put his coat back on. I think I told you about his attaché case, which he didn't so much carry when abroad as he wore it, as diplomats wear theirs, carrying (I mean Ned's Bible and the two tablespoonfuls of—probably—Grandfather's best whiskey) I suspect at times even less in them.

Then we ate lunch—the ham and fried chicken and biscuits and homemade pear preserves and cake and the jug of buttermilk—and put back the emergency mud-defying gear (which in the end had been not a defiance but an inglorious brag) and measured the gasoline tank—a gesture not to distance but to time—and went on. Because the die was indeed cast now; we looked not back to remorse or regret or might-have-been; if we crossed Rubicon when we crossed the Iron Bridge into another county, when we conquered Hell Creek we locked the portcullis and set the bridge on fire. And it did seem as though we had won to reprieve as a reward for invincible determination, or refusal to recognise defeat when we faced it or it faced us. Or maybe it was just Virtue who had given up, relinquished us to Non-virtue to cherish and nurture and coddle in the style whose right we had won with the now irrevocable barter of our souls.

The very land itself seemed to have changed. The farms were bigger, more prosperous, with tighter fences and painted houses and even barns; the very air was urban. We came at last to a broad highway running string-straight into distance and heavily marked with wheel prints; Boon said, with a kind of triumph, as if we had doubted him or as if he had invented it to disprove us, created it, cleared and graded and smoothed it with his own hands (and perhaps even added the wheel marks): "What did I tell you? The highway to Memphis." We could see for miles; much closer than that was a rapid and mounting cloud of dust like a portent, a promise. It was indubitable, travelling that fast and that much of it; we were not even surprised when it contained an automobile; we passed each other, commingling our dust into one giant cloud like a pillar, a signpost raised and set to cover the land with the adumbration of the future: the antlike to and fro, the incurable down-payment itch-foot; the mechanised, the mobilised, the inescapable destiny of America.

And now, gray with dust from toes to eyelids (particularly Boon's still-damp clothes), we could make time, even if, for a while, not speed; without switching off the engine Boon got out and walked briskly around the car to my side, saying briskly to me: "All right. Slide over. You know how. Just dont get the idea you're a forty-mile-a-hour railroad engine." So I drove, on across the sunny May afternoon. I couldn't look at it though, I was too busy, too concentrated (all right, too nervous and proud): the Sabbath afternoon, workless, the cotton and corn growing unvexed now, the mules themselves Sabbatical and idle in the pastures, the people still in their Sunday clothes on galleries and in shady yards with glasses of lemonade or saucers of the ice cream left from dinner. Then we made speed too; Boon said, "We're coming to some towns now. I better take it." We went on. Civilisation was now constant: single country stores and crossroads hamlets; we were barely free of one before here was another; commerce was rife about us, the air was indeed urban, the very dust itself which we raised and moved in had a metropolitan taste to tongue and nostrils; even the little children and the dogs no longer ran to the gates and fences to watch us and the three other automobiles we had passed in the last thirteen miles.

Then the country itself was gone. There were no longer intervals between the houses and shops and stores; suddenly before us was a wide tree-bordered and ordered boulevard with car tracks in the middle; and sure enough, there was the streetcar itself, the conductor and motorman just lowering the back trolley and raising the front one to turn it around and go back to Main Street. "Two minutes to five oclock," Boon said. "Twenty-three and a half hours ago we were in Jefferson, Missippi, eighty miles away. A record." I had been in Memphis before (so had Ned. This morning he had told us so; thirty minutes from now he would prove it) but always by train, never like this: to watch Memphis grow, increase; to assimilate it deliberately like a spoonful of ice cream in the mouth. I had never thought about it other than to assume we would go to the Gayoso Hotel as we—I anyway—always had. So I dont know what mind Boon read this time. "We're going to a kind a boarding house I know," he said. "You'll like it. I had a letter last week from one of the g— ladies staying there that she's got her nephew visiting her so you'll even have somebody to play with. The cook can locate a place for Ned to sleep too."

"Hee hee hee," Ned said. Besides the streetcars there

were buggies and surreys—phaetons, traps, stanhopes, at least one victoria, the horses a little white-eyed at us but still collected; evidently Memphis horses were already used to automobiles—so Boon couldn't turn his head to look at Ned. But he could turn one eye.

"Just what do you mean by that?" he said.

"Nothing," Ned said. "Mind where you're going and nemmine me. Nemmine me nohow. I got friends here too. You just show me where this automobile gonter be at tomorrow morning and I'll be there too."

"And you damn well better be," Boon said. "If you aim to go back to Jefferson in it. Me and Lucius never invited you on this trip so you aint none of mine and his responsibility. As far as me and Jefferson are concerned, I dont give a damn whether you come back or not."

"When we gets this automobile back in Jefferson and has to try to look Boss Priest and Mr Maury in the eye, aint none of us gonter have time to give a damn who is back and who aint," Ned said. But it was too late now, far too late to keep on bringing that up. So Boon just said,

"All right, all right. All I said was, if you want to be back in Jefferson when you start doing your not having time to give a damn, you better be where I can see you when I start back." We were getting close to Main Street now—the tall buildings, the stores, the hotels: the Gaston (gone now) and the Peabody (they have moved it since) and the Gayoso, to which all us McCaslins-Edmondses-Priests devoted our allegiance as to a family shrine because our remote uncle and cousin, Theophilus McCaslin, Cousin Ike's father, had been a member of the party of horsemen which legend said (that is, legend to some people maybe. To us it was historical fact) General Forrest's brother led at a gallop into the lobby itself and almost captured a Yankee general. We didn't go that

far though. Boon turned into a side street, almost a back
alley, with two saloons at the corner and lined with
houses that didn't look old or new either, all very quiet,
as quiet as Jefferson itself on Sunday afternoon. Boon in
fact said so. "You ought to seen it last night, I bet. On
any Saturday night. Or even on a week night when there's
a fireman's or policeman's or a Elk or something conven-
tion in town."

"Maybe they've all gone to early prayer meeting,"
I said.

"No," Boon said. "I dont think so. Likely they're just
resting."

"From what?" I said.

"Hee hee hee," Ned said in the back seat. Obviously,
we were learning, Ned had been in Memphis before.
Though probably even Grandfather, though he might
have known when, didn't know how often. And you
see, I was only eleven. This time, the street being empty,
Boon did turn his head.

"Just one more out of you," he told Ned.

"One more which?" Ned said. "All I says is, point
out where this thing gonter be at tomorrow morning,
and I'll already be setting in it when it leaves." So Boon
did. We were almost there: a house needing about the
same amount of paint the others did, in a small grassless
yard but with a sort of lattice vestibule like a well house
at the front door. Boon stopped the car at the curb. Now
he could turn and look at Ned.

"All right," he said. "I'm taking you at your word. And
you better take me at mine. On the stroke of eight oclock
tomorrow morning. And I mean the first stroke, not the
last one. Because I aint even going to be here to hear
it."

Ned was already getting out, carrying his little grip and
his muddy shirt. "Aint you got enough troubles of your

own on your mind, without trying to tote mine too?" he said. "If you can finish your business here by eight oclock tomorrow morning, how come you think I cant neither?" He walked on. Then he said, still walking on and not looking back: "Hee hee hee."

"Come on," Boon said. "Miss Reba'll let us wash up." We got out. Boon reached into the back and started to pick up his grip and said, "Oh yes," and reached to the dashboard and took the switch key out of the slot and put it in his pocket and started to pick up the grip and stopped and took the switch key out of his pocket and said, "Here. You keep it. I might lay it down somewhere and mislay it. Put it in your pocket good so it wont fall out. You can wad your handkerchief on top of it." I took the key and he started to reach for the grip again and stopped again and looked quick over his shoulder at the boarding house and turned sideways a little and took his wallet out of his hind pocket and opened it close to him and took out a five-dollar bill and stopped and then took out a one-dollar bill also and closed the wallet and slid it toward me behind his body, saying, not quick so much as quiet: "Keep this too. I might forget it somewhere too. Whenever we need money out of it I'll tell you how much to give me." Because I had never been inside a boarding house either; and remember, I was just eleven. So I put the wallet into my pocket too and Boon took the grip and we went through the gate and up the walk and into the lattice vestibule, and there was the front door. Boon had barely touched the bell when we heard feet inside. "What did I tell you?" Boon said rapidly. "They probably are all peeping from behind the window curtains at that automobile." The door opened. It was a young Negro woman but before she could open her mouth a white woman pushed her aside —a young woman too, with a kind hard handsome face and hair that was too red, with two of the biggest yellowish-colored diamonds I ever saw in her ears.

"Dammit, Boon," she said. "The minute Corrie got that dispatch yesterday I told her to telegraph you right back not to bring that child here. I've already had one in the house for a week now, and one hell-on-wheels is enough for any house or street either for that matter. Or even all Memphis, providing it's that one we already got. And dont lie that you never got the message neither."

"I didn't," Boon said. "We must have already left Jefferson before it got there. What do you want me to do with him then? tie him out in the yard?"

"Come on in," she said. She moved out of the door so we could enter; as soon as we did so, the maid locked the door again. I didn't know why then; maybe that was the way all people in Memphis did, even while they were at home. It was like any other hall, with a stairway going up, only at once I smelled something; the whole house smelled that way. I had never smelled it before. I didn't dislike it; I was just surprised. I mean, as soon as I smelled it, it was like a smell I had been waiting all my life to smell. I think you should be tumbled pell-mell, without warning, only into experience which you might well have spent the rest of your life not having to meet. But with an inevitable (ay, necessary) one, it's not really decent of Circumstance, Fate, not to prepare you first, especially when the preparation is as simple as just being fifteen years old. That was the kind of smell it was. The woman was still talking. "You know as well as I do that Mr Binford disapproves like hell of kids using houses for holiday vacations; you heard him last summer when Corrie brought that little s.o.b. in here the first time because she claims he dont get enough refinement on that Arkansas tenant farm. Like Mr Binford says, they'll be in here soon enough anyhow, so why rush them until at least they have some jack and are capable of spending it. Not to mention the customers, coming in here for business and finding instead we're running a damn kindergarden." We were in the dining room now. It had a Pianola in it. The woman was still talking. "What's his name?"

"Lucius," Boon said. "Make your manners to Miss Reba," he told me. I did so, the way I always did: that I reckon Grandfather's mother taught him and Grandmother taught Father and Mother taught us: what Ned called "drug my foot." When I straightened up, Miss Reba was watching me. She had a curious look on her face.

"I'll be damned," she said. "Minnie, did you see that? Is Miss Corrie—"

"She dressing as fast as she can," the maid said. And that was when I saw it. I mean, Minnie's tooth. I mean, that was how—yes, why—I, you, people, everybody, remembered Minnie. She had beautiful teeth anyhow, like small richly alabaster matched and evenly serrated headstones against the rich chocolate of her face when she smiled or spoke. But she had more. The middle right-hand upper one was gold; in her dark face it reigned like a queen among the white dazzle of the others, seeming actually to glow, gleam as with a slow inner fire or lambence of more than gold, until that single tooth appeared even bigger than both of Miss Reba's yellowish diamonds put together. (Later I learned—no matter how—that she had had the gold one taken out and an ordinary white one, like anybody else's, put in; and I grieved. I thought that, had I been of her race and age group, it would have been worth being her husband just to watch that tooth in action across the table every day; a child of eleven, it seemed to me that the very food it masticated must taste different, better.)

Miss Reba turned to Boon again. "What you been doing? wrassling with hogs?"

"We got in a mudhole back down the road. We drove up. The automobile's outside now."

"I saw it," Miss Reba said. "We all did. Dont tell me it's yours. Just tell me if the police are after it. If they are, get it away from my door. Mr Binford's strict about having police around here too. So am I."

"The automobile's all right," Boon said.

"It better be," Miss Reba said. She was looking at me again. She said, "Lucius," not to anybody. "Too bad you didn't get here sooner. Mr Binford likes kids. He still likes them even after he begins to have doubts, and this last week would have raised doubts in anybody that aint a ossified corpse. I mean, he was still willing to give Otis the benefit of the doubt to take him to the zoo right after dinner. Lucius could have gone too. But then on the other hand, maybe not. If Otis is still using up doubts at the same rate he was before they left here, he aint coming back—providing there's some way to get him up close enough to the cage for one of them lions or tigers to reach him—providing a lion or tiger would want him, which they wouldn't if they'd ever spent a week in the same house with him." She was still looking at me. She said, "Lucius," again, not at anybody. Then she said to Minnie: "Go up and tell everybody to stay out of the bathroom for the next half an hour." She said to Boon: "You got a change of clothes with you?"

"Yes," Boon said.

"Then wash yourself off and put them on; this is a decent place: not a joint. Let them use Vera's room, Minnie. Vera's visiting her folks up in Paducah." She said to Boon or maybe to both of us: "Minnie fixed a bed for Otis up in the attic. Lucius can sleep with him tonight—"

There were feet on the stairs, then in the hall and in

the door. This time it was a big girl. I dont mean fat: just big, like Boon was big, but still a girl, young too, with dark hair and blue eyes and at first I thought her face was plain. But she came into the room already looking at me, and I knew it didn't matter what her face was. "Hi, kiddo," Boon said. But she didn't pay any attention to him at all yet; she and Miss Reba were both looking at me.

"Watch now," Miss Reba said. "Lucius, this is Miss Corrie." I made my manners again. "See what I mean?" Miss Reba said. "You brought that nephew of yours over here hunting refinement. Here it is, waiting for him. He wont know what it means, let alone why he's doing it. But maybe Lucius could learn him to at least ape it. All right," she said to Boon. "Go get cleaned up."

"Maybe Corrie'll come help us," Boon said. He was holding Miss Corrie's hand. "Hi, kiddo," he said again.

"Not looking like a shanty-boat swamp rat," Miss Reba said. "I'll keep this damned place respectable on Sunday anyhow."

Minnie showed us where the room and the bathroom were upstairs and gave us soap and a towel apiece and went out. Boon put his grip on the bed and opened it and took out a clean shirt and his other pants. They were his everyday pants but the Sunday ones he had on wouldn't be fit to wear anywhere until they were cleaned with naphtha probably. "You see?" he said. "I told you so. I done the best I could to make you bring at least a clean shirt."

"My blouse aint muddy," I said.

"But you ought to have a fresh one just on principle to put on after you bathe."

"I aint going to bathe," I said. "I had a bath yesterday."

"So did I," he said. "But you heard what Miss Reba said, didn't you?"

"I heard her," I said. "I never knew any ladies anywhere that wasn't trying to make somebody take a bath."

"By the time you've known Miss Reba a few hours longer, you'll find out you done learned something else about ladies too: that when she suggests you to do something, it's a good idea to do it while you're still deciding whether you're going to or not." He had already unpacked his other pants and shirt. It doesn't take long to unpack one pair of pants and one shirt from one grip, but he seemed to be having trouble, mainly about putting them down after he took them out, not looking at me, bending over the open grip, busy, holding the shirt in his hand while he decided where to put the pants, then putting the shirt on the bed and picking up the pants again and moving them about a foot further along the bed, then picking up the shirt again and putting it where the pants were; then he cleared his throat loud and hard and went to the window and opened it and leaned out and spit and closed the window and came back to the bed, not looking at me, talking loud, like somebody that comes upstairs first on Christmas morning and tells you what you're going to get on the Christmas tree that's not the thing you wrote Santa Claus for:

"Dont it beat all how much a fellow can learn and in what a short time, about something he not only never knowed before, he never even had no idea he would ever want to know it, let alone would find it useful to him for the rest of his life—providing he kept it, never let it get away from him. Take you, for instance. Just think. Here it aint but yesterday morning, not even two days back yet, and think how much you have learned: how to drive a automobile, how to go to Memphis across the country without depending on the railroad, even how to get a automobile out of a mudhole. So that when you get big and own a automobile of your own, you will not only already know how to drive it but the road to Memphis too and even how to get it out of a mudhole."

"Boss says that when I get old enough to own an automobile, there wont be any more mudholes to get into. That all the roads everywhere will be so smooth and hard that automobiles will be foreclosed and reclaimed by the bank or even wear out without ever seeing a mudhole."

"Sure, sure," Boon said, "all right, all right. Say there aint no more need to know how to get out of a mudhole, at least you'll still know how to. Because why? Because you aint give the knowing how away to nobody."

"Who could I give it to?" I said. "Who would want to know how, if there aint any more mudholes?"

"All right, all right," Boon said. "Just listen to me a minute, will you? I aint talking about mudholes. I'm talking about the things a fellow—boy can learn that he never even thought about before, that forever afterward, when he needs them he will already have them. Because there aint nothing you ever learn that the day wont come when you'll need it or find use for it—providing you've still got it, aint let it get away from you by chance or, worse than that, give it away from carelessness or pure and simple bad judgment. Do you see what I mean now? Is that clear?"

"I dont know," I said. "It must be, or you couldn't keep on talking about it."

"All right," he said. "That's point number one. Now for point number two. Me and you have been good friends as long as we have known each other, we're having a nice trip together; you done already learned a few things you never seen nor heard of before, and I'm proud to be the one to be along and help you learn them. And tonight you're fixing to learn some more things I dont think you have thought about before neither—things and information and doings that a lot of folks in Jefferson and other places too will try to claim you aint old enough yet to be bothered with knowing about them. But shucks, a boy that not only learned to run a automobile but how to drive it to Memphis and get it out of that son of a bitch's private mudhole too, all in one day, is plenty old enough to handle anything he'll meet. Only—" He had to cough again, hard, and clear his throat and then go to the window and open it and spit again and close it again. Then he came back.

"And that's point number three. That's what I'm trying to impress on you. Everything a m— fel— boy sees and learns and hears about, even if he dont understand it at the time and cant even imagine he will ever have any use to know it, some day he will have a use for it and will need it, providing he has still got it and aint give it away to nobody. And then he will thank his stars for the good friend that has been his friend since he had to be toted around that livery stable on his back like a baby and held him on the first horse he ever rode, that warned him in time not to throw it away and lose it for good by forgetfulness or accident or mischance or maybe even just friendly blabbing about what aint nobody else's business but theirs—"

"What you mean is, whatever I see on this trip up here, not to tell Boss or Father or Mother or Grandmother when we get back home. Is that it?"

"Dont you agree?" Boon said. "Aint that not a bit more than just pure and sensible good sense and nobody's business but yours and mine? Dont you agree?"

"Then why didn't you just come right out and say so?" I said. Only he still remembered to make me take another bath; the bathroom smelled even more. I dont mean stronger: I just mean more. I didn't know much about boarding houses, so maybe they could have one with just ladies in it. I asked Boon; we were on the way back downstairs then; it was beginning to get dark and I was hungry.

"You damn right they're ladies," he said. "If I so much as catch you trying to show any sass to any of them—"

"I mean, dont any men board here? live here?"

"No. Dont no men actively live here except Mr Binford, and there aint no boarding to speak of neither. But they have plenty of company here, in and out after supper and later on; you'll see. Of course this is Sunday night, and Mr Binford is pretty strict about Sunday: no dancing and frolicking: just visiting their particular friends quiet and polite and not wasting too much time, and Mr Binford sees to it they damn sure better keep on being quiet and polite while they are here. In fact, he's a good deal that way even on week nights. Which reminds me. All you need to do is be quiet and polite yourself and enjoy yourself and listen good in case he happens to say anything to you in particular, because he dont talk very loud the first time and he dont never like it when somebody makes him have to talk twice. This way. They're likely in Miss Reba's room."

They were: Miss Reba, Miss Corrie, Mr Binford and Otis. Miss Reba had on a black dress now, and three more diamonds, yellowing too. Mr Binford was little, the littlest one in the room above Otis and me. He had on a black Sunday suit and gold studs and a big gold watch chain and a heavy moustache, and a gold-headed cane and his derby hat and a glass of whiskey on the table at his elbow. But the first thing you noticed about him was his eyes because the first thing you found out was that he was already looking at you. Otis had his Sunday clothes on too. He was not even as big as me but there was something wrong about him.

"Evening, Boon," Mr Binford said.

"Evening, Mr Binford," Boon said. "This is a friend of mine. Lucius Priest." But when I made my manners to him, he didn't say anything at all. He just quit looking at me. "Reba," he said, "buy Boon and Corrie a drink. Tell Minnie to make these boys some lemonade."

"Minnie's putting supper on," Miss Reba said. She unlocked the closet door. It had a kind of bar in it—one shelf with glasses, another with bottles. "Besides, that one of Corrie's dont want lemonade no more than Boon does. He wants beer."

"I know it," Mr Binford said. "He slipped away from me out at the park. He would have made it only he couldn't find anybody to go into the saloon for him. Is yours a beer-head too, Boon?"

"No sir," I said. "I dont drink beer."

"Why?" Mr Binford said. "You dont like it or you cant get it?"

"No sir," I said. "I'm not old enough yet."

"Whiskey, then?" Mr Binford said.

"No sir," I said. "I dont drink anything. I promised my mother I wouldn't unless Father or Boss invited me."

"Who's his boss?" Mr Binford said to Boon.

"He means his grandfather," Boon said.

"Oh," Mr Binford said. "The one that owns the automobile. So evidently nobody promised him anything."

"You dont need to," Boon said. "He tells you what to do and you do it."

"You sound like you call him boss too," Mr Binford said. "Sometimes."

"That's right," Boon said. That's what I meant about Mr Binford: he was already looking at me before I even knew it.

"But your mother's not here now," he said. "You're on a tear with Boon now. Eighty—is it?—miles away."

"No sir," I said. "I promised her."

"I see," Mr Binford said. "You just promised her you wouldn't drink with Boon. You didn't promise not to go whore-hopping with him."

"You son of a bitch," Miss Reba said. I dont know how to say it. Without moving, she and Miss Corrie jumped, sprang, confederated, Miss Reba with the whiskey bottle in one hand and three glasses in the other.

"That'll do," Mr Binford said.

"Like hell," Miss Reba said. "I can throw you out too. Dont think I wont. What the hell kind of language is that?"

"And you too!" Miss Corrie said; she was talking at Miss Reba. "You're just as bad! Right in front of them—"

"I said, that'll do," Mr Binford said. "One of them cant get beer and the other dont drink it so maybe they both just come here for refinement and education. Call it they just got some. They just learned that whore and son of a bitch are both words to think twice before pulling the trigger on because both of them can backfire."

"Aw, come on, Mr Binford," Boon said.

"Why, be damned if here aint still another hog in this wallow," Mr Binford said. "A big one, too. Wake up, Miss Reba, before these folks suffocate for moisture." Miss Reba poured the whiskey, her hand shaking, enough to clink the bottle against the glass, saying son of a bitch. son of a bitch. son of a bitch. in a thick fierce whisper.

"That's better," Mr Binford said. "Let's have peace around here. Let's drink to it." He raised his glass and was saying, "Ladies and gents all," when somebody—Minnie I suppose—began to ring a hand bell somewhere in the back. Mr Binford got up. "That's better still," he said. "Hash time. Learn us all the refinement and education that there's a better use for the mouth than running private opinions through it."

We went back toward the dining room, not fast, Mr

Binford leading the way. There were feet again, going fast; two more ladies, girls—that is, one of them was still a girl—hurried down the stairs, still buttoning their clothes, one in a red dress and the other in pink, panting a little. "We hurried as fast as we could," one of them said quickly to Mr Binford. "We're not late."

"I'm glad of that," Mr Binford said. "I dont feel like lateness tonight." We went in. There were more than enough places at the table, even with Otis and me. Minnie was still bringing things, all cold—fried chicken and biscuits and vegetables left over from dinner, except Mr Binford's. His supper was hot: not a plate, a dish of steak smothered in onions at his place. (You see? how much ahead of his time Mr Binford was? Already a Republican. I dont mean a 1905 Republican—I dont know what his Tennessee politics were, or if he had any— I mean a 1961 Republican. He was more: he was a Conservative. Like this: a Republican is a man who made his money; a Liberal is a man who inherited his; a Democrat is a barefooted Liberal in a cross-country race; a Conservative is a Republican who has learned to read and write.) We all sat down, the two new ladies too; I had met so many people by now that I couldn't get names any more and had stopped trying; besides, I never saw these two again. We began to eat. Maybe the reason Mr Binford's steak smelled so extra was that the rest of the food had smelled itself out at noon. Then one of the new ladies—the one who was no longer a girl—said,

"Were we, Mr Binford?" Now the other one, the girl, had stopped eating too.

"Were you what?" Mr Binford said.

"You know what," the girl said, cried. "Miss Reba," she said, "you know we do the best we can—dont dare make no extra noise—no music on Sunday when all the other places do—always shushing our customers up every time they just want to have a little extra fun—but if we aint already setting down at our places in this dining room when he sticks his nose in the door, next Saturday we got to drop twenty-five cents into that God damned box—"

"They are house rules," Mr Binford said. "A house without rules is not a house. The trouble with you bitches is, you have to act like ladies some of the time but you dont know how. I'm learning you how."

"You cant talk to me that way," the older one said.

"All right," Mr Binford said. "We'll turn it around. The trouble with you ladies is, you dont know how to quit acting like bitches."

The older one was standing now. There was something wrong about her too. It wasn't that she was old, like Grandmother is old, because she wasn't. She was alone. It was just that she shouldn't have had to be here, alone, to have to go through this. No, that's wrong too. It's that nobody should ever have to be that alone, nobody, not ever. She said, "I'm sorry, Miss Reba. I'm going to move out. Tonight."

"Where?" Mr Binford said. "Across the street to Birdie Watts's? Maybe she'll let you bring your trunk back with you this time—unless she's already sold it."

"Miss Reba," the woman said quietly. "Miss Reba."

"All right," Miss Reba said briskly. "Sit down and eat your supper; you aint going nowhere. Yes," she said, "I like peace too. So I'm going to mention just one more thing, then we'll close this subject for good." She was talking up the table at Mr Binford now. "What the hell's wrong with you? What the hell happened this afternoon to get you into this God damned humor?"

"Nothing that I noticed," Mr Binford said.

"That's right," Otis said suddenly. "Nothing sure didn't happen. He wouldn't even run." There was something, like a quick touch of electricity; Miss Reba was sitting

with her mouth open and her fork halfway in it. I didn't
understand yet but everybody else, even Boon, did. And
in the next minute I did too.

"Who wouldn't run?" Miss Reba said.

"The horse," Otis said. "The horse and buggy we bet
on in the race. Did they, Mr Binford?" Now the silence
was no longer merely electric: it was shocked, electro-
cuted. Remember I told you there was something wrong
somewhere about Otis. Though I still didn't think this was
quite it, or at least all of it. But Miss Reba was still
fighting. Because women are wonderful. They can bear
anything because they are wise enough to know that all
you have to do with grief and trouble is just go on through
them and come out on the other side. I think they can do
this because they not only decline to dignify physical
pain by taking it seriously, they have no sense of shame at
the idea of being knocked out. She didn't quit, even
then.

"A horse race," she said. "At the zoo? in Overton Park?"

"Not Overton Park," Otis said. "The driving park. We
met a man on the streetcar that knowed which horse
and buggy was going to win, and changed our mind
about Overton Park. Only, they didn't win, did they,
Mr Binford? But even then, we never lost as much as
the man did, we didn't even lose forty dollars because
Mr Binford give me twenty-five cents of it not to tell,
so all we lost was just thirty-nine dollars and seventy-five
cents. Only, on top of that, my twenty-five cents got
away from me in that beer mix-up Mr Binford was telling
about. Didn't it, Mr Binford?" And then some more
silence. It was quite peaceful. Then Miss Reba said,

"You son of a bitch." Then she said, "Go on. Finish
your steak first if you want." And Mr Binford wasn't a
quitter either. He was proud too: that gave no quarter
and accepted none, like a gamecock. He crossed his

knife and fork neatly and without haste on the steak he had barely cut into yet; he even folded his napkin and pushed it back through the ring and got up and said,

"Excuse me, all," and went out, looking at nobody, not even Otis.

"Well, Jesus," the younger of the two late ones, the girl, said; it was then I noticed Minnie standing in the half-open kitchen door. "What do you know?"

"Get to hell out of here," Miss Reba said to the girl. "Both of you." The girl and the woman rose quickly.

"You mean . . . leave?" the girl said.

"No," Miss Corrie said. "Just get out of here. If you're not expecting anybody in the next few minutes, why dont you take a walk around the block or something?" They didn't waste any time either. Miss Corrie got up. "You too," she told Otis. "Go upstairs to your room and stay there."

"He'll have to pass Miss Reba's door to do that," Boon said. "Have you forgot about that quarter?"

"It was more than a quarter," Otis said. "There was them eighty-five cents I made pumping the pee a noler for them to dance Saturday night. When he found out about the beer, he taken that away from me too." But Miss Reba looked at him.

"So you sold him out for eighty-five cents," she said.

"Go to the kitchen," Miss Corrie told Otis. "Let him come back there, Minnie."

"All right," Minnie said. "I'll try to keep him out of the icebox. But he's too fast for me."

"Hell, let him stay here," Miss Reba said. "It's too late now. He should have been sent somewhere else before he ever got off that Arkansas train last week." Miss Corrie went to the chair next to Miss Reba.

"Why dont you go and help him pack?" she said, quite gently.

"Who the hell are you accusing?" Miss Reba said. "I will trust him with every penny I've got. Except for those God damn horses." She stood up suddenly, with her trim rich body and the hard handsome face and the hair that was too richly red. "Why the hell cant I do without him?" she said. "Why the hell cant I?"

"Now, now," Miss Corrie said. "You need a drink. Give Minnie the keys— No, she cant go to your room yet—"

"He gone," Minnie said. "I heard the front door. It dont take him long. It never do."

"That's right," Miss Reba said. "Me and Minnie have been here before, haven't we, Minnie?" She gave Minnie the keys and sat down and Minnie went out and came back with a bottle of gin this time and they all had a glass of gin, Minnie too (though she declined to drink with this many white people at once, each time carrying her full glass back to the kitchen then reappearing a moment later with the glass empty), except Otis and me. And so I found out about Mr Binford.

He was the landlord. That was his official even if unwritten title and designation. All places, houses like this, had one, had to have one. In the alien outside world fortunate enough not to have to make a living in this hard and doomed and self-destroying way, he had a harder and more contemptuous name. But here, the lone male not even in a simple household of women but in a hysteria of them, he was not just lord but the unthanked and thankless catalyst, the single frail power wearing the shape of respectability sufficient to compel enough of order on the hysteria to keep the unit solvent or anyway eating—he was the agent who counted down the money and took the receipt for the taxes and utilities, who dealt with the tradesmen from the liquor dealers through the grocers and coal merchants, down through the plumbers who thawed the frozen pipes in winter and the casual labor which cleaned the chimneys and gutters and cut the weeds out of the yard; his was the hand which paid the blackmail to the law; it was his voice which fought the losing battles with the street- and assessment-commissioners and cursed the newspaper boy the day after the paper wasn't delivered. And of these (I mean, landlords) in this society, Mr Binford was the prince and paragon: a man of style and presence and manner and ideals; incorruptible in principles, impeccable in morals, more faithful than many husbands during the whole five years he had been Miss Reba's lover: whose sole and only vice was horses running in competition on which bets could be placed. This he could not resist; he knew it was his weakness and he fought against it. But each time, at the cry of "They're off!" he was putty in the hands of any stranger with a dollar to bet.

"He knowed it his-self," Minnie said. "He was ashamed of his-self and for his-self both, for being so weak, of there being anything bigger than him; to find out he aint bigger than anything he could meet up with, he dont care where nor what, even if on the outside, to folks that didn't know him, he just looked like a banty rooster. So he would promise us and mean it, like he done that time two years ago when we finally had to throw him out. You remember how much work it taken to get him back that time," she told Miss Reba.

"I remember," Miss Reba said. "Pour another round."

"I dont know how he'll manage it," Minnie said. "Because when he leaves, he dont take nothing but his clothes, I mean, just the ones he's got on since it was Miss Reba's money that paid for them. But wont two days pass before a messenger will be knocking on the door with every cent of them forty dollars—"

"You mean thirty-nine, six bits," Boon said.

"No," Minnie said. "Every one of them forty dollars,

even that quarter, was Miss Reba's. He wont be satisfied less. Then Miss Reba will send for him and he wont come; last year when we finally found him he was working in a gang laying a sewer line way down past the Frisco depot until she had to beg him right down on her bended knee—"

"Come on," Miss Reba said. "Stop running your mouth long enough to pour the gin, anyway." Minnie began to pour. Then she stopped, the bottle suspended.

"What's that hollering?" she said. Now we all heard it— a faint bawling from somewhere toward the back.

"Go and see," Miss Reba said. "Here, give me the bottle." Minnie gave her the bottle and went back to the kitchen. Miss Reba poured and passed the bottle.

"He's two years older now," Miss Corrie said. "He'll have more sense—"

"What's he saving it for?" Miss Reba said. "Go on. Pass it." Minnie came back. She said:

"Man standing in the back yard hollering Mr Boon Hogganbeck at the back wall of the house. He got something big with him."

We ran, following Boon, through the kitchen and out onto the back gallery. It was quite dark now; the moon was not high enough yet to do any good. Two dim things, a little one and a big one, were standing in the middle of the back yard, the little one bawling "Boon Hogganbeck! Mister Boon Hogganbeck! Hellaw. Hellaw" toward the upstairs windows until Boon overrode him by simple volume:

"Shut up! Shut up! Shut up!"

It was Ned. What he had with him was a horse.

6

◆◆◆◆

We were all in the kitchen. "Good Godalmighty," Boon
said. "You swapped Boss's automobile for a *horse?*" He
had to say it twice even. Because Ned was still looking
at Minnie's tooth. I mean, he was waiting for it again.
Maybe Miss Reba had said something to her or maybe
Minnie had spoken herself. What I do remember is the
rich instantaneous glint of gold out of the middle of
whatever Minnie said, in the electric light of the kitchen,
as if the tooth itself had gained a new luster, lambence
from the softer light of the lamp in the outside darkness,
like the horse's eyes had—this, and its effect on Ned.

It had stopped him cold for that moment, instant, like
basilisk. So had it stopped me when I first saw it, so I
knew what Ned was experiencing. Only his was more
so. Because I realised this dimly too, even at only eleven:

that I was too far asunder, not merely in race but in age, to feel what Ned felt; I could only be awed, astonished and pleased by it; I could not, like Ned, participate in that tooth. Here, in the ancient battle of the sexes, was a foeman worthy of his steel; in the ancient mystic solidarity of race, here was a high priestess worth dying for—if such was your capacity for devotion: which, it was soon obvious, was not what Ned intended (anyway hoped) to do with Minnie. So Boon had to repeat before Ned heard—or anyway noticed—him.

"You know good as me," Ned said, "that Boss dont want no automobile. He bought that thing because he had to, because Colonel Sartoris made him. He had to buy that automobile to put Colonel Sartoris back in his place he had done upstarted from. What Boss likes is a *horse*—and I dont mean none of these high-named harness plugs you and Mr Maury has in that livery stable: but a *horse*. And I got him one. The minute he sees this horse, he's gonter say right down much oblige to me just for being where I could get a-holt of it before somebody else done it—" It was like a dream, a nightmare; you know it is, and if you can only touch something hard, real, actual, unaltered, you can wake yourself; Boon and I had the same idea, instantaneous: I moved quicker only because there was less of me to put in motion. Ned stopped us; he read two minds: "No need to go look," he said. "He done already come and got it." Boon, frozen in midstride, glared at me, the two of us mutual in one horrified unbelief while I fumbled in my pocket. But the switch key was there. "Sho," Ned said, "he never needed that thing. He was a expert. He claimed he knowed how to reach his hand in behind the lock and turn it on from the back. He done it, too. I didn't believe it neither, until I seen it. It never give him no trouble a-tall. He even throwed in the halter with the horse—"

We—Boon and I—were not running, but fast enough, Miss Reba and Miss Corrie too, to the front door. The automobile was gone. That was when I realised that Miss Reba and Miss Corrie were there too, and that they had said nothing whatever themselves—no surprise, shock; watching and listening, not missing any part of it but not saying anything at all, as if they belonged to a different and separate society, kind, from Boon and me and Ned and Grandfather's automobile and the horse (whoever it belonged to) and had no concern with us and our doings but entertainment; and I remembered how that was exactly the way Mother would watch me and my brothers and whatever neighborhood boys were involved, not missing anything, quite constant and quite dependable, even warmly so, bright and kind but insulate until the moment, the need arrived to abolish the bone and (when necessary) stanch the consequent blood.

We went back to the kitchen, where we had left Ned and Minnie. We could already hear Ned: "—money you talking about, Good-looking, I got it or I can get it. Lemme get this horse put up and fed and me and you gonter step out and let that tooth do its shining amongst something good enough to match it, like a dish of catfish or maybe hog meat if it likes hog meat better—"

"All right," Boon said. "Go get that horse. Where does the man live?"

"Which man?" Ned said. "What you want with him?"

"To get Boss's automobile back. I'll decide then whether to send you to jail here or take you back to Jefferson and let Boss have the fun."

"Whyn't you stop talking a minute and listen to me?" Ned said. "In course I knows where the man lives: didn't I just trade a horse from him this evening? Let him alone. We dont want him yet. We wont need him until after the race. Because we aint just got the horse: he throwed in the horse race too. A man at Possum got a horse waiting right this minute to run against him as soon as we get there. In case you ladies dont know where Possum's at, it's where the railroad comes up from Jefferson and crosses the Memphis one where you changes cars unlessen you comes by automobile like we done—"

"All right," Boon said. "A man at Possum—"

"Oh," Miss Reba said. "Parsham."

"That's right," Ned said. "Where they has the bird-dog trials. It aint no piece. —got a horse done already challenged this un to a three-heat race, fifty dollars a heat, winner take all. But that aint nothing: just a hundred and fifty dollars. What we gonter do is win back that automobile."

"How?" Boon said. "How the hell are you going to use the horse to win the automobile back from the man that has already give you the horse for it?"

"Because the man dont believe the horse can run. Why you think he swapped me as cheap as a automobile? Why didn't he just keep the horse and win him a automobile of his own, if he wanted one, and have both of them—a horse and a automobile too?"

"I'll bite," Boon said. "Why?"

"I just told you. This horse done already been beat twice by that Possum horse because never nobody knowed how to make him run. So naturally the man will believe that if the horse wouldn't run them other two times, he aint gonter run this time neither. So all we got to do is, bet him the horse against Boss's automobile. Which he will be glad to bet because naturally he wouldn't mind owning the horse back too, long as he's already got the automobile, especially when it aint no more risk than just having to wait at the finish line until the horse finally comes up to where he can catch him and tie him behind the automobile and come on back to Memphis—"

This was the first time Miss Reba spoke. She said, "Jesus."

"—because he dont believe I can make that horse run neither. But unlessen I done got rusty on my trading and made a mistake I dont know about, he dont disbelieve it enough not to be at Possum day after tomorrow to find out. And if you cant scrap up enough extra boot amongst these ladies here to make him good interested in betting that automobile against it, you better hadn't never laid eyes on Boss Priest in your born life. It would have tooken a braver man than me to just took his automobile back to him. But maybe this horse will save you. Because the minute I laid my eyes on that horse, it put me in mind of—"

"Hee hee hee," Boon said, in that harsh and savage parody. "You give away Boss's automobile for a horse that cant run, and now you're fixing to give the horse back providing I can scrape up enough boot to interest him—"

"Let me finish," Ned said. Boon stopped. "You gonter let me finish?" Ned said.

"Finish then," Boon said. "And make it—"

"—put me in mind of a mule I use to own," Ned said. Now they both stopped, looking at each other; we all watched them. After a moment Ned said, gently, almost dreamily: "These ladies wasn't acquainted with that mule. Naturally, being young ladies like they is, not to mention so fur away as Yoknapatawpha County. It's too bad Boss or Mr Maury aint here now to tell them about him."

I could have done that. Because the mule was one of our family legends. It was back when Father and Ned were young men, before Grandfather moved in from Mc-Caslin to become a Jefferson banker. One day, during Cousin McCaslin's (Cousin Zack's uncle's) absence, Ned bred the mare of his matched standard-bred carriage team to the farm jack. When the consequent uproar exhausted itself and the mule colt was foaled, Cousin McCaslin made Ned buy it from him at ten cents a week subtracted from Ned's wages. It took Ned three years, by which time the mule had consistently beaten every mule matched against him for fifteen or twenty miles around, and was now being challenged by mules from forty and fifty, and beating them.

You were born too late to be acquainted with mules and so comprehend the startling, the even shocking, import of this statement. A mule which will gallop for a half-mile in the single direction elected by its rider even one time becomes a neighborhood legend; one that will do it consistently time after time is an incredible phenomenon. Because, unlike a horse, a mule is far too intelligent to break its heart for glory running around the rim of a mile-long saucer. In fact, I rate mules second only to rats in intelligence, the mule followed in order by cats, dogs, and horses last—assuming of course that you accept my definition of intelligence: which is the ability to cope with environment: which means to accept environment yet still retain at least something of personal liberty.

The rat of course I rate first. He lives in your house without helping you to buy it or build it or repair it or keep the taxes paid; he eats what you eat without helping you raise it or buy it or even haul it into the house; you cannot get rid of him; were he not a cannibal, he would long since have inherited the earth. The cat is third, with some of the same qualities but a weaker, punier creature; he neither toils nor spins, he is a parasite on you but he does not love you; he would die, cease to exist, vanish from the earth (I mean, in his so-called domestic form) but so far he has not had to. (There is the fable, Chinese

I think, literary I am sure: of a period on earth when the dominant creatures were cats: who after ages of trying to cope with the anguishes of mortality—famine, plague, war, injustice, folly, greed—in a word, civilised government—convened a congress of the wisest cat philosophers to see if anything could be done: who after long deliberation agreed that the dilemma, the problems themselves were insoluble and the only practical solution was to give it up, relinquish, abdicate, by selecting from among the lesser creatures a species, race optimistic enough to believe that the mortal predicament could be solved and ignorant enough never to learn better. Which is why the cat lives with you, is completely dependent on you for food and shelter but lifts no paw for you and loves you not; in a word, why your cat looks at you the way it does.)

The dog I rate fourth. He is courageous, faithful, monogamous in his devotion; he is your parasite too: his failure (as compared to the cat) is that he will work for you—I mean, willingly, gladly, ape any trick, no matter how silly, just to please you, for a pat on the head; as sound and first-rate a parasite as any, his failure is that he is a sycophant, believing that he has to show gratitude also; he will debase and violate his own dignity for your amusement; he fawns in return for a kick, he will give his life for you in battle and grieve himself to starvation over your bones. The horse I rate last. A creature capable of but one idea at a time, his strongest quality is timidity and fear. He can be tricked and cajoled by a child into breaking his limbs or his heart too in running too far too fast or jumping things too wide or hard or high; he will eat himself to death if not guarded like a baby; if he had only one gram of the intelligence of the most backward rat, he would be the rider.

The mule I rate second. But second only because you

can make him work for you. But that too only within his own rigid self-set regulations. He will not permit himself to eat too much. He will draw a wagon or a plow, but he will not run a race. He will not try to jump anything he does not indubitably know beforehand he can jump; he will not enter any place unless he knows of his own knowledge what is on the other side; he will work for you patiently for ten years for the chance to kick you once. In a word, free of the obligations of ancestry and the responsibilities of posterity, he has conquered not only life but death too and hence is immortal; were he to vanish from the earth today, the same chanceful biological combination which produced him yesterday would produce him a thousand years hence, unaltered, unchanged, incorrigible still within the limitations which he himself had proved and tested; still free, still coping. Which is why Ned's mule was unique, a phenomenon. Put a dozen mules on a track and when the word Go is given, a dozen different directions will be taken, like a scattering of disturbed bugs on the surface of a pond; the one of the twelve whose direction happens to coincide with the track, will inevitably win.

But not Ned's mule. Father said it ran like a horse, but without the horse's frantic frenzy, the starts and falterings and the frightened heartbreaking bursts of speed. It ran a race like a job: it sprang into what it had already calculated would be the exact necessary speed at Ned's touch (or voice or whatever his signal was) and that speed never altered until it crossed the finish line and Ned stopped it. And nobody, not even Father—who was Ned's, well, not groom exactly but rather his second and betting agent—knew just what Ned did to it. Naturally the legend of that grew and mounted (doing no harm to their stable either) also. I mean, of just what magic Ned had found or invented to make the mule run

completely unlike any known mule. But they—we—
never learned what it was, nor did anybody else ever
ride as its jockey, even after Ned began to put on years
and weight, until the mule died, unbeaten at twenty-two
years of age; its grave (any number of Edmondses have
certainly already shown it to you) is out there at Mc-
Caslin now.

That's what Ned meant and Boon knew it, and Ned
knew he knew it. They stared at each other. "This aint
that mule," Boon said. "This is a horse."

"This horse got the same kind of sense that mule had,"
Ned said. "He aint got as much of it but it's the same
kind." They stared at each other. Then Boon said,

"Let's go look at him." Minnie lighted a lamp. With
Boon carrying it, we all went out to the back porch and
into the yard, Minnie and Miss Corrie and Miss Reba
too. The moon was just getting up now and we could
see a little. The horse was tied beneath a locust tree in
the corner. Its eyes glowed, then flashed away; it snorted
and we could hear one nervous foot.

"You ladies kindly stand back a minute, please," Ned
said. "He aint used to much society yet." We stopped,
Boon holding the lamp high; the eyes glowed coldly and
nervously again as Ned walked toward it, talking to it
until he could touch its shoulder, stroking it, still talking
to it until he had the halter in his hand. "Now, dont run
that lamp at him," he told Boon. "Just walk up and hold
the light where the ladies can see a *horse* if they wants
to. And when I says horse, I means *horse*. Not them
plugs they calls horses back yonder in Jefferson."

"Stop talking and bring him out where we can see him,"
Boon said.

"You're looking at him now," Ned said. "Hold the lamp
up." Nevertheless he brought the horse out and moved
him a little. Oh yes, I remember him: a three-year-old

three-quarters-bred (at least, maybe more: I wasn't expert enough to tell) chestnut gelding, not large, not even sixteen hands, but with the long neck for balance and the laid-back shoulders for speed and the big hocks for drive (and, according to Ned, Ned McCaslin for heart and will). So that even at only eleven, I believe I was thinking exactly what Boon proved a moment later that he was. He looked at the horse. Then he looked at Ned. But when he spoke his voice was no more than a murmur:

"This horse is—"

"Wait," Miss Corrie said. That's right. I hadn't even noticed Otis. That was something else about him: when you noticed him, it was just a second before it would have been too late. But that was still not what was wrong about him.

"God, yes," Miss Reba said. I tell you, women are wonderful. "Get out of here," she told Otis.

"Go in the house, Otis," Miss Corrie said.

"You bet," Otis said. "Come on, Lucius."

"No," Miss Corrie said. "Just you. Go on now. You can go up to your room now."

"It's early yet," Otis said. "I aint sleepy neither."

"I aint going to tell you twice," Miss Reba said. Boon waited until Otis was in the house. We all did, Boon holding the lamp high so its light fell mostly on his and Ned's faces, speaking again in that heatless monotone, he and Ned both:

"This horse is stolen," Boon murmured.

"What would you call that automobile?" Ned murmured.

Yes, wonderful; Miss Reba's tone was no more than Boon's and Ned's: only brisker: "You got to get it out of town."

"That's just exactly the idea I brought him here with,"

Ned said. "Soon as I eats my supper, me and him gonter start for Possum."

"Have you got any idea how far it is to Possum, let alone in what direction?" Boon said.

"Does it matter?" Ned said. "When Boss left town without taking that automobile with him right in his hand, did your mind worry you about how far Memphis was?"

Miss Reba moved. "Come in the house," she said. "Can anybody see him here?" she said to Ned.

"Nome," Ned said. "I got that much sense. I done already seen to that." He tied the horse to the tree again and we followed Miss Reba up the back steps.

"The kitchen," she said. "It's getting time for company to start coming in." In the kitchen she said to Minnie: "Sit in my room where you can answer the door. Did you give me the keys back or have you— All right. Dont give no credit to anybody unless you know them; make the change before you even pull the cork if you can. See who's in the house now too. If anybody asks for Miss Corrie, just say her friend from Chicago's in town."

"In case any of them dont believe you, tell them to come around the alley and knock on the back door," Boon said.

"For Christ's sake," Miss Reba said. "Haven't you got troubles enough already to keep you busy? If you dont want Corrie having company, why the hell dont you buy her outright instead of just renting her once every six months?"

"All right, all right," Boon said.

"And see where everybody in the house is, too," Miss Reba told Minnie.

"I'll see about him, myself," Miss Corrie said.

"Make him stay there," Miss Reba said. "He's already played all the hell with horses I'm going to put up with in one day." Miss Corrie went out. Miss Reba went herself and closed the door and stood looking at Ned. "You mean, you were going to walk to Parsham and lead that horse?"

"That's right," Ned said.

"Do you know how far it is to Parsham?"

"Do it matter?" Ned said again. "I dont need to know how far it is to Possum. All I needs is Possum. That's why I changed my mind about leading him: it might be far. At first I thought, being as you're in the connection business—"

"What the hell do you mean?" Miss Reba said. "I run a house. Anybody that's too polite to call it that, I dont want in my front door or back door neither."

"I mean, one of your ladies' connections," Ned said. "That might have a saddle horse or even a plow horse or even a mule I could ride whilst Lucius rides the colt, and go to Possum that way. But we aint only got to run a solid mile the day after tomorrow, we got to do it three times and at least two of them gonter have to be before the next horse can. So I'm gonter walk him to Possum."

"All right," Miss Reba said. "You and the horse are in Parsham. All you need now is a horse race."

"Any man with a horse can find a horse race anywhere," Ned said. "All he needs is for both of them to be able to stand up long enough to start."

"Can you make this one stand up that long?"

"That's right," Ned said.

"Can you make him run while he's standing up?"

"That's right," Ned said.

"How do you know you can?"

"I made that mule run," Ned said.

"What mule?" Miss Reba said. Miss Corrie came in, shutting the door behind her. "Shut it good," Miss Reba said. She said to Ned: "All right. Tell me about that race." Now Ned looked at her, for a full quarter of a minute; the spoiled immune privileged-retainer impudence of his relations with Boon and the avuncular bossiness of those with me, were completely gone.

"You sounds like you want to talk sense for a while," he said.

"Try me," Miss Reba said.

"All right," Ned said. "A man, another rich white man, I dont call his name but I can find him; aint but one horse like that in twenty miles of Possum, let alone ten—owns a blood horse too that has already run twice against this horse last winter and beat him twice. That Possum horse beat this horse just enough bad the first time, for the other rich white man that owned this horse to bet twice as much the second time. And got beat just enough more bad that second time, that when this horse turns up in Possum day after tomorrow, wanting to run him another race, that Possum rich white man wont be just willing to run his horse again, he'll likely be proud and ashamed both to take the money."

"All right," Miss Reba said. "Go on."

"That's all," Ned said. "I can make this horse run. Only dont nobody but me know it yet. So just in case you ladies would like to make up a little jackpot, me and Lucius and Mr Hogganbeck can take that along with us too."

"That includes the one that's got that automobile now too?" Miss Reba said. "I mean, among the ones that dont know you can make it run?"

"That's right," Ned said.

"Then why didn't he save everybody trouble and send you and the horse both to Parsham, since he believes all he's got to do to have the horse and the automobile both, is to run that race?" Now there was no sound; they just looked at each other. "Come on," Miss Reba said. "You got to say something. What's your name?"

"Ned William McCaslin Jefferson Missippi," Ned said.

"Well?" Miss Reba said.

"Maybe he couldn't afford it," Ned said.

"Hell," Boon said. "Neither have we—"

"Shut up," Miss Reba said to Boon. She said to Ned: "I thought you said he was rich."

"I'm talking about the one I swapped with,'" Ned said.

"Did he buy the horse from the rich one?"

"He had the horse," Ned said.

"Did he give you a paper of any kind when you swapped?"

"I got the horse," Ned said.

"You cant read," Miss Reba said. "Can you?"

"I got the horse," Ned said. Miss Reba stared at him.

"You've got the horse. You've got him to Parsham. You say you got a system that will make him run. Will the same system get that automobile to Parsham too?"

"Use your sense," Ned said. "You got plenty of it. You done already seen more and seen it quicker than anybody else here. Just look a little harder and see that them folks I swapped that horse from—"

"Them?" Miss Reba said. "You said a man." But Ned hadn't even stopped:

"—is in exactly the same fix we is: they got to go back home sometime too sooner or later."

"Whether his name is Ned William McCaslin or Boon Hogganbeck or whether it's them folks I swapped the horse from, to go back home with just the horse or just the automobile aint going to be enough: he's got to have both of them. Is that it?" Miss Reba said.

"Not near enough," Ned said. "Aint that what I been trying to tell you for two hours now?" Miss Reba stared at Ned. She breathed quietly, once.

"So now you're going to walk him to Parsham, with

every cop in west Tennessee snuffing every road out of Memphis for horse—"

"Reba!" Miss Corrie said.

"—by daylight tomorrow morning."

"That's right," Ned said. "It's long past too late for nobody to get caught now. But you doing all right. You doing fine. You tell me." She was looking at him; she breathed twice this time; she didn't even move her eyes when she spoke to Miss Corrie:

"That brakeman—"

"What brakeman?" Miss Corrie said.

"You know the one I mean. That his mother's uncle or cousin or something—"

"He's not a brakeman," Miss Corrie said. "He's a flagman. On the Memphis Special, to New York. He wears a uniform too, just like the conductor—"

"All right," Miss Reba said. "Flagman." Now she was talking to Boon: "One of Corrie's . . ." She looked at Ned a moment. "Connections. Maybe I like that word of yours, after all. —His mother's uncle or something is vice president or something of the railroad that goes through Parsham—"

"His uncle is division superintendent," Miss Corrie said.

"Division superintendent," Miss Reba said. "That is, between the times when he's out at the driving park here or in any of the other towns his trains go through where he can watch horse races while his nephew is working his way up from the bottom with the silver spoon already in his mouth as long as he dont bite down on it hard enough to draw too much notice. See what I mean?"

"The baggage car," Boon said.

"Right," Miss Reba said. "Then they'll be in Parsham and already out of sight by daylight tomorrow."

"Even with the baggage car, it will still cost money," Boon said. "Then to stay hid until the race, and then we got to put up a hundred and fifty for the race itself and all I got is fifteen or twenty dollars." He rose. "Go get that horse," he told Ned. "Where did you say the man you gave that automobile lives?"

"Sit down," Miss Reba said. "Jesus, the trouble you're already in when you get back to Jefferson, and you still got time to count pennies." She looked at Ned. "What did you say your name was?"

Ned told her again. "You wants to know about that mule. Ask Boon Hogganbeck about him."

"Dont you ever make him call you mister?" she said to Boon.

"I always does," Ned said. "Mister Boon Hogganbeck. Ask him about that mule."

She turned to Miss Corrie. "Is Sam in town tonight?"

"Yes," Miss Corrie said.

"Can you get hold of him now?"

"Yes," Miss Corrie said.

Miss Reba turned to Boon. "You get out of here. Take a walk for a couple of hours. Or go over to Birdie Watts's if you want. Only, for Christ's sake dont get drunk. What the hell do you think Corrie eats and pays her rent with while you're down there in that Missippi swamp stealing automobiles and kidnapping children? air?"

"I aint going nowhere," Boon said. "God damn it," he said to Ned, "go get that horse."

"I dont need to entertain him," Miss Corrie said. "I can use the telephone." It was not smug nor coy: it was just serene. She was much too big a girl, there was much too much of her, for smugness or coyness. But she was exactly right for serenity.

"You sure?" Miss Reba said.

"Yes," Miss Corrie said.

"Then get at it," Miss Reba said.

"Come here," Boon said. Miss Corrie stopped. "Come

here, I said," Boon said. She approached then, just outside Boon's reach; I noticed suddenly that she wasn't looking at Boon at all: she was looking at me. Which was perhaps why Boon, still sitting, was able to reach suddenly and catch her arm before she could evade him, drawing her toward him, she struggling belatedly, as a girl that big would have to, still watching me.

"Turn loose," she said. "I've got to telephone."

"Sure, sure," Boon said, "plenty of time for that," drawing her on; until, with that counterfeit composure, that desperate willing to look at once forceful and harmless, with which you toss the apple in your hand (or any other piece of momentary distraction) toward the bull you suddenly find is also on your side of the fence, she leaned briskly down and kissed him, pecked him quickly on the top of the head, already drawing back. But again too late, his hand dropping and already gripping one cheek of her bottom, in sight of us all, she straining back and looking at me again with something dark and beseeching in her eyes—shame, grief, I don't know what— while the blood rushed slowly into her big girl's face that was not really plain at all except at first. But only a moment; she was still going to be a lady. She even struggled like a lady. But she was simply too big, too strong for even anyone as big and strong as Boon to hold with just one hand, with no more grip than that; she was free.

"Aint you ashamed of yourself," she said.

"Cant you save that long enough for her to make one telephone call even?" Miss Reba said to Boon. "If you're going to run fevers over her purity, why the hell dont you set her up in a place of her own where she can keep pure and still eat?" Then to Miss Corrie: "Go on and telephone. It's already nine oclock."

Already late for all we had to do. The place had begun

to wake up—"jumping," as you say nowadays. But decorously: no uproar either musical or simply convivial; Mr Binford's ghost still reigned, still adumbrated his callipygian grottoes since only two of the ladies actually knew he was gone and the customers had not missed him yet; we had heard the bell and Minnie's voice faintly at the front door and the footsteps of the descending nymphs themselves had penetrated from the stairs; and even as Miss Corrie stood with the knob in her hand, the chink of glasses interspersed in orderly frequence the bass rumble of the entertained and the shriller pipes of their entertainers beyond the door she opened and went through and then closed again. Then Minnie came back too; it seems that the unoccupied ladies would take turnabout as receptionists during the emergency.

You see how indeed the child is father to the man, and mother to the woman also. Back there in Jefferson I had thought that the reason corruption, Non-virtue, had met so puny a foeman in me as to be not even worthy of the name, was because of my tenderness and youth's concomitant innocence. But that victory at least required the three hours between the moment I learned of Grandfather Lessep's death and that one when the train began to move and I realised that Boon would be in unchallenged possession of the key to Grandfather's automobile for at least four days. While here were Miss Reba and Miss Corrie: foemen you would say already toughened, even if not wisened, by constant daily experience to any wile or assault Non-virtue (or Virtue) might invent against them, already sacked and pillaged: who thirty minutes before didn't even know that Ned existed, let alone the horse. Not to mention the complete stranger whom Miss Corrie had just left the room tranquilly confident to conquer with no other weapon than the telephone.

She had been gone nearly two minutes now. Minnie had taken the lamp and gone back to the back porch; I noticed that Ned was not in the room either. "Minnie," Miss Reba said toward the back door, "was any of that chicken—"

"Yessum," Minnie said. "I already fixed him a plate. He setting down to it now." Ned said something. We couldn't hear it. But we could hear Minnie: "If all you got to depend on for appetite is me, you gonter starve twice between here and morning." We couldn't hear Ned. Now Miss Corrie had been gone almost four minutes. Boon stood up, quick.

"God damn it—" he said.

"Are you even jealous of a telephone?" Miss Reba said. "What the hell can he do to her through that damn gutta-percha earpiece?" But we could hear Minnie: a quick sharp flat sound, then her feet. She came in. She was breathing a little quick, but not much. "What's wrong?" Miss Reba said.

"Aint nothing wrong," Minnie said. "He like most of them. He got plenty of appetite but he cant seem to locate where it is."

"Give him a bottle of beer. Unless you're afraid to go back out there."

"I aint afraid," Minnie said. "He just nature-minded. Maybe a little extra. I'm used to it. A heap of them are that way: so nature-minded dont nobody get no rest until they goes to sleep."

"I bet you are," Boon said. "It's that tooth. That's the hell of women: you wont let well enough alone."

"What do you mean?" Miss Reba said.

"You know damn well what I mean," Boon said. "You dont never quit. You aint never satisfied. You dont never have no mercy on a damn man. Look at her: aint satisfied until she has saved and scraped to put a gold tooth, a *gold tooth* in the middle of her face just to drive crazy a poor ignorant country nigger—"

"—or spending five minutes talking into a wooden box just to drive crazy another poor ignorant country bastard that aint done nothing in the world but steal an automobile and now a horse. I never knew anybody that needed to get married as bad as you do."

"He sure do," Minnie said from the door. "That would cure him. I tried it twice and I sho learned my lesson—" Miss Corrie came in.

"All right," she said: serene, no more plain than a big porcelain lamp with the wick burning inside is plain. "He's coming too. He's going to help us. He—"

"Not me," Boon said. "The son of a bitch aint going to help me."

"Then beat it," Miss Reba said. "Get out of here. How you going to do it? walk back to Missippi or ride the horse? Go on. Sit down. You might as well while we wait for him. Tell us," she said to Miss Corrie.

You see? "He's *not* a brakeman! He's a *flagman!* He wears a uniform just the same as the conductor's. He's going to help us." All the world loves a lover, quoth (I think) the Swan: who saw deeper than any into the human heart. What pity he had no acquaintance with horses, to have added, All the world apparently loves a stolen race horse also. Miss Corrie told us; and Otis was in the room now though I hadn't seen him come in, with something still wrong about him though not noticing him until it was almost too late still wasn't it:

"We'll have to buy at least one ticket to Possum to have—"

"It's Parsham," Miss Reba said.

"All right," Miss Corrie said. "—something to check him as baggage on, like you do a trunk; Sam will bring the ticket and the baggage check with him. But it will be all right; an empty boxcar will be on a side track—Sam will know where—and all we have to do is get the horse in it and Sam said wall him up in one corner with planks so he cant slip down; Sam will have some planks and nails ready too; he said this was the best he could do at short notice because he didn't dare tell his uncle any more than he had to or his uncle would want to come too. So Sam says the only risk will be getting the horse from here to where the boxcar is waiting. He says it wont do for . . ." She stopped, looking at Ned.

"Ned William McCaslin Jefferson Missippi," Ned said.

". . . Ned to be walking along even a back street this late at night leading a horse; the first policeman they pass will stop him. So he—Sam—is bringing a blanket and he's going to wear his uniform and him and Boon and me will lead the horse to the depot and nobody will notice anything. Oh yes; and the passenger train will—"

"Jesus," Miss Reba said. "A whore, a pullman conductor and a Missippi swamp rat the size of a water tank leading a race horse through Memphis at midnight Sunday night, and nobody will notice it?"

"You stop!" Miss Corrie said.

"Stop what?" Miss Reba said.

"You know. Talking like that in front of—"

"Oh," Miss Reba said. "If he just dropped up here from Missippi with Boon on a friendly visit you might say, we might of could protected his ears. But using this place as headquarters while they steal automobiles and horses, he's got to take his chances like anybody else. What were you saying about the train?"

"Yes. The passenger train that leaves for Washington at four A.M. will pick the boxcar up and we'll all be in Possum before daylight."

"Parsham, God damn it," Miss Reba said. "We?"

"Aint you coming too?" Miss Corrie said.

7

◆◆◆◆

That's what we did. Though first Sam had to see the horse. He came in the back way, through the kitchen, carrying the horse blanket. He was in his uniform. He was almost as big as Boon.

So we—all of us again—stood once more in the back yard, Ned holding the lamp this time, to shine its light not on the horse but on Sam's brass-buttoned coat and vest and the flat cap with the gold lettering across the front. In fact, I had expected trouble with Ned over Sam and the horse, but I was wrong. "Who, me?" Ned said. "What for? We couldn't be no better off with a policeman himself leading that horse to Possum." On the contrary, the trouble we were going to have about Sam would be with Boon. Sam looked at the horse.

"That's a good horse," Sam said. "He looks like a damn good horse to me."

"Sure," Boon said. "He aint got no whistle nor bell neither on him. He aint even got a headlight. I'm surprised you can see him a-tall."

"What do you mean by that?" Sam said.

"I dont mean nothing," Boon said. "Just what I said. You're an iron-horse man. Maybe you better go on to the depot without waiting for us."

"You bas—" Miss Reba said. Then she started over: "Cant you see, the man's just trying to help you? going out of his way so that the minute you get back home, the first live animal you'll see wont be the sheriff? He's the one to be inviting you to get to hell back where you came from and take your goddamn horse along with you. Apologise."

"All right," Boon said. "Forget it."

"You call that an apology?" Miss Reba said.

"What do you want?" Boon said. "Me to bend over and invite him to—"

"You hush! Right this minute!" Miss Corrie said.

"And you dont help none neither," Boon said. "You already got me and Miss Reba both to where we'll have to try to forget the whole English language before we can even pass the time of day."

"That's no lie," Miss Reba said. "That one you brought here from Arkansas was bad enough, with one hand in the icebox after beer and the other one reaching for whatever was little and not nailed down whenever anybody wasn't looking. And now Boon Hogganbeck's got to bring another one that's got me scared to even open my mouth."

"He didn't!" Miss Corrie said. "Otis dont take anything without asking first! Do you, Otis?"

"That's right," Miss Reba said. "Ask him. He certainly ought to know."

"Ladies, ladies, ladies," Sam said. "Does this horse want to go to Parsham tonight, or dont he?"

So we started. But at first Miss Corrie was still looking at Otis and me. "They ought to be in bed," she said.

"Sure," Miss Reba said. "Over in Arkansas or back down there in Missippi or even further than that, if I had my way. But it's too late now. You cant send one to bed without the other, and that one of Boon's owns part of the horse." Only at the last, Miss Reba couldn't go either. She and Minnie couldn't be spared. The place was jumping indeed now, but still discreetly, with Sabbath decorum: Saturday night's fading tide rip in one last spumy upfling against the arduous humdrum of day-by-day for mere bread and shelter.

So Ned and Boon put the blanket on the horse. Then from the sidewalk we—Ned and Otis and me—watched Boon and Sam in polyandrous . . . maybe not amity but at least armistice, Miss Corrie between them, leading the horse down the middle of the street from arc light to arc light through the Sunday evening quiet of Second and Third streets, toward the Union depot. It was after ten now; there were few lights, these only in the other boarding houses (I was experienced now; I was a sophisticate —not a connoisseur of course but at least cognizant; I recognised a place similar to Miss Reba's when I saw one). The saloons though were all dark. That is, I didn't know a saloon just by passing it; there were still a few degrees yet veiled to me; it was Ned who told us—Otis and me—they were saloons, and that they were closed. I had expected them to be neither one: neither closed nor open; remember, I had been in Memphis (or in Catalpa Street) less than six hours, without my mother or father either to instruct me; I was doing pretty well.

"They calls it the blue law," Ned said.

"What's a blue law?" I said.

"I dont know neither," Ned said. "Lessen it means they blewed in all the money Saturday night and aint none of them got enough left now to make it worth burning the coal oil."

"That's just the saloons," Otis said. "It dont hurt nobody that way. What they dont sell Sunday night they can just save it and sell it to somebody, maybe the same folks, Monday. But pugnuckling's different. You can sell it tonight and turn right around again and sell the same pugnuckling again tomorrow. You aint lost nothing. Likely if they tried to put that blue law onto pugnuckling, the police would come in and stop them."

"What's pugnuckling?" I said.

"You knows a heap, dont you?" Ned said to Otis. "No wonder Arkansaw cant hold you. If the rest of the folks there knows as much as you do at your age, time they's twenty-one even Texas wont be big enough."

"——t," Otis said.

"What's pugnuckling?" I said.

"Try can you put your mind on knuckling up some feed for that horse," Ned said to me, still louder. "To try to keep him quiet long enough to get him to Possum, let alone into that train in the first place. That there railroad-owning conductor, flinging boxcars around without even taking his hand out of his pocket, is somebody reminded him of that? Maybe even a bucket of soap and water too, so your aunt"—he was talking to Otis now—"can take you around behind something and wash your mouth out."

"——t," Otis said.

"Or maybe even the nearest handy stick," Ned said.

"——t," Otis said. And sure enough, we met a police-man. I mean, Otis saw the policeman even before the policeman saw the horse. "Twenty-three skiddoo," Otis said. The policeman knew Miss Corrie. Then apparently he knew Sam too.

"Where you taking him?" he said. "Did you steal him?"

"Borrowed him," Sam said. They didn't stop. "We rode him to prayer meeting tonight and now we're taking him back home." We went on. Otis said Twenty-three skiddoo again.

"I never seen that before," he said. "Every policeman I ever seen before speaking to anybody, they give him something. Like Minnie and Miss Reba already having a bottle of beer waiting for him before he could even get his foot inside, even if Miss Reba cussed him before he come and cussed him again after he left. And ever since I got here last summer and found out about it, every day I go up to Court Square where that I-talian wop has got that fruit and peanut stand and, sho enough, here the policeman comes and without even noticing it, takes a apple or a handful of peanuts." He was almost trotting to keep up with us; he was that much smaller than me. I mean, he didn't seem so much smaller until you saw him trotting to keep up. There was something wrong about him. When it's you, you say to yourself *Next year I'm going to be bigger than I am now* simply because being bigger is not only natural, it's inevitable; it doesn't even matter that you cant imagine to yourself how or what you will look like then. And the same with other children; they cant help it either. But Otis looked like two or three years ago he had already reached where you wont be until next year, and since then he had been going backward. He was still talking. "So what I thought back then was that the only thing to be was a policeman. But I never taken long to get over that. It's too limited."

"Limited to what?" Ned said.

"To beer and apples and peanuts," Otis said. "Who's going to waste his time on beer and apples and peanuts?" He said Twenty-three skiddoo three times now. "This town is where the jack's at."

"Jacks?" Ned said. "In course they has jacks here. Dont Memphis need mules the same as anybody else?"

"Jack," Otis said. "Spondulicks. Cash. When I think about all that time I wasted in Arkansas before anybody ever told me about Memphis. That tooth. How much do you reckon that tooth by itself is worth? if she just walked into the bank and taken it out and laid it on the counter and said, Gimme change for it?"

"Yes," Ned said. "I mind a boy like you back there in Jefferson used to keep his mind on money all the time too. You know where he's at now?"

"Here in Memphis, if he's got any sense," Otis said.

"He never got that far," Ned said. "The most he could get was into the state penitentiary at Parchman. And at the rate you sounds like going, that's where you'll wind up too."

"But not tomorrow," Otis said. "Maybe not the next day neither. Twenty-three skiddoo, where even a durn policeman cant even pass by without a bottle of beer or a apple or a handful of peanuts put right in his hand before he can even ask for it. Them eighty-five cents them folks give me last night for pumping the pee a noler that that son of a bitch taken away from me this evening. That I might a even pumped that pee a noler free for nothing if I hadn't found out by pure accident that they was aiming to pay me for it; if I had just happened to step out the door a minute, I might a missed it. And if I hadn't even been there, they would still a give it to somebody, anybody that just happened to pass by. See what I mean? Sometime just thinking about it, I feel like just giving up, just quitting."

"Quitting what?" Ned said. "Quitting for what?"

"Just quitting," Otis said. "When I think of all them years I spent over there on a durn farm in Arkansas with Memphis right here across the river and I never even knowed it. How if I had just knowed when I was four or five years old, what I had to wait until just last year to find out about, sometimes I just want to give up and quit. But I reckon I wont. I reckon maybe I can make it up. How much you folks figger on making out of that horse?"

"Never you mind about that horse," Ned said. "And the making up you needs to do is to make back up that street to wherever it is you gonter sleep tonight, and go to bed." He even paused, half turning. "Do you know the way back?"

"There aint nothing there," Otis said. "I already tried it. They watch too close. It aint like over in Arkansas, when Aunt Corrie was still at Aunt Fittie's and I had that peephole. If you swapped that automobile for him, you must be figgering on at least two hundred—" This time Ned turned completely around. Otis sprang, leaped away, cursing Ned, calling him nigger—something Father and Grandfather must have been teaching me before I could remember because I dont know when it began, I just knew it was so: that no gentleman ever referred to anyone by his race or religion.

"Go on," I said. "They're leaving us." They were: almost two blocks ahead now and already turning a corner; we ran, trotted, Ned too, to catch up and barely did so: the depot was in front of us and Sam was talking to another man, in greasy overalls, with a lantern—a switchman, a railroad man anyway.

"See what I mean?" Ned said. "Can you imagine police sending out a man with a lantern to show us the way?" And you see what I mean too: all the world (I mean about a stolen race horse); who serves Virtue works alone, unaided, in a chilly vacuum of reserved judgment; where, pledge yourself to Non-virtue and the whole countryside boils with volunteers to help you. It seems that Sam was trying to persuade Miss Corrie to wait in the depot with Otis and me while they located the box-car and loaded the horse into it, even voluntarily suggesting that Boon attend us with the protection of his size and age and sex: proving that Sam's half anyway of the polyandrous stalemate was amicable and trusting. But Miss Corrie would have no part of it, speaking for all of us. So we turned aside, following the lantern, through a gate into a maze of loading platforms and tracks; now Ned himself had to come forward and take the halter and quiet the horse to where we could move again in the aura now of the horse's hot ammoniac reek (you never smelled a frightened horse, did you?) and the steady murmur of Ned's voice talking to it, both of them—murmur and smell—thickened, dense, concentrated now between the loom of lightless baggage cars and passenger coaches among the green-and-ruby gleams of switch points; on until we were clear of the passenger yard and were now following a cinder path beside a spur track leading to a big dark warehouse with a loading platform in front of it. And there was the boxcar too, with a good twenty-five feet of moonlit (that's right. We were in moonlight now. Free of the street- and depot-lights, we—I—could see it now) vacancy between it and the nearest point of the platform—a good big jump for even a jumping horse, let alone a three-year-old flat racer that (according to Ned) had a little trouble running anyway. Sam cursed quietly the entire depot establishment: switchmen, yard crews, ticket sellers and all.

"I'll go get the goat," the man with the lantern said.

"We dont need no goat," Ned said. "No matter how far he can jump. What we needs is to either move that flat-form or that boxcar."

"He means the switch engine," Sam told Ned. "No," he told the man with the lantern. "I expected this. For a switching crew to miss just twenty-five feet is practically zero. That's why I told you to bring the key to the section house. Get the crowbars. Maybe Mr Boon wont mind helping you."

"Why dont you go yourself?" Boon said. "It's your railroad. I'm a stranger here."

"Why dont you take these boys on back home to bed, if you're all that timid around strangers?" Miss Corrie said.

"Why dont you take them back home yourself?" Boon said. "Your old buddy-boy there has already told you once you aint got no business here."

"I'll go with him to get the crowbars," Miss Corrie told Sam. "Will you keep your eye on the boys?"

"All right, all right," Boon said. "Let's do something, for Christ's sake. That train will be along in four or five hours while we're still debating who's first at the lick dog. Where's that tool shed, Jack?" So he and the man with the lantern went on; we had only moonlight now. The horse hardly smelled at all now and I could see it nuzzling at Ned's coat like a pet. And Sam was thinking what I had been thinking ever since I saw the platform.

"There's a ramp around at the back," he said. "Did he ever walk a ramp before? Why dont you take him on now and let him look at it. When we get the car placed, we can all help you carry him up if we have to—"

"Dont you waste your time worrying about us," Ned said. "You just get that boxcar to where we wont have to jump no ten-foot gash into it. This horse wants to get out of Memphis as bad as you does." Only I was afraid Sam would say, Dont you want this boy to go with you? Because I wanted to see that boxcar moved. I didn't believe it. So we waited. It wasn't long; Boon and the man with the lantern came back with two crowbars that looked at least eight feet long and I watched (Miss Corrie and Otis too) while they did it. The man set his lantern down and climbed the ladder onto the roof and released the brake wheel and Sam and Boon jammed the ends of the bars between the back wheels and the rails, pinching and nudging in short strokes like pumping and I still didn't believe it: the car looming black and square and high in the moon, solid and rectangular as a black wall inside the narrow silver frame of the moonlight, one high puny figure wrenching at the brake wheel on top and two more puny figures crouching, creeping, nudging the silver-lanced iron bars behind the back wheels; so huge and so immobile that at first it looked, not like the car was moving forward, but rather Boon and Sam in terrific pantomimic obeisance were pinching infinitesimally rearward past the car's fixed and foundationed mass, the moon-mazed panoramic earth: so delicately balanced now in the massive midst of Motion that Sam and Boon dropped the bars and Boon alone pressed the car gently on with his hands as though it were a child's perambulator, up alongside the platform and into position and Sam said,

"All right," and the man on top set the brake wheel again. So all we had to do now was get the horse into it. Which was like saying, Here we are in Alaska; all we have to do now is find the gold mine. We went around to the back of the warehouse. There was a cleated ramp. But the platform had been built at the right height for the drays to load and unload from it, and the ramp was little more than a track for hand trucks and wheelbarrows, stout enough but only about five feet wide, rail-less. Ned was standing there talking to the horse. "He done seen it," he said. "He know we want him to walk up it but he aint decided yet do he want to. I wish now Mr Boxcar Man had went a little further and borried a whup too."

"You got one," Boon said. He meant me—one of my tricks, graces. I made it with my tongue, against the sounding board of my mouth, throat, gorge—a sound quite sharp and loud, as sharp and loud when done right as the crack of a whip; Mother finally forbade me to do it anywhere inside our yard, let alone in the house. Then it made Grandmother jump once and use a swear word. But just once. That was almost a year ago so I might have forgotten how by this time.

"That's right," Ned said. "So we has." He said to me: "Get you a long switch. They ought to be one in that hedge bush yonder." There was: a privet bush; all this was probably somebody's lawn or garden before progress, industry, commerce, railroads came. I cut the switch and came back. Ned led the horse up, facing the ramp. "Now you big folks, Mr Boon and Mr Boxcar, come up one on either side like you was the gateposts." They did so, Ned halfway up the ramp now, with the lead rope, facing the horse and talking to it. "There you is," he said. "Right straight up this here chicken walk to glory and Possum, Tennessee, by sunup tomorrow." He came back down, already turning the horse, moving fairly rapidly, speaking to me now: "He done seen the switch. Fall right in behind him. Dont touch him nor pop till I tell you to." I did that, the three of us—Ned, the horse, then me—moving directly away from the ramp for perhaps twenty yards, when without stopping Ned turned and wheeled the horse, I still following, until it faced the rise of the ramp between Boon and Sam twenty yards away. When it saw the ramp, it checked. "Pop," Ned said. I made the sound, a good one; the horse sprang a little, Ned already moving on, a little faster now, back toward the ramp. "When I tells you to pop this time, touch him with the switch. Dont hit: just tap him at the root of his tail a second after you pops." He had already passed between Boon and Sam and was on the ramp. The horse was now trying to decide which to do: refuse, or run out (with the addi-

tional confusion of having to decide which of Boon and
Sam would run over the easiest) or simply bolt over and
through us all. You could almost see it happening: which
was maybe what Ned was counting on: an intelligence
panicky and timorous and capable of only one idea at a
time, in which the intrusion of a second one reduces all
to chaos. "Pop," Ned said. This time I tapped the horse
too, as Ned had told me. It surged, leaped, its forefeet
halfway up the ramp, the near hind foot (Boon's side)
striking the edge of the ramp and sliding off until Boon,
before Ned could speak, grasped the leg in both hands
and set it back on the ramp, leaning his weight against
the flank, the horse motionless now, trembling, all four
feet on the ramp now. "Now," Ned said, "lay your switch
right across his hocks so he'll know he got something
behind him to not let him fall."

"To not let him back off the ramp, you mean," Sam
said. "We need one of the crowbars. Go get it, Charley."

"That's right," Ned said. "We gonter need that crowbar
in a minute. But all we needs right now is that switch.
You's too little," he told me. "Let Mr Boon and Mr Boxcar have it. Loop it behind his hocks like britching." They
did so, one at each end of the limber switch. "Now, walk
him right on up. When I say pop this time, pop loud, so
he will think the lick gonter be loud too." But I didn't
need to pop at all again. Ned said to the horse: "Come
on, son. Let's go to Possum," and the horse moved, Boon
and Sam moving with it, the switch like a loop of string
pressing it on, its forefeet on the solid platform now, then
one final scuffling scrabbling surge, the platform resound-
ing once as if it had leaped onto a wooden bridge.

"It's going to take more than this switch or that boy
popping his tongue either, to get him into that car," Sam
said.

"What gonter get him into that boxcar is that crowbar,"

Ned said. "Aint it come yet?" It was here now. "Prize that-ere chicken walk loose," Ned said.

"Wait," Sam said. "What for?"

"So he can walk on it into that boxcar," Ned said. "He's used to it now. He's done already found out aint nothing at the other end gonter hurt or skeer him."

"He aint smelled the inside of an empty boxcar yet though," Sam said. "That's what I'm thinking about." But Ned's idea did make sense. Besides, we had gone much too far now to boggle even if Ned had commanded us to throw down both walls of the warehouse so the horse wouldn't have to turn corners. So Boon and the railroad man prized the ramp away from the platform.

"God damn it," Sam said. "Do it quiet, cant you?"

"Aint you right here with us?" Ned said. "Sholy you can get a little more benefit outen them brass buttons than just walking around in them." Though it took all of us, including Miss Corrie, to lift the ramp onto the platform and carry it across and lay it like a bridge from the platform into the black yawn of the open car door. Then Ned led the horse up and at once I understood what Sam had meant. The horse had not only never smelled an empty boxcar before, but unlike mere humans it could see inside too; I remember thinking *Now that we've torn up the ramp, we cant even get it down off the platform again before daylight catches us.* But nothing like that happened. I mean, nothing happened. I mean, I dont know what happened; none of us did. Ned led the horse, its hooves ringing loud and hollow on the planks, up to the end of the ramp which was now a bridge, Ned standing on the bridge just inside the door, talking to the horse, pulling lightly on the halter until the horse put one foot forward onto the bridge and I dont know what I was thinking; a moment ago I had believed that not in all Memphis were there enough people to get that horse into

that black orifice, then the next instant I was expecting
that same surge and leap which would have taken the
horse inside the boxcar as it had up the ramp; when the
horse lifted the foot and drew it back to the platform, it
and Ned facing each other like a tableau. I heard Ned
breathe once. "You folks just step back to the wall," he
said. We did so. I didn't know then what he did. I just
saw him, one hand holding the lead rope, the other stroking, touching the horse's muzzle. Then he stepped back
into the car and vanished; the lead rope tightened but
only his voice came out: "Come on, son. I got it."

"I'll be God damned," Sam said. Because that was all.
The loose bridge clattered a little, the cavernous black-
ness inside the car boomed to the hooves, but no more.
We carried the lantern in; the horse's eyes glowed coldly
and vanished where Ned stood with it in the corner.

"Where's them planks and nails you talked about?" he
asked Sam. "Bring that chicken walk on in; that's already
one whole wall."

"Hell," Sam said. "Hold on now."

"Folks coming in here tomorrow morning already missing a whole boxcar," Ned said, "aint gonter have time to
be little-minded over a homemade ladder outen somebody's henhouse." So all of us again except Ned—including Miss Corrie—carried the ravished ramp into the car
and set it up and held it in place while Boon and Sam
and the railroad man (Sam had the planks and nails
ready too) built a stall around the horse in the corner of
the car; before Ned could even complain, Sam had a
bucket for water and a box for grain and even a bundle of
hay too; we all stood back now in the aura of the horse's
contented munching. "He just the same as in Possum right
this minute," Ned said.

"What you folks better wish is that he has already
crossed that finish line first day after tomorrow," Sam
said. "What time is it?" Then he told us himself: "Just

past midnight. Time for a little sleep before the train leaves at four." He was talking to Boon now. "You and Ned will want to stay here with your horse of course; that's why I brought all that extra hay. So you bed down here and I'll take Corrie and the boys on back home and we'll all meet here at—"

"You says," Boon said, not harshly so much as with a kind of cold grimness. "You do the meeting here at four oclock. If you dont oversleep, maybe we'll see you." He was already turning. "Come on, Corrie."

"You're going to leave your boss's automobile—I mean your boss's horse—I mean this horse, whoever it really belongs to—here with nobody to watch it but this colored boy?" Sam said.

"Naw," Boon said. "That horse belongs to the railroad now. I got a baggage check to prove it. Maybe you just borrowed that railroad suit to impress women and little boys in but as long as you're in it you better use it to impress that baggage check or the railroad might not like it."

"Boon!" Miss Corrie said. "I'm not going home with anybody! Come on, Lucius, you and Otis."

"It's all right," Sam said. "We keep on forgetting how Boon has to slave for five or six months in that cotton patch or whatever it is, to make one night on Catalpa Street. You all go on. I'll see you at the train."

"Cant you even say much obliged?" Miss Corrie said to Boon.

"Sure," Boon said. "Who do I owe one to? the horse?"

"Try one on Ned," Sam said. He said to Ned: "You want me to stay here with you?"

"We'll be all right," Ned said. "Maybe if you go too it might get quiet enough around here to where somebody can get some sleep. I just wish now I had thought in time to—"

"I did," Sam said. "Where's that other bucket, Charley?"

The railroad man—switchman, whatever he was—had it too; it was in the same corner of the car with the planks and nails and tools and the feed; it contained a thick crude ham sandwich and a quart bottle of water and a pint bottle of whiskey. "There you are," Sam said. "Breakfast too."

"I see it," Ned said. "What's your name, Whitefolks?"

"Sam Caldwell," Sam said.

"Sam Caldwell," Ned said. "It strikes me that Sam Caldwell is a better name for this kind of horse business than twice some others a man could mention around here. A little more, and I could be wishing me and you was frequent enough to be permanent. Kindly much obliged."

"You're kindly welcome," Sam said. So we said good night to Sam and Ned and Charley (all of us except Boon and Otis, that is) and went back to Miss Reba's. The streets were empty and quiet now; Memphis was using the frazzled worn-out end of the week to get at least a little sleep and rest to face Monday morning with; we walked quietly too from vacant light to light between the dark windows and the walls: but one faint single light dimly visible in what my new infallible roué's instinct recognised immediately as a competitor of Miss Reba; a single light similar in wanness behind Miss Reba's curtains because even here throe must by this time have spent itself; even Minnie herself gone to bed or home or wherever she retired to at her and Miss Reba's trade's evensong. Because Miss Reba herself unlocked the front door to us, smelling strongly of gin and, in her hard handsome competent way, even beginning to look like it. She had changed her dress too. This one didn't have hardly any top to it at all, and in those days ladies— women—didn't really paint their faces, so that was the first time I ever saw that too. And she had on still more diamonds, as big and yellowish as the first two. No: five.

But Minnie hadn't gone to bed either. She was standing in the door to Miss Reba's room, looking just about worn out.

"All fixed?" Miss Reba said, locking the door behind us.

"Yes," Miss Corrie said. "Why dont you go to bed? Minnie, make her go to bed."

"You could a asked me that a hour back from now," Minnie said. "I just wish wouldn't nobody still be asking it two hours ahead from now. But you wasn't here that other time two years ago."

"Come on to bed," Miss Corrie said. "When we get back from Possum Wednesday—"

"God damn it, Parsham," Miss Reba said.

"All right," Miss Corrie said. "—Wednesday, Minnie will have found out where he is and we can go and get him."

"Sure," Miss Reba said. "And bury him right there in the same ditch this time, pick and shovel and all, if I had any sense. You want a drink?" she said to Boon. "Minnie's a damn christian scientist or republican or something and wont take one."

"Somebody around here has got to not take one," Minnie said. "It dont need no republican for that. All it needs is just to be wore out and want to go to bed."

"That's what we all need," Miss Corrie said. "That train leaves at four, and it's already after one. Come on, now."

"Go to bed then," Miss Reba said. "Who the hell's stopping you?" So we went upstairs. Then Otis and I went upstairs again; he knew the way: an attic, with nothing in it but some trunks and boxes and a mattress made up into a bed on the floor. Otis had a nightshirt but (the nightshirt still had the creases in it where Miss Corrie I suppose had bought it off the shelf in the store) he went to bed just like I had to: took off his pants and shoes and turned off the light and lay down too. There

was one little window and now we could see the moon
and then I could even see inside the room because of the
moonlight; there was something wrong with him; I was
tired and coming up the stairs I had thought I would be
asleep almost before I finished lying down. But I could
feel him lying there beside me, not just wide awake, but
rather like something that never slept in its life and didn't
even know it never had. And suddenly there was something wrong with me too. It was like I didn't know what
it was yet: only that there was something wrong and in a
minute now I would know what and I would hate it; and
suddenly I didn't want to be there at all, I didn't want to
be in Memphis or ever to have heard of Memphis: I
wanted to be at home. Otis said Twenty-three skiddoo
again.

"The jack that's here," he said. "You can even smell it.
It aint fair that it's just women can make money pugnuckling while all a man can do is just try to snatch onto
a little of it while it's passing by—" There was that word
again, that I had asked twice what it meant. But not any
more, not again: lying there tense and rigid with the
moon-shaped window lying across mine and Otis's legs,
trying not to hear him but having to: "—one of the rooms
is right under here; on a busy night like Sad-dy was you
can hear them right up through the floor. But there aint
no chance here. Even if I could get a auger and bore a
peephole through it, that nigger and Miss Reba wouldn't
let me bring nobody up here to make no money off of and
even if I did they would probably take the money away
from me like that son of a bitch done that pee a noler
money today. But it was different back home at Aunt
Fittie's, when Bee—" He stopped. He lay perfectly still.
He said Twenty-three skiddoo again.

"Bee?" I said. But it was too late. No, it wasn't too late.
Because I already knew now.

"How old are you?" he said.

"Eleven," I said.

"You got a year on me then," he said. "Too bad you aint going to be here after tonight. If you just stayed around here next week, we might figger that peephole out some way."

"What for?" I said. You see, I had to ask it. Because what I wanted was to be back home. I wanted my mother. Because you should be prepared for experience, knowledge, knowing: not bludgeoned unaware in the dark as by a highwayman or footpad. I was just eleven, remember. There are things, circumstances, conditions in the world which should not be there but are, and you cant escape them and indeed, you would not escape them even if you had the choice, since they too are a part of Motion, of participating in life, being alive. But they should arrive with grace, decency. I was having to learn too much too fast, unassisted; I had nowhere to put it, no receptacle, pigeonhole prepared yet to accept it without pain and lacerations. He was lying face up, as I was. He hadn't moved, not even his eyes. But I could feel him watching me.

"You dont know much, do you?" he said. "Where did you say you was from?"

"Missippi," I said.

"——t," he said. "No wonder you dont know nothing."

"All right," I said. "Bee is Miss Corrie."

"Here I am, throwing money away like it wasn't nothing," he said. "But maybe me and you both can make something out of it. Sure. Her name is Everbe Corinthia, named for Grandmaw. And what a hell of a name that is to have to work under. Bad enough even over there around Kiblett, where some of them already knowed it and was used to it and the others was usually in too much of a hurry to give a hoot whether she called herself nothing or not. But here in Memphis, in a house like this that they tell me every girl in Memphis is trying to get into it as soon as a room is vacant. So it never made much difference over there around Kiblett after her maw died and Aunt Fittie taken her to raise and started her out soon as she got big enough. Then when she found out how much more money there was in Memphis and come over here, never nobody knowed about the Everbe and so she could call herself Corrie. So whenever I'm over here visiting her, like last summer and now, since I know about the Everbe, she gives me five cents a day not to tell nobody. You see? Instead of telling you like I slipped up and done, if I had just went to her instead and said, At five cents a day I can try not to forget, but ten cents a day would make it twice as hard to. But never mind; I can tell her tomorrow that you know it too, and maybe we both can—"

"Who was Aunt Fittie?" I said.

"I dont know," he said. "Folks just called her Aunt Fittie. She might have been kin to some of us, but I dont know. Lived by herself in a house on the edge of town until she taken Bee in after Bee's maw died and soon as Bee got big enough, which never taken long because Bee was already a big girl even before she got to be ten or eleven or twelve or whenever it was and got started—"

"Started at what?" I said. You see? I had to. I had gone too far to stop now, like in Jefferson yesterday—or was it yesterday? last year: another time: another life: another Lucius Priest. "What is pugnuckling?"

He told me, with some of contempt but mostly a sort of incredulous, almost awed, almost respectful amazement. "That's where I had the peephole—a knothole in the back wall with a tin slide over it that never nobody but me knowed how to work, while Aunt Fittie was out in front collecting the money and watching out. Folks

your size would have to stand on a box and I would
charge a nickel until Aunt Fittie found out I was letting
grown men watch for a dime that otherwise might have
went inside for fifty cents, and started hollering like a
wildcat—"

Standing now, I was hitting him, so much to his surprise (mine too) that I had had to stoop and take hold
of him and jerk him up within reach. I knew nothing
about boxing and not too much about fighting. But I
knew exactly what I wanted to do: not just hurt him but
destroy him; I remember a second perhaps during which
I regretted (from what ancient playing-fields-of-Eton avatar) that he was not nearer my size. But not longer than
a second; I was hitting, clawing, kicking not at one
wizened ten-year-old boy, but at Otis and the procuress
both: the demon child who debased her privacy and the
witch who debauched her innocence—one flesh to bruise
and burst, one set of nerves to wrench and anguish; more:
not just those two, but all who had participated in her
debasement: not only the two panders, but the insensitive
blackguard children and the brutal and shameless men
who paid their pennies to watch her defenseless and un-
defended and unavenged degradation. He had plunged
sprawling across the mattress, on his hands and knees
now, scrabbling at his discarded trousers; I didn't know
why (nor care), not even when his hand came out and up.
Only then did I see the blade of the pocketknife in his
fist, nor did I care about that either; that made us in a
way the same size; that was my *carte blanche*. I took the
knife away from him. I dont know how; I never felt the
blade at all; when I flung the knife away and hit him
again, the blood I saw on his face I thought was his.

Then Boon was holding me clear of the floor, struggling and crying now. He was barefoot, wearing only his
pants. Miss Corrie was there too, in a kimono, with her

hair down; it reached further than her waist. Otis was scrunched back against the wall, not crying but cursing like he had cursed at Ned. "What the damned hell," Boon said.

"His hand," Miss Corrie said. She paused long enough to look back at Otis. "Go to my room," she said. "Go on." He went out. Boon put me down. "Let me see it," she said. That was the first I knew where the blood came from— a neat cut across the cushions of all four fingers; I must have grasped the blade just as Otis tried to snatch it away. It was still bleeding. That is, it bled again when Miss Corrie opened my hand.

"What the hell were you fighting about?" Boon said.

"Nothing," I said. I drew my hand back.

"Keep it closed till I get back," Miss Corrie said. She went out and came back with a basin of water and a towel and a bottle of something and what looked like a scrap of a man's shirt. She washed the blood off and uncorked the bottle. "It's going to sting," she said. It did. She tore a strip from the shirt and bound my hand.

"He still wont tell what they were fighting about," Boon said. "At least I hope he started it: not half your size even if he is a year older. No wonder he pulled a knife—"

"He aint even as old," I said. "He's ten."

"He told me he was twelve," Boon said. Then I found out what was wrong about Otis.

"Twelve?" Miss Corrie said. "He'll be fifteen years old next Monday." She was looking at me. "Do you want—"

"Just keep him out of here," I said. "I'm tired. I want to go to sleep."

"Don't worry about Otis," she said. "He's going back home this morning. There's a train that leaves at nine oclock. I'm going to send Minnie to the depot with him and tell her to watch him get on it and stand where she can see his face through the window until the train moves."

"Sure," Boon said. "And he can have my grip to carry the refinement and culture back in. Bringing him over here to spend a week in a Memphis—"

"You hush," Miss Corrie said.

"—house hunting refinement and culture. Maybe he found it; he might a hunted for years through Arkansas cat-cribs and still not found nobody near enough his size to draw that pocketknife on—"

"Stop it! Stop it!" Miss Corrie said.

"Sure sure," Boon said. "But after all, Lucius has got to know the name of where he's at in order to brag about where he's been." Then they turned the light out and were gone. Or so I thought. It was Boon this time, turning the light on again. "Maybe you better tell me what it was," he said.

"Nothing," I said. He looked down at me, huge, naked to the waist, his hand on the light to turn it out again.

"Eleven years old," he said, "and already knife-cut in a whorehouse brawl." He looked at me. "I wish I had knowed you thirty years ago. With you to learn me when I was eleven years old, maybe by this time I'd a had some sense too. Good night."

"Good night," I said. He turned off the light. Then I had been asleep, it was Miss Corrie this time, kneeling beside the mattress; I could see the shape of her face and the moon through her hair. She was the one crying this time—a big girl, too big to know how to cry daintily: only quietly.

"I made him tell me," she said. "You fought because of me. I've had people—drunks—fighting over me, but you're the first one ever fought for me. I aint used to it, you see. That's why I dont know what to do about it. Except one thing. I can do that. I want to make you a promise. Back there in Arkansas it was my fault. But it wont be my fault any more." You see? You have to learn too fast; you have to leap in the dark and hope that Something—It—They—will place your foot right. So maybe there are after all other things besides just Poverty and Non-virtue who look after their own.

"It wasn't your fault then," I said.

"Yes it was. You can choose. You can decide. You can say No. You can find a job and work. But it wont be my fault any more. That's the promise I want to make you. For me to keep like you kept that one you told Mr Binford about before supper tonight. You'll have to take it. Will you take it?"

"All right," I said.

"But you'll have to say you'll take it. You'll have to say it out loud."

"Yes," I said. "I'll take it."

"Now try to get back to sleep," she said. "I've brought a chair and I'm going to sit here where I'll be ready to wake you in time to go to the depot."

"You go back to bed too," I said.

"I aint sleepy," she said. "I'll just sit here. You go on back to sleep." And this time, Boon again. The moon-shaped square of window had shifted, so I had slept this time, his voice trying at least for whisper or anyway monotone, looming still naked from the waist up over the kitchen chair where Everbe (I mean Miss Corrie) sat, his hand grasping the backward-straining of her arm:

"Come on now. We aint got but a hour left."

"Let me go." She whispered too. "It's too late now. Let me go, Boon." Then his rasping murmur, still trying for, calling itself whisper:

"What the hell do you think I came all the way for, waited all this long for, all this working and saving up and waiting for—" Then the shape of the mooned window

had moved still more and I could hear a rooster somewhere and my cut hand was partly under me and hurting,
which was maybe what waked me. So I couldn't tell if
this was the same time or he had gone and then come
back: only the voices, still trying for whisper and if a
rooster was crowing, it was time to get up. And oh yes,
she was crying again.

"I wont! I wont! Let me alone!"

"All right, all right. But tonight is just tonight; tomorrow night, when we're settled down in Possum—"

"No! Not tomorrow either! I cant! I cant! Let me alone!
Please, Boon. Please!"

8

◆◆◆◆

We—Everbe and Boon and I—were at the depot in plenty
of time—or so we thought. The first person we saw was
Ned, waiting for us in front of it. He had on a clean white
shirt—either a new one, or he had managed somehow to
get the other one washed. But almost at once things
began to go too fast for anyone to learn yet that the new
shirt was one of Sam's. Ned didn't even give Boon time
to open his mouth. "Calm yourself," he said. "Mr Sam
is keeping Lightning whilst I finishes the outside arrange-
ments. The boxcar has done already been picked up and
switched onto the train waiting behind the depot right
now for you all to get on. When Mr Sam Caldwell runs
a railroad, it's run, mon. We done already named him too
—Forkid Lightning." Then he saw my bandage. He almost pounced. "What you done to it?"

"I cut it," I said. "It's all right."

"How bad?" he said.

"Yes," Everbe said. "It's cut across all four fingers. He ought not to move it even." Nor did Ned waste any more time there either. He looked quickly about us.

"Where's that other one?" he said.

"That other what?" Boon said.

"Whistle-britches," Ned said. "That money-mouthed runt boy that was with us last night. I may need two hands on that horse. Who do you think is gonter ride that race? me and you that's even twice as heavy as me? Lucius was going to, but being as we already got that other one, we dont need to risk it. He's even less weight than Lucius and even if he aint got as much sense as Lucius, he's at least old enough in meanness to ride a horse race, and wropped up enough in money to want to win it, and likely too much of a coward to turn loose and fall off. Which is all we needs. Where is he?"

"Gone back to Arkansas," Boon said. "How old do you think he is?"

"What he looks like," Ned said. "About fifteen, aint he? Gone to Arkansaw? Then somebody better go get him quick."

"Yes," Everbe said. "I'll bring him. There wont be time to go back and get him now. So I'll stay and bring him on the next train this afternoon."

"Now you talking," Ned said. "That's Mr Sam's train. Just turn Whistle-britches over to Mr Sam; he'll handle him."

"Sure," Boon said to Everbe. "That'll give you a whole hour free to practise that No on Sam. Maybe he's a better man than me and wont take it." But she just looked at him.

"Then why dont you wait and bring Otis on and we'll

meet you in Parsham tonight," I said. Now Boon looked at me.

"Well well," he said. "What's that Mr Binford said last night? If here aint still another fresh hog in this wallow. Except that this one's still just a shoat yet. That is, I thought it was."

"Please, Boon," Everbe said. Like that: "Please, Boon."

"Take him too and the both of you get to hell back to that slaughterhouse that maybe you ought not to left in the first place," Boon said. She didn't say anything this time. She just stood there, looking down a little: a big girl that stillness suited too. Then she turned, already walking.

"Maybe I will," I said. "Right on back home. Ned's got somebody else to ride the horse and you dont seem to know what to do with none of the folks trying to help us."

He looked, glared at me: a second maybe. "All right," he said. He strode past me until he overtook her. "I said, all right," he said. "Is it all right?"

"All right," she said.

"I'll meet the first train today. If you aint on it, I'll keep on meeting them. All right?"

"All right," she said. She went on.

"I bet aint none of you thought to bring my grip," Ned said.

"What?" Boon said.

"Where is it?" I said.

"Right there in the kitchen where I set it," Ned said. "That gold-tooth high-brown seen it."

"Miss Corrie'll bring it tonight," I said. "Come on." We went into the depot. Boon bought our tickets and we went out to where the train was waiting, with people already getting on it. Up ahead we could see the boxcar. Sam and the conductor and two other men were standing by the open door; one of them must have been the engineer. You see? not just one casual off-duty flagman, but a functioning train crew.

"You going to run him today?" the conductor said.

"Tomorrow," Boon said.

"Well, we got to get him there first," the conductor said, looking at his watch. "Who's going to ride with him?"

"Me," Ned said. "Soon as I can find a box or something to climb up on."

"Gimme your foot," Sam said. Ned cocked his knee and Sam threw him up into the car. "See you in Parsham tomorrow," he said.

"I thought you went all the way to Washington," Boon said.

"Who, me?" Sam said. "That's just the train. I'm going to double back from Chattanooga tonight on Two-O-Nine. I'll be back in Parsham at seven oclock tomorrow morning. I'd go with you now and pick up Two-O-Eight in Parsham tonight, only I got to get some sleep. Besides, you wont need me anyhow. You can depend on Ned until then."

So did Boon and I. I mean, need sleep. We got some, until the conductor waked us and we stood on the cinders at Parsham in the first light and watched the engine (there was a cattle-loading chute here) spot the boxcar, properly this time, and take its train again and go on, clicking car by car across the other tracks which went south to Jefferson. Then the three of us dismantled the stall and Ned led the horse out; and of course, naturally, materialised from nowhere, a pleasant-looking Negro youth of about nineteen, standing at the bottom of the chute, said, "Howdy, Mr McCaslin."

"That you, son?" Ned said. "Whichaway?" So we left Boon for that time; his was the Motion role now, the doing: to find a place for all of us to live, not just him and me, but Otis and Everbe when they came tonight: to locate a man whose name Ned didn't even know, whom nobody but Ned said owned a horse, and then persuade him to run it, race it—one figment of Ned's imagination to race another figment—in a hypothetical race which was in the future and therefore didn't exist, against a horse it had already beaten twice (this likewise according only to Ned, or Figment Three), as a result of which Ned intended to recover Grandfather's automobile; all this Boon must do while still keeping clear of being challenged about who really did own the horse. We—Ned and the youth and me—were walking now, already out of town, which didn't take long in those days—a hamlet, two or three stores where the two railroads crossed, the depot and loading chute and freight shed and a platform for cotton bales. Though some of it has not changed: the big rambling multigalleried multistoried steamboat-gothic hotel where the overalled aficionados and the professionals who trained the fine bird dogs and the northern millionaires who owned them (one night in the lounge in 1933, his Ohio business with everybody else's under the Damocles sword of the federally closed banks, I myself heard Horace Lytle refuse five thousand dollars for Mary Montrose) gathered for two weeks each February; Paul Rainey also, who liked our country enough —or anyway our bear and deer and panther enough—to use some of the Wall Street money to own enough Mississippi land for him and his friends to hunt them in: a hound man primarily, who took his pack of bear hounds to Africa to see what they would do on lion or vice versa.

"This white boy's going to sleep walking," the youth said. "Aint you got no saddle?" But I wasn't going to sleep yet. I had to find out, to ask:

"I didn't even know you knew anybody here, let alone getting word ahead to them."

Ned walked on as if I had not even spoken. After a

while he said over his shoulder: "So you wants to know how, do you?" He walked on. He said: "Me and that boy's grandpappy are Masons."

"Why are you whispering?" I said. "Boss is a Mason too but I never heard him whisper about it."

"I didn't know I was," Ned said. "But suppose I was. What do you want to belong to a lodge for, unless it's so secret cant hardly nobody else get in it? And how are you gonter keep it secret unless you treat it like one?"

"But how did you get word to him?" I said.

"Let me tell you something," Ned said. "If you ever need to get something done, not just done but done quick and quiet and so you can depend on it and not no blabbing and gabbling around about it neither, you hunt around until you finds somebody like Mr Sam Caldwell, and turn it over to him. You member that. Folks around Jefferson could use some of him. They could use a heap of Sam Caldwells."

Then we were there. The sun was well up now. It was a dog-trot house, paintless but quite sound and quite neat among locust and chinaberry trees, in a swept yard inside a fence which had all its palings too and a hinged gate that worked, with chickens in the dust and a cow and a pair of mules in the stable lot behind it, and two pretty good hounds which had already recognised the youth with us, and an old man at the top of the gallery steps above them—an old man very dark in a white shirt and galluses and a planter's hat, with perfectly white moustaches and an imperial, coming down the steps now and across the yard to look at the horse. Because he knew, remembered the horse, and so one at least of Ned's figment's vanished.

"You all buy him?" he said.

"We got him," Ned said.

"Long enough to run him?"

"Once, anyway," Ned said. He said to me: "Make your manners to Uncle Possum Hood." I did so.

"Rest yourself," Uncle Parsham said. "You all about ready for breakfast, aint you?" I could already smell it —the ham.

"All I want is to go to sleep," I said.

"He's been up all night," Ned said. "Both of us. Only he had to spend his in a house full of women hollering why and how much whilst all I had was just a quiet empty boxcar with a horse." But I was still going to help stable and feed Lightning. They wouldn't let me. "You go with Lycurgus and get some sleep," Ned said. "I'm gonter need you soon, before it gets too hot. We got to find out about this horse, and the sooner we starts, the sooner it will be." I followed Lycurgus. It was a lean-to room, a bed with a bright perfectly clean harlequin-patched quilt; it seemed to me I was asleep before I even lay down, and that Ned was shaking me before I had ever slept. He had a clean heavy wool sock and a piece of string. I was hungry now. "You can eat your breakfast afterwards," Ned said. "You can learn a horse better on a empty stomach. Here—" holding the sock open. "Whistle-britches aint showed up yet. It might be better if he dont a-tall. He the sort that no matter how bad you think you need him, you find out afterward you was better off. Hold out your hand." He meant the bandaged one. He slipped the sock over it, bandage and all, and tied it around my wrist with the string. "You can still use your thumb, but this'll keep you from forgetting and trying to open your hand and bust them cuts again."

Uncle Parsham and Lycurgus were waiting with the horse. He was bridled now, under an old, used, but perfectly cared-for McClellan saddle. Ned looked at it. "We might run him bareback, unless they makes us. But leave it on. We can try him both ways and let him learn us which he likes best."

It was a small pasture beside the creek, flat and smooth, with good footing. Ned shortened the leathers, to suit not me so much as him, and threw me up. "You know what to do: the same as with them colts out at McCaslin. Let him worry about which hand he's on; likely all anybody ever tried to learn him is just to run as fast as the bit will let him, whichever way somebody points his head. Which is all we wants too. You dont need no switch yet. Besides, we dont want to learn a switch: we wants to learn him. Go on."

I moved him out, into the pasture, into a trot. He was nothing on the bit; a cobweb would have checked him. I said so. "I bet," Ned said. "I bet he got a heap more whip calluses on his behind than bit chafes in his jaw. Go on. Move him." But he wouldn't. I kicked, pounded my heels, but he just trotted, a little faster in the back stretch (I was riding a circular course like the one we had beaten out in Cousin Zack's paddock) until I realised suddenly that he was simply hurrying back to Ned. But still behind the bit; he had never once come into the bridle, his whole head bent around and tucked but with no weight whatever on the hand, as if the bit were a pork rind and he a Mohammedan (or a fish spine and he a Mississippi candidate for constable whose Baptist opposition had accused him of seeking the Catholic vote, or one of Mrs Roosevelt's autographed letters and a secretary of the Citizens Council, or Senator Goldwater's cigar butt and the youngest pledge to the A.D.A.), on until he reached Ned, and with a jerk I felt clean up to my shoulder, snatched his head free and began to nuzzle at Ned's shirt. "U-huh," Ned said. He had one hand behind him; I could see a peeled switch in it now. "Head him back." He said to the horse: "You got to learn, son, not to run back to me until I sends for you." Then to me: "He aint gonter stop this time. But you make like he is: just one stride ahead of where, if you was him, you would think about turning to come to me, reach back with your hand and whop him hard as you can. Now set tight," and stepped back and cut the horse quick and hard across the buttocks.

It leapt, sprang into full run: the motion (not our speed nor even our progress: just the horse's motion) seemed terrific: graceless of course, but still terrific. Because it was simple reflex from fright, and fright does not become horses. They are built wrong for it, being merely mass and symmetry, while fright demands fluidity and grace and bizarreness and the capacity to enchant and enthrall and even appall and aghast, like an impala or a giraffe or a snake; even as the fright faded I could feel, sense the motion become simply obedience, no more than an obedient hand gallop, on around the back turn and stretch and into what would be the home stretch, when I did as Ned ordered: one stride before the point at which he had turned to Ned before, I reached back and hit him as hard as I could with the flat of my sound hand; and again the leap, the spring, but only into willingness, obedience, alarm: not anger nor even eagerness. "That'll do," Ned said. "Bring him in." We came up and stopped. He was sweating a little, but that was all. "How do he feel?" Ned said.

I tried to tell him. "The front half of him dont want to run."

"He reached out all right when I touched him," Ned said.

I tried again. "I dont mean his front end. His legs feel all right. His head just dont want to go anywhere."

"U-huh," Ned said. He said to Uncle Parsham: "You seen one of them races. What happened?"

"I saw both of them," Uncle Parsham said. "Nothing happened. He was running good until all of a sudden he must have looked up and seen there wasn't nothing in front of him but empty track."

"U-huh," Ned said. "Jump down." I got down. He stripped off the saddle. "Hand me your foot."

"How do you know that horse has been ridden bareback before?" Uncle Parsham said.

"I dont," Ned said. "We gonter find out."

"This boy aint got but one hand," Uncle Parsham said. "Here, Lycurgus—"

But Ned already had my foot. "This boy learnt holding on riding Zack Edmonds's colts back in Missippi. I watched him at least one time when I didn't know what he was holding on with lessen it was his teeth." He threw me up. The horse did nothing: it squatted, flinched a moment, trembling a little; that was all. "U-huh," Ned said. "Let's go eat your breakfast. Whistle-britches will be here to work him this evening, then maybe Lightning will start having some fun outen this too."

Lycurgus's mother, Uncle Parsham's daughter, was cooking dinner now; the kitchen smelled of the boiling vegetables. But she had kept my breakfast warm—fried sidemeat, grits, hot biscuits and buttermilk or sweet milk or coffee; she untied my riding-glove from my hand so I could eat, a little surprised that I had never tasted coffee since Lycurgus had been having it on Sunday morning since he was two years old. And I thought I was just hungry until I went to sleep right there in the plate until Lycurgus half dragged, half carried me to his bed in the lean-to. And, as Ned said, Mr Sam Caldwell was some Sam Caldwell; Everbe and Otis got down from the caboose of a freight train which stopped that long at Parsham a few minutes before noon. It was a through freight, not intended to stop until it reached Florence, Alabama,

or some place like that. I dont know how much extra coal
it took to pump up the air brakes to stop it dead still at
Parsham and then fire the boiler enough to regain speed
and make up the lost time. Some Sam Caldwell. Twenty-
three skiddoo, as Otis said.

So when the loud unfamiliar voice waked me and
Lycurgus's mother tied the riding-sock back on from
where she had put it away when I went to sleep in my
plate, and I went outside, there they all were: a surrey
tied outside the gate and Uncle Parsham standing again
at the top of his front steps, still wearing his hat, and Ned
sitting on the next-to-bottom step and Lycurgus standing
in the angle between steps and gallery as if the three of
them were barricading the house; and in the yard facing
them Everbe (yes, she brought it. I mean, Ned's grip)
and Otis and Boon and the one who was doing the loud
talking—a man almost as big as Boon and almost as ugly,
with a red face and a badge and a holstered pistol stuck
in his hind pocket, standing between Boon and Everbe,
who was still trying to pull away from the hand which
was holding her arm.

"Yep," he was saying, "I know old Possum Hood. And
more than that, old Possum Hood knows me, dont you,
boy?"

"We all knows you here, Mr Butch," Uncle Parsham
said with no inflection whatever.

"If any dont, it's just a oversight and soon corrected,"
Butch said. "If your womenfolks are too busy dusting and
sweeping to invite us in the house, tell them to bring
some chairs out here so this young lady can set down.
You, boy," he told Lycurgus, "hand down two of them
chairs on the gallery there where me and you"—he was
talking at Everbe now—"can set in the cool and get acquainted while Sugar Boy"—he meant Boon. I dont know
how I knew it—"takes these boys down to look at that

horse. Huh?" Still holding Everbe's elbow, he would tilt
her gently away from him until she was almost off
balance; then, a little faster though still not a real jerk,
pull her back again, she still trying to get loose; now she
used her other hand, pushing at his wrist. And now I was
watching Boon. "You sure I aint seen you somewhere? at
Birdie Watts's maybe? Where you been hiding, anyway?
a good-looking gal like you?" Now Ned got up, not
fast.

"Morning, Mr Boon," he said. "You and Mr Shurf want
Lucius to bring the horse out?" Butch stopped tilting
Everbe. He still held her though.

"Who's he?" he said. "As a general rule, we dont take
to strange niggers around here. We dont object though,
providing they notify themselves and then keep their
mouths shut."

"Ned William McCaslin Jefferson Missippi," Ned said.

"You got too much name," Butch said. "You want something quick and simple to answer to around here until
you can raise a white mush-tash and goat whisker like
old Possum there, and earn it. We dont care where you
come from neither; all you'll need here is just somewhere
to go back to. But you'll likely do all right; at least you
got sense enough to recognise Law when you see it."

"Yes sir," Ned said. "I'm acquainted with Law. We got
it back in Jefferson too." He said to Boon: "You want the
horse?"

"No," Everbe said; she had managed to free her arm;
she moved quickly away; she could have done it sooner
by just saying Boon: which was what Butch—deputy,
whatever he was—wanted her to do, and we all knew
that too. She moved, quickly for a big girl, on until she
had me between her and Butch, holding my arm now; I
could feel her hand trembling a little as she gripped me.
"Come on, Lucius. Show us the way." She said, her voice

tense: a murmur, almost passionate: "How's your hand?
Does it hurt?"

"It's all right," I said.

"You sure? You'd tell me? Does wearing that sock on
it help?"

"It's all right," I said. "I'd tell you." We went back to
the stable that way, Everbe almost dragging me to keep
me between her and Butch. But it was no good; he simply
walked me off; I could smell him now—sweat and
whiskey—and now I saw the top of the pint bottle in his
other hind pocket; he (Butch) holding her elbow again
and suddenly I was afraid, because I knew I didn't—and
I wasn't sure Boon did—know Everbe that well yet. No:
not afraid, that wasn't the word; not afraid, because we—
Boon alone—would have taken the pistol away from him
and then whipped him, but afraid for Everbe and Uncle
Parsham and Uncle Parsham's home and family when it
happened. But I was more than afraid. I was ashamed
that such a reason for fearing for Uncle Parsham, who
had to live here, existed; hating (not Uncle Parsham doing
the hating, but me doing it) it all, hating all of us for
being the poor frail victims of being alive, having to be
alive—hating Everbe for being the vulnerable helpless
lodestar victim; and Boon for being the vulnerable and
helpless victimised; and Uncle Parsham and Lycurgus
for being where they had to, couldn't help but watch
white people behaving exactly as white people bragged
that only Negroes behaved—just as I had hated Otis for
telling me about Everbe in Arkansas and hated Everbe
for being that helpless lodestar for human debasement
which he had told me about and hated myself for listening, having to hear about it, learn about it, know about
it; hating that such not only was, but must be, had to be
if living was to continue and mankind be a part of it.

And suddenly I was anguished with homesickness,

wrenched and wrung and agonised with it: to be home, not just to retrace but to retract, obliterate: make Ned take the horse back to wherever and whoever and however he had got it and get Grandfather's automobile and take it back to Jefferson, in reverse if necessary, travelling backward to unwind, ravel back into No-being, Never-being, that whole course of dirt roads, mudholes, the man and the color-blind mules, Miss Ballenbaugh and Alice and Ephum, so that, as far as I was concerned, they had never been; when sudden and quiet and plain inside me something said *Why dont you?* Because I could; I needed only say to Boon, "We're going home," and Ned would have returned the horse and my own abject confession would have the automobile located and recovered by the police at the price of merely my shame. Because I couldn't now. It was too late. Maybe yesterday, while I was still a child, but not now. I knew too much, had seen too much. I was a child no longer now; innocence and childhood were forever lost, forever gone from me. And Everbe was loose again. I had missed seeing how she did it this time: only that she was free, facing him; she said something inaudible, quick; anyway he was not even touching her now, just looking down at her, grinning.

"Sure, sure," he said. "Thrash around a little; maybe I like that too; makes it look a little better to old Sugar Boy too. All right, boy," he said to Ned. "Let's see that horse."

"You stay here," Ned told me. "Me and Lycurgus will get him." So I stood, next to Everbe at the fence; she was holding my arm again, her hand still shaking a little. Ned and Lycurgus led the horse out. Ned was already looking toward us; he said quickly: "Where's that other one?"

"Dont tell me you got two of them," Butch said. But I knew what Ned meant. So did Everbe. She turned quickly.

"Otis!" she said. But he was nowhere in sight.

"Run," Ned told Lycurgus. "If he aint got into the house yet, maybe you can cut him off. Tell him his aunt wants him. And you stay right with him." Lycurgus didn't even wait to say Yes sir: he just gave the lead rope to Ned and departed running. The rest of us stood along the fence— Everbe trying for immobility since that was all she had to find effacement in, but too big for it like the doe is too big for the plum thicket which is all she has available for safety; Boon furious and seething, restraining himself who never before had restrained himself from anything. Not from fear; I tell you, he was not afraid of that gun and badge: he could and would have taken them both away from Butch and, in a kind of glory, tossed the pistol on the ground halfway between them and then given Butch the first step toward it; and only half from the loyalty which would shield me—and my family (his family)—from the result of such a battle, no matter who won it. Because the other half was chivalry: to shield a woman, even a whore, from one of the predators who debase police badges by using them as immunity to prey on her helpless kind. And a little further along, dissoci- ated though present, Uncle Parsham, the patrician (he bore in his Christian name the patronymic of the very land we stood on), the aristocrat of us all and judge of us all.

"Hell," Butch said. "He cant win races standing still in a halter. Go on. Trot him across the lot."

"We just sent for his jockey," Ned said. "Then you can see him work." Then he said, "Unlessen you in a hurry to get back to yourn."

"My what?" Butch said.

"Your law work," Ned said. "Back in Possum or wher- ever it is."

"After coming all the way out here to see a race horse?"

Butch said. "All I see so far is a plug standing half asleep in a lot."

"I'm sho glad you told me that," Ned said. "I thought maybe you wasn't interested." He turned to Boon. "So maybe what you and Miss Corrie better do is go on back to town now and be ready to meet the others when the train comes. You can send the surrey back for Mr Butch and Lucius and that other boy after we breezes Lightning."

"Ha ha ha," Butch said, without mirth, without anything. "How's that for a idea? Huh, Sugar Boy? You and Sweet Thing bobbasheely on back to the hotel now, and me and Uncle Remus and Lord Fauntleroy will mosey along any time up to midnight, providing of course we are through here." He moved easily along the fence to where Boon stood, watching Boon though addressing Ned: "I cant let Sugar Boy leave without me. I got to stay right with him, or he might get everybody in trouble. They got a law now, about taking good-looking gals across state lines for what they call immortal purposes. Sugar Boy's a stranger here; he dont know exactly where that state line's at, and his foot might slip across it while his mind's on something else—something that aint a foot. At least we dont call it foot around here. Huh, Sugar Boy?" He slapped Boon on the back, still grinning, watching Boon—one of those slaps which jovial men give one another, but harder, a little too hard but not quite too hard. Boon didn't move, his hands on the top rail of the gate. They were too sunburned or maybe too ingrained with dirt to turn white. But I could see the muscles. "Yes sir," Butch said, watching Boon, grinning, "all friends together for a while yet anyhow. Come one, come all, or come none—for a while longer anyhow. At least until something happens that might put a man not watching what he was doing out of circulation—say a stranger that wouldn't be

missed nohow. Huh, Sugar Boy?" and slapped Boon again
on the back, still harder this time, watching him, grinning.
And Everbe saw Boon's hand this time too; she said,
quick, not loud:

"Boon." Like that: "Boon." So had Uncle Parsham.

"Here come the other boy," he said. Otis was just
coming around the corner of the house, Lycurgus looming almost twice as tall right behind him. Even knowing
what was wrong about him didn't help Otis much. But
Ned was the one who was looking at him hard. He came
up gently; strolling, in fact.

"Somebody want me?" he said.

"It was me," Ned said. "But I aint seed you in daylight
before and maybe my mind gonter change." He said to
Lycurgus: "Get the tack." So we—they—tacked up and
Lycurgus and Ned led the way back along the lane to
the creek pasture, we following, even Butch giving his
attention to the matter in hand now; unless, as the angler
does, he was deliberately giving Everbe a little rest to
build up her strength to rush and thrash once more
against the hook of that tin star on his sweaty shirt. When
we reached the pasture, Ned and Otis were already
facing each other about eight feet apart; behind them,
Lycurgus stood with the horse. Ned looked strained and
tired. As far as I knew, he had had no sleep at all unless
he actually had slept for an hour or so on the hay in the
boxcar. But that's all he was: not exhausted by sleeplessness, just annoyed by it. Otis was picking his nose,
still gently. "A know-boy," Ned was saying. "As knowing
a boy as I ever seed. I just hopes that when you're twice
your age, you will still know half as much."

"Much obliged," Otis said.

"Can you ride a horse?" Ned said.

"I been living on a Arkansas farm for a right smart number of years," Otis said.

"Can you ride a horse?" Ned said. "Nemmine where you used to live or still does."

"Now, that depends, as the fellow says," Otis said. "I figgered I was going back home this morning. That I would a long been in Kiblett, Arkansas, right this minute. But since my plans got changed without nobody asking me, I aint decided quite yet just what I'm going to do next. How much you paying to get that horse rode?"

"Otis!" Everbe said.

"We aint come to that yet," Ned said, as gentle as Otis. "The first thing is to get them three heats run and to be in front when at least two of them is finished. Then we'll git around to how much."

"Heh heh heh," Otis said, not laughing either. "That is, there aint going to be nothing to pay nobody with until you win it—that's you. And you cant even run at it without somebody setting on the horse—that's me. Is that right?"

"Otis!" Everbe said.

"That's right," Ned said. "We all of us working on shares so we'll have something to divide afterward. Your share will have to wait too, like ourn."

"Yeah," Otis said. "I seen that kind of share dividing in the Arkansas cotton business. The trouble is, the share of the fellow that does the sharing is always a little different from the share of the fellow that done the dividing. The fellow that done the sharing is still waiting for his share because he aint yet located where it's at. So from now on, I'll just take the cash-in-advance share and let you folks keep all the dividing."

"How much do that come to?" Ned said.

"You cant be interested, because you aint even run the first heat yet, let alone won it. But I dont mind telling you, in confidence, you might say. It'll be ten dollars."

"Otis!" Everbe said. She moved now; she cried, "Aint you ashamed?"

"Hold up, Miss," Ned said. "I'll handle it." He looked tired, but that was all. Without haste he drew a folded flour sack from his hip pocket and unfolded it and took out his worn snap purse and opened it. "Hold out your hand," he told Lycurgus, who did so while Ned counted slowly onto the palm six frayed dollar bills and then about a cupful of coins of various denominations. "It's gonter be fifteen cents short, but Mr Hogganbeck will make it up."

"Make it up to what?" Otis said.

"To what you said. Ten dollars," Ned said.

"You cant seem to hear neither," Otis said. "What I said was twenty dollars." Now Boon moved.

"God damn it," he said.

"Just hold up," Ned told him. His hand didn't even stop, now returning the coins one by one from Lycurgus's hand, and then the frayed bills, back into the purse, and closed it and folded it back into the flour sack and put the sack back into his pocket. "So you aint gonter ride the horse," he said to Otis.

"I aint seen my price—" Otis said.

"Mr Boon Hogganbeck there is fixing to hand it to you right now," Ned said. "Whyn't you just come right out like a man and say you aint gonter ride that horse? It dont matter why you aint." They looked at each other. "Come on. Say it out."

"Naw," Otis said. "I aint going to ride it." He said something else, foul, which was his nature; vicious, which was his nature; completely unnecessary, which was his nature too. Yes, even finally knowing what it was didn't help with him. By this time Everbe had him. She snatched him, hard. And this time he snarled. He cursed her. "Watch out. I aint near done talking yet—if I'm a mind."

"Say the word," Butch said. "I'll beat the hell out of him just on principle; I wont even bother with pleasure. How the hell did Sugar Boy ever let him get this far without at least one whelp on him?"

"No!" Everbe said to Butch. She still held Otis by the arm. "You're going back home on the next train!"

"Now you're tooting," Otis said. "I'd a been there right now except for you." She released him.

"Go on back to the surrey," she said.

"You cant risk it," Boon said rapidly to her. "You'll have to go with him." He said: "All right. You all go back to town. You can send for me and Lucius about sundown."

And I knew what that meant, what decision he had wrestled with and licked. But Butch fooled us; the confident angler was letting his fish have the backing too. "Sure," he said. "Send back for us." Everbe and Otis went on. "Now that that's settled, who is going to ride the horse?"

"This boy here," Ned said. "He a one-handed horse."

"Heh heh heh," Butch said; he was laughing this time. "I seen this horse run here last winter. If one hand can even wake him up, it will take more hands than a spider or a daddy longlegs to get him out in front of that horse of Colonel Linscomb's."

"Maybe you right," Ned said. "That's what we gonter find out now. Son," he said to Lycurgus, "hand me my coat." I had not even noticed the coat yet, but now Lycurgus had it; also the peeled switch. Ned took both and put the coat on. He said to Boon and Butch: "Yawl stand over yonder under them trees with Uncle Possum where you'll be in the shade and wont distract his mind. Hand me your foot," he told me. We did so. I mean, Ned threw me up and Boon and Butch and Lycurgus went back to the tree where Uncle Parsham was already standing. Even though we had made only three trips around the pasture this morning, we had a vestigial path which Lightning would remember whether I could see it or not. Ned led him out to what had been our old starting point this morning. He spoke, quiet and succinct. He was not Uncle Remus now. But then, he never was when it was just me and members of his own race around:

"That track tomorrow aint but a half a mile, so you gonter go around it twice. Make like this is it, so when he sees that real track tomorrow, he'll already know beforehand what to expect and to do. You understand?"

"Yes," I said. "Ride him around it twice—"

He handed me the switch. "Get him going quick and hard. Cut him once with this before he even knows it. Then dont touch him again with it until I tells you to. Keep him going as fast as you can with your heels and talking to him but dont bother him: just set there. Keep your mind on it that you're going around twice, and try to think his mind onto that too, like you done with them colts out at McCaslin. You cant do it, but you got the switch this time. But dont touch him with it until I tells you to." He turned his back; he was doing something now inside the shelter of his coat—something infinitesimal with his hidden hands; suddenly I smelled something, faint yet sharp; I realise now that I should have recognised it at once but I didn't have time then. He turned back; as when he had coaxed the horse into the boxcar this morning, his hand touched, caressed Lightning's muzzle for maybe a second, then he stepped back, Lightning already trying to follow him had I not reined him back. "Go!" Ned said. "Cut him!"

I did. He leapt, sprang, out of simple fright: nothing else; it took a half-stride to get his head back and another stride before he realised we wanted to follow the track, path again, at full gallop now, on just enough outside rein to hold him on the course; I already heeling him as hard as I could even before the fright began to fade. Only, there we were again, just like this morning: going good, obedient enough, plenty of power, but once more with that sense that his head didn't really want to go anywhere; until we entered the back stretch and he saw Ned again on the opposite side of the ring. It was the explosion again; he had taken the bit away from me; he had already left the path and was cutting straight across to Ned before I got balance enough to reach my good hand down and take the rein short and haul, wrench him angling back into the track, going hard now; I had to hold him on the outside to make the back turn and into the stretch where he could see Ned again and once more reached for the bit to go straight to him; I was using the cut hand too now to hold him onto the track; it seemed forever until Ned spoke. "Cut him," he said. "Then throw the switch away."

I did so and flung the switch backward; the leap again but I had him now since it only took one rein, the outside one, to keep him on the course, going good now, around the first turn and I was ready for him this time when he would see Ned, on through the back stretch still going, into and around the last turn, still going, Ned standing now about twenty yards beyond where our finish line would be, speaking just exactly loud enough for Lightning to hear him and just exactly as he had spoken to him in the boxcar door last night—and I didn't need the switch now; I wouldn't have had time to use it if I had had it and I thought until then that I had ridden at least one horse that I called hot anyway: a half-bred colt of Cousin Zack's with Morgan on the bottom: but nothing like this, this burst, surge, as if until now we had been dragging a rope with a chunk of wood at the end of it behind us and Ned's voice had cut the rope: "Come on, son. I got it."

So we were standing there, Lightning's muzzle buried to the nostrils in Ned's hand, though all I could smell now was horse-reek and all I could see was the handful of grass which Lightning was eating; Ned himself saying "Hee hee hee" so gentle and quiet that I whispered too:

"What?" I said. "What?" But Boon didn't whisper, coming up.

"I'll be God damned. What the hell did you tell him?"

"Nothing," Ned said. "Just if he want his supper, to come on and get it." And not Butch either: bold, confident, unconvinceable, without scruple or pity.

"Well, well," he said. He didn't draw Lightning's head up out of Ned's hand: he jerked it up, then rammed the bit home when Lightning started back.

"Lemme do it," Ned said quickly. "What you want to find out?"

"Any time I need help handling horses around here, I'll holler," Butch said. "And not for you. I'll save you to holler for down in Missippi." He lifted Lightning's lip and looked at his gums, then at his eyes. "Dont you know it's against the law to dope a horse for a race? Maybe you folks down there in them swamps aint heard about it, but it's so."

"We got horse doctors in Missippi though," Ned said. "Send for one of them to come and see if he been doped."

"Sure, sure," Butch said. "Only, why did you give it to him a day ahead of the race? to see if it would work?"

"That's right," Ned said. "If I give him nothing. Which I aint. Which if you knows horses, you already knows."

"Sure, sure," Butch said again. "I dont interfere with no man's business secrets—providing they work. Is this horse going to run like that again tomorrow? I dont mean once: I mean three times."

"He dont need to do it but twice," Ned said.

"All right," Butch said. "Twice. Is he?"

"Ask Mr Hogganbeck there if he hadn't better do it twice," Ned said.

"I aint asking Mr Sugar Boy," Butch said. "I'm asking you."

"I can make him do it twice," Ned said.

"Fair enough," Butch said. "In fact, if all you got is three more doses, I wouldn't even risk but twice. Then if he misses the second one, you can use the last one to get back to Missipi on."

"I done thought of that too," Ned said. "Walk him back to the barn," he said to me. "Cool him out. Then we'll bath him."

Butch watched that too, some of it. We went back to the barn and untacked and Lycurgus brought a bucket and a rag and Lycurgus washed him down and dried him with crokersacks before stalling and feeding him—or had started to. Because Butch said, "Here, boy, run to the house and set the water bucket and some sugar on the front gallery. Me and Mr Sugar Boy are going to have a toddy." Though Lycurgus didn't move until Uncle Parsham said,

"Go." He went then, Boon and Butch following. Uncle Parsham stood at the door of the stable, watching them (Butch, that is)—a lean dramatic old man all black-and-white: black pants, white shirt, black face and hat behind the white hair and moustache and imperial. "Law," he said. He said it calmly, with cold and detached contempt.

"A man that never had nothing in it nohow, one of them little badges goes to his head so fast it makes yourn swim too," Ned said. "Except it aint the badge so much as that pistol, that likely all the time he was a little boy, he wanted to tote, only he knowed all the time that soon as he got big enough to own one, the law wouldn't let him tote it. Now with that badge too, he dont run no risk of being throwed in jail and having it took away from him; he can still be a little boy in spite of he had to grow up. The risk is, that pistol gonter stay on that little boy mind just so long before some day it gonter shoot at something alive before he even knowed he aimed to." Then Lycurgus came back.

"They waiting for you," he told me. "The surrey."

"It's back from town already?" I said.

"It never went to town," Lycurgus said. "It never left. She been setting in it out there with that-ere boy all the time, waiting for you all. She say to come on."

"Wait," Ned said. I stopped; I still had the riding-sock on and I thought he meant that. But he was looking at me. "You gonter start running into folks now."

"What folks?" I said.

"That word has done got around to. About this race."

"How got around?" I said.

"How do word ever get around?" he said. "It dont need no messenger; all it needs is two horses that can run to be inside the same ten miles of each other. How you reckon that Law got here? maybe smelled that white girl four or five miles away like a dog? I know; maybe I hoped like Boon Hogganbeck still believes: that we could get these two horses together here all nice and private and run that race, win or lose, and me and you and him could either go back home or go any other place we wants providing it's longer away than Boss Priest's arm. But not now. You gonter start meeting them from now on. And tomorrow they gonter be thicker still."

"You mean we can run the race?"

"We got to now. Maybe we been had to ever since me and Boon realised that Boss had done took his hand off of that automobile for as long as twenty-four hours. But now we sho got to run it."

"What do you want me to do?" I said.

"Nothing. I'm just telling you so you wont be surprised in advance. All we got to do is get them two horses on the same track and pointed the same way and you just set there on Lightning and do like I tell you. Go on, now, before they start hollering for you."

9

◆◆◆◆

Ned was right. I mean, about word already being around.
There was nothing wrong with my hand when Everbe
took the riding-sock off. I mean, it felt like anybody's
hand would that had been cut across the inside of the
fingers yesterday. I dont believe it had bled any more
even when I used it against Lightning's pulling this afternoon. But not Everbe. So we stopped at the doctor's first,
about a mile this side of town. Butch knew him, knew
where but I dont know how Everbe persuaded him to
take us there—nagged him or threatened or promised or
maybe just did it like a big girl trout so busy fussing
around a child trout that she quit behaving like there was
any such thing in existence as a barbed hook with a line
fastened to it and so the fisherman had to do something
even if only getting rid of the child trout. Or maybe it

was not Everbe but rather the empty flask, since the next drink would have to be at the hotel in Parsham. Because as I came around the house, Lycurgus's mother was standing at the edge of the gallery holding a sugar bowl and a water bucket with a gourd dipper and Butch and Boon were just draining the two tumblers and Lycurgus was just picking up the empty flask where Butch had flung it into a rosebush.

So Butch took us to the doctor's—a little once-white house in a little yard filled with the kind of rank-growing rank-smelling dusty flowers that bloom in the late summer and fall, a fat iron-gray woman in pince-nez like a retired schoolteacher who even fifteen years later still hated eight-year-old children, who came to the door and looked at us once (Ned was right) and said back into the house, "It's them race-horse folks," and turned and vanished toward the back, Butch moving right on in before she could turn, jovial, already welcome—or somebody damn well better see that he was (the badge again, you see; wearing it or simply being known to possess one, to enter any house in any other manner would be not a mere individual betrayal but a caste betrayal and debasement) —saying,

"Howdy, Doc; got a patient for you," to an iron-gray man too if the tobacco juice were bleached out of his unshaven whiskers, in a white shirt like Ned's but not as clean, and a black coat too with a long streak of day before yesterday's egg on it, who looked and smelled like something also, except it wasn't just alcohol, or anyway all ₁alcohol. "Me and Brother Hogganbeck will wait in the parlor," Butch said. "Dont bother; I know where the bottle's at. Dont worry about Doc," he said to Boon. "He dont hardly ever touch whiskey unless he just has to. The law allows him one shot of ether as a part of the cure for every patient that can show blood or a broken bone. If it's

just a little old cut or broke finger or ripped hide like this,
Doc divides the treatment with the patient: he drinks all
the ether and lets the patient have all the cure. Haw haw
haw. This way."

So Butch and Boon went that way, and Everbe and I
(you have doubtless noticed that nobody had missed Otis
yet. We got out of the surrey; it appeared to be Butch's;
anyway he was driving it; there had been some delay at
Uncle Parsham's while Butch tried to persuade, then ca-
jole, then force Everbe to get in the front seat with him,
which she foiled by getting into the back seat and holding
me by one arm and holding Otis in the surrey with her
other hand, until Boon got in front with Butch—and first
Butch, then the rest of us were somehow inside the doctor's hall but nobody remembered Otis at that moment)
followed the doctor into another room containing a horse-
hair sofa with a dirty pillow and a wadded quilt on it, and
a roll-top desk cluttered with medicine bottles and more
of them on the mantel beneath which the ashes of last
winter's final fire had not yet been disturbed, and a wash-
stand with a bowl and pitcher and a chamber pot that
somebody hadn't emptied yet either in one corner and a
shotgun in the other; and if Mother had been there his
fingernails would have touched no scratch belonging to
her, let alone four cut fingers, and evidently Everbe
agreed with her; she—Everbe—said, "I'll unwrap it," and
did so. I said the hand was all right. The doctor looked at
it through his steel-rimmed spectacles.

"What did you put on it?" he said. Everbe told him. I
know what it is now. The doctor looked at her. "How'd
you happen to have that handy?" he said. Then he lifted
the spectacles by one corner and looked at her again and
said, "Oh." Then he said, "Well, well," and lowered the
spectacles again and—yes he did: it was a sigh—said,
"I aint been to Memphis in thirty-five years," and stood

there a minute and—I tell you, it was a sigh—said, "Yes.
Thirty-five years," and said, "If I was you I wouldn't do
anything to it. Just bandage it again." Yes, exactly like
Mother: he got the bandage out but she put it on. "You
the boy going to ride that horse tomorrow?" he said.

"Yes," Everbe said.

"Beat that Linscomb horse this time, durn him."

"We'll try," Everbe said. "How much do we owe you?"

"Nothing," he said. "You already cured it. Just beat that
durn Linscomb horse tomorrow."

"I want to pay you something for looking at it," Everbe
said. "For telling us it's all right."

"No," he said. He looked at her: the old man's eyes behind the spectacles magnified yet unfocusable, as irre-
parable as eggs, until you would think they couldn't
possibly grasp and hold anything as recent as me and
Everbe.

"Yes," Everbe said. "What is it?"

"Maybe if you had a extra handkerchief or something . . ." He said: "Yes, thirty-five years. I had one once,
when I was a young man, thirty, thirty-five years ago.
Then I got married, and it . . ." He said, "Yes. Thirty-five
years."

"Oh," Everbe said. She turned her back to us and bent
over; her skirts rustled; it was not long; they rustled again
and she turned back. "Here," she said. It was a garter.

"Beat that durn horse!" he said. "Beat him! You can do
it!" Now we heard the voices—voice, that is, Butch's—
loud in the little hall before we got there:

"What do you know? Sugar Boy wont take a drink no
more. All boys together, give and take, never snatch without whistling first, and now he insults me." He stood grinning at Boon, triumphant, daring. Boon looked really
dangerous now. Like Ned (all of us) he was worn out for
sleep too. But all the load Ned had to carry was the horse;

Everbe and Butch's badge were not his burden. "Huh, boy?" Butch said; now he was going to slap Boon on the back again with that jovial force which was just a little too hard but not quite.

"Dont do it again," Boon said. Butch stopped. He didn't retract the motion: he just stopped it, grinning at Boon.

"My name's Mister Lovemaiden," he said. "But call me Butch."

After a while Boon said, "Lovemaiden."

"Butch," Butch said.

After a while Boon said, "Butch."

"That's a boy," Butch said. He said to Everbe: "Doc fix you up all right? Maybe I ought to warned you about Doc. They claim when he was a young squirt fifty-sixty years ago, he would a had one snatch at your drawers before he even tipped his hat."

"Come on," Boon said. "You paid him?"

"Yes," Everbe said. We went outside. And that was when somebody said, Where is Otis? No, it was Everbe of course; she just looked once and said, "Otis!" quite loud, strong, not to say urgent, not to say alarmed and desperate.

"Dont tell me he's scared of horses even tied to a gatepost," Butch said.

"Come on," Boon said. "He's just gone on ahead; he aint got nowhere else to go. We'll pick him up."

"But why?" Everbe said. "Why didn't he—"

"How do I know?" Boon said. "Maybe he's right." He meant Butch. Then he meant Otis: "For all he's as knowing a little son of a bitch as ever come out of Arkansas or Missippi either for that matter, he's still a arrant coward. Come on." So we got in the surrey and went on to town. Except that I was on Everbe's side about Otis; when you couldn't see him was a good time to be already wondering where he was and why. I never saw anybody lose public confidence as fast as he could; he would have had a hard time now finding anybody in this surrey to take him to another zoo or anywhere else. And it wasn't going to be much longer before he couldn't have found anybody in Parsham either.

Only we didn't overtake him. He wasn't on the road all the way to the hotel. And Ned was wrong. I mean about the increasing swarm of horse-race devotees we would be running into from now on. Maybe I had expected to find the entire hotel veranda lined with them, waiting for us and watching us arrive. If so, I was wrong; there was nobody there at all. In the winter of course, during the quail season and especially during the two weeks of the National Trials, it would be different. But in those days, unlike London, Parsham had no summer season; people went elsewhere: to water or mountains: Raleigh, near Memphis, or Iuka not far away in Mississippi, or to the Ozarks or Cumberlands. (Nor, for that matter, does it have one now, nor indeed does any place else, either winter or summer season; there are no seasons at all any more, with interiors artificially contrived at sixty degrees in summer and ninety degrees in winter, so that mossbacked recidivists like me must go outside in summer to escape cold and in winter to escape heat; including the automobiles also which once were mere economic necessities but are now social ones, the moment already here when, if all the human race ever stops moving at the same instant, the surface of the earth will seize, solidify: there are too many of us; humanity will destroy itself not by fission but by another beginning with f which is a verb-active also as well as a conditional state; I wont see it but you may: a law compelled and enforced by dire and frantic social—not economic: social—desperation permitting a woman but one child as she is now permitted but one husband.)

But in winter of course (as now), it was different, with the quail season and the Grand National Trials, with the rich money of oil and wheat barons from Wall Street and Chicago and Saskatchewan, and the fine dogs with pedigrees more jealous than princes, and the fine breeding and training kennels only minutes away now by automobile—Red Banks and Michigan City and La Grange and Germantown, and the names—Colonel Linscomb, whose horse (we assumed) we were going to race against tomorrow, and Horace Lytle and George Peyton as magical among bird-dog people as Babe Ruth and Ty Cobb among baseball aficionados, and Mr Jim Avant from Hickory Flat and Mr Paul Rainey just a few miles down Colonel Sartoris's railroad toward Jefferson—hound men both, who (I suppose) among these mere pedigreed pointers and setters, called themselves slumming; the vast rambling hotel booming then, staffed and elegant, the very air itself suave and murmurous with money, littered with colored ribbons and cluttered with silver cups.

But there was nobody there now, the quiet street empty with May dust (it was after six now; Parsham would be at home eating—or preparing to eat—supper), vacant even of Otis, though he could be, probably was, inside. And what was even more surprising, to me anyway, vacant also of Butch. He simply drove us up to the door and put us out and drove away, pausing only long enough to give Everbe one hard jeering leer and Boon one hard leering jeer, if anything a little harder than Everbe's, saying, "Dont worry, boy, I'll be back. If you got any business still hanging, better get it unhung before I get back or something might get tore," and drove away. So apparently he also had somewhere he had to be occasionally: a home; I was still ignorant and innocent (not as much as I was twenty-four hours ago, but still tainted) but I was on Boon's side, my loyalty was to him, not to mention to

Everbe, and I had assimilated enough (whether I had digested all of it yet or not) since yesterday, to know exactly what I meant when I hoped that maybe he had a wife in it—some innocent ravished out of a convent whose friendless avengeless betrayal would add another charge to the final accounting of his natural ruthless baseness; or better: an ambidextrous harridan who could cope with him by at least recording into his face each one of his countermarital victories. Because probably half the pleasure he got out of fornication was having it known who the victim was. But I wronged him. He was a bachelor.

But Otis was not inside either: only the single temporary clerk in the half-shrouded lobby and the single temporary waiter flapping his napkin in the door of the completely shrouded dining room save for a single table set out for such anonymous passers-by as we were—so far were, that is. But Otis had not been seen. "I aint wondering so much where he's at," Boon said, "as I am about what the hell he has done this time that we aint found out about yet."

"Nothing!" Everbe said. "He's just a child!"

"Sure," Boon said. "Just a little armed child. When he gets big enough to steal—"

"Stop!" Everbe said. "I wont—"

"All right, all right," Boon said. "Find, then. Find enough money to buy a knife with a six-inch blade in place of that two-inch pocketknife, anybody that turns his back on him had sho enough better be wearing one of them old-time iron union suits like you see in museums. I got to talk to you," he told her. "Supper'll be soon, and then we got to meet the train. And that tin-badge stallion will be neighing and prancing back here any time now." He took her arm. "Come on."

That was when I had to begin to listen to Boon. I mean, I had to. Everbe compelled it. She wouldn't even go with him unless I came too. We—they—went to the ladies' parlor; there wasn't much time now; we would have to eat supper and then go to the depot to meet Miss Reba. In those days females didn't run in and out of gentlemen's rooms in hotels as, I am told, they do now, even wearing, I am told, what the advertisements call the shorts or scanties capable of giving women the freedom they need in their fight for freedom; in fact, I had never seen a woman alone in a hotel before (Mother would not have been here without Father) and I remember how I wondered how Everbe without a wedding ring even could have got in. They—the hotels—had what were known as ladies' parlors, like this one where we now were—a smaller though still more elegant room, most of it likewise shrouded in holland bags. But I was still on Boon's side; I didn't pass the doorway but stopped outside, where Everbe could know where I was, within call, even if she couldn't actually see me. So I heard. Oh yes, listened. I would have listened anyway; I had gone too far by now in sophistication and the facts of life to stop now, just as I had gone too far in stealing automobiles and race horses to quit now. So I could hear them: Everbe; and almost at once she was crying again:

"No! I wont! Let me alone!" Then Boon:

"But why? You said you loved me. Was that just lying too?" Then Everbe:

"I do love you. That's why. Let me alone! Turn me loose! Lucius! Lucius!" Then Boon:

"Shut up. Stop now." Then nothing for a minute. I didn't look, peep, I just listened. No: just heard: "If I thought you were just two-timing me with that God damned tin-badged—" Then Everbe:

"No! No! I'm not!" Then something I couldn't hear, until Boon said:

"What? Quit? What do you mean, quit?" Then Everbe:

"Yes! I've quit! Not any more. Never!" Then Boon:

"How're you going to live? What will you eat? Where you going to sleep?" And Everbe:

"I'm going to get a job. I can work."

"What can you do? You aint got no more education than me. What can you do to make a living?"

"I can wash dishes. I can wash and iron. I can learn to cook. I can do something, I can even hoe and pick cotton. Let me go, Boon. Please. Please. I've got to. Cant you see I've got to?" Then her feet running, even on the thick carpet; she was gone. So Boon caught me this time. His face was pretty bad now. Ned was lucky; all he had to frazzle over was just a horse race.

"Look at me," Boon said. "Look at me good. What's wrong with me? What the hell's wrong with me? It used to be that I . . ." His face looked like it was going to burst. He started again: "And why me? Why the hell me? Why the hell has she got to pick out me to reform on? God damn it, she's a whore, cant she understand that? She's in the paid business of belonging to me exclusive the minute she sets her foot where I'm at like I'm in the paid business of belonging to Boss and Mr Maury exclusive the minute I set my foot where they're at. But now she's done quit. For private reasons. She cant no more. She aint got no more private rights to quit without my say-so too than I got to quit without Boss's and Mr Maury's say-so too—" He stopped, furious and baffled, raging and helpless; and more: terrified. It was the Negro waiter, flapping his napkin in this doorway now. Boon made a tremendous effort; Ned with nothing but a horse race to win didn't even know what trouble was. "Go tell her to come on to supper. We got to meet that train. Her room is Number Five."

But she wouldn't come out. So Boon and I ate alone. His face still didn't look much better. He ate like you put meat into a grinder: not like he either wanted it or didn't want it, but it was just time to eat. After a while I said, "Maybe he started walking back to Arkansas. He said two or three times this afternoon that that's where he would have been by now if folks hadn't kept on interfering with him."

"Sure," Boon said. "Maybe he just went on ahead to locate that dish-washing job for her. Or maybe he reformed too and they're both going right straight to heaven without stopping off at Arkansas or nowhere else, and he just went ahead to find out how to pass Memphis without nobody seeing them." Then it was time to go. I had been watching the edge of her dress beyond the dining-room door for about two minutes, but now the waiter himself came.

"Two-O-Eight, sir," he said. "Just blowed for One Mile Crossing." So we went across to the depot, not far, the three of us walking together, mutual overnight hotel guests. I mean we—they—were not fighting now; we— they—could even have talked, conversed, equable and inconsequential. Everbe would have, only Boon would need to speak first. Not far: merely to cross the tracks to reach the platform, the train already in sight now, the two of them (Boon and Everbe) shackled yet estranged, alien yet indissoluble, confounded yet untwainable by no more than what Boon thought was a whim: who (Boon) for all his years was barely older than me and didn't even know that women no more have whims than they have doubts or illusions or prostate troubles; the train, the engine passing us in hissing thunder, sparks flying from the brake shoes; it was the long one, the big one, the cannonball, the Special: the baggage cars, the half Jim Crow smoker, then the day coaches and the endless pullmans, the dining car at the end, slowing; it was Sam Caldwell's train and if Everbe and Otis had travelled to

Parsham in the caboose of a scheduled through freight, Miss Reba would be in a drawing room, if indeed she was not in the president's private car; the train stopping at last though still no vestibule opened, no white-jacketed porter nor conductor, though certainly Sam would have been watching for us; until Boon said, "Hell. The smoker," and began to run. Then we all saw them, far ahead: Sam Caldwell in his uniform on the cinders helping Miss Reba down, someone—another woman—following her, and not from the smoking car at all but from the Jim Crow half of it where Negroes travelled; the train—it was the Special for Washington and New York, the cannonball wafting the rich women in diamonds and the men with dollar cigars in suave and insulate transmigration across the earth—already moving again so that Sam had only time to wave back at us from the step, diminishing eastward behind the short staccato puffs and the long whistle blasts and at last the red diminishing twin lamps, and the two women standing among the grips and bags on the vacant cinders, Miss Reba bold and handsome and chic and Minnie beside her looking like death.

"We've had trouble," Miss Reba said. "Where's the hotel?" We went there. Now, in the lighted lobby, we could see Minnie. Her face was not like death. Death is peaceful. What Minnie's fixed close-lipped brooding face boded was not peaceful and it wasn't boded at her either. The clerk came. "I'm Mrs Binford," Miss Reba said. "You got my wire about a cot in my room for my maid?"

"Yes, Mrs Binford," the clerk said. "We have special quarters for servants, with their own dining room—"

"Keep them," Miss Reba said. "I said a cot in my room. I want her with me. We'll wait in the parlor while you make it up. Where is it?" But she had already located the ladies' parlor, we following. "Where is he?" she said.

"Where is who?" Everbe said.

"You know who," Miss Reba said. And suddenly I knew who, and that in another moment I would know why. But I didn't have time. Miss Reba sat down. "Sit down," she told Minnie. But Minnie didn't move. "All right," Miss Reba said. "Tell them." Minnie smiled at us. It was ghastly: a frantic predatory rictus, an anguished ravening gash out of which the beautiful and matchless teeth arched outward to the black orifice where the gold one had been; I knew now why Otis had fled Parsham even though he had had to do it on foot; oh yes, at that moment fifty-six years ago I was one with you now in your shocked and horrified unbelief, until Minnie and Miss Reba told us.

"It was him!" Minnie said. "I know it was him! He taken it while I was asleep!"

"Hell fire," Boon said. "Somebody stole a tooth out of your mouth and you didn't even know it?"

"God damn it, listen," Miss Reba said. "Minnie had that tooth made that way, so she could put it in and take it out—worked extra and scrimped and saved for—how many years was it, Minnie? three, wasn't it?—until she had enough money to have her own tooth took out and that God damned gold one put in. Oh sure, I tried my best to talk her out of it—ruin that set of natural teeth that anybody else would give a thousand dollars apiece, and anything else she had too; not to mention all the extra it cost her to have it made so she could take it out when she ate—"

"Took it out when she ate?" Boon said. "What the hell is she saving her teeth for?"

"I wanted that tooth a long time," Minnie said, "and I worked and saved to get it, extra work. I aint going to have it all messed up with no spit-mixed something to eat."

"So she would take it out when she ate," Miss Reba said,

"and put it right there in front of her plate where she could see it, not only watch it but enjoy it too while she was eating. But that wasn't the way he got it; she says she put it back in when she finished breakfast, and I believe her; she aint never forgot it before because she was proud of it, it was valuable, it had cost her too much; no more than you would put that God damned horse down somewhere that's probably cost you a damned sight more than a gold tooth, and forget it—"

"I know I never," Minnie said. "I put it back as soon as I ate. I remember. Only I was plumb wore out and tired—"

"That's right," Miss Reba said. She was talking to Everbe now: "I reckon I was going good when you all come in last night. It was daybreak before I come to my senses enough to quit, and the sun was up when I finally persuaded Minnie to take a good slug of gin and see the front door was bolted and go on back to bed, and I went up myself and woke Jackie and told her to keep the place shut, I didn't care if every horny bastard south of St Louis come knocking, not to let nobody in before six oclock this evening. So Minnie went back and laid down on her cot in the storeroom off the back gallery and I thought at first maybe she forgot to lock that door—"

"Course I locks it," Minnie said. "That's where the beer's at. I been keeping that door locked ever since that boy got here because I remembered him from last summer when he come to visit."

"So there she was," Miss Reba said, "wore out and dead asleep on that cot with the door locked and never knowed nothing until—"

"I woke up," Minnie said. "I was still so tired and wore out that I slept too hard, like you do; I just laid there and I knowed something felt a little funny in my mouth. But I just thought maybe it was a scrap of something had done got caught in it no matter how careful I was, until I got up and went to the looking glass and looked—"

"I wonder they never heard her in Chattanooga, let alone just in Parsham," Miss Reba said. "And the door still locked—"

"It was him!" Minnie said, cried. "I know it was! He been worrying me at least once every day how much it cost and why didn't I sell it and how much could I get for it and where would I go to sell it at—"

"Sure," Miss Reba said. "That's why he squalled like a wildcat this morning when you told him he wasn't going back home but would have to come on to Parsham with you," she told Everbe. "So when he heard the train whistle, he run, huh? Where do you figger he is? Because I'm going to have Minnie's tooth back."

"We dont know," Everbe said. "He just disappeared out of the surrey about half past five oclock. We thought he would have to be here, because he aint got anywhere else to go. But we haven't found him yet."

"Maybe you aint looked right," Miss Reba said. "He aint the kind you can whistle out. You got to smoke him out like a rat or a snake." The clerk came back. "All right now?" Miss Reba said.

"Yes, Mrs Binford," the clerk said. Miss Reba got up.

"I'll get Minnie settled down and stay with her until she goes to sleep. Then I'd like some supper," she told the clerk. "It dont matter what it is."

"It's a little late," the clerk said. "The dining room—"

"And it's going to be still later after a while," Miss Reba said. "It dont matter what it is. Come on, Minnie." She and Minnie went out. Then the clerk was gone too. We stood there; none of us had sat down; she—Everbe— just stood there: a big girl that stillness looked well on; grief too, as long as it was still, like this. Or maybe not grief so much as shame.

"He never had no chance back there," she said. "That's why I thought . . . To get him away even for just a week last summer. And then this year, especially after you all came too and as soon as I saw Lucius I knew that that was the way I had been wanting him to be all the time, only I didn't know neither how to tell him, learn him. And so I thought maybe just being around Lucius, even for just two or three days—"

"Sure," Boon said. "Refinement." Now he went to her, awkward. He didn't offer to put his arms around her again. He didn't even touch her, really. He just patted her back; it looked almost as hard, his hand did, as insensitive and heavy, as when Butch had slapped his this afternoon. But it wasn't at all. "It's all right," he said. "It aint nothing, see. You were doing the best you knowed. You done good. Come on, now." It was the waiter again.

"Your coachman's in the kitchen, sir," he said. "He says it's important."

"My coachman?" Boon said. "I aint got no coachman."

"It's Ned," I said, already moving. Then Everbe was too, ahead of Boon. We followed the waiter back to the kitchen. Ned was standing quite close to the cook, a tremendous Negro woman who was drying dishes at the sink. He was saying,

"If it's money worrying your mind, Good-looking, I'm the man what—" and saw us and read Boon's mind like a flash: "Ease your worry. He's out at Possum's. What's he done this time?"

"What?" Boon said.

"It's Otis," I said. "Ned found him."

"I didn't," Ned said. "I hadn't never lost him. Uncle Possum's hounds did. Put him up a gum sapling behind the henhouse about a hour ago, until Lycurgus went and got him. He wouldn't come in with me. In fact, he acted like he didn't aim to go nowhere right away. What's he done this time?" We told him. "So she's here too," he said. He said quietly: "Hee hee hee." He said: "Then he wont be there when I get back."

"What do you mean?" Boon said.

"Would you still be there, if you was him?" Ned said. "He knows that by this time that gal's done woke up and found that tooth missing. He must a been knowing that Miss Reba long enough by now to know she aint gonter stop until she gets her hand on him and turns him upside down and shake until that tooth falls out of wherever he's got it. I told him myself where I was going on that mule, and anybody there can tell him what time that train got in and how long it will take somebody to get back out there. Would you still be there if you had that tooth?"

"All right," Boon said. "What's he going to do with it?"

"If it was anybody else but him," Ned said, "I'd say he had three chances with it: sell it or hide it or give it away. But since it's him, he aint got but two: sell it or hide it, and if it's got to just stay hid somewhere, it might just as well be back in that gal's mouth as fur as he's concerned. So the best place to sell a gold tooth quick would be back in Memphis. Only Memphis is too fur to walk, and to get on the train (which would cost money, which he likely is got providing he is desperate enough to spend some of hisn) he would have to come back to Possum, where somebody might see him. So the next best quick place to sell that gold tooth will be at that race track tomorrow. If it was you or me, we might likely bet that tooth on one of them horses tomorrow. But he aint no betting man. Betting's too slow for him, not to mention uncertain. But that race track will be a good place to start looking for him. It's too bad I didn't know about that tooth whilst I had my hand on him tonight. Maybe I could a reasoned it out of him. Then, if he belonged to me, Mr Sam Caldwell gonter be through here on that west-bound train at six-fawty tomorrow morning and I'd a had him at the depot and turned him over to Mr Sam and told Mr Sam not to lift his hand offen him until the door shut on the first train leaving for Arkansas tomorrow."

"Can you find him tomorrow?" Everbe said. "I've got to find him. He's just a child. I'll pay for the tooth, I'll buy Minnie another one. But I've got to find him. He'll say he hasn't got it, he never saw it, but I've got—"

"Sho," Ned said. "That's what I'd say too if it was me. I'll try. I'll be in early tomorrow morning to get Lucius, but the best chance gonter be at that track tomorrow just before the race." He said to me: "Folks is already kind of dropping by Possum's lot like they wasn't noticing themselves doing it, likely trying to find out who it is this time that still believes that horse can run a race. So likely we gonter have a nice crowd tomorrow. It's late now, so you go get some sleep whilst I takes that mule of Possum's back home to bed too. Where's your sock? You aint lost it?"

"It's in my pocket," I said.

"Be sho you dont," he said. "The mate to it is the left-footed one and a left-footed sock is unlucky unlessen you wears both of them." He turned, but no further than the fat cook; he said to her now: "Unlessen my mind changes to staying in town tonight. What time you setting breakfast, Good-looking?"

"The soonest time after your jaws is too far away to chomp it," the cook said.

"Good night, all," Ned said. Then he was gone. We went back to the dining room, where the waiter, in his short sleeves now and without his collar and tie, brought Miss Reba a plate of the pork chops and grits and biscuits and blackberry jam we had had for supper,

neither hot nor cold now but lukewarm, in deshabille
like the waiter, you might say.

"Did you get her to sleep?" Everbe said.

"Yes," Miss Reba said. "That little son of a—" and cut
it off and said, "Excuse me. I thought I had seen everything in my business, but I never thought I'd have a
tooth stolen in one of my houses. I hate little bastards.
They're like little snakes. You can handle a big snake
because you been already warned to watch out. But a
little one has already bit you behind before you even
knew it had teeth. Where's my coffee?" The waiter
brought it and went away. And then even that big
shrouded dining room was crowded; it was like every
time Boon and Butch got inside the same four walls everything compounded, multiplied, leaving not really room
for anything else. He—Butch—had been back to the
doctor's, or maybe in the tin badge business you knew
everybody who didn't dare refuse you a free drink. And
it was getting late, and I was tired, but here he was
again; and suddenly I knew that up to now he hadn't
really been anything and that we were only just starting
with him now, standing in the door, bulging, bright-eyed,
confident, breezy and a little redder, the badge itself
seeming to bulge at us as with a life of its own on his
sweaty shirt, he—Butch—wearing it not as the official au-
thorisation of his unique dedication, but as a boy scout
wears his merit badge: as both the unique and hard-won
reward and emblem of a specialisation and the pre-absolu-
tion for any other activities covered or embraced by its
mystic range; at that moment Everbe rose quickly across
the table and almost scuttled around it and into the chair
next Miss Reba, whom Butch was looking at, bulging
at now. And that was when I rated Boon down a notch
and left Everbe first for trouble. All Boon had was Butch;
she had Boon and Butch both.

"Well well," Butch said, "is all Catalpa Street moving east to Possum?" So that at first I thought he might be a friend or at least a business acquaintance of Miss Reba's. But if he was, he didn't remember her name. But then even at eleven I was learning that there are people like Butch who don't remember anybody except in the terms of their immediate need of them, and what he needed now (or anyway could use) was another woman, he didn't care who provided she was more or less young and pleasing. No: he didn't really need one: he just happened to find one already in the path, like one lion on his way to fight another lion over an antelope that he never had any doubts about licking (I mean licking the lion, not the antelope) would still be a fool not to try throwing in, just for luck you might say, another antelope if he happened to find one straying in the path. Except that Miss Reba turned out not to be an antelope. What Butch found was another lion. He said: "This is what I call Sugar Boy using his head; what's the use of him and me being all racked up over one hunk of meat when here's another exactly like it in all important details except maybe a little difference in the pelt."

"Who's that?" Miss Reba said to Everbe. "Friend of yours?"

"No," Everbe said; she was actually crouching: a big girl, too big to crouch. "Please—"

"She's telling you," Boon said. "She aint got no friends no more. She dont want none. She's quit, gone out of business. Soon as we finish losing this horse race, she's going away somewhere and get a job washing dishes. Ask her."

Miss Reba was looking at Everbe. "Please," Everbe said.

"What do you want?" Miss Reba asked Butch.

"Nothing," Butch said. "Nothing a-tall. Me and Sugar

Boy was kind of bollixed up at one another for a while. But now you showed up, everything is hunky-dory. Twenty-three skiddoo." He came and took hold of Everbe's arm. "Come on. The surrey's outside. Let's give them a little room."

"Call the manager," Miss Reba said, quite loud, to me. I didn't even have to move; likely, if I had been looking, I could have seen the edge of him too beyond the door. He came in. "Is this man the law here?" Miss Reba said.

"Why, we all know Butch around here, Mrs Binford," the clerk said. "He's got as many friends in Parsham as anybody I know. Of course he's from up at Hardwick; properly speaking, we dont have a law officer right here in Parsham; we aint quite that big yet." Butch's rich and bulging warmth had embraced, invited the clerk almost before he could enter the door, as though he—the clerk—had fallen headlong into it and vanished like a mouse into a lump of still-soft ambergris. But now Butch's eyes were quite cold, hard.

"Maybe that's what's wrong around here," he told the clerk. "Maybe that's why you dont have no progress and advancement: what you need is a little more law."

"Aw, Butch," the clerk said.

"You mean, anybody that wants to can walk in off the street and drag whichever one of your women guests he likes the looks of best, off to the nearest bed like you were running a cat-house?" Miss Reba said.

"Drag who where?" Butch said. "Drag with what? a two-dollar bill?" Miss Reba rose.

"Come on," she said to Everbe. "There's a train back to Memphis tonight. I know the owner of this dump. I think I'll go see him tomorrow—"

"Aw, Butch," the clerk said. "Wait, Mrs Binford—"

"You go back out front, Virgil," Butch told the clerk.

"It aint only four months to November; some millionaire with two registered bird dogs might walk in any minute, and there wont be nobody out there to show him where to sign his name at. Go on. We're all friends here." The clerk went. "Now that that's all out of the way," Butch said, reaching for Everbe's arm again.

"Then you'll do," Miss Reba said to Butch. "Let's me and you go out front, or anywhere else that's private, too. I got a word for you."

"About what?" Butch said. She didn't answer, already walking toward the door. "Private, you say?" Butch said. "Why, sure; any time I cant accommodate a good-looking gal private, I'll give Sugar Boy full lief to step in." They went out. And now, from the lobby, we couldn't see them beyond the door of the ladies' parlor, for almost a minute in fact, maybe even a little more, before Miss Reba came back out, still walking steadily, hard and handsome and composed; then Butch a second later, saying, "Is that so, huh? We'll just see about that," Miss Reba coming steadily on to where we waited, watching Butch go on across the lobby without even looking at us.

"All right?" Everbe said.

"Yes," Miss Reba said. "And that goes for you too," she told Boon. She looked at me. "Jesus," she said.

"What the hell did you do to him?" Boon said.

"Nothing," she said over her shoulder, because she was looking at me. "—thought I had seen all the cat-house problems possible. Until I had one with children in it. You brought one in"—she was talking to Everbe now—"that run the landlord off and robbed all the loose teeth and fourteen dollars' worth of beer; and if that wasn't enough, Boon Hogganbeck brings one that's driving my damned girls into poverty and respectability. I'm going to bed and you—"

"Come on," Boon said. "What did you tell him?"

"What's that town of yours?" Miss Reba said.

"Jefferson," Boon said.

"You big-town folks from places like Jefferson and Memphis, with your big-city ideas, you don't know much about Law. You got to come to little places, like this. I know, because I was raised in one. He's the constable. He could spend a week in Jefferson or Memphis, and you wouldn't even see him. But here among the folks that elected him (the majority of twelve or thirteen that voted for him, and the minority of nine or ten or eleven that didn't and are already sorry for it or damned soon will be) he dont give a damn about the sheriff of the county nor the governor of the state nor the president of the United States all three rolled into one. Because he's a Baptist. I mean, he's a Baptist first, and then he's the Law. When he can be a Baptist and the Law both at the same time, he will. But any time the law comes conflicting up where nobody invited it, the law knows what it can do and where to do it. They tell how that old Pharaoh was pretty good at kinging, and another old one back in the Bible times named Caesar, that did the best he knew how. They should have visited down here and watched a Arkansas or Missippi or Tennessee constable once."

"But how do you know who he is?" Everbe said. "How do you even know there's one here?"

"There's one everywhere," Miss Reba said. "Didn't I just tell you I grew up in a place like this—as long as I could stand it? I dont need to know who he is. All I needed was to let that bastard know I knew there was one here too. I'm going—"

"But what did you tell him?" Boon said. "Come on. I may want to remember it."

"Nothing, I told you," Miss Reba said. "If I hadn't learned by now how to handle these damned stud horses with his badge in one hand and his fly in the other, I'd been in the poorhouse years ago. I told him if I saw his mug around here again tonight, I would send that sheep-faced clerk to wake the constable up and tell him a deputy sheriff from Hardwick has just registered a couple of Memphis whores at the Parsham Hotel. I'm going to bed, and you better too. Come on, Corrie. I put your outraged virtue on record with that clerk and now you got to back it up, at least where he can see you." They went on. Then Boon was gone too; possibly he had followed Butch to the front door just to make sure the surrey was gone. Then suddenly Everbe swooped down at me, that big: a big girl, muttering rapidly:

"You didn't bring anything at all, did you? I mean, clothes. You been wearing the same ones ever since you left home."

"What's wrong with them?" I said.

"I'm going to wash them," she said. "Your underthings and stockings, your blouse. And the sock you ride with too. Come on and take them off."

"But I aint got any more," I said.

"That's all right. You can go to bed. I'll have these all ready again when you get up. Come on." So she stood outside the door while I undressed and shoved my blouse and underwear and stockings and the riding-sock through the crack in the door to her and she said Good night and I closed the door and got into bed; and still there was something unfinished, that we hadn't done, attended to yet: the secret pre-race conference; the close, grim, fierce murmurous plotting of tomorrow's strategy. Until I realised that, strictly speaking, we had no strategy; we had nothing to plan for nor even with: a horse whose very ownership was dubious and even (unless Ned himself really knew) unknown, of whose past we knew only that he had consistently run just exactly fast enough to finish second to the other horse in the race; to be raced tomorrow, exactly where I anyway didn't know, against a horse none of us had ever seen and whose very existence (as far as we were concerned) had to be taken on trust. Until I realised that, of all human occupations, the racing of horses, and all concerned or involved in it, were the most certainly in God's hands. Then Boon came in; I was already in bed, already half asleep.

"What've you done with your clothes?" he said.

"Everbe's washing them," I said. He had taken off his pants and shoes and was already reaching to turn out the light. He stopped, dead still.

"Who did you say?" I was awake now but it was already too late. I lay there with my eyes closed, not moving. "What name did you say?"

"Miss Corrie is," I said.

"You said something else." I could feel him looking at me. "You called her Everbe." I could feel him looking at me. "Is that her name?" I could feel him looking at me. "So she told you her real name." Then he said, quite gently: "God damn," and I saw through my eyelids the room go dark, then the bed creaked as he lay down on it, as beds always do since there is so much of him, as I have heard them ever since I can remember when I would sleep with him: once or twice at home when Father would be away and he would stay in the house so Mother wouldn't be afraid, and at Miss Ballenbaugh's two nights ago, and in Memphis last night, until I remembered that I hadn't slept with him in Memphis: it was Otis. "Good night," he said.

"Good night," I said.

10

◆◆◆◆

Then it was morning, it was tomorrow: THE day on which I would ride my first actual horse race (and by winning it, set Boon and Ned—me too of course, but then I was safe, immune; I was not only just a child, I was kin to them—free to go home again, not with honor perhaps, not even unscathed, but at least they could go back) toward which all the finagling and dodging and manipulating and scrabbling around (what other crimes subsequent to—all right, consequent to—the simple and really spontaneous and in a way innocent stealing of Grandfather's automobile, I didn't even know) had been leading up to; now it was here. "So she told you what her real name is," Boon said. Because you see, it was too late now; I had been half asleep last night and off my guard.

"Yes," I said; whereupon I realised that that was completely false: she hadn't told me; she didn't even know I knew it, that I had been calling her Everbe ever since Sunday night. But it was too late now. "But you've got to promise," I said. "Not promise her: promise me. Never to say it out loud until she tells it first."

"I promise," he said. "I aint never lied to you yet. I mean, lied bad. I mean . . . I aint . . . All right," he said. "I done promised." Then he said again, like last night, gentle and almost amazed: "God damn." And my clothes —blouse, stockings and underwear and the riding-sock —were neatly folded, laundered and ironed, on a chair just outside our door. Boon handed them in to me. "With all them clean clothes, you got to bathe again," he said.

"You just made me bathe Saturday," I said.

"We was on the road Saturday night," he said. "We never even got to Memphis until Sunday."

"All right. Sunday," I said.

"This is Tuesday," he said. "Two days."

"Just one day," I said. "Two nights, but just one day."

"You been travelling since," Boon said. "You got two sets of dirt now."

"It's almost seven oclock," I said. "We're already late for breakfast."

"You can bathe first," he said.

"I got to get dressed so I can thank Everbe for washing my clothes."

"Bathe first," Boon said.

"I'll get my bandage wet."

"Hold your hand on your neck," Boon said "You aint going to wash that nohow."

"Why dont you bathe then?" I said.

"We aint talking about me. We're talking about you." So I went to the bathroom and bathed and put my clothes back on and went to the dining room. And Ned was right. Last night there had been just the one table, the end of it cleared and set up for us. Now there were seven or eight people, all men (but not aliens, foreigners, mind you; in fact they were strangers only to us who didn't live in Parsham. None of them had got down from pullmans in silk underclothes and smoking Upmann cigars; we had not opened the cosmopolitan Parsham winter sporting season here in the middle of May. Some were in overalls, all but one were tieless: people like us except that they lived here, with the same passions and hopes and dialect, enjoying—Butch too—our inalienable constitutional right of free will and private enterprise which has made our country what it is, by holding a private horse race between two local horses; if anyone, committee or individual, from no further away than the next county, had come to interfere or alter or stop it or even participate beyond betting on the horse of his choice, all of us, partisans of either horse, would have risen as one man and repulsed him). And besides the waiter, I saw the back of a maid in uniform just going through the swing door to the pantry or kitchen, and there were two men (one of them had the necktie) at our table talking to Boon and Miss Reba. But Everbe wasn't there, and for an instant, second, I had a horrified vision of Butch finally waylaying and capturing her by force, ambushing her in the corridor perhaps while she was carrying the chair to mine and Boon's door with my laundered clothes on it. But only for a second, and too fantastical; if she had washed for me last night, she had probably, doubtless been up quite late washing for herself and maybe Miss Reba too, and was still asleep. So I went on to the table, where one of the men said,

"This the boy going to ride him? Looks more like you got him taped up for a fist fight."

"Yes," Boon said, shoving the dish of ham toward me

as I sat down; Miss Reba passed the eggs and grits across. "He cut himself eating peas last night."

"Haw haw," the man said. "Anyway, he'll be carrying less weight this time."

"Sure," Boon said. "Unless he eats the knives and forks and spoons while we aint watching him and maybe takes along one of the fire dogs for a snack."

"Haw haw," the man said. "From the way he run here last winter, he's going to need a good deal more than just less weight. But then, that's the secret, huh?"

"Sure," Boon said; he was eating again now. "Even if we never had no secret, we would have to act like we did."

"Haw haw," the man said again; they got up. "Well, good luck, anyway. That might be as good for that horse as less weight." The maid came, bringing me a glass of milk and carrying a plate of hot biscuits. It was Minnie, in a fresh apron and cap where Miss Reba had either loaned or hired her to the hotel to help out, with her ravished and unforgiving face, but calm and quiet now; evidently she had rested, even slept some even if she hadn't forgiven anybody yet. The two strangers went away.

"You see?" Miss Reba said to nobody. "All we need is the right horse and a million dollars to bet."

"You heard Ned Sunday night," Boon said. "You were the one that believed him. I mean, decided to believe him. I was different. After that God damned automobile vanished and all we had was the horse, I had to believe him."

"All right," Miss Reba said. "Keep your shirt on."

"And you can stop worrying too," Boon said to me. "She just went to the depot in case them dogs caught him again last night and Ned brought him in to the train. Or so she said—"

"Did Ned find him?" I said.

"Naw," Boon said. "Ned's in the kitchen now. You can ask him—or so she said. Yes. So maybe you had better worry some, after all. Miss Reba got shut of that tin badge for you, but that other one—what's his name: Caldwell— was on that train this morning."

"What are you talking about now?" Miss Reba said.

"Nothing," Boon said. "I aint got nothing to talk about now. I've quit. Lucius is the one that's got tin badge and pullman cap rivals now." But I was already getting up because I knew now where she was.

"Is that all the breakfast you want?" Miss Reba said.

"Let him alone," Boon said. "He's in love." I crossed the lobby. Maybe Ned was right, and all it took for a horse race was two horses with the time to run a race, within ten miles of each other, and the air itself spread the news of it. Though not as far as the ladies' parlor yet. So maybe what I meant by crying looking well on Everbe was that she was big enough to cry as much as she seemed to have to do, and still have room for that many tears to dry off without streaking. She was sitting by herself in the ladies' parlor and crying again, the third time—no: four, counting two Sunday night. Until you wondered why. I mean, nobody made her come with us and she could have gone back to Memphis on any train that passed. Yet here she was, so she must be where she wanted to be. Yet this was the second time she had cried since we reached Parsham. I mean, anybody with as many extra tears as she had, still didn't have enough to waste that many on Otis. So I said,

"He's all right. Ned will find him today. Much obliged for washing my clothes. Where's Mr Sam? I thought he was going to be on that train."

"He had to take the train on to Memphis and take his uniform off," she said. "He cant go to a horse race in it. He'll be back on the noon freight. I can't find my handkerchief."

I found it for her. "Maybe you ought to wash your face," I said. "When Ned finds him, he will get the tooth back."

"It aint the tooth," she said. "I'm going to buy Minnie another tooth. It's that . . . He never had no chance. He . . . Did you promise your mother you wouldn't never take things too?"

"You dont have to promise anybody that," I said. "You dont take things."

"But you would have promised, if she had asked you?"

"She wouldn't ask me," I said. "You dont take things."

"Yes," she said. She said: "I aint going to stay in Memphis. I talked to Sam at the depot this morning and he says that's a good idea too. He can find me a job in Chattanooga or somewhere. But you'll still be in Jefferson, so maybe I could write you a post card where I'm at and then if you took a notion—"

"Yes," I said. "I'll write to you. Come on. They're still eating breakfast."

"There's something about me you dont know. You couldn't even guess it."

"I know it," I said. "It's Everbe Corinthia. I been calling you that two or three days now. That's right. It was Otis. But I wont tell anybody. But I dont see why."

"Why? A old-timey countrified name like that? Can you imagine anybody in Reba's saying, Send up Everbe Corinthia? They would be ashamed. They would die laughing. So I thought of changing it to Yvonne or Billie or Ken. But Reba said Corrie would do."

"Shucks," I said.

"You mean, it's all right? You say it." I said it. She listened. Then she kept on listening, exactly as you wait for an echo. "Yes," she said. "That's what it can be now."

"Then come on and eat breakfast," I said. "Ned's waiting for me and I got to go." But Boon came in first.

"There are too many people out there," he said. "Maybe I shouldn't a told that damn fellow you were going to ride him today." He looked at me. "Maybe I shouldn't a never let you leave Jefferson." There was a small door behind a curtain at the back of the room. "Come on," he said. It was another corridor. Then we were in the kitchen. The vast cook was at the sink again. Ned was sitting at a table finishing his breakfast, but mainly saying,

"When I sugars up a woman, it aint just empty talk. They can buy something with it too—" and stopped and rose at once; he said to me: "You ready? Time you and me was getting back to the country. They's too many folks around here. If they all had money and would bet it, and the horse they bet on would just be the wrong horse, and we just had the money to cover it and knowed the right horse to cover it with, we wouldn't just take no automobile back to Jefferson tonight: we'd take all Possum too, to maybe sugar back Boss Priest's nature. He aint never owned a town before, and he might like it."

"Wait," Boon said. "Aint we got to make some plans?"

"The onliest one that needs any plan is Lightning," Ned said. "And the only plan he needs is to plan to get out in front and stay there until somebody tells him to stop. But I know what you mean. We gonter run on Colonel Linscomb's track. The first heat is at two oclock. That's four miles from here. Me and Lightning and Lucius gonter show up there about two minutes beforehand. You better get out there earlier. You better leave here soon as Mr Sam gets off that freight train. Because that's yourn and his plan: to get to that track in time to bet the money, and to have some money to bet when you get there."

"Wait," Boon said. "What about that automobile? What the hell good will money do us if we go back home without—"

"Stop fretting about that automobile," Ned said. "Aint I told you them boys got to go back home not much longer than tonight too?"

"What boys?" Boon said.

"Yes sir," Ned said. "The trouble with Christmas is the first of January; that's what's wrong with it." Minnie came in with a tray of dirty dishes—the brown calm tragic hungry and inconsolable mask. "Come on," Ned told her, "gimme that smile again so I'll have the right measure to fit that tooth when I brings it back tonight."

"Dont do it, girl," the fat cook said. "Maybe that Missippi sugar will spend where it come from, but it wont buy nothing up here in Tennessee. Not in this kitchen, nohow."

"But wait," Boon said.

"You wait for Mr Sam," Ned said. "He can tell you. In fact, whilst me and Lucius are winning this race, maybe you and Mr Sam can locate around amongst the folks for Whistle-britches and that tooth." He had Uncle Parsham's buggy this time, with one of the mules. And he was right: the little hamlet had changed overnight. It was not that there were so many people in sight, any more than yesterday. It was the air itself—an exhilaration, almost; for the first time I really realised that I was going to ride in a horse race before many more hours, and I could taste my spit sudden and sharp around my tongue.

"I thought you said last night that Otis would be gone when you got back from town," I said.

"He was," Ned said. "But not far. He aint got nowhere

to go neither. The hounds give mouth twice during the night back toward the barn; them hounds taken the same quick mislike to him that human folks does. Likely soon as I left this morning, he come up for his breakfast."

"But suppose he sells the tooth before we can catch him."

"I done fixed that," Ned said. "He aint gonter sell it. He aint gonter find nobody to buy it. If he aint come up for breakfast, Lycurgus gonter take the hounds and tree him again, and tell him that when I come back from Parsham last night, I said a man in Memphis offered that gal twenty-eight dollars for that tooth, cash. He'll believe that. If it had been a hundred dollars or even fifty, he wouldn't believe it. But he'll believe a extra number like twenty-eight dollars, mainly because he'll think it aint enough: that that Memphis man was beating Minnie down. And when he tries to sell it at that race track this evening, wont nobody give him even that much, so wont be nothing left for him to do but wait until he can get back to Memphis with it. So you get your mind off that tooth and put it on this horse race. On them last two heats, I mean. We gonter lose the first one, so you dont need to worry about that—"

"What?" I said. "Why?"

"Why not?" Ned said. "All we needs to win is two of them."

"But why lose the first one? Why dont we win that one, get that much ahead as soon as we can—" He drove on, maybe a half a minute.

"The trouble with this race, it's got too many different things mixed up in it."

"Too many what?" I said.

"Too many of everything," he said. "Too many folks. But mainly, too many heats. If it was just one heat, one run, off in the bushes somewhere and not nobody around but me and you and Lightning and that other horse and whoever gonter ride him, we would be all right. Because we found out yestiddy we can make Lightning run one time. Only, now he got to run three of them."

"But you made that mule run every time," I said.

"This horse aint that mule," Ned said. "Aint no horse ever foaled was that mule. Or any other mule. And this horse we got to depend on now aint even got as much sense as some horses. So you can see what our fix is. We knows I can make him run once, and we hopes I can make him run twice. But that's all. We just hopes. So we cant risk that one time we *knows* I can make him run, until we got to have it. So the most we got at the best, is two times. And since we got to lose one of them, no matter what, we gonter lose the one we can maybe learn something from to use next time. And that's gonter be the first one."

"Have you told Boon that? so he wont—"

"Let him lose on the first heat, providing he dont put up all the money them ladies scraps up for him to bet. Which, from what I seen of that Miss Reba, he aint gonter do. That will make the odds that much better for them next two. Besides, we can tell him all he needs to know when the time comes. So you just—"

"I didn't mean that," I said. "I meant Boss's—"

"Didn't I tell you I was tending to that?" he said. "Now you quit worrying. I dont mean quit thinking about the race, because you cant do that. But quit worrying about winning it. Just think about what Lightning taught you yesterday about riding him. That's all you got to do. I'll tend to all the rest of it. You got your sock, aint you?"

"Yes," I said. Only we were not going back to Uncle Parsham's; we were not even going in that direction now.

"We got our own private stable for this race," Ned said. "A spring branch in a hollow that belongs to one of Possum's church members, where we can be right there not half a quarter from the track without nobody knowing to bother us until we wants them. Lycurgus and Uncle Possum went on with Lightning right after breakfast."

"The track," I said. Of course, there would have to be a track. I had never thought of that. If I thought at all, I reckon I simply assumed that somebody would ride or lead the other horse up, and we would run the race right there in Uncle Parsham's pasture.

"That's right," Ned said. "A regular track, just like a big one except it's just a half a mile and aint got no grandstands and beer-and-whiskey counters like anybody that wants to run horse racing right ought to have. It's right there in Colonel Linscomb's pasture, that owns the other horse. Me and Lycurgus went and looked at it last night. I mean the track, not the horse. I aint seen the horse yet. But we gonter have a chance to look at him today, leastways, one end of him. Only what we want is to plan for that horse to spend the last half of two of these heats looking at that end of Lightning. So I need to talk to the boy that's gonter ride him. A colored boy; Lycurgus knows him. I want to talk to him in a way that he wont find out until afterward that I talked to him."

"Yes," I said. "How?"

"Let's get there first," Ned said. We went on; it was new country to me, of course. Obviously we were now crossing Colonel Linscomb's plantation, or anyway somebody's— big neat fields of sprouting cotton and corn, and pastures with good fences and tenant cabins and cotton houses at the turnrow ends; and now I could see the barns and stables and sure enough, there was the neat white oval of the small track; we—Ned—turning now, following a faint road, on into a grove; and there it was, isolate and secure, even secret if we wished: a grove of beeches about a spring, Lightning standing with Lycurgus at his head, groomed and polished and even glowing faintly in the dappled light, the other mule tied in the background and Uncle Parsham, dramatic in black and white, even regal, prince and martinet in the dignity of solvent and workless age, sitting on the saddle which Lycurgus had propped against a tree into a sort of chair for him, all waiting for us. And then in the next instant I knew what was wrong: they were all waiting for me. And that was the real moment when—Lightning and me standing in (not to mention breathing it) the same air not a thousand feet from the race track and not much more than a tenth of that in minutes from the race itself—when I actually realised not only how Lightning's and my fate were now one, but that the two of us together carried that of the rest of us too, certainly Boon's and Ned's, since on us depended under what conditions they could go back home, or indeed if they could go back home—a mystical condition which a boy of only eleven should not really be called to shoulder. Which is perhaps why I noticed nothing, or anyway missed what I did see: only that Lycurgus handed Lightning's lead rope to Uncle Parsham and came and took our bridle and Ned said, "You get that message to him all right?" and Lycurgus said Yes sir, and Ned said to me, "Whyn't you go and take Lightning offen Uncle Possom so he wont have to get up?" and I did so, leaving Ned and Lycurgus standing quite close together at the buggy; and that not long before Ned came on to us, leaving Lycurgus to take the mule out of the buggy and loop the lines and traces up and tie the mule beside its mate and come on to us, where Ned was now squatting beside Uncle Parsham. He said: "Tell again about them two races last winter. You said nothing happened. What kind of nothing?"

"Ah," Uncle Parsham said. "It was a three-heat race just like this one, only they never run but two of them.

By that time there wasn't no need to run the third one. Or maybe somebody got tired."

"Tired reaching into his hind pocket, maybe," Ned said.

"Maybe," Uncle Parsham said. "The first time, your horse run too soon, and the second time he run too late. Or maybe it was the whip whipped too soon the first time and not soon enough the second. Anyhow, at the first lick your horse jumped out in front, a good length, and stayed there all the way around the first lap, even after the whipping had done run out, like it does with a horse or a man either: he can take just so much whipping and after that it aint no more than spitting on him. Then they come into the home stretch and it was like your horse saw that empty track in front of him and said to himself, This aint polite; I'm a stranger here, and dropped back just enough to lay his head more or less on Colonel Linscomb's boy's knee, and kept it there until somebody told him he could stop. And the next time your horse started out like he still thought he hadn't finished that first heat, his head all courteous and polite about opposite Colonel Linscomb's boy's knee, on into the back turn of the last lap, where that Memphis boy hit him the first lick, not late enough this time, because all that full-length jump done this time was to show him that empty track again."

"Not too late to scare McWillie," Lycurgus said.

"Skeer him how much?" Ned said.

"Enough," Lycurgus said. Ned squatted there. He must have got a little sleep last night, even with the hounds treeing Otis every now and then. He didn't look it too much though.

"All right," he said to me. "You and Lycurgus just stroll up yonder to that stable awhile. All you're doing is taking your natural look at the horse you gonter ride against this evening. For the rest of it, let Lycurgus do the talking, and dont look behind you on the way back." I didn't even ask him why. He wouldn't have told me. It was not far: past the neat half-mile track with its white-painted rails that it would be nice to be rich too, on to the barns, the stable that if Cousin Zack had one like it out at Mc-Caslin, Cousin Louisa would probably have them living in it. There was nobody in sight. I dont know what I had expected: maybe still more of the overalled and tieless aficionados squatting and chewing tobacco along the wall as we had seen them in the dining room at breakfast. Maybe it was too early yet: which, I now realised, was probably exactly why Ned had sent us; we—Lycurgus— lounging into the hallway which—the stable—was as big as our dedicated-to-a-little-profit livery one in Jefferson and a good deal cleaner—a tack room on one side and what must have been an office on the other, just like ours; a Negro stableman cleaning a stall at the rear and a youth who for size and age and color might have been Lycurgus's twin, lounging on a bale of hay against the wall, who said to Lycurgus: "Hidy, son. Looking for a horse?"

"Hidy, son," Lycurgus said. "Looking for two. We thought maybe the other one might be here too."

"You mean Mr van Tosch aint even come yet?"

"He aint coming a-tall," Lycurgus said. "Some other folks running Coppermine this time. Whitefolks named Mr Boon Hogganbeck. This white boy gonter ride him. This is McWillie," he told me. McWillie looked at me a minute. Then he went back to the office door and opened it and said something inside and stood back while a white man ("Trainer," Lycurgus murmured. "Name Mr Walter") came out and said,

"Morning, Lycurgus. Where you folks keeping that horse hid, anyway? You aint ringing in a sleeper on us, are you?"

"No sir," Lycurgus said. "I reckon he aint come out

from town yet. We thought they might have sent him
out here. So we come to look."

"You walked all the way here from Possum's?"

"No sir," Lycurgus said. "We rid the mules."

"Where'd you tie them? I cant even see them. Maybe
you painted them with some of that invisible paint you
put on that horse when you took him out of that boxcar
yesterday morning."

"No sir," Lycurgus said. "We just rid as far as the pasture and turned them loose. We walked the balance of
the way."

"Well, anyway, you come to see a horse, so we wont
disappoint you. Bring him out, McWillie, where they can
look at him."

"Look at his face for a change," McWillie said. "Folks
on that Coppermine been looking at Akron's hind end
all winter, but aint none of them seen his face yet."

"Then at least this boy can start out knowing what
he looks like in front. What's your name, son?" I told him.
"You aint from around here."

"No sir. Jefferson, Mississippi."

"He travelling with Mr Hogganbeck that's running
Coppermine now," Lycurgus said.

"Oh," Mr Walter said. "Mr Hogganbeck buy him?"

"I dont know, sir," Lycurgus said. "Mr Hogganbeck's
running him." McWillie brought the horse out; he and
Mr Walter stripped off the blanket. He was black, bigger
than Lightning but very nervous; he came out showing
eye-white; every time anybody moved or spoke near
him his ears went back and he stood on the point of one
hind foot as though ready to lash out with it, Mr Walter
and McWillie both talking, murmuring at him but both
of them always watching him.

"All right," Mr Walter said. "Give him a drink and
put him back up." We followed him toward the front.

"Dont let him discourage you," he said. "After all, it's just a horse race."

"Yes sir," Lycurgus said. "That's what they says. Much oblige for letting us look at him."

"Thank you, sir," I said.

"Good-bye," Mr Walter said. "Dont keep them mules waiting. See you at post time this afternoon."

"No sir," Lycurgus said.

"Yes sir," I said. We went on, past the stables and the track once more.

"Mind what Mr McCaslin told us," Lycurgus said.

"Mr McCaslin?" I said. "Oh yes," I said. I didn't ask What? this time either. I think I knew now. Or maybe I didn't want to believe I knew; didn't want to believe even yet that at a mere eleven you could progress that fast in weary unillusion; maybe if I had asked What? it would have been an admission that I had. "That horse is bad," I said.

"He's scared," Lycurgus said. "That's what Mr McCaslin said last night."

"Last night?" I said. "I thought you all came to look at the track."

"What do he want to look at that track for?" Lycurgus said. "That track dont move. He come to see that horse."

"In the dark?" I said. "Didn't they have a watchman or wasn't the stable locked or anything?"

"When Mr McCaslin make up his mind to do something, he do it," Lycurgus said. "Aint you found out that about him yet?" So we—I—didn't look back. We went on to our sanctuary, where Lightning—I mean Coppermine —and the two mules stamped and swished in the dappled shade and Ned squatted beside Uncle Parsham's saddle and another man sat on his heels across the spring from them—another Negro; I almost knew him, had known him, seen him, something—before Ned spoke:

"It's Bobo," he said. And then it was all right. He was a McCaslin too, Bobo Beauchamp, Lucas's cousin—Lucas Quintus Carothers McCaslin Beauchamp, that Grandmother, whose mother had described old Lucius to her, said looked (and behaved: just as arrogant, just as ironheaded, just as intolerant) exactly like him except for color. Bobo was another motherless Beauchamp child whom Aunt Tennie raised until the call of the out-world became too much for him and he went to Memphis three years ago. "Bobo used to work for the man that used to own Lightning," Ned said. "He come to watch him run." Because it was all right now: the one remaining thing which had troubled us—me: Bobo would know where the automobile was. In fact, he might even have it. But that was wrong, because in that case Boon and Ned would simply have taken it away from him—until suddenly I realised that the reason it was wrong was, I didn't want it to be; if we could get the automobile back for no more than just telling Bobo to go get it and be quick about it, what were we doing here? what had we gone to all this trouble and anxiety for? camouflaging and masquerading Lightning at midnight through the Memphis tenderloin to get him to the depot; ruthlessly using a combination of uxoriousness and nepotism to disrupt a whole boxcar from the railroad system to get him to Parsham; not to mention the rest of it: having to cope with Butch, Minnie's tooth, invading and outraging Uncle Parsham's home, and sleeplessness and (yes) homesickness and (me again) not even a change of underclothes; all that striving and struggling and finagling to run a horse race with a horse which was not ours, to recover an automobile we had never had any business with in the first place, when all we had to do to get the automobile was to send one of the family colored boys to fetch it. You see what I mean? if the successful outcome of the race this afternoon wasn't really the pivot; if Lightning and I were not the last desperate barrier between Boon and Ned and Grandfather's anger, even if not his police; if without winning the race or even having to run it, Ned and Boon could go back to Jefferson (which was the only home Ned knew, and the only milieu in which Boon could have survived) as if nothing had happened, and take up again as though they had never been away, then all of us were engaged in a make-believe not too different from a boys' game of cops and robbers. But Bobo could know where the automobile was; that would be allowable, that would be fair; and Bobo was one of us. I said so to Ned. "I thought I told you to stop worrying about that automobile," he said. "Aint I promised you I'd tend to it when the right time come? You got plenty other things to fret your mind over: you got a horse race. Aint that enough to keep it busy?" He said to Lycurgus: "All right?"

"I think so," Lycurgus said. "We never looked back to see."

"Then maybe," Ned said. But Bobo had already gone. I neither saw nor heard him; he was just gone. "Get the bucket," Ned told Lycurgus. "Now is a good time to eat our snack whilst we still got a little peace and quiet around here." Lycurgus brought it—a tin lard bucket with a clean dishcloth over it, containing pieces of corn bread with fried sidemeat between; there was another bucket of buttermilk sitting in the spring.

"You et breakfast?" Uncle Parsham said to me.

"Yes sir," I said.

"Then dont eat no more," he said. "Just nibble a piece of bread and a little water."

"That's right," Ned said. "You can ride better empty." So he gave me a single piece of corn bread and we all squatted now around Uncle Parsham's saddle, the two buckets on the ground in the center; we heard one step or maybe two up the bank behind us, then McWillie said,

"Hidy, Uncle Possum, morning, reverend" (that was Ned), and came down the bank, already—or still—looking at Lightning. "Yep, that's Coppermine, all right. These boys had Mr Walter skeered this morning that maybe yawl had rung in another horse on him. You running him, reverend?"

"Call him Mr McCaslin," Uncle Parsham said.

"Yes sir," McWillie said. "Mr McCaslin. You running him?"

"White man named Mr Hogganbeck is," Ned said. "We waiting on him now."

"Too bad you aint got something else besides Coppermine to wait with, that would maybe give Akron a race," McWillie said.

"I already told Mr Hogganbeck that, myself," Ned said. He swallowed. Without haste he lifted the bucket of buttermilk and drank, still without haste. McWillie watched him. He set the bucket down. "Set down and eat something," he said.

"Much obliged," McWillie said, "I done et. Maybe that's why Mr Hogganbeck's late, waiting to bring out that other horse."

"There aint time now," Ned said. "He'll have to run this one now. The trouble is, the only one around here that knows how to rate this horse, is the very one that knows better than to let him run behind. This horse dont like to be in front. He wants to run right behind up until he can see the finish line, and have something to run at. I aint seen him race yet, but I'd be willing to bet that the slower the horse in front of him goes, the more carefuller he is not to get out in front where he aint got no company—until he can see that finish line and find out it's a race he's in and run at it. All anybody got to do to beat him is to keep his mind so peaceful that when he does notice he's in a race, it's too late. Some day somebody gonter let him get far enough behind to scare him, then look out. But it wont be this race. The trouble is, the onliest one around here that knows that too, is the wrong one."

"Who's that?" McWillie said.

Ned took another bite. "Whoever's gonter ride that other horse today."

"That's me," McWillie said. "Dont tell me Uncle Possum and Lycurgus both aint already told you that."

"Then you oughter be talking to me instead," Ned said. "Set down and eat; Uncle Possum got plenty here."

"Much obliged," McWillie said again. "Well," he said. "Mr Walter'll be glad to know it aint nobody but Coppermine. We was afraid we would have to break in a new one. See yawl at the track." Then he was gone. But I waited another minute.

"But why?" I said.

"I dont know," Ned said. "We may not even need it. But if we does, we already got it there. You mind I told you this morning how the trouble with this race was, it had too many different things all mixed up in it? Well, this aint our track and country, and it aint even our horse except just in a borried manner of speaking, so we cant take none of them extra things out. So the next best we can do is, to put a few extry ones into it on our own account. That's what we just done. That horse up yonder is a Thoroughbred paper horse; why aint he in Memphis or Louisville or Chicago running races, instead of back here in a homemade country pasture running races against whoever can slip in the back way, like us? Because why, because I felt him last night and he's weedy, like a horse that cant nothing catch for six furlongs, but fifty foot more and he's done folded up right under you before you knowed it. And so far, all that boy—"

"McWillie," I said.

"—McWillie has had to worry about is just staying on top of him and keeping him headed in the right direction; he's won twice now and likely he thinks if he just had the chance, he would run Earl Sande and Dan Patch both clean outen the horse business. Now we've put something else in his mind; he's got two things in it now that dont quite fit one another. So we'll just wait and see. And whilst we're waiting, you go over behind them bushes yonder and lay down and rest. Word's out now, and folks gonter start easing in and out of here to see what they can find out, and over there they wont worry you."

Which I did. Though not always asleep; I heard the voices; I wouldn't have needed to see them even if I had raised onto one elbow and opened one eye past a bush: the same overalls, tieless, the sweated hats, the chewing tobacco, squatting, unhurried, not talking very much, looking inscrutably at the horse. Nor always awake, because Lycurgus was standing over me and time had passed; the very light looked postmeridian. "Time to go," he said. There was nobody with Lightning now but Ned and Uncle Parsham; if they were all up at the track already, it must be even later still. I had expected Boon and Sam and probably Everbe and Miss Reba too. (But not Butch. I hadn't even thought of him; maybe Miss Reba had really got rid of him for good, back up to Hardwick or wherever it was the clerk said last night he really belonged. I had forgotten him; I realised now what the morning's peace actually was.) I said so.

"Haven't they come yet?"

"Aint nobody told them where to come yet," Ned said. "We dont need Boon Hogganbeck now. Come on. You can walk him up and limber him on the way." I got up: the worn perfectly cared-for McClellan saddle and the worn perfectly cared-for cavalry bridle which was the other half of Uncle Parsham's (somebody's) military loot from that Cause which, the longer I live the more convinced I am, your spinster aunts to the contrary, that whoever lost it, it wasn't us.

"Maybe they're looking for Otis," I said.

"Maybe they are," Ned said. "It's a good place to hunt for him, whether they finds him or not." We went on, Uncle Parsham and Ned walking at Lightning's head; Lycurgus would bring the buggy and the other mule around by the road, provided he could find enough clear space to hitch them in. Because already the pasture next to the track was filled up—wagons, the teams unhitched and reversed and tied to the stanchions and tail gates; buggies, saddle-horses and -mules hitched to the fence itself; and now we—I—could see the people, black and white, the tieless shirts and the overalls, already dense along the rail and around the paddock. Because this race was homemade, remember; this was democracy, not triumphant, because anything can be triumphant provided it is tenderly and firmly enough protected and guarded and shielded in its innocent fragility, but democracy working: Colonel Linscomb, the aristocrat, the baron, the suzerain, was not even present. As far as I knew, nobody knew where he was. As far as I knew, nobody cared. He owned one of the horses (I still didn't know for certain just who owned the one I was sitting on) and the dirt we were going to race on and the nice white rail enclosing it and the adjacent pasture which the tethered wagons and buggies were cutting up and the fence one entire panel of which a fractious or frightened saddle-horse had just wrenched into kindling, but nobody knew where he was or seemed to bother or care.

We went to the paddock. Oh yes, we had one; we had everything a race track should have except, as Ned said, grandstands and stalls for beer and whiskey; we had everything else that any track had, but we had democracy too: the judges were the night telegraph operator at the depot and Mr McDiarmid, who ran the depot eating room, who, the legend went, could slice a ham so thin that his entire family had made a summer trip to Chicago on the profits from one of them; our steward and marshal was a dog trainer who shot quail for the market and was now out on bond for his part in (participation in or maybe just his presence at) a homicide which had occurred last winter at a neighboring whiskey still; did I not tell you this was free and elective will and choice and private enterprise at its purest? And there were Boon and Sam waiting for us. "I cant find him," Boon said. "Aint you seen him?"

"Seen who?" Ned said. "Jump down," he told me. The other horse was there too, still nervous, still looking what I would have called bad but that Lycurgus said Ned said was afraid. "Now, what did this horse—"

"That damn boy!" Boon said. "You said this morning he would be out here."

"Maybe he's behind something," Ned said. He came back to me. "What did this horse learn you yesterday? You was on a twice-around track that time too. What did he learn you? Think." I thought hard. But there still wasn't anything.

"Nothing," I said. "All I did was to keep him from going straight to you whenever he saw you."

"And that's exactly what you want to do this first heat: just keep him in the middle of the track and keep him going and then dont bother him. Dont bother nohow; we gonter lose this first heat anyway and get shut of it—"

"Lose it?" Boon said. "What the hell—"

"Do you want to run this horse race, or do you want me to?" Ned asked him.

"All right," Boon said. "But, God damn it—" Then he said: "You said that damn boy—"

"Lemme ask you another way then," Ned said. "Do you want to run this horse race and lemme go hunt for that tooth?"

"Here they come," Sam said. "We aint got time now. Gimme your foot." He threw me up. So we didn't have time, for Ned to instruct me further or for anything else. But we didn't need it; our victory in the first heat (we didn't win it; it was only a dividend which paid off later) was not due to me or even to Lightning, but to Ned and McWillie; I didn't even really know what was happening until afterward. Because of my (indubitable) size and (more than indubitable) inexperience, not to mention the unmanageable state toward which the other horse was now well on his way, it was stipulated and agreed that we should be led up to the wire by grooms, and there released at the word Go. Which we did (or were), Lightning behaving as he always did when Ned was near enough for him to nuzzle at his coat or hand, Acheron behaving as (I assumed, having seen him but that once) he always did when anyone was near his head, skittering, bouncing, snatching the groom this way and that but gradually working up to the wire; it would be any moment now; it seemed to me that I actually saw the marshal-murderer fill his lungs to holler Go! when I dont know what happened, I mean the sequence: Ned said suddenly:

"Set tight," and my head, arms, shoulders and all, snapped; I dont know what it was he used—awl, ice pick, or maybe just a nail in his palm, the spring, the leap; the voice not hollering Go! because it never had, hollering instead:

"Stop! Stop! Whoa! Whoa!" which we—Lightning and me—did, to see Acheron's groom still on his knees where Acheron had flung him, and Acheron and McWillie al-

ready at top speed going into the first turn, McWillie
sawing back on him, wrenching Acheron's whole neck
sideways. But he already had the bit, the marshal and
three or four spectators cutting across the ring to try to
stop him in the back stretch, though they might as well
have been hollering at Sam's cannonball limited between
two flag stops. But McWillie had slowed him now, though
it was now a matter of mere choice: whether to come on
around the track or turn and go back, the distance being
equal, McWillie (or maybe it was Acheron) choosing
the former, Ned murmuring rapidly at my knee now:

"Anyhow, we got one extra half a mile on him. This
time you'll have to do it yourself because them judges
gonter—" They were; they were already approaching.
Ned said: "Just remember. This un dont matter nohow—"
Then they did: disqualified him. Though they had seen
nothing: only that he had released Lightning's head before the word Go. So this time I had a volunteer from the
crowd to hold Lightning's head, McWillie glaring at me
while Acheron skittered and plunged under him while
the groom gradually worked him back toward position.
And this time the palm went to McWillie. You see what
I mean? Even if Non-virtue knew nothing about back-
country horse racing, she didn't need to: all necessary
was to supply me with Sam, to gain that extra furtherance
in evil by some primeval and insentient process like os-
mosis or maybe simple juxtaposition. I didn't even wait
for Lightning to come in to the bridle, I didn't know why:
I brought the bit back to him and (with no little, in fact
considerable, help from the volunteer who was mine and
Lightning's individual starter) held so, fixed; and sure
enough, I saw the soles of Acheron's groom's feet and
Acheron himself already two leaps on his next circuit of
the track, Lightning and me still motionless. But Mc-
Willie was on him this time, before he reached the turn,

so that the emergency squad not only reached the back stretch first but even stopped and caught Acheron and led him back. So our—mine and Ned's—net was only six furlongs, and the last one of them debatable. Though our main gain was McWillie; he was not just mad now, he was scared too, glaring at me again but with more than just anger in it, two grooms holding Acheron now long enough for us to be more or less in position, Lightning and me well to the outside to give them room, when the word Go came.

And that's all. We were off, Lightning strong and willing, every quality you could want in fact except eagerness, his brain not having found out yet that this was a race, McWillie holding Acheron back now so that we were setting the pace, on around the first lap, Lightning moving slower and slower, confronted with all that solitude, until Acheron drew up and passed us despite all McWillie could do; whereupon Lightning also moved out again, with companionship now, around the second lap and really going now, Acheron a neck ahead and our crowd even beginning to yell now as though they were getting their money's worth; the wire ahead now and McWillie, giving Acheron a terrific cut with his whip, might as well have hit Lightning too; twenty more feet, and we would have passed McWillie on simple momentum. But the twenty more feet were not there, McWillie giving me one last glare over his shoulder of rage and fright, but triumph too now as I slowed Lightning and turned him and saw it: not a fight but rather a turmoil, a seething of heads and shoulders and backs out of the middle of the crowd around the judges' stand, out of the middle of which Boon stood suddenly up like a pine sapling out of a plum thicket, his shirt torn half off and one flailing arm with two or three men clinging to it: I could see him bellowing. Then he vanished and I saw Ned

running toward me up the track. Then Butch and another
man came out of the crowd toward us. "What?" I said
to Ned.

"Nemmine that," he said. He took the bridle with one
hand, his other hand already digging into his hip pocket.
"It's that Butch again; it dont matter why. Here." He held
his hand up to me. He was not rushed, hurried: he was
just rapid. "Take it. They aint gonter bother you." It was
a cloth tobacco sack containing a hardish lump about the
size of a pecan. "Hide it and keep it. Dont lose it. Just
remember who it come from: Ned William McCaslin.
Will you remember that? Ned William McCaslin Jefferson Missippi."

"Yes," I said. I put it in my hip pocket. "But what—"
He didn't even let me finish.

"Soon as you can, find Uncle Possum and stay with
him. Nemmine about Boon and the rest of them. If they
got him, they got all the others too. Go straight to Uncle
Possum and stay with him. He will know what to do."

"Yes," I said. Butch and the other man had reached the
gate onto the track; part of Butch's shirt was gone too.
They were looking at us.

"That it?" the man with him said.

"Yep," Butch said.

"Bring that horse here, boy," the man said to Ned. "I
want it."

"Set still," Ned told me. He led the horse up to where
they waited.

"Jump down, son," the man told me, quite kindly. "I
dont want you." I did so. "Hand me the reins," he told
Ned. Ned did so. "I'll take you bareback," the man told
Ned. "You're under arrest."

11

◆◆◆◆

We were going to have all the crowd too presently. We just stood there, facing Butch and the other man, who now held Lightning. "What's it for, Whitefolks?" Ned said.

"It's for jail, son," the other man said. "That's what we call it here. I dont know what you call it where you come from."

"Yes sir," Ned said. "We has that back home too. Only they mentions why, even to niggers."

"Oh, a lawyer," Butch said. "He wants to see a paper. Show him one. —Never mind, I'll do it." He took something from his hip pocket: a letter in a soiled envelope. Ned took it. He stood there quietly, holding it in his hand. "What do you think of that," Butch said. "A man that cant even read, wanting to see a paper. Smell it then. Maybe it smells all right."

"Yes sir," Ned said. "It's all right."

"Dont say you are satisfied if you aint," Butch said.

"Yes sir," Ned said. "It's all right." We had the crowd now. Butch took the envelope back from Ned and put it back in his pocket and spoke to them: "It's all right, boys; just a little legal difficulty about who owns this horse. The race aint cancelled. The first heat will still stand; the next ones are just put off until tomorrow. Can you hear me back there?"

"We likely cant, if the bets is cancelled too," a voice said. There was a guffaw, then two or three.

"I dont know," Butch said. "Anybody that seen this Memphis horse run against Akron them two heats last winter and still bet on him, has done already cancelled his money out before he even got it put up." He waited, but there was no laughter this time; then the voice—or another—said:

"Does Walter Clapp think that too? Ten foot more, and that chestnut would a beat him today."

"All right, all right," Butch said. "Settle it tomorrow. Aint nothing changed; the next two heats is just put off until tomorrow. The fifty-dollar heat bets is still up and Colonel Linscomb aint won but one of them. Come on, now; we got to get this horse and these witnesses in to town where we can get everything cleared up and be ready to run again tomorrow. Somebody holler back there to send my surrey." Then I saw Boon, a head above them. His face was quite calm now, still blood-streaked, and somebody (I had expected him to be handcuffed, but he wasn't; we were still democracy; he was still only a minority and not a heresy) had tied the sleeves of his torn shirt around his neck so that he was covered. Then I saw Sam too; he was barely marked; he was the one who pushed through first. "Now, Sam," Butch said. "We been trying for thirty minutes to step around you, but you wont let us."

"You damn right I wont," Sam said. "I'll ask you again, and let this be the last one. Are we under arrest?"

"Are who under arrest?" Butch said.

"Hogganbeck. Me. That Negro there."

"Here's another lawyer," Butch said to the other man. I learned quite quick now that he was the Law in Parsham; he was who Miss Reba had told us about last night: the elected constable of the Beat, where Butch for all his badge and pistol was just another guest like we were, being (Butch) just one more tenureless appointee from the nepotic files of the County Sheriff's office in the county seat at Hardwick thirteen miles away. "Maybe he wants to see a paper too."

"No," the other man, the constable, told Sam. "You can go whenever you want to."

"Then I'm going back to Memphis to find some law," Sam said. "I mean the kind of law a man like me can approach without having his britches and underwear both ripped off. If I aint back tonight, I'll be here early tomorrow morning." He had already seen me. He said, "Come on. You come with me."

"No," I said. "I'm going to stay here." The constable was looking at me.

"You can go with him, if you want," he said.

"No sir," I said. "I'm going to stay here."

"Who does he belong to?" the constable said.

"He's with me," Ned said. The constable said, as though Ned had not spoken, there had been no sound:

"Who brought him here?"

"Me," Boon said. "I work for his father."

"I work for his grandfather," Ned said. "We done already fixed to take care of him."

"Just hold on," Sam said. "I'll try to get back tonight. Then we can attend to everything."

"And when you come back," the constable said, "remember that you aint in Memphis or Nashville either. That you aint even in Hardwick County except primarily. What you're in right now, and what you'll be in every time you get off of a train at that depot yonder, is Beat Four."

"That's telling them, judge," Butch said. "The free state of Possum, Tennessee."

"I was talking to you too," the constable told Butch. "You may be the one that better try hardest to remember it." The surrey came up to where they were holding Boon. The constable gestured Ned toward it. Suddenly Boon was struggling; Ned was saying something to him. Then the constable turned back to me. "That Negro says you are going home with old Possum Hood."

"Yes sir," I said.

"I dont think I like that—a white boy staying with a family of niggers. You come home with me."

"No sir," I said.

"Yes," he said, but still really kind. "Come on. I'm busy."

"There's somewhere you stops," Ned said. The constable became completely motionless, half turned.

"What did you say?" he said.

"There's somewhere the Law stops and just people starts," Ned said. And still for another moment the constable didn't move—an older man than you thought at first, spare, quite hale, but older, who wore no pistol, in his pocket or anywhere else, and if he had a badge, it wasn't in sight either.

"You're right," he said. He said to me: "That's where you want to stay? with old Possum?"

"Yes sir," I said.

"All right," he said. He turned. "Get in, boys," he said.

"What you going to do with the nigger?" Butch said. He had taken the lines from the man who brought the surrey up; his foot was already on the stirrup to get into the driver's seat; Boon and Sam were already in the back. "Let him ride your horse?"

"You're going to ride my horse," the constable said. "Jump up, son," he told Ned. "You're the horse expert around here." Ned took the lines from Butch and got up and cramped the wheel for the constable to get up beside him. Boon was still looking down at me, his face battered and bruised but quiet now under the drying blood.

"Come on with Sam," he said.

"I'm all right," I said.

"No," Boon said. "I cant—"

"I know Possum Hood," the constable said. "If I get worried about him, I'll come back tonight and get him. Drive on, son." They went on. They were gone. I was alone. I mean, if I had been left by myself like when two hunters separate in the woods or fields, to meet again later, even as late as camp that night, I would not have been so alone. As it was, I was anything but solitary. I was an island in that ring of sweated hats and tieless shirts and overalls, the alien nameless faces already turning away from me as I looked about at them, and not one word to me of Yes or No or Go or Stay: who—me— was being reabandoned who had already been abandoned once: and at only eleven you are not really big enough in size to be worth that much abandonment; you would be obliterated, effaced, dissolved, vaporised beneath it. Until one of them said:

"You looking for Possum Hood? I think he's over yonder by his buggy, waiting for you." He was. The other wagons and buggies were pulling out now; most of them and all the saddled horses and mules were already gone.

I went up to the buggy and stopped. I dont know why:
I just stopped. Maybe there was nowhere else to go. I
mean, there was no room for the next step forward until
somebody moved the buggy.

"Get in," Uncle Parsham said. "We'll go home and wait
for Lycurgus."

"Lycurgus," I said as though I had never heard the
name before even.

"He rode on to town on the mule. He will find out what
all this is about and come back and tell us. He's going
to find out what time a train goes to Jefferson tonight."

"To Jefferson?" I said.

"So you can go home." He didn't quite look at me. "If
you want to."

"I cant go home yet," I said. "I got to wait for Boon."

"I said if you want to," Uncle Parsham said. "Get in."
I got in. He drove across the pasture, into the road. "Close
the gate," Uncle Parsham said. "It's about time somebody
remembered to." I closed the gate and got back in the
buggy. "You ever drive a mule to a buggy?"

"No sir," I said. He handed me the lines. "I dont know
how," I said.

"Then you can learn now. A mule aint like a horse.
When a horse gets a wrong notion in his head, all you
got to do is swap him another one for it. Most anything
will do—a whip or spur or just scare him by hollering
at him. A mule is different. He can hold two notions at
the same time and the way to change one of them is to
act like you believe he thought of changing it first. He'll
know different, because mules have got sense. But a mule
is a gentleman too, and when you act courteous and respectful at him without trying to buy him or scare him,
he'll act courteous and respectful back at you—as long
as you dont overstep him. That's why you dont pet a mule
like you do a horse: he knows you dont love him: you're

just trying to fool him into doing something he already dont aim to do, and it insults him. Handle him like that. He knows the way home, and he will know it aint me holding the lines. So all you need to do is tell him with the lines that you know the way too but he lives here and you're just a boy so you want him to go in front."

We went on, at a fair clip now, the mule neat and nimble, raising barely half as much dust as a horse would; already I could feel what Uncle Parsham meant; there came back to me through the lines not just power, but intelligence, sagacity; not just the capacity but the willingness to choose when necessary between two alternatives and to make the right decision without hesitation. "What do you do at home?" Uncle Parsham said.

"I work on Saturdays," I said.

"Then you going to save some of the money. What are you going to buy with it?" And so suddenly I was talking, telling him: about the beagles: how I wanted to be a fox hunter like Cousin Zack and how Cousin Zack said the way to learn was with a pack of beagles on rabbits; and how Father paid me ten cents each Saturday at the livery stable and Father would match whatever I saved of it until I could buy the first couple to start my pack, which would cost twelve dollars and I already had eight dollars and ten cents; and then, all of a sudden too, I was crying, bawling: I was tired, not from riding a mile race because I had ridden more than that at one time before, even though it wasn't real racing; but maybe from being up early and chasing back and forth across the country without any dinner but a piece of corn bread. Maybe that was it: I was just hungry. But anyway, there I sat, bawling like a baby, worse than Alexander and even Maury, against Uncle Parsham's shirt while he held me with one arm and took the lines from me with his other hand, not saying anything at all, until he said, "Now you can quit.

We're almost home; you'll have just time to wash your
face at the trough before we go in the house. You dont
want womenfolks to see it like that."

Which I did. That is, we unhitched the mule first and
watered him and hung the harness up and wiped him
down and stalled and fed him and pushed the buggy back
under its shed and then I smeared my face with water
at the trough and dried it (after a fashion) with the riding-sock and we went into the house. And the evening
meal—supper—was ready although it was barely five
oclock, as country people, farmers, ate; and we sat down:
Uncle Parsham and his daughter and me since Lycurgus
was not yet back from town, and Uncle Parsham said,
"You gives thanks at your house too," and I said,

"Yes sir," and he said,

"Bow your head," and we did so and he said grace,
briefly, courteously but with dignity, without abasement
or cringing: one man of decency and intelligence to another: notifying Heaven that we were about to eat and
thanking It for the privilege, but at the same time remind-
ing It that It had had some help too; that if someone
named Hood or Briggins (so that was Lycurgus's and his
mother's name) hadn't sweated some, the acknowledg-
ment would have graced mainly empty dishes, and said
Amen and unfolded his napkin and stuck the corner in
his collar exactly as Grandfather did, and we ate: the
dishes of cold vegetables which should have been eaten
hot at the country hour of eleven oclock, but there were
hot biscuits and three kinds of preserves, and buttermilk.
And still it wasn't even sundown: the long twilight and
even after that, still the long evening, the long night and
I didn't even know where I was going to sleep nor even
on what, Uncle Parsham sitting there picking his teeth
with a gold toothpick just like Grandfather's and reading
my mind like it was a magic-lantern slide: "Do you like

to go fishing?" I didn't really like it. I couldn't seem to learn to want—or maybe want to learn—to be still that long. I said quickly:

"Yes sir."

"Come on then. By that time Lycurgus will be back." There were three cane poles, with lines floats sinkers hooks and all, on two nails in the wall of the back gallery. He took down two of them. "Come on," he said. In the tool shed there was a tin bucket with nail holes punched through the lid. "Lycurgus's cricket bucket," he said. "I like worms myself." They were in a shallow earth-filled wooden tray; he—no: I; I said,

"Lemme do it," and took the broken fork from him and dug the long frantic worms out of the dirt, into a tin can.

"Come on," he said, shouldering his pole, passing the stable but turning sharp away and down toward the creek bottom, not far; there was a good worn path among the blackberry thickets and then the willows, then the creek, the water seeming to gather gently the fading light and then as gently return it; there was even a log to sit on. "This is where my daughter fishes," he said, "We call it Mary's hole. But you can use it now. I'll be on down the bank." Then he was gone. The light was going fast now; it would be night before long. I sat on the log, in a gentle whine of mosquitoes. It wouldn't be too difficult; all I would have to do would just be to say *I wont think* whenever it was necessary. After a while I thought about putting the hook into the water, then I could watch how long it would take the float to disappear into darkness when night finally came. Then I even thought about putting one of Lycurgus's crickets on the hook, but crickets were not always easy to catch and Lycurgus lived by a creek and would have more time to fish and would need them. So I just thought *I wont think*; I could see the float plainer than ever, now that it was on the water; it would probably be the last of all to vanish into the darkness, since the water itself would be next to last; I couldn't see or hear Uncle Parsham at all, I didn't know how much further he called on down the bank and now was the perfect time, chance to act like a baby, only what's the good of acting like a baby, of wasting it with nobody there to know it or offer sympathy—if anybody ever wants sympathy or even in fact really to be back home because what you really want is just a familiar soft bed to sleep in for a change again, to go to sleep in; there were whippoorwills now and back somewhere beyond the creek an owl too, a big one by his voice; maybe there were big woods there and if Lycurgus's (or maybe they were Uncle Parsham's) hounds were all that good on Otis last night, they sure ought to be able to handle rabbits or coons or possums. So I asked him. It was full night now for some time. He said quietly behind me; I hadn't even heard him until then:

"Had a bite yet?"

"I aint much of a fisherman," I said. "How do your hounds hunt?"

"Good," he said. He didn't even raise his voice: "Pappy." Uncle Parsham's white shirt held light too, up to us where Lycurgus took the two poles and we followed, up the path again where the two hounds met us, on into the house again, into the lamplight, a plate of supper with a cloth over it ready for Lycurgus.

"Sit down," Uncle Parsham said. "You can talk while you eat." Lycurgus sat down.

"They're still there," he said.

"They aint took them to Hardwick yet?" Uncle Parsham said. "Possum hasn't got a jail," he told me. "They lock them in the woodshed behind the schoolhouse until they can take them to the jail at Hardwick. Men, that is. They aint had women before."

"No sir," Lycurgus said. "The ladies is still in the hotel, with a guard at the door. Just Mr Hogganbeck is in the woodshed. Mr Caldwell went back to Memphis on Number Thirty-one. He taken that boy with him."

"Otis?" I said. "Did they get the tooth back?"

"They never said," Lycurgus said, eating; he glanced briefly at me. "And the horse is all right too. I went and seen him. He's in the hotel stable. Before he left, Mr Caldwell made a bond for Mr McCaslin so he can watch the horse." He ate. "A train leaves for Jefferson at nine-forty. We could make it all right if we hurry." Uncle Parsham took a vast silver watch from his pocket and looked at it. "We could make it," Lycurgus said.

"I cant," I said. "I got to wait." Uncle Parsham put the watch back. He rose. He said, not loud:

"Mary." She was in the front room; I hadn't heard a sound. She came to the door.

"I already did it," she said. She said to Lycurgus: "Your pallet's ready in the hall." Then to me: "You sleep in Lycurgus's bed where you was yestiddy."

"I dont need to take Lycurgus's bed," I said. "I can sleep with Uncle Parsham. I wont mind." They looked at me, quite still, quite identical. "I sleep with Boss a lot of times," I said. "He snores too. I dont mind."

"Boss?" Uncle Parsham said.

"That's what we call Grandfather," I said. "He snores too. I wont mind."

"Let him," Uncle Parsham said. We went to his room. His lamp had flowers painted on the china shade and there was a big gold-framed portrait on a gold easel in one corner: a woman, not very old but in old-timey clothes; the bed had a bright patchwork quilt on it like Lycurgus's and even in May there was a smolder of fire on the hearth. There was a chair, a rocking chair too, but I didn't sit down. I just stood there. Then he came in again. He wore a nightshirt now and was winding the silver watch. "Undress," he said. I did so. "Does your mother let you sleep like that at home?"

"No sir," I said.

"You aint got anything with you, have you?"

"No sir," I said. He put the watch on the mantel and went to the door and said,

"Mary." She answered. "Bring one of Lycurgus's clean shirts." After a while her hand held the shirt through the door crack. He took it. "Here," he said. I came and put it on. "Do you say your Now I lay me in bed or kneeling down?"

"Kneeling down," I said.

"Say them," he said. I knelt beside the bed and said my prayers. The bed was already turned back. I got into it and he blew out the lamp and I heard the bed again and then—the moon would be late before it was very high tonight but there was already enough light—I could see him, all black and white against the white pillow and the white moustache and imperial, lying on his back, his hands folded on his breast. "Tomorrow morning I'll take you to town and we'll see Mr Hogganbeck. If he says you have done all you can do here and for you to go home, will you go then?"

"Yes sir," I said.

"Now go to sleep," he said. Because even before he said it, I knew that that was exactly what I wanted, what I had been wanting probably ever since yesterday: to go home. I mean, nobody likes to be licked, but maybe there are times when nobody can help being; that all you can do about it is not quit. And Boon and Ned hadn't quit, or they wouldn't be where they were right now. And maybe they wouldn't say that I had quit either, when it was them who told me to go home. Maybe I was just too little, too young; maybe I just wasn't able to tote whatever my share was, and if they had had somebody else bigger or older or maybe just smarter, we wouldn't have been licked. You see? like that: all specious and rational; unimpugnable even, when the simple truth was, I wanted to go home and just wasn't brave enough to say so, let alone do it. So now, having admitted at last that I was not only a failure but a coward too, my mind should be peaceful and easy and I should go on to sleep like a baby: where Uncle Parsham already was, just barely snoring (who should hear Grandfather once). Not that that mattered either, since I would be home tomorrow with nothing—no stolen horses nor chastity-stricken prostitutes and errant pullman conductors and Ned and Boon Hogganbeck in his normal condition once he had slipped Father's leash—to interfere with sleep, hearing the voice, the bawling two or three times before I struggled up and out, into daylight, sunlight; Uncle Parsham's side of the bed was empty and now I could hear the bawling from outside the house:

"Hellaw. Hellaw. Lycurgus. Lycurgus," and leapt, sprang from the bed, already running, across to the window where I could look out into the front yard. It was Ned. He had the horse.

12

◆◆◆◆

So once again, at two oclock in the afternoon, McWillie
and I sat our (his was anyway) skittering mounts—we
had scared Mr Clapp enough yesterday to where we had
drawn for pole position this time and McWillie won it—
poised for the steward-starter's (the bird-dog trainer-
market hunter–homicidist's) Go!

A few things came before that though. One of them
was Ned. He looked bad. He looked terrible. It wasn't
just lack of sleep; we all had that lack. But Boon and I
had at least spent the four nights in bed since we left
Jefferson, where Ned had spent maybe two, one of the
others in a boxcar with a horse and the other in a stable
with him, both on hay if on anything. It was his clothes
too. His shirt was filthy and his black pants were not
much better. At least Everbe had washed some of mine

night before last, but Ned hadn't even had his off until now: sitting now in a clean faded suit of Uncle Parsham's overalls and jumper while Mary was washing his shirt and doing what she could with his pants, at the kitchen table now, he and I eating our breakfast while Uncle Parsham sat and listened.

He said that a little before daylight one of the white men—it wasn't Mr Poleymus, the constable—woke him where he was asleep on some bales of hay and told him to take the horse and get out of town with it—

"Just you and Lightning, and not Boon and the others?" I said. "Where are they?"

"Where them white folks put um," Ned said. "So I said, Much oblige, Whitefolks, and took Lightning in my hand and—"

"Why?" I said.

"What do you care why? All we need to do now is be up behind that starting wire at two oclock this afternoon and win them two heats and get a holt of Boss's automobile and get on back to Jefferson that we hadn't ought to never left nohow—"

"We cant go back without Boon," I said. "If they let you and Lightning go, why didn't they let him go?"

"Look," Ned said. "Me and you got enough to do just running that horse race. Why dont you finish your breakfast and then go back and lay down and rest until I calls you in time—"

"Stop lying to him," Uncle Parsham said. Ned ate, his head bent over his plate, eating fast. He was tired; his eye-whites were not even just pink any more: they were red.

"Mr Boon Hogganbeck aint going anywhere for a while. He's in jail good this time. They gonter take him to Hardwick this morning where they can lock him up sho enough. But forget that. What you and me have got to do is—"

"Tell him," Uncle Parsham said. "He's stood everything else you folks got him into since you brought him here; what makes you think he cant stand the rest of it too, until you manage somehow to come out on the other side and can take him back home? Didn't he have to watch it too, right here in my yard and my house, and down yonder in my pasture both, not to mention what he might have seen in town since—that man horsing and studding at that gal, and her trying to get away from him, and not nobody but this eleven-year-old boy to run to? not Boon Hogganbeck and not the Law and not the grown white folks to count on and hope for, but just him? Tell him." And already the thing inside me saying *No No Dont ask Leave it Leave it.* I said,

"What did Boon do?" Ned chewed over his plate, blinking his reddened eyes like when you have sand in them.

"He whupped that Law. That Butch. He nigh ruint him. They let him out before they done me and Lightning. He never even stopped. He went straight to that gal—"

"It was Miss Reba," I said. "It was Miss Reba."

"No," Ned said. "It was that other one. That big one. They never called her name to me. —and whupped her and turned around—"

"He hit her?" I said. "Boon hit Ever— Miss Corrie?"

"Is that her name? Yes. —and turned around and went straight back until he found that Law and whupped him, pistol and all, before they could pull him off—"

"Boon hit her," I said. "He hit her."

"That's right," Ned said. "She is the reason me and Lightning are free right now. That Butch found out he couldn't get to her no other way, and when he found out that me and you and Boon had to win that race today before we could dare to go back home, and all we had to win it with was Lightning, he took Lightning and locked him up. That's what happened. That's all it was; Uncle Possum just told you how he watched it coming Monday, and maybe I ought to seen it too and maybe I would if I hadn't been so busy with Lightning, or maybe if I had been a little better acquainted with that Butch—"

"I dont believe it," I said.

"Yes," he said. "That's what it was. It was just bad luck, the kind of bad luck you cant count against beforehand. He likely just happened to be wherever he was just by chance when he seen her Monday and figgered right off that that badge and pistol would be all he would need, being likely used to having them be enough around here. Only this time they wasn't and so he had to look again, and sho enough, there was Lightning that we had to depend on to win that race so we could get back Boss's automobile and maybe go back home—"

"No!" I said. "No! It wasn't her! She's not even here! She went back to Memphis with Sam yesterday evening! They just didn't tell you! It was somebody else! It was another one!"

"No," Ned said. "It was her. You seen it Monday out here." Oh yes; and on the way back in the surrey that afternoon, and at the doctor's, and at the hotel that night until Miss Reba frightened him away, we—I anyway—thought for good. Because Miss Reba was only a woman too. I said:

"Why didn't somebody else help her? a man to help her—that man, that man that took you and Lightning, that told Sam and Butch both they could be whatever they wanted in Memphis or Nashville or Hardwick either, but that here in Possum he was the one—" I said, cried: "I dont believe it!"

"Yes," Ned said. "It was her that bought Lightning loose to run again today. I aint talking about me and

Boon and them others; Butch never cared nothing about us, except to maybe keep Boon outen the way until this morning. All he needed was Lightning, only he had to throw in me and Boon and the rest to make Mr Poleymus believe him. Because Butch tricked him too, used him too, until whatever it was that happened this morning— whether that Butch, having done been paid off now, said it was all a mistake or it was the wrong horse, or maybe by that time Mr Poleymus his-self had added one to one and smelled a mouse and turned everybody loose and before he could turn around, Boon went and whupped that gal and then come straight back without even stopping and tried to tear that Butch's head off, pistol and all, with his bare hands, and Mr Poleymus smelled a whole rat. And Mr Poleymus may be little, and he may be old; but he's a man, mon. They told me how last year his wife had one of them strokes and cant even move her hand now, and all the chillen are married and gone, so he has to wash her and feed her and lift her in and outen the bed day and night both, besides cooking and keeping house too unlessen some neighbor woman comes in to help. But you dont know it to look at him and watch him act. He come in there—I never seen none of it; they just told me: two or three holding Boon and another one trying to keep that Butch from whupping him with the pistol whilst they was holding him—and walked up to Butch and snatched that pistol outen his hand and reached up and ripped that badge and half his shirt off too and telefoamed to Hardwick to send a automobile to bring them all back to jail, the women too. When it's women, they calls it fragrancy."

"Vagrancy," Uncle Parsham said.

"That's what I said," Ned said. "You call it whatever you want. I calls it jail."

"I dont believe it," I said. "She quit."

"Then we sho better say much obliged that she started again," Ned said. "Else me and you and Lightning—"

"She's quit," I said. "She promised me."

"Aint we got Lightning back?" Ned said. "Aint all we got to do now is just run him? Didn't Mr Sam say he will be back today and will know what to do, and then me and you and Boon will be just the same as already back home?"

I sat there. It was still early. I mean, even now it was still only eight oclock. It was going to be hot today, the first hot day, precursor of summer. You see, just to keep on saying *I dont believe it* served only for the moment; as soon as the words, the noise, died, there it still was— anguish, rage, outrage, grief, whatever it was—unchanged. "I have to go to town right away," I said to Uncle Parsham. "If I can use one of the mules, I'll send you the money as soon as I get home." He rose at once.

"Come on," he said.

"Hold on," Ned said. "It's too late now, Mr Poleymus sent for a automobile. They've already left before now."

"He can cut them off," Uncle Parsham said. "It aint a half a mile from here to the road they'll be on."

"I got to get some sleep," Ned said.

"I know it," Uncle Parsham said. "I'm going with him. I told him last night I would."

"I'm not going home yet," I said. "I'm just going to town for a minute. Then I'll come back here."

"All right," Ned said. "At least lemme finish my coffee." We didn't wait for him. One of the mules was gone, probably to the field with Lycurgus. But the other was there. Ned came out before we had the gear on. Uncle Parsham showed us the short cut to the Hardwick road, but I didn't care. I mean, it didn't matter to me now where I met him. If I hadn't been just about worn out with race horses and women and deputy sheriffs and everybody else that wasn't back home where they belonged, I might have preferred to hold my interview with Boon in some quick private place for both our sakes. But it didn't matter now; it could be in the middle of the big road or in the middle of the Square either, as far as I was concerned; there could be a whole automobile full of them. But we didn't meet the automobile; obviously I was being protected; to have had to do it in public would have been intolerable, gratuitously intolerable for one who had served Non-virtue this faithfully for four days and asked so little in return. I mean, not to have to see any more of them than I had to. Which was granted; the still-empty automobile had barely reached the hotel itself when we got there: a seven-passenger Stanley Steamer: enough room even for the baggage of two—no, three: Minnie too—women on a two-day trip from Memphis to Parsham, which they would all be upstairs packing now, so even horse stealing took care of its own. Ned cramped the wheel for me to get down. "You still dont want to tell me what you come for?" he said.

"No," I said. None of the long row of chairs on the gallery were occupied, Caesar could have held his triumph there and had all the isolation Boon's and Butch's new status required; the lobby was empty, and Mr Poleymus could have used that. But he was a man, mon; they were in the ladies' parlor—Mr Poleymus, the driver of the car (another deputy; anyway, in a badge), Butch and Boon fresh and marked from battle. Though only Boon for me, who read my face (he had known it long enough) or maybe it was his own heart or anyway conscience; he said quickly:

"Look out, now, Lucius; look out!" already flinging up one arm as he rose quickly, already stepping back, retreating, I walking at him, up to him, not tall enough by more than half and nothing to stand on either (that ludicrous anticlimax of shame), having to reach, to jump even, stretch the best I could to strike at his face; oh yes, I was crying, bawling again; I couldn't even see him now: just hitting as high as I could, having to jump at him to do so, against his Alp-hard Alp-tall crags and cliffs, Mr Poleymus saying behind me:

"Hit him again. He struck a woman, I dont care who she is," and (or somebody) holding me until I wrenched, jerked free, turning, blind, for the door or where I thought I remembered it, the hand guiding me now.

"Wait," Boon said. "Dont you want to see her?" You see, I was tired and my feet hurt. I was about worn out, and I needed sleep too. But more: I was dirty. I wanted fresh clothes. She had washed for me Monday night but I didn't want just rewashed clothes: I wanted a change of clothes that had had time to rest for a while, like at home, smelling of rest and quiet drawers and starch and bluing; but mainly my feet; I wanted fresh stockings and my other shoes.

"I dont want to see nobody!" I said. "I want to go home!"

"All right," Boon said. "Here—anybody—will somebody put him on that train this morning? I got money—can get it—"

"Shut up," I said. "I aint going nowhere now." I went on, still blind; or that is, the hand carried me.

"Wait," Boon said. "Wait, Lucius."

"Shut up," I said. The hand curved me around; there was a wall now.

"Wipe your face," Mr Poleymus said. He held out a bandanna handkerchief but I didn't take it; my bandage would sop it up all right. Anyway, the riding-sock did. It was used to being cried into. Who knew? if it stayed with me long enough, it might even win a horse race. I could see now; we were in the lobby. I started to turn but he held me. "Hold up a minute," he said. "If you still dont want to see anybody." It was Miss Reba and Everbe coming down the stairs carrying their grips but Minnie wasn't with them. The car-driving deputy was waiting. He took the grips and they went on; they didn't look toward us, Miss Reba with her head mad and hard and high; if the deputy hadn't moved quick she would have tromped right over him, grips and all. They went out. "I'll buy you a ticket home," Mr Poleymus said. "Get on that train." I didn't say Shut up to him. "You've run out of folks sure enough now, I'll stay with you and tell the conductor—"

"I'm going to wait for Ned," I said. "I cant go without him. If you hadn't ruined everything yesterday, we'd all been gone by now."

"Who's Ned?" he said. I told him. "You mean you're going to run that horse today anyhow? you and Ned by yourself?" I told him. "Where's Ned now?" I told him. "Come on," he said. "We can go out the side door." Ned was standing at the mule's head. The back of the automobile was toward us. And Minnie still wasn't with them. Maybe she went back to Memphis yesterday with Sam and Otis; maybe now that she had Otis again she wasn't going to lift her hand off of him until it had that tooth in it. That's what I would have done, anyway.

"So Mr Poleymus finally caught you too, did he?" Ned said. "What's the matter? aint he got no handcuffs your size?"

"Shut up," I said.

"When you going to get him back home, son?" Mr Poleymus said to Ned.

"I hope tonight," Ned said; he wasn't being Uncle Remus or smart or cute or anything now. "Soon as I get rid of this horse race and can do something about it."

"Have you got enough money?"

"Yes sir," Ned said. "Much oblige. We'll be all right

after this race." He cramped the wheel and we got in. Mr Poleymus stood with his hand on the top stanchion. He said:

"So you really are going to race that Linscomb horse this afternoon."

"We gonter beat that Linscomb horse this afternoon," Ned said.

"You hope so," Mr Poleymus said.

"I know so," Ned said.

"How much do you know so?" Mr Poleymus said.

"I wish I had a hundred dollars of my own to bet on it," Ned said. They looked at each other; it was a good while. Then Mr Poleymus turned loosed the stanchion and took from his pocket a worn snap purse that when I saw it I thought I was seeing double because it was exactly like Ned's, scuffed and worn and even longer than the riding-sock, that you didn't even know who was paying who for what, and unsnapped it and took out two one-dollar bills and snapped the purse shut and handed the bills to Ned.

"Bet this for me," he said. "If you're right, you can keep half of it." Ned took the money.

"I'll bet it for you," he said. "But much oblige. By sun-down tonight I can lend you half of three or four times this much." We drove on then—I mean, Ned drove on—turning; we didn't pass the automobile at all. "Been crying again," he said. "A race-horse jockey and still aint growed out of crying."

"Shut up," I said. But he was turning the buggy again, on across the tracks and on along what would have been the other side of the Square if Parsham ever got big enough to have a Square, and stopped; we were in front of a store.

"Hold him," Ned said and got out and went in the store, not long, and came back with a paper sack and got in and took the lines, back toward home—I mean Uncle

Parsham's—now and with his free hand took from the big bag a small one; it was peppermint drops. "Here," he said. "I got some bananas too and soon as we get Lightning back to that private spring-branch paddock we uses, we can set down and eat um and then maybe I can get some sleep before I forget how to. And meanwhiles, stop fretting about that gal, now you done said your say to Boon Hogganbeck. Hitting a woman dont hurt her because a woman dont shove back at a lick like a man do; she just gives to it and then when your back is turned, reaches for the flatiron or the butcher knife. That's why hitting them dont break nothing; all it does is just black her eye or cut her mouf a little. And that aint nothing to a woman. Because why? Because what better sign than a black eye or a cut mouf can a woman want from a man that he got her on his mind?"

So once more, in the clutch of our respective starting grooms, McWillie and I sat our skittering and jockeying mounts behind that wire. (That's right, skittering and jockeying, Lightning too; at least he had learned—anyway remembered from yesterday—that he was supposed to be at least up with Acheron when the running started, even if he hadn't discovered yet that he was supposed—hoped—to be in front when it stopped.)

This time Ned's final instructions were simple, explicit, and succinct: "Just remember, I knows I can make him run once, and I believes I can make him run twice. Only, we wants to save that once I *knows*, until we knows we needs it. So here's what I want you to do for this first heat: Just before them judges and such hollers Go! you say to yourself *My name is Ned William McCaslin* and then do it."

"Do what?" I said.

"I dont know yet neither," he said. "But Akrum is a horse, and with a horse anything can happen. And with a nigger boy on him, it's twice as likely to. You just got to watch and be ready, so that when it do happen, you done already said *My name is Ned William McCaslin* and then do it and do it quick. And dont worry. If it dont work and dont nothing happen, I'll be waiting right there at the finish, where I come in. Because we knows I can make him run once."

Then the voice hollered Go! and our grooms sprang for their lives and we were off (as I said, we had drawn this time and McWillie had the pole). Or McWillie was off, that is. Because I dont remember: whether I had planned it or just did it by instinct, so that when McWillie broke, I was already braced and Lightning's first spring rammed him into the bridle all the way up to my shoulders, bad hand and all. Acheron already in full run and three lengths ahead when I let Lightning go, but still kept the three-length gap, both of us going now but three horses apart, when I saw McWillie do what you call nowadays a double-take: a single quick glance aside, using only his eyeballs, expecting to see me of course more or less at his knee, then seeming to drive on at full speed for another stride or so before his vision told his intelligence that Lightning and I were not there. Then he turned, jerked his whole head around to look back and I remember still the whites of his eyes and his open mouth; I could see him sawing frantically at Acheron to slow him; I sincerely believe I even heard him yell back at me: "Goddammit, white boy, if you gonter race, race!" the gap between us closing fast now because he now had Acheron wrenched back and crossways until he was now at right angles to the course, more or less filling the track sideways from rail to rail it looked like and facing the outside rail and for that moment, instant, second, motionless; I am convinced that McWillie's now frantic mind actually toyed with the idea of turning and running back until he could turn again with Lightning in front. Nor no premeditation, nothing: I just said in my mind *My name is Ned William McCaslin* and cut Lightning as hard as I could with the switch, pulling his head over so that when he sprang for the gap between Acheron's stern and the inside rail, we would scrape Acheron; I remember I thought *My leg will be crushed* and I sat there, the switch poised again, in complete detachment, waiting in nothing but curiosity for the blow, shock, crack, spurt of blood and bones or whatever it would be. But we had just exactly room enough or speed enough or maybe it was luck enough: not my leg but Lightning's hip which scraped across Acheron's buttocks: at which second I cut again with the switch as hard as I could. Nor any judge or steward, dog trainer, market hunter or murderer, nor purist or stickler of the most finicking and irreproachable, to affirm it was not my own mount I struck; in fact, we were so inextricable at that second that, of the four of us, only Acheron actually knew who had been hit.

Then on. I mean, Lightning and me. I didn't—couldn't —look back yet, so I had to wait to learn what happened. They said that Acheron didn't try to jump the rail at all: he just reared and fell through it in a kind of whirling dust of white planks, but still on his feet, frantic now, running more or less straight out into the pasture, spectators scattering before him, until McWillie wrenched him around; and they said that this time McWillie actually set him quartering at the fence (it was too late now to go back to the gap in it he had already made; we—Lightning —were too far ahead by this time) as though he were a hunter. But he refused it, running instead at full speed along the rail, but still on the outside of it, the spectators hollering and leaping like frogs from in front of him as he cleared his new path or precedent. That was when I began to hear him again. He—they: McWillie and Acheron—was closing fast now, though with the outside rail between us: Lightning with the whole track to himself now and going with that same fine strong rhythm and reach and power to which it had simply not occurred yet that there was any hurry about it; in the back stretch now and Acheron, who had already run at least one extra fifty yards and would have to run another one before he finished, already abreast of us beyond the rail; around the far turn of the first lap now and now I could actually see McWillie's desperate mind grappling frantically with the rapidly diminishing choice of whether to swing Acheron wide enough to bring him back through his self-made gap and onto the track again and have him refuse its jumbled wreckage, or play safe and stay where they were in the new track which they had already cleared of obstacles.

Conservatism won (as it should and does); again the back stretch (second lap now); now the far turn (second one also) and even on the outside longer curve, they were drawing ahead; there was the wire and Acheron a length at least ahead and I believe I thought for an instant of going to the whip just for the looks of the thing; on; our crowd was yelling now and who could blame them? few if any had seen a heat like this before between two horses running on opposite sides of the rail; on, Acheron still at top speed along his path as empty and open for him as the path to heaven; two lengths ahead when we—Lightning—passed under the wire, and (Acheron: evidently he liked running outside) already into his third lap when McWillie dragged him by main strength away and into the pasture and into a tightening circle which even he could no longer negotiate. And much uproar behind us now: shouts: "Foul! Foul! No! No! Yes! No heat! No heat! Yes it was! No it wasn't! Ask the judge! Ask Ed! What was it, Ed?"—that part of the crowd which Acheron had scattered from the outside rail now pouring across the track through the shattered gap to join the others in the infield; I was looking for Ned; I thought I saw him but it was Lycurgus, trotting up the track toward me until he could take Lightning's bit, already turning him back.

"Come on," he said. "You can stop. You got to cool him out. Mr McCaslin said to get him away from the track, take him over yonder to them locust trees where the buggy's at, where he can be quiet and we can rub him down." But I tried to hold back.

"What happened?" I said. "Is it going to count? We won, didn't we? We went under the wire. They just went around it. Here," I said, "you take him while I go back and see."

"No, I tell you," Lycurgus said. He had Lightning trotting now. "Mr McCaslin dont want you there neither. He said for me and you to stay right with Lightning and have him ready to run again; that next heat's in less than a hour now and we got to win that one now, because if this throws this one out, we got to win the next one no matter what happens." So we went on. He lifted down a rail at the end of the track and we went through, on to the clump of locust trees about two hundreds yards away; now I could see Uncle Parsham's buggy hitched to one of them. And I could still hear the voices from the judges' stand in the infield and I still wanted to go back and find out. But Lycurgus had forestalled that too: he had the pails and sponges and cloths and even a churn of water in the buggy for us to strip Lightning and go to work on him.

So I had to get my first information about what had happened (and was still happening too) from hearsay— what little Lycurgus had seen before Ned sent him to meet me, and from others later—before Ned came up: the uproar, vociferation of protest and affirmation (oh yes, even after losing two races—heats, whatever they were—last winter, and the first heat of this one yesterday, there were still people who had bet on Lightning. Because I was only eleven; I had not learned yet that no horse ever walked to post, provided he was still on his feet when he got there, that somebody didn't bet on), coming once or twice almost to blows, with Ned in the center of it, in effect the crux of it, polite and calm but dogged and insistent too, rebutting each attack: "It wasn't a race. It takes at least two horses to make a race, and one of these wasn't even on the track." And Ned:

"No sir. The rule book dont mention how many horses. It just talks about one horse at a time: that if it dont commit fouls and dont stop forward motion and the jockey dont fall off and it cross the finish line first, it wins." Then another:

"Then you just proved yourself that black won: it never fouled nothing but about twenty foot of that fence and it sho never stopped forward motion because I myself seen a least a hundred folks barely get out from under it in time and you yourself seen it pass that finish line a good two lengths ahead of that chestnut." And Ned:

"No sir. That finish wire just runs across that track from one rail to the other. It dont run on down into Missippi too. If it done that, there are horses down there been crossing it ever since sunup this morning that we aint even heard about yet. No sir. It's too bad about that little flimsy railing, but we was too busy running our horse to have time to stop and wait for that other one to come back." When suddenly three newcomers were on the scene, or anyway in the telling of it: not three strangers, because one of them was Colonel Linscomb himself and they all knew him since they were his neighbors. So probably what they meant was that the other two were simply his guests, city men too or very likely simply of Colonel Linscomb's age and obvious solvency and likewise wearing coats and neckties, who—one of them—seemed to take charge of the matter, coming into the crowd clamoring around Ned and the harassed officials and saying,

"Gentlemen, let me offer a solution. As this man"—meaning Ned—"says, his horse ran according to the rules and went under the wire first. Yet we all saw the other horse run the fastest race and was in the lead at the finish. The owners of the horses are these gentlemen right here behind me: Colonel Linscomb, your neighbor, and Mr van Tosch from Memphis, near enough to be your neighbor too when you get to know him better. They have agreed, and your judges will approve it, to put this heat that was just run, into what the bankers call escrow. You all have done business with bankers whether you wanted to or not"—they said he even paused for the guffaw, and got it—"and you know how they have a name for everything—"

"Interest on it too," a voice said, and so he got that guffaw free and joined it.

"What escrow means this time is, suspended. Not abolished or cancelled: just suspended. The bets still stand just as you made them; nobody won and nobody lost; you can increase them or hedge them or whatever you want to; the stake money for the last heat still stands and the owners are already adding another fifty a side for the next heat, the winner of this next heat to be the winner of the one that was just run. Win this next heat, and win all. What do you say?"

That's what I—we—Lycurgus and me—heard later. Right now we knew nothing: just waiting for Ned or somebody to come for us or send for us, Lightning cleaned and blanketed now and Lycurgus leading him up and down, keeping him moving, and I sitting against a tree with my riding-sock off to dry out my bandage; it seemed hours, forever, then in the next thinking it seemed no time, collapsed, condensed. Then Ned came up, walking fast. I told you how he had looked terrible this morning, but that was partly because of his clothes. His shirt was white (or almost) again now, and his pants were clean too. But it would not have been his clothes this time, even if they were still filthy. It was his face. He didn't look like he had seen a simple and innocent hant: he looked like he had without warning confronted Doom itself, except that Doom had said to him: *Calm down. It will be thirty or forty minutes yet before I will want you. Be ready then but in the meantime stop worrying and tend to your business.* But he gave me—us—no time. He went to the buggy and took his black coat out and put it on, already talking:

"They put it in what they calls escrow. That means whoever loses this next one has done lost everything. Tack up." But Lycurgus already had the blanket off; it didn't take us long. Then I was up, Ned standing at Lightning's head, holding the bridle with one hand, his other hand in the pocket of the coat, fumbling at something. "This one is gonter be easy for you. We nudged him a little yestiddy, then you fooled him bad today. So you aint gonter trick him again. But it wont matter. We wont need to trick him now; I'll tend to this one myself. All you got to do is, still be on him at the finish. Dont fall off: that's all you got to do until right at the last. Just keep him between them two rails, and dont fall off of him. Remember what he taught you Monday. When you comes around the first lap, and just before he will think about where I was standing Monday, hit him. Keep him going; dont worry about that other horse, no matter where he is or what he's doing: just tend to yourn. You mind that?"

"Yes," I said.

"All right. Then here's the onliest other thing you got to do. When you comes around the last lap and around the back turn into the home stretch toward that wire,

dont just believe, *know* that Lightning is where he can see
the whole track in front of him. When you get there, you
will know why. But before that, dont just think maybe he
can, or that by now he sholy ought to, but *know* he can
see that whole track right up to the wire and beyond it.
If that other horse is in front of you, pull Lightning all
the way across the track to the outside rail if you needs
to where there wont be nothing in the way to keep him
from seeing that wire and on beyond it too. Dont worry
about losing distance; just have Lightning where he can
see everything in front of him." His other hand was out
now; Lightning was nuzzling his nose into it again and
again I smelled that faint thin odor which I had smelled
in Uncle Parsham's pasture Monday, that I or anybody
else should recognise at once, and that I would recognise
if it would only happen when I had time. "Can you remember that?"

"Yes," I said.

"Then go on," he said. "Lead him on, Lycurgus."

"Aint you coming?" I said. Lycurgus pulled at the
bridle; he had to get Lightning's muzzle out of Ned's hand
by force; finally Ned had to put his hand back in his
pocket.

"Go on," he said. "You knows what to do." Lycurgus led
on; he had to for a while; Lightning even tried once to
whirl back until Lycurgus snatched him.

"Hit him a little," Lycurgus said. "Get his mind back on
what he's doing." So I did and we went on and so for the
third time McWillie and I crouched our poised thunder-
bolts behind that wire. McWillie's starting groom having
declined to be hurled to earth three times, and nobody
else either volunteering or even accepting conscription,
they used a piece of cotton-bagging jute stretched from
rail to rail in the hands of two more democrats facing each
other across the track. It was probably the best start we

had had yet. Acheron, who had thought nothing of diving through a six-inch plank, naturally wouldn't go within six feet of it, and Lightning, though with his nose almost touching it, was standing as still as a cow now, I suppose scanning the crowd for Ned, when the starter hollered Go! and the string dropped and in the same second Acheron and McWillie shot past us, McWillie shouting almost in my ear:

"I'll learn you this time, white boy!" and already gone, though barely a length before Lightning pulled obediently up to McWillie's knee—the power, the rhythm, everything in fact except that still nobody had told his head yet this was a race. And, in fact, for the first time, at least since I had participated, been a factor, we even looked like a race, the two horses as though bolted together and staggered a little, on into the back stretch of the first lap, our relative positions, in relation to our forward motion, changing and altering with almost dreamlike indolence, Acheron drawing ahead until it would look like he really was about to leave us, then Lightning would seem to notice the gap and close it. It would even look like a challenge; I could hear them along the rail, who didn't really know Lightning yet: that he just didn't want to be that far back by himself; on around the back turn and into the home stretch of the first lap and I give you my word Lightning came into it already looking for Ned; I give you my word he whinnied; going at a dead run, he whinnied: the first time I ever heard a horse nicker while running. I didn't even know they could.

I cut him as hard as I could. He broke, faltered, sprang again; we had already made McWillie a present of two lengths so I cut him again; we went into the second lap two lengths back and traveling now on the peeled switch until the gap between him and Acheron replaced Ned in what Lightning called his mind, and he closed it again until his head was once more at McWillie's knee, completely obedient but not one inch more—this magnificently equipped and organised organisation whose muscles had never been informed by their brain, or whose brain had never been informed by its outposts of observation and experience, that the sole aim and purpose of this entire frantic effort was to get somewhere first. McWillie was whipping now, so I didn't need to; he could no more have drawn away from Lightning than he could have dropped behind him, through the back stretch again and around the back turn again, me still on Lightning and Lightning still between the rails, so all that remained from here out were Ned's final instructions: to pull, ease him out, presenting McWillie again with almost another length, until nothing impeded his view of the track, the wire, and beyond it. He—Lightning—even saw Ned first. The first I knew was that neck-snapping surge and lunge as though he—Lightning—had burst through some kind of invisible band or yoke. Then I saw Ned myself, maybe forty yards beyond the wire, small and puny and lonely in the track's vacancy while Acheron and McWillie's flailing arm fled rapidly back to us; then McWillie's wrung face for an instant too, then gone too; the wire flashed overhead. "Come on, son," Ned said. "I got it."

He—Lightning—almost unloaded me stopping, cutting back across the track (Acheron was somewhere close behind us, trying—I hoped—to stop too) and went to Ned at that same dead run, bit bridle and all notwithstanding, and simply stopped running, his nose already buried in Ned's hand, and me up around his ears grabbing at whatever was in reach, sore hand too. "We did it!" I said, cried. "We did it! We beat him!"

"We done this part of it," Ned said. "Just hope to your stars it's gonter be enough." Because I had just ridden and won my first race, you see. I mean, a man-size race,

with people, grown people, more people than I could remember at one time before, watching me win it and
(some of them anyway) betting their money that I would.
Also, I didn't have time to notice, remark anything in his
face or voice or what he said, because they were already
through the rail and on the track, coming toward us: the
whole moil and teem of sweated hats and tieless shirts
and faces still gaped with yelling. "Look out now," Ned
said; and still to me, nothing: only the faces and the voices
like a sea:

"That's riding him, boy! That's bringing him in!" but
we not stopping, Ned leading Lightning on, saying,

"Let us through, Whitefolks; let us through, Whitefolks," until they gave back enough to let us go on, but
still moving along with us, like the wave, until we reached
the gate to the infield where the judges were waiting, and
Ned said again: "Look out, now"; and now I dont remember: only the stopped horse with Ned at the bit like a
tableau, and me looking past Lightning's ears at Grandfather leaning a little on his cane (the gold-headed one)
and two other people whom I had known somewhere a
long time ago just behind him.

"Boss," I said.

"What did you do to your hand?" he said.

"Yes sir," I said. "Boss."

"You're busy now," he said. "So am I." It was quite
kind, quite cold. No: it wasn't anything. "We'll wait until
we get home," he said. Then he was gone. Now the two
people were Sam and Minnie looking up at me with her
calm grim inconsolable face for it seemed to me a long
time while Ned was still pawing at my leg.

"Where's that tobacco sack I give you to keep yestiddy?" he said. "You sholy aint lost it?"

"Oh yes," I said, reaching it from my pocket.

13

◆◆◆◆

"Show them," Miss Reba told Minnie. They were in our—
I mean Boon's—no, I mean Grandfather's—automobile:
Everbe and Miss Reba and Minnie and Sam and Colonel
Linscomb's chauffeur; he was McWillie's father; Colonel
Linscomb had an automobile too. They—the chauffeur
and Sam and Minnie—had gone up to Hardwick to get
Miss Reba and Everbe and Boon and bring them all back
to Parsham, where Miss Reba and Minnie and Sam could
take the train for Memphis. Except that Boon didn't come
back with them. He was in jail again, the third time now,
and they had stopped at Colonel Linscomb's to tell Grandfather. Miss Reba told it, sitting in the car, with Grandfather and Colonel Linscomb and me standing around it
because she wouldn't come in; she told about Boon and
Butch.

"It was bad enough in the automobile going up there. But at least we had that deputy, let alone that little old constable you folks got that dont look like much but I'd say people dont fool around with him much either. When we got to Hardwick, they at least had sense enough to lock them in separate cells. The trouble was, they never had no way to lock up Corrie's new friend's mouth—" and stopped; and I didn't want to have to look at Everbe either: a big girl, too big for little things to have to happen to like the black eye or the cut mouth, whichever one she would have, unless maybe she wouldn't, couldn't, be content with less than both; sitting there, having to, without anywhere to go or room to do it even, with the slow painful blood staining up the cheek I could see from here. "I'm sorry, kid; forget it," Miss Reba said. "Where was I?"

"You were telling what Boon did this time," Grandfather said.

"Oh yes," Miss Reba said. "—locked them up in separate cells across the corridor and they were taking Corrie and me—sure; they treated us fine: just like ladies—down to the jailor's wife's room where we were going to stay, when what's-his-name—Butch—pipes up and says, 'Well, there's one thing about it: me and Sugar Boy lost some blood and skin and a couple of shirts too, but at least we got these excuse my French," Miss Reba said, " 'Memphis whores off the street.' So Boon started in right away to tear that steel door down but they had remembered to already lock it, so you would think that would have calmed him: you know: having to sit there and look at it for a while. Anyhow, we thought so. Then when Sam came with the right papers or whatever they were—and much obliged to you," she told Grandfather. "I dont know how much you had to put up, but if you'll send the bill to me when I get home, I'll attend to it. Boon knows the address and knows me."

"Thank you," Grandfather said. "If there's any charge, I'll let you know. What happened to Boon? You haven't told me yet."

"Oh yes. They unlocked What's-his-name first; that was the mistake, because they hadn't even got the key back out of Boon's lock before he was out of the cell and on—"

"Butch," I said.

"Butch," Miss Reba said. "—one good lick anyhow, knocked him down and was right on top of him before anybody woke up. So they never even let Boon stop; all the out he got was that trip across the corridor and back, into the cell and locked up again before they even had time to take the key out of the lock. But at least you got to admire him for it." But she stopped.

"For what?" I said.

"What did you say?" she said.

"What he did that we're going to admire him for. You didn't tell us that. What did he do?"

"You think that still trying to tear that—"

"Butch," I said.

"—Butch's head off before they even let him out of jail, aint nothing?" Miss Reba said.

"He had to do that," I said.

"I'll be damned," Miss Reba said. "Let's get started; we got to catch that train. You wont forget to send that bill," she told Grandfather.

"Get out and come in," Colonel Linscomb said. "Supper's about ready. You can catch the midnight train."

"No much obliged," Miss Reba said. "No matter how long your wife stays at Monteagle, she'll come back home some day and you'll have to explain it."

"Nonsense," Colonel Linscomb said. "I'm boss in my house."

"I hope you'll keep on being," Miss Reba said. "Oh

yes," she said to Minnie. "Show them." She—Minnie—didn't smile at us: she smiled at me. It was beautiful: the even, matched and matchless unblemished porcelain march, curving outward to embrace, almost with passion, the restored gold tooth which looked bigger than any three of the natural merely white ones possibly could. Then she closed her lips again, serene, composed, once more immune, once more invulnerable to that extent which our frail webs of bone and flesh and coincidence ever hold or claim on Invulnerability. "Well," Miss Reba said. McWillie's father cranked the engine and got back in; the automobile moved on. Grandfather and Colonel Linscomb turned and went back toward the house and I had begun to move too when the automobile horn tooted, not loud, once, and I turned back. It had stopped and Sam was standing beside it, beckoning to me.

"Come here," he said. "Miss Reba wants to see you a minute." He watched me while I came up. "Why didn't you and Ned tell me that horse was really going to run?" he said.

"I thought you knew," I said. "I thought that was why we came here."

"Sure, sure," he said. "Ned told me. You told me. Everybody told me. Only, why didn't somebody make me believe it? Oh sure, I never broke a leg. But if I'd just had Miss Reba's nerve, maybe I could have got that boxcar covered too. Here," he said. It was a tight roll of money, bills. "This is Ned's. Tell him the next time he finds a horse that wont run, not to wait to come and get me: just telegraph me." Miss Reba was leaning out, hard and handsome. Everbe was on the other side of her, not moving but still too big not to notice. Miss Reba said:

"I didn't expect to wind up in jail here too. But then, maybe I didn't expect not to, neither. Anyway, Sam bet for me too. I put up fifty for Mr Binford and five for

Minnie. Sam got three for two. I—I mean we—want to split fifty-fifty with you. I aint got that much cash now, what with this unexpected side trip I took this morning—"

"I dont want it," I said.

"I thought you'd say that," she said. "So I had Sam put up another five for you. You got seven-fifty coming. Here." She held out her hand.

"I dont want it," I said.

"What did I tell you?" Sam said.

"Is it because it was gambling?" she said. "Did you promise that too?" I hadn't. Maybe Mother hadn't thought about gambling yet. But I wouldn't have needed to have promised anybody anyway. Only, I didn't know how to tell her when I didn't know why myself: only that I wasn't doing it for money: that money would have been the last thing of all; that once we were in it, I had to go on, finish it, Ned and me both even if everybody else had quit; it was as though only by making Lightning run and run first could we justify (not escape consequences: simply justify) any of it. Not to hope to make the beginning of it any less wrong—I mean, what Boon and I had deliberately, of our own free will, to do back there in Jefferson four days ago; but at least not to shirk, dodge— at least to finish—what we ourselves had started. But I didn't know how to say it. So I said,

"Nome. I dont want it."

"Go on," Sam said. "Take it so we can go. We got to catch that train. Give it to Ned, or maybe to that old boy who took care of you last night. They'll know what to do with it." So I took the money; I had two rolls of it now, the big one and this little one. And still Everbe hadn't moved, motionless, her hands in her lap, big, too big for little things to happen to. "At least pat her on the head," Sam said. "Ned never taught you to kick dogs too, did he?"

"He wont though," Miss Reba said. "Watch him. Jesus, you men. And here's another one that aint but eleven years old. What the hell does one more matter? aint she been proving ever since Sunday she's quit? If you'd been sawing logs as long as she has, what the hell does one more log matter when you've already cancelled the lease and even took down the sign?" So I went around the car to the other side. Still she didn't move, too big for little things to happen to, too much of her to have to be the recipient of things petty and picayune, like bird splashes on a billboard or a bass drum; just sitting there, too big to shrink even, shamed (because Ned was right), her mouth puffed a little but mostly the black eye; with her, even a simple shiner was not content but must look bigger, more noticeable, more unhidable, than on anyone else.

"It's all right," I said.

"I thought I had to," she said. "I didn't know no other way."

"You see?" Miss Reba said. "How easy it is? That's all you need to tell us; we'll believe you. There aint the lousiest puniest bastard one of you, providing he's less than seventy years old, that cant make any woman believe there wasn't no other way."

"You did have to," I said. "We got Lightning back in time to run the race. It dont matter now any more. You better go on or you'll miss that train."

"Sure," Miss Reba said. "Besides, she's got supper to cook too. You aint heard that yet; that's the surprise. She aint going back to Memphis. She aint just reformed from the temptation business: she's reformed from temptation too, providing what they claim, is right: that there aint no temptation in a place like Parsham except a man's own natural hopes and appetites. She's got a job in Parsham washing and cooking and lifting his wife in and out of bed and washing her off, for that constable. So she's even reformed from having to divide half she makes and half she has with the first tin badge that passes, because all she'll have to do now is shove a coffeepot or a greasy skillet in the way. Come on," she told Sam. "Even you cant make that train wait from here."

Then they were gone. I turned and went back toward the house. It was big, with columns and porticoes and formal gardens and stables (with Lightning in one of them) and carriage houses and what used to be slave quarters—the (still is) old Parsham place, what remains of the plantation of the man, family, which gave its name to the town and the countryside and to some of the people too, like Uncle Parsham Hood. The sun was gone now, and soon the day would follow. And then, for the first time, I realised that it was all over, finished—all the four days of scuffling and scrabbling and dodging and lying and anxiety; all over except the paying-for. Grandfather and Colonel Linscomb and Mr van Tosch would be somewhere in the house now, drinking presupper toddies; it might be half an hour yet before the supper bell rang, so I turned aside and went through the rose garden and on to the back. And, sure enough, there was Ned sitting on the back steps.

"Here," I said, holding out the big roll of money. "Sam said this is yours." He took it. "Aint you going to count it?" I said.

"I reckon he counted it," Ned said. I took the little one from my pocket. Ned looked at it. "Did he give you that too?"

"Miss Reba did. She bet for me."

"It's gambling money," Ned said. "You're too young to have anything to do with gambling money. Aint nobody ever old enough to have gambling money, but you sho aint." And I couldn't tell him either. Then I realised that

I had expected him, Ned anyway, to already know without having to be told. And in the very next breath he did know. "Because we never done it for money," he said.

"You aint going to keep yours either?"

"Yes," he said. "It's too late for me. But it aint too late for you. I'm gonter give you a chance, even if it aint nothing but taking a chance away from you."

"Sam said I could give it to Uncle Parsham. But he wouldn't take gambling money either, would he?"

"Is that what you want to do with it?"

"Yes," I said.

"All right," he said. He took the little roll too and took out his snap purse and put both the rolls into it and now it was almost dark but I could certainly hear the supper bell here.

"How did you get the tooth back?" I said.

"It wasn't me," he said. "Lycurgus done it. That first morning, when I come back to the hotel to get you. It wasn't no trouble. The hounds had already treed him once, and Lycurgus said he thought at first he would just use them, put him up that gum sapling again and not call off the hounds until Whistle-britches wropped the tooth up in his cap or something, and dropped it. But Lycurgus said he was still a little rankled up over the upstarty notions Whistle-britches had about horses, mainly about Lightning. So, since Lightning was gonter have to run a race that afternoon and would need his rest, Lycurgus said he decided to use one of the mules. He said how Whistle-britches drawed a little old bitty pocketknife on him, but Lycurgus is gonter take good care of it until he can give it back to some of them." He stopped. He still looked bad. He still hadn't had any sleep. But maybe it is a relief to finally meet doom and have it set a definite moment to start worrying at.

"Well?" I said. "What?"

"I just told you. The mule done it."

"How?" I said.

"Lycurgus put Whistle-britches on the mule without no bridle or saddle and tied his feet underneath and told him any time he decided to wrop that tooth up in his cap and drop it off, he would stop the mule. And Lycurgus give the mule a light cut, and about halfway round the first circle of the lot Whistle-britches dropped the cap, only there wasn't nothing in it that time. So Lycurgus handed the cap back up to him and give the mule another cut and Lycurgus said he had disremembered that this was the mule that jumped fences until it had already jumped that four-foot bobwire and Lycurgus said it looked like it was fixing to take Whistle-britches right on back to Possum. But it never went far until it turned around and come back and jumped back into the lot again so next time Whistle-britches dropped the cap the tooth was in it. Only he might as well kept it, for all the good it done me. She went back to Memphis too, huh?"

"Yes," I said.

"That's what I figgered. Likely she knows as good as I do it's gonter be a long time before Memphis sees me or Boon Hogganbeck either again. And if Boon's back in jail again, I dont reckon Jefferson, Missippi's gonter see us tonight neither."

I didn't know either; and suddenly I knew that I didn't want to know; I not only didn't want to have to make any more choices, decisions, I didn't even want to know the ones being made for me until I had to face the results. Then McWillie's father came to the door behind us, in a white coat; he was the houseman too. Though I hadn't heard any bell. I had already washed (changed my clothes too; Grandfather had brought a grip for me, and even my other shoes), so the houseman showed me the way to the dining room and I stood there; Grandfather and Mr van Tosch and Colonel Linscomb came in, the old fat Llewellin setter walking at Colonel Linscomb's hand, and we all stood while Colonel Linscomb said grace. Then we sat down, the old setter beside Colonel Linscomb's chair, and ate, with not just Mc-Willie's father but a uniformed maid too to change the plates. Because I had quit; I wasn't making choices and decisions any more. I almost went to sleep in my plate, into the dessert, when Grandfather said:

"Well, gentlemen, shall the guard fire first?"

"We'll go to the office," Colonel Linscomb said. It was the best room I ever saw. I wished Grandfather had one like it. Colonel Linscomb was a lawyer too, so there were cases of law books, but there were farm- and horse-papers too and a glass case of jointed fishing rods and guns, and chairs and a sofa and a special rug for the old setter to lie on in front of the fireplace, and pictures of horses and jockeys on the walls, with the rose wreaths and the dates they won, and a bronze figure of Manassas (I didn't know until then that Colonel Linscomb was the one who had owned Manassas) on the mantel, and a special table for the big book which was his stud book, and another table with a box of cigars and a decanter and water pitcher and sugar bowl and glasses already on it, and a French window that opened onto the gallery above the rose garden so that you could smell the roses even in the house, and honeysuckle too and a mockingbird some-where outside.

Then the houseman came back with Ned and set a chair at the corner of the hearth for him, and they—we—sat down—Colonel Linscomb in a white linen suit and Mr van Tosch in the sort of clothes they wore in Chicago (which was where he came from until he visited Memphis and liked it and bought a place to breed and raise and train race horses too, and gave Bobo Beauchamp a job on it five or six years ago) and Grandfather in the Confederate-gray pigeon-tailed suit that he inherited (I mean, inherited not the suit but the Confederate gray because he hadn't been a soldier himself; he was only fourteen in Carolina, the only child, so he had to stay with his mother while his father was a color sergeant of Wade Hampton's until a picket of Fitz-John Porter's shot him out of his saddle at one of the Chickahominy crossings the morning after Gaines's Mill, and Grandfather stayed with his mother until she died in 1864, and still stayed until General Sherman finally eliminated him completely from Carolina in 1865 and he came to Mississippi hunting for the descendants of a distant kinsman named McCaslin—he and the kinsman even had the same baptismal names: Lucius Quintus Carothers—and found one in the person of a great-granddaughter named Sarah Edmonds and in 1869 married her).

"Now," Grandfather told Ned, "begin at the beginning."

"Wait," Colonel Linscomb said. He leaned and poured whiskey into a glass and held it out toward Ned. "Here," he said.

"Thank you kindly," Ned said. But he didn't drink it. He set the glass on the mantel and sat down again. He had never looked at Grandfather and he didn't now: he just waited.

"Now," Grandfather said.

"Drink it," Colonel Linscomb said. "You may need it." So Ned took the drink and swallowed it at one gulp and sat holding the empty glass, still not looking at Grandfather.

"Now," Grandfather said. "Begin—"

"Wait," Mr van Tosch said. "How did you make that horse run?"

Ned sat perfectly still, the empty glass motionless in

his hand while we watched him, waiting. Then he said, addressing Grandfather for the first time: "Will these white gentlemen excuse me to speak to you private?"

"What about?" Grandfather said.

"You will know," Ned said. "If you thinks they ought to know too, you can tell them."

Grandfather rose. "Will you excuse us?" he said. He started toward the door to the hall.

"Why not the gallery?" Colonel Linscomb said. "It's dark there; better for conspiracy or confession either." So we went that way. I mean, I was already up too. Grandfather paused again. He said to Ned:

"What about Lucius?"

"He used it too," Ned said. "Anybody got a right to know what his benefits is." We went out onto the gallery, into the darkness and the smell of the roses and the honeysuckle too, and besides the mockingbird which was in a tree not far away, we could hear two whippoor-wills and, as always at night in Mississippi and so Tennessee wasn't too different, a dog barking. "It was a sour dean," Ned said quietly.

"Don't lie to me," Grandfather said. "Horses dont eat sardines."

"This one do," Ned said. "You was there and saw it. Me and Lucius tried him out beforehand. But I didn't even need to try him first. As soon as I laid eyes on him last Sunday, I knowed he had the same kind of sense my mule had."

"Ah," Grandfather said. "So that's what you and Maury used to do to that mule."

"No sir," Ned said. "Mr Maury never knowed it neither. Nobody knowed it but me and that mule. This horse was just the same. When he run that last lap this evening, I had that sour dean waiting for him and he knowed it."

We went back inside. They were already looking at

us. "Yes," Grandfather said. "But it's a family secret. I wont withhold it if it becomes necessary. But will you let me be the judge, under that stipulation? Of course, Van Tosch has the first claim on it."

"In that case, I'll either have to buy Ned or sell you Coppermine," Mr van Tosch said. "But shouldn't all this wait until your man Hogganbeck is here too?"

"You dont know my man Hogganbeck," Grandfather said. "He drove my automobile to Memphis. When I take him out of jail tomorrow, he will drive it back to Jefferson. Between those two points in time, his presence would have been missed no more than his absence is." Only this time he didn't have to even start to tell Ned to begin.

"Bobo got mixed up with a white man," Ned said. And this time it was Mr van Tosch who said Ah. And that was how we began to learn it: from Ned and Mr van Tosch both. Because Mr van Tosch was an alien, a foreigner, who hadn't lived in our country long enough yet to know the kind of white blackguard a young country-bred Negro who had never been away from home before, come to a big city to get more money and fun for the work he intended to do, would get involved with. It was probably gambling, or it began with gambling; that would be their simplest mutual meeting ground. But by this time, it was more than just gambling; even Ned didn't seem to know exactly what it was—unless maybe Ned did know exactly what it was, but it was in a white man's world. Anyway, according to Ned, it was by now so bad—the money sum involved was a hundred and twenty-eight dollars—that the white man had convinced Bobo that, if the law found out about it, merely being fired from his job with Mr van Tosch would be the least of Bobo's troubles; in fact, he had Bobo believing that his real trouble wouldn't even start until after he no longer had a white man to front for him. Until at last, the situation, crisis, so desperate and the threat so great, Bobo went to Mr van Tosch and asked for a hundred and twenty-eight dollars, getting the answer which he had probably expected from the man who was not only a white man and a foreigner, but settled too, past the age when he could remember a young man's passions and predicaments, which was No. That was last fall—

"I remember that," Mr van Tosch said. "I ordered the man never to come on my place again. I thought he was gone." You see what I mean. He—Mr van Tosch—was a good man. But he was a foreigner. —Then Bobo, abandoned by that last hope, which he had never really believed in anyway, "got up" as he put it (Ned didn't know how either or perhaps he did know or perhaps the way in which Bobo "got it up" was such that he wouldn't even tell a member of his own race who was his kinsman too) fifteen dollars and gave it to the man, and bought with it just what you might expect and what Bobo himself probably expected. But what else could he do, where else turn? only more threat and pressure, having just proved that he could get money when driven hard enough— "But why didn't he come to me?" Mr van Tosch said.

"He did," Ned said. "You told him No." They sat quite still. "You're a white man," Ned said gently. "Bobo was a nigger boy."

"Then why didn't he come to me," Grandfather said. "Back where he should never have left in the first place, instead of stealing a horse?"

"What would you a done?" Ned said. "If he had come in already out of breath from Memphis and told you, Dont ask me no questions: just hand me a hundred and a few extra dollars and I'll go back to Memphis and start paying you back the first Saturday I gets around to it?"

"He could have told me why," Grandfather said, "I'm a McCaslin too."

"You're a white man too," Ned said.

"Go on," Grandfather said. —So Bobo discovered that the fifteen dollars which he had thought might save him, had actually ruined him. Now, according to Ned, Bobo's demon gave him no rest at all. Or perhaps the white man began to fear Bobo—that a mere dribble, a few dollars at a time, would take too long; or perhaps that Bobo, because of his own alarm and desperation, plus what the white man doubtless considered the natural ineptitude of Bobo's race, would commit some error or even crime which would blow everything up. Anyway, this was when he—the white man—began to work on Bobo to try for a one-stroke killing which would rid him of the debt, creditor, worry and all. His first idea was to have Bobo rifle Mr van Tosch's tack room, load into the buggy or wagon or whatever it would be, as many saddles and bridles and driving harnesses as it would carry, and clear out; Bobo of course would be suspected at once, but the white man would be safely away by then; and if Bobo moved fast enough, which even he should have the sense to do, he had all the United States to flee into and find another job. But (Ned said) even the white man abandoned this one; he would not only have a buggy- or wagon-load of horseless horse gear and daylight coming, it would have taken days to dispose of it piecemeal, even if he had had days to do it in.

So that was when they thought of a horse: to condense the wagon- or buggy-load of uncohered fragments of leather into one entity which could be sold in a lump, and—if the white man worked fast enough and didn't haggle over base dollars—without too much delay. That is, the white man, not Bobo, believed that Bobo was going to steal a horse for him. Only, Bobo knew, if he didn't steal the horse, he could see the end of everything —job, liberty, all—when next Monday morning (the crisis had reached its crux last Saturday, the same day Boon and I—and Ned—left Jefferson in the automobile) came. And the reason for the crisis at this particular moment, what made it so desperate, was that there was a horse of Mr van Tosch's so available for safe stealing that it might almost have been planted for that purpose. This of course was Lightning (I mean, Coppermine) himself, who at the moment was in a sales stable less than half a mile away, where, as Mr van Tosch's known groom (it was Bobo who had delivered the horse to the sales stable in the first place) Bobo could go and get him at any time for no more trouble than putting a halter on him and leading him away. Which by itself might have been tolerable. The trouble was, the white man knew it—a horse bred and trained for running, but which would not run, and which in consequence was in such bad repute with Mr van Tosch and Mr Clapp, the trainer, that it was at the sales stable waiting for the first to come along who would make an offer for it; in further consequence of which, Bobo could go and remove it and it would very likely not even be reported to Mr van Tosch unless he happened to inquire; in still further consequence of which, Bobo had until tomorrow morning (Monday) to do something about it, or else.

That was the situation when Ned left us in front of Miss Reba's Sunday afternoon and walked around the corner to Beale Street and entered the first blind tiger he came to and found Bobo trying to outface his doom through the bottom of a whiskey bottle. Grandfather said:

"So that's what it was. Now I'm beginning to understand. A nigger Saturday night. Bobo already drunk, and your tongue hanging out all the way from Jefferson to get to the first saloon you could reach—" and stopped and said, pounced almost: "Wait. That's wrong. It wasn't even Saturday. You got to Memphis Sunday evening," and Ned sitting there, quite still, the empty glass in his hand. He said,

"With my people, Saturday night runs over into Sunday."

"And into Monday morning too," Colonel Linscomb said. "You wake up Monday morning, sick, with a hangover, filthy in a filthy jail, and lie there until some white man comes and pays your fine and takes you straight back to the cotton field or whatever it is and puts you back to work without even giving you time to eat breakfast. And you sweat it out there, and maybe by sundown you feel you are not really going to die; and the next day, and the day after that, and after that, until it's Saturday again and you can put down the plow or the hoe and go back as fast as you can to that stinking jail cell on Monday morning. Why do you do it? I dont know."

"You cant know," Ned said. "You're the wrong color. If you could just be a nigger one Saturday night, you wouldn't never want to be a white man again as long as you live."

"All right," Grandfather said. "Go on." —So Bobo told Ned of his predicament: the horse less than half a mile away, practically asking to be stolen; and the white man who knew it and who had given Bobo an ultimatum measurable now in mere hours— "All right," Grandfather said. "Now get to my automobile."

"We're already to it," Ned said. They—he and Bobo— went to the stable to look at the horse. "And soon as I laid eyes on him, I minded that mule I used to own." And Bobo, like me, was too young actually to remember the mule; but, also like me, he had grown up with its legend. "So we decided to go to that white man and tell him something had happened and Bobo couldn't get that horse outen that stable for him like Bobo thought he could, but we could get him a automobile in place of it. —Now, wait," he told Grandfather quickly. "We knowed as good as you that that automobile would be safe at least long enough for us to finish. Maybe in thirty or forty years you can stand on a Jefferson street corner and count a dozen automobiles before sundown, but you cant yet. Maybe then you can steal a automobile and find somebody to buy it that wont worry you with a lot of how-come and who and why. But you cant now. So for a man that looked like I imagined he looked (I hadn't never seen him yet) to travel around trying to sell a automobile quick and private, would be about as hard as selling a elephant quick and private. You never had no trouble locating where it was at and getting your hand on it, once you and Mr van Tosch got started, did you?"

"Go on," Grandfather said. Ned did.

"Then the white man would ask what automobile? and Bobo would let me tend to that; and then the white man would maybe ask what I'm doing in it nohow, and then Bobo would tell him that I want that horse because I know how to make it run; that we already got a match race waiting Tuesday, and if the white man wanted, he could come along too and win enough on the horse to pay back three or four times them hundred and thirteen dollars, and then he wouldn't even have to worry with the automobile if he didn't want to. Because he would be the kind of a white man that done already had enough experience to know what would sell easy and what would be a embarrassment to get caught with. So that's what we were gonter do until yawl come and ruint it: let that white man just watch the first heat without betting yes or no, which he would likely do, and see Lightning lose it like he always done, which the white man would a heard all about too, by now; then we would say Nemmine, just wait to the next heat, and then bet him the horse against the automobile on that one without needing to remind him that when Lightning got beat this time, he would own him too." They—Grandfather and Colonel Linscomb and Mr van Tosch—looked at Ned. I wont try to describe their expressions. I cant. "Then yawl come and ruint it," Ned said.

"I see," Mr van Tosch said. "It was all just to save Bobo. Suppose you had failed to make Coppermine run, and lost him too. What about Bobo then?"

"I made him run," Ned said. "You seen it."

"But just suppose, for the sake of the argument," Mr van Tosch said.

"That would a been Bobo's lookout," Ned said. "It wasn't me advised him to give up Missippi cotton farming and take up Memphis frolicking and gambling for a living in place of it."

"But I thought Mr Priest said he's your cousin," Mr van Tosch said.

"Everybody got kinfolks that aint got no more sense than Bobo," Ned said.

"Well," Mr van Tosch said.

"Let's all have a toddy," Colonel Linscomb said briskly. He got up and mixed and passed them. "You too," he told Ned. Ned brought his glass and Colonel Linscomb poured. This time when Ned set the untasted glass on the mantel, nobody said anything.

"Yes," Mr van Tosch said. Then he said: "Well, Priest, you've got your automobile. And I've got my horse. And maybe I frightened that damn scoundrel enough to stay clear of my stable hands anyway." They sat there. "What shall I do about Bobo?" They sat there. "I'm asking you," Mr van Tosch said to Ned.

"Keep him," Ned said. "Folks—boys and young men anyhow—in my people dont convince easy—"

"Why just Negroes?" Mr van Tosch said.

"Maybe he means McCaslins," Colonel Linscomb said.

"That's right," Ned said. "McCaslins and niggers both act like the mixtry of the other just makes it worse. Right now I'm talking about young folks, even if this one is a nigger McCaslin. Maybe they dont hear good. Anyhow, they got to learn for themselves that roguishness dont pay. Maybe Bobo learnt it this time. Aint that easier for you than having to break in a new one?"

"Yes," Mr van Tosch said. They sat there. "Yes," Mr van Tosch said again. "So I'll either have to buy Ned, or sell you Coppermine." They sat there. "Can you make him run again, Ned?"

"I made him run that time," Ned said.

"I said, again," Mr van Tosch said. They sat there. "Priest," Mr van Tosch said, "do you believe he can do it again?"

"Yes," Grandfather said.

"How much do you believe it?" They sat there.

"Are you addressing me as a banker or a what?" Grandfather said.

"Call it a perfectly normal and natural northwest Mississippi countryman taking his perfectly normal and natural God-given and bill-of-rights-defended sabbatical among the fleshpots of southwestern Tennessee," Colonel Linscomb said.

"All right," Mr van Tosch said. "I'll bet you Coppermine against Ned's secret, one heat of one mile. If Ned can make Coppermine beat that black of Linscomb's again, I get the secret and Coppermine is yours. If Coppermine loses, I dont want your secret and you take or leave Coppermine for five hundred dollars—"

"That is, if he loses, I can have Coppermine for five

hundred dollars, or if I pay you five hundred dollars, I dont have to take him," Grandfather said.

"Right," Mr van Tosch said. "And to give you a chance to hedge, I will bet you two dollars to one that Ned cant make him run again." They sat there.

"So I've either got to win that horse or buy him in spite of anything I can do," Grandfather said.

"Or maybe you didn't have a youth," Mr van Tosch said. "But try to remember one. You're among friends here; try for a little while not to be a banker. Try." They sat there.

"Two-fifty," Grandfather said.

"Five," Mr van Tosch said.

"Three-fifty," Grandfather said.

"Five," Mr van Tosch said.

"Four-and-a-quarter," Grandfather said.

"Five," Mr van Tosch said.

"Four-fifty," Grandfather said.

"Four-ninety-five," Mr van Tosch said.

"Done," Grandfather said.

"Done," Mr van Tosch said.

So for the fourth time McWillie on Acheron and I on Lightning (I mean Coppermine) skittered and jockeyed behind that taut little frail jute string. McWillie wasn't speaking to me at all now; he was frightened and outraged, baffled and determined; he knew that something had happened yesterday which should not have happened; which in a sense should not have happened to anyone, certainly not to a nineteen-year-old boy who was simply trying to win what he had thought was a simple horse race: no holds barred, of course, but at least a mutual agreement that nobody would resort to necromancy. We had not drawn for position this time. We—McWillie and I—had been offered the privilege, but Ned said at once: "Nemmine this time. McWillie needs to feel better after yesterday, so let him have the pole where he can start feeling better now." Which, from rage or chivalry, I didn't know which, McWillie refused, bringing us to what appeared insoluble impasse, until the official—the pending homicide one—solved it quick by saying,

"Here, you boys, if you aim to run this race, get on up behind that-ere bagging twine where you belong." Nor had Ned gone through his preliminary incantation or ritual of rubbing Lightning's muzzle. I dont say, forgot to; Ned didn't forget things. So obviously I hadn't been watching, noticing closely enough; anyway, it was too late now. Nor had he given me any last-minute instructions this time either; but then, what was there for him to say? And last night Mr van Tosch and Colonel Linscomb and Grandfather had agreed that, since this was a private running, almost you might say a grudge match, effort should be made and all concerned cautioned to keep it private. Which would have been as easy to do in Parsham as to keep tomorrow's weather private and restricted to Colonel Linscomb's pasture, since—a community composed of one winter-resort hotel and two stores and a cattle chute and depot at a railroad intersection and the churches and schools and scattered farmhouses of a remote countryside—any news, let alone word of any horse race, not to mention a repeat between these two horses, spread across Parsham as instantaneously as weather does. So they were here today too, including the night-telegraphist judge who really should sleep sometimes: not as many as yesterday, but a considerable more than Grandfather and Mr van Tosch had given the impression of wanting—the stained hats, the tobacco, the tieless shirts and overalls—when somebody hollered Go! and the string snatched away and we were off.

We were off, McWillie as usual two strides out before Lightning seemed to notice we had started, and pulled quickly and obediently up until he could more or less lay his cheek against McWillie's knee (in case he wanted to), near turn, back stretch, mine and McWillie's juxtaposition altering, closing and opening with that dreamlike and unhurried quality probably quite familiar to people who fly aeroplanes in close formation; far turn and into the stretch for the first lap, I by simple rote whipping Lightning onward about one stride before he would remember to begin to look for Ned; I took one quick raking glance at the faces along the rail looking for Ned's and Lightning ran that whole stretch not watching where he was going at all but scanning the rush of faces for Ned's, likewise in vain; near turn again, the back stretch again and into the far turn, the home stretch; I was already swinging Lightning out toward the outside rail where (Acheron might be beating us but at least he wouldn't obstruct our view) he could see. But if he had seen Ned this time, he didn't tell me. Nor could I tell him, Look! Look yonder! There he is! because Ned wasn't there: only the vacant track beyond the taut line of the wire as fragile-looking as a filtered or maybe attenuated moonbeam, McWillie whipping furiously now and Lightning responding like a charm, exactly one neck back; if Acheron had known any way to run sixty miles an hour, we would too— one neck back; if Acheron had decided to stop ten feet before the wire, so would we—one neck back. But he didn't. We went on, still paired but staggered a little, as though bolted together; the wire flicked overhead, McWillie and I speaking again now—that is, he was, yelling back at me in a kind of cannibal glee: "Yah-yah-yah, yah-yah-yah," slowing also but not stopping, going straight on (I suppose) to the stable; he and Acheron certainly deserved to. I turned Lightning and walked back. Ned was trotting toward us, Grandfather behind him though not trotting; our sycophants and adulators of yesterday had abandoned us; Caesar was not Caesar now.

"Come on," Ned said, taking the bit, rapid but calm: only impatient, almost inattentive. "Hand—"

"What happened?" Grandfather said. "What the devil happened?"

"Nothing," Ned said. "I never had no sour dean for him this time, and he knowed it. Didn't I tell you this horse got sense?" Then to me: "There's Bobo over yonder waiting. Hand this plug back to him so he can take it on to Memphis. We're going home tonight."

"But wait," I said. "Wait."

"Forget this horse," Ned said. "We dont want him. Boss has got his automobile back and all he lost was four hundred and ninety-six dollars and it's worth four hundred and ninety-six dollars not to own this horse. Because what in the world would we do with him, supposing they was to quit making them stinking little fishes? Let Mr van Man have him back; maybe some day Coppermine will tell him and Bobo what happened here yesterday."

We didn't go home tonight though. We were still at Colonel Linscomb's, in the office again, after supper again. Boon looked battered and patched up and a considerable subdued, but he was calm and peaceful enough. And clean too: he had shaved and had on a fresh shirt. I mean, a new shirt that he must have bought in Hardwick, sitting on the same straight hard chair Ned had sat on last night.

"Naw," he said. "I wasn't fighting him about that. I wasn't even mad about that no more. That was her business. Besides, you cant just cut right off: you got to—got—"

"Taper off?" Grandfather said.

"No sir," Boon said. "Not taper off. You quit, only you still got to clean up the trash, litter, no matter how good you finished. It wasn't that. What I aimed to break his neck for was for calling my wife a whore."

"You mean you're going to marry her?" Grandfather said. But it was not Grandfather: it was me that Boon pounced, almost jumped at.

"God damn it," he said, "if you can go bare-handed against a knife defending her, why the hell cant I marry her? Aint I as good as you are, even if I aint eleven years old?"

And that's about all. About six the next afternoon we came over the last hill, and there was the clock on the courthouse above the trees around the Square. Ned said, "Hee hee hee." He was in front with Boon. He said: "Seems like I been gone two years."

"When Delphine gets through with you tonight, maybe you'll wish you had," Grandfather said.

"Or maybe not come back a-tall," Ned said. "But a woman, got to keep sweeping and cooking and washing and dusting on her mind all day long, I reckon she needs a little excitement once in a while."

Then we were there. The automobile stopped. I didn't move. Grandfather got out, so I did too. "Mr. Ballott's got the key," Boon said.

"No he hasn't," Grandfather said. He took the key from his pocket and gave it to Boon. "Come on," he said. We crossed the street toward home. And do you know what I thought? I thought *It hasn't even changed*. Because it should have. It should have been altered, even if only a little. I dont mean it should have changed of itself, but that I, bringing back to it what the last four days must have changed in me, should have altered it. I mean, if those four days—the lying and deceiving and tricking and decisions and undecisions, and the things I had done and seen and heard and learned that Mother and Father wouldn't have let me do and see and hear and learn—

the things I had had to learn that I wasn't even ready for yet, had nowhere to store them nor even anywhere to lay them down; if all that had changed nothing, was the same as if it had never been—nothing smaller or larger or older or wiser or more pitying—then something had been wasted, thrown away, spent for nothing; either it was wrong and false to begin with and should never have existed, or I was wrong or false or weak or anyway not worthy of it.

"Come on," Grandfather said—not kind, not unkind, not anything; I thought *If Aunt Callie would just come out whether she's carrying Alexander or not and start hollering at me*. But nothing: just a house I had known since before I could have known another, at a little after six oclock on a May evening, when people were already thinking about supper; and Mother should have had a few gray hairs at least, kissing me for a minute, then looking at me; then Father, whom I had always been a little . . . afraid is not the word but I cant think of another—afraid of because if I hadn't been, I think I would have been ashamed of us both. Then Grandfather said, "Maury."

"Not this time, Boss," Father said. Then to me: "Let's get it over with."

"Yes sir," I said, and followed him, on down the hall to the bathroom and stopped at the door while he took the razor strop from the hook and I stepped back so he could come out and we went on; Mother was at the top of the cellar stairs; I could see the tears, but no more; all she had to do would be to say Stop or Please or Maury or maybe if she had just said Lucius. But nothing, and I followed Father on down and stopped again while he opened the cellar door and we went in, where we kept the kindling in winter and the zinc-lined box for ice in summer, and Mother and Aunt Callie had shelves for preserves and jelly and jam, and even an old rocking chair for Mother and Aunt Callie while they were putting up the jars, and for Aunt Callie to sleep in sometimes after dinner, though she always said she hadn't been asleep. So here we were at last, where it had taken me four days of dodging and scrabbling and scurrying to get to; and it was wrong, and Father and I both knew it. I mean, if after all the lying and deceiving and disobeying and conniving I had done, all he could do about it was to whip me, then Father was not good enough for me. And if all that I had done was balanced by no more than that shaving strop, then both of us were debased. You see? it was impasse, until Grandfather knocked. The door was not locked, but Grandfather's father had taught him, and he had taught Father, and Father had taught me that no door required a lock: the closed door itself was sufficient until you were invited to enter it. But Grandfather didn't wait, not this time.

"No," Father said. "This is what you would have done to me twenty years ago."

"Maybe I have more sense now," Grandfather said. "Persuade Alison to go on back upstairs and stop snivelling." Then Father was gone, the door closed again. Grandfather sat in the rocking chair: not fat, but with just the right amount of paunch to fill the white waistcoat and make the heavy gold watch chain hang right.

"I lied," I said.

"Come here," he said.

"I cant," I said. "I lied, I tell you."

"I know it," he said.

"Then do something about it. Do anything, just so it's something."

"I cant," he said.

"There aint anything to do? Not anything?"

"I didn't say that," Grandfather said. "I said I couldn't. You can."

"What?" I said. "How can I forget it? Tell me how to."

"You cant," he said. "Nothing is ever forgotten. Nothing is ever lost. It's too valuable."

"Then what can I do?"

"Live with it," Grandfather said.

"Live with it? You mean, forever? For the rest of my life? Not ever to get rid of it? Never? I cant. Dont you see I cant?"

"Yes you can," he said. "You will. A gentleman always does. A gentleman can live through anything. He faces anything. A gentleman accepts the responsibility of his actions and bears the burden of their consequences, even when he did not himself instigate them but only acquiesced to them, didn't say No though he knew he should. Come here." Then I was crying hard, bawling, standing (no: kneeling; I was that tall now) between his knees, one of his hands at the small of my back, the other at the back of my head holding my face down against his stiff collar and shirt and I could smell him—the starch and shaving lotion and chewing tobacco and benzine where Grandmother or Delphine had cleaned a spot from his coat, and always a faint smell of whiskey which I always believed was from the first toddy which he took in bed in the morning before he got up. When I slept with him, the first thing in the morning would be Ned (he had no white coat; sometimes he didn't have on any coat or even a shirt, and even after Grandfather sent the horses to stay at the livery stable, Ned still managed to smell like them) with the tray bearing the decanter and water jug and sugar bowl and spoon and tumbler, and Grandfather would sit up in bed and make the toddy and drink it, then put a little sugar into the heel-tap and stir it and add a little water and give it to me until Grand-

mother came suddenly in one morning and put a stop
to it. "There," he said at last. "That should have emptied
the cistern. Now go wash your face. A gentleman cries
too, but he always washes his face."

And this is all. It was Monday afternoon, after school
(Father wouldn't let Mother write me an excuse, so I
had to take the absent marks. But Miss Rhodes was going
to let me make up the work) and Ned was sitting on the
back steps again, Grandmother's steps this time, but in
the shade this time too. I said:

"If we'd just thought to bet that money Sam gave us
on Lightning that last time, we could have settled what
to do about it good."

"I did settle it good," Ned said. "I got five for three this
time. Old Possum Hood's got twenty dollars for his church
now."

"But we lost," I said.

"You and Lightning lost," Ned said. "Me and that
money was on Akrum."

"Oh," I said. Then I said, "How much was it?" He
didn't move. I mean, he didn't do anything. I mean, he
looked no different at all; it might have been last Friday
instead of this one; all the four days of dodging and
finagling and having to guess right and guess fast and
not having but one guess to do it with, had left no mark
on him, even though I had seen him once when he not
only had had no sleep, he didn't even have any clothes to
wear. (You see, how I keep on calling it four days? It was
Saturday afternoon when Boon and I—we thought—
left Jefferson, and it was Friday afternoon when Boon
and Ned and I saw Jefferson again. But to me, it was
the four days between that Saturday night at Miss
Ballenbaugh's when Boon would have gone back home
tomorrow if I had said so, and the moment when I looked
down from Lightning Wednesday and saw Grandfather

and passed to him, during which Ned had carried the load alone, held back the flood, shored up the crumbling levee with whatever tools he could reach—including me— until they broke in his hand. I mean, granted we had no business being behind that levee: a gentleman always sticks to his lie whether he told it or not.) And I was only eleven; I didn't know how I knew that too, but I did: that you never ask anyone how much he won or lost gambling. So I said: "I mean, would there be enough to pay back Boss his four hundred and ninety-six dollars?" And he still sat there, unchanged; so why should Mother have a gray hair since I saw her last? since I would have to be unchanged too? Because now I knew what Grandfather meant: that your outside is just what you live in, sleep in, and has little connection with who you are and even less with what you do. Then he said:

"You learned a considerable about folks on that trip; I'm just surprised you aint learnt more about money too. Do you want Boss to insult me, or do you want me to insult Boss, or do you want both?"

"How do you mean?" I said.

"When I offers to pay his gambling debt, aint I telling him to his face he aint got enough sense to bet on horses? And when I tells him where the money come from I'm gonter pay it with, aint I proving it?"

"I still dont see where the insult to you comes in," I said.

"He might take it," Ned said.

Then the day came at last. Everbe sent for me and I walked across town to the little back-street almost doll-size house that Boon was buying by paying Grandfather fifty cents every Saturday. She had a nurse and she should have been in bed. But she was sitting up, waiting for me, in a wrapper; she even walked across to the cradle and stood with her hand on my shoulder while we looked at it.

"Well?" she said. "What do you think?"

I didn't think anything. It was just another baby, already as ugly as Boon even if it would have to wait twenty years to be as big. I said so. "What are you going to call it?"

"Not it," she said. "Him. Cant you guess?"

"What?" I said.

"His name is Lucius Priest Hogganbeck," she said.

"For range of effect, philosophical weight, originality of style, variety of characterization, humor, and tragic intensity, Faulkner's works are without equal in our time and country."

—Robert Penn Warren

Absalom, Absalom!

One of Faulkner's finest achievements, *Absalom, Absalom!* is the story of Thomas Sutpen and his ruthless, single-minded pursuit of his grand design—to forge a dynasty in Jefferson, Mississippi, in 1830—which is ultimately destroyed (along with Sutpen himself) by his own sons.

Fiction/Literature/0-679-73218-7

As I Lay Dying

As I Lay Dying is Faulkner's harrowing and deeply affecting account of the Bundren family's odyssey across the Mississippi countryside to bury Addie, their wife and mother. Told in turns by each of the family members—including Addie herself—the novel ranges in mood from dark comedy to the deepest pathos.

Fiction/Literature/0-679-73225-x

A Fable

Winner of the Pulitzer and the National Book Award, this allegorical novel about World War I is set in the trenches in France and deals with a mutiny in a French regiment.

Fiction/Literature/0-394-72413-5

Go Down, Moses

Composed of seven interrelated stories (including the acclaimed "The Bear"), all of them set in Faulkner's mythic Yoknapatawpha County, *Go Down, Moses* reveals the complex, changing relationships between blacks and whites, between man and nature, weaving a cohesive novel rich in implication and insight.

Fiction/Literature/0-679-73217-9

If I Forget Thee, Jerusalem [The Wild Palms]

In Depression-era New Orleans, two lovers set forth on an odyssey of illicit passion. Ten years earlier a convict risks his one chance for freedom to rescue a pregnant woman from the flooded Mississippi. These two stories, alternately woven, describe desperate people, attempting to escape the poverty and seething violence of a world from which there is no escape.

Fiction/Literature/0-679-74193-3

Intruder in the Dust

At once an engrossing murder mystery and an unflinching portrait of racial injustice, *Intruder in the Dust* is the story of Lucas Beauchamp, a black man wrongly arrested for the murder of a white man. Confronted by the threat of lynching, Lucas sets out to prove his innocence, aided by a white lawyer and his young nephew.

Fiction/Literature/0-679-73651-4

Light in August

A novel about hopeful perseverance in the face of mortality, *Light in August* tells the tale of guileless, dauntless Lena Grove, in search of the father of her unborn child; Reverend Gail Hightower, who is plagued by visions of Confederate horsemen; and Joe Christmas, a desperate, enigmatic drifter consumed by his mixed ancestry.

Fiction/Literature/0-679-73226-8

The Reivers

One of Faulkner's comic masterpieces and winner of a Pulitzer Prize, *The Reivers* is a picaresque tale that tells of three unlikely car thieves from rural Mississippi and their wild misadventures in the fast life of Memphis—from horse smuggling to bawdy houses.

Fiction/Literature/0-679-74192-5

Sanctuary

A powerful novel examining the nature of evil, *Sanctuary* is the dark, at times brutal, story of the kidnapping of Mississippi debutante Temple Drake, who introduces her own form of venality into the Memphis underworld where she is being held.

Fiction/Literature/0-679-74814-8

The Sound and the Fury

One of the greatest novels of the twentieth century, *The Sound and the Fury* is the tragedy of the Compson family, featuring some of the most memorable characters in American literature: beautiful, rebellious Caddy; the manchild Benjy; haunted, neurotic Quentin; Jason, the brutal cynic; and Dilsey, their black servant.

Fiction/Literature/0-679-73224-1

The Unvanquished

The Unvanquished is a novel of the Satoris family, who embody the ideal of Southern honor and its transformation through war, defeat, and Reconstruction: Colonel John Sartoris, who is murdered by a business rival after the war; his son Bayard, who finds an alternative to bloodshed; and Granny Millard, the matriarch, who must put aside her code of gentility in order to survive.

Fiction/Literature/0-679-73652-2

Also available:

Big Woods   0-679-75252-8

The Collected Stories   0-679-76403-8

Flags in the Dust   0-394-71239-0

The Hamlet   0-679-73653-0

Knight's Gambit   0-394-72729-0

The Mansion   0-394-70282-4

Pylon   0-394-74741-0

Requiem for a Nun   0-394-71412-1

Three Famous Short Novels   0-394-70149-6

The Town   0-394-70184-4

The Uncollected Stories of William Faulkner   0-394-74656-2

Available at your local bookstore, or call toll-free to order:
1-800-793-2665 (credit cards only).

Catamarán

Serie Roja

Catamarán

Serie Naranja

Catamarán

Serie Azul

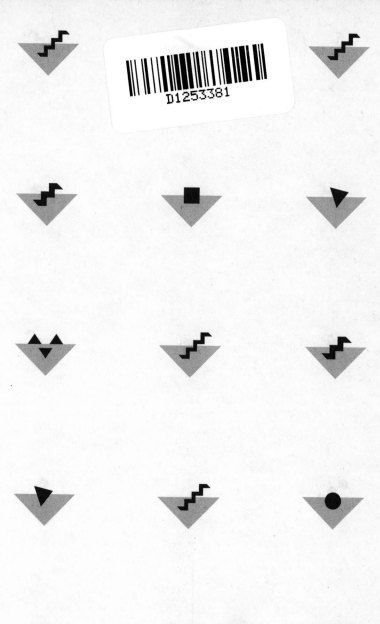

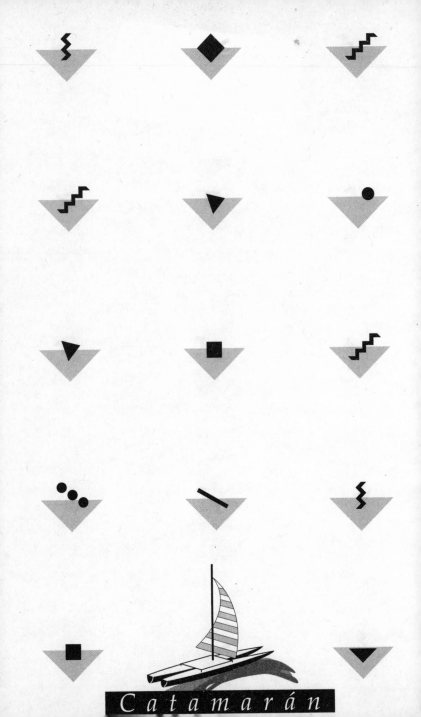

GUILLE Y LA CREMA DE SÉMOLA
y otras historias

Roger
Collinson

ilustraciones de
David McKee

Colección dirigida por **Isabel Cano**

Traducción del inglés: *Miguel Azaola*
Diseño de la colección: *Alfonso Ruano*

Título original: *Willy and the semolina pudding and other Stories*
Publicado por Andersen Press Ltd., Londres
© del texto: Roger Collinson, 1994
© de las ilustraciones: David McKee, 1994
© Ediciones SM, 1995
  Joaquín Turina, 39 - 28044 Madrid

Comercializa: CESMA, SA - Aguacate, 43 - 28044 Madrid

ISBN: 84-348-4659-4
Depósito legal: M-14441-1995
Fotocomposición: Grafilia, SL
Impreso en España/Printed in Spain
Imprenta SM - Joaquín Turina, 39 - 28044 Madrid

1 GUILLE Y LA CREMA DE SÉMOLA

GUILLE no era un chico difícil para comer. Comía de todo. Bueno, quizá no absolutamente de todo. No se comía la costra seca del arroz con leche, ni la de las natillas. La verdad es que tampoco se comía las natillas. Ni el arroz con leche. Pero, aparte de eso, había muy pocas cosas que no se le pudieran dar para comer, quitando la carne cuando tenía grasa, claro. Y el repollo, y el apio, y el pescado, y el hígado, y los huevos pasados por agua, y el pan integral, y la coliflor, y los raviolis, y las ciruelas, y el queso, y el pudin, y las espinacas, y... la sémola. Excepto esas pocas cosas, Guille comía cualquier plato que le pusieran delante; cual-

quiera, siempre que fueran salchichas, claro está, o palitos de merluza, o hamburguesas, o patatas fritas. Y también le gustaba la mermelada si era de fresa.

Las comidas del colegio eran de lo más ricas, pero raro era el día que Guille no se dejaba algo en el plato. Y no valía de nada que las cuidadoras del comedor lo intentaran con halagos o con broncas. Si a Guille no le gustaba, no se lo comía y punto.

Sobre todo, una de las cuidadoras parecía tomárselo como cosa personal. Cualquiera hubiera pensado que la comida la había hecho ella especialmente para Guille.

—Ya sé lo que haría yo si fueras mío —farfullaba.

Guille sabía lo que él haría si fuera suyo: pólvora y cartuchos de dinamita eran de las primeras cosas que formaban parte de su plan.

Las cosas llegaron a su punto álgido de forma inesperada un viernes a la hora de la comida. El primer plato había sido totalmente aceptable: palitos de pescado y patatas fritas con aros de pasta como guarnición. Los

aros de pasta no tenían un sabor demasiado bueno, pero eran buenísimos para jugar con ellos. Fue «lo de después» lo que, de pronto, hizo que la tensión subiera al máximo.

Después de llevarse los platos sucios, las cuidadoras volvieron con una gran perola llena de crema de sémola y la plantaron en mitad de la mesa. Se veía, por la forma en que temblequeó la superficie de la crema, que la sémola estaba aquel día especialmente espesa. La cuidadora rompió la costra y empezó a repartir con su cucharón grandes pegotes de aquel amasijo grisáceo en los platos que aguardaban.

—Ahí tienes lo tuyo —dijo la chica, y descargó la ración de Guille justo debajo de sus narices.

Guille frunció el ceño a la vista de la sémola, y la sémola también pareció mirarle con desconfianza. Guille hizo caso omiso de su cuchara. Si alguna cosa era cierta en el ancho mundo, era que Guille y la crema de sémola iban a permanecer totalmente separados la una del otro. Para no ser injustos con la sémola, hay que hacer constar que los otros niños estaban zampándose vorazmente la suya.

Una niña pequeña que se sentaba frente a Guille no podía esperar a tragarse un bocado para engullir otro. Sus mandíbulas trabajaban sin descanso como una hormigonera.

—Eztá buenízima —observó, escupiendo perdigones de aquella pasta en todas direcciones.

La cara de Guille era la viva imagen de la repugnancia, no por los modales de la jovencita, sino ante la posibilidad de que alguien pudiera disfrutar de aquella forma comiéndose la sémola.

—Vamos —dijo la cuidadora—, déjate de aspavientos y trágatela.

Guille no se movió.

—He dicho que te la tragues.

—No me gusta —dijo Guille.

—Me da igual que te guste o no —se enfureció la cuidadora—. Te vas a comer esa crema o vas a saber lo que es bueno.

—Ya sé lo que es bueno —dijo Guille—, y esta crema no me gusta.

—¿Ah sí? ¡Pues se acabó! Vamos a ver qué piensa de esto la señora Remartínez.

A los pocos minutos, la cuidadora volvía con la directora.

—Vamos a ver, Guille —dijo la señora Remartínez—. La señora Tortajada dice que no quieres comerte tu sémola.

—No es sólo la sémola —interrumpió la señora Tortajada—. No es sólo la sémola. Le pasa con casi todo. No come de esto, no come de aquello... Si los demás niños fueran iguales, aquí no comería nadie...

—No me gusta y no tengo hambre —dijo Guille.

—Vamos a ver, Guille —dijo la señora Remartínez—, creo que debes comértela para dar ejemplo a los demás niños.

A Guille le pareció que los demás niños no necesitaban que les diera ningún ejemplo. La niña pequeña de enfrente estaba ya terminando de rebañar el cuenco «de repetir» y empezaba a mirar con avidez la ración de Guille.

—La comida no se deja en el plato, Guille —dijo la señora Remartínez—. En esta vida, a veces tenemos que hacer cosas que no nos gustan.

—¿Por qué? —preguntó Guille.

—¡Ya basta! —dijo la señora Remartínez—. Te vas a comer tu crema antes de le-

vantarte de la mesa, y pienso volver luego para asegurarme de que te la has comido. No te atrevas a marcharte antes de que yo te vea.

La señora Remartínez se fue, dejando a la señora Tortajada radiante de satisfacción. Los otros niños iban terminando y las cuidadoras les dejaban marcharse. Quitaron el mantel. Pronto sólo quedó Guille sentado a la mesa. Las cuidadoras se habían retirado a comer a la cocina. Guille estaba solo. Delante de él seguía la crema de sémola informe, fría y asquerosa.

Ahora había ya dos cosas ciertas en el ancho mundo. La primera seguía siendo que Guille no iba a comerse su crema; y la segunda, que la señora Remartínez no tenía que encontrar la crema en el plato cuando volviese. Estas dos certidumbres juntas planteaban un problema, y Guille se estrujaba la sesera buscando la solución. ¿Dónde se podría dejar la sémola sin que la descubrieran?

Guille miró a su alrededor. No había ningún sitio. Alzó con desgana su cuchara y empujó la repugnante masa. ¡Puaj! La crema parecía mirarle burlonamente y decirle, sofocando la risa: «¡Vas a tener que comerme...!

¡Cucharada pringosa a cucharada viscosa...! ¡Ja, ja, ja...!»

«¡Puaj!», pensó Guille. «Parece la pasta que usamos para empapelar el techo del cuarto de baño... Huele exactamente igual que la pasta que usamos para empapelar el techo del cuarto de baño... Pero apuesto a que no sabe tan bien como la pasta que usamos para empapelar el techo del cuarto de baño...». Y, según iba empujando la sémola y *puajeaba*, Guille empezó a recordar otra cosa: «Es casi igual de espesa que la pasta que usamos para empapelar el techo del cuarto de baño...».

¿Y qué era lo que les había dicho el abuelo el día que les había concedido a Guille y a su mamá el privilegio de sus consejos...? «Hacedla bien espesa; así, cuando la pongáis en el techo, no se desprenderá». Y por una vez, el abuelo había tenido razón. Habían embadurnado el papel con pasta, lo habían alisado contra el techo, y allí seguía, bien pegado...

Guille miró hacia el techo. Parecía muy lejos. Nunca lo alcanzaría, aunque se pusiera de pie en una silla colocada encima de la mesa... Y, de todas maneras, había un peligro enorme de que le vieran. Era una aventura

desesperada... Y si algo fallaba... Bueno, ni se atrevía a pensarlo... Claro que, si estaba dispuesto a correr el riesgo, no tenía un momento que perder...

Primero llenó bien la cuchara; luego, sujetando firmemente el mango con una mano, con la otra tiró hacia atrás de la cazoleta, apuntó con cuidado y disparó.

La sémola saltó en el aire, se remontó hacia el techo, lo golpeó con un ruido que sonó algo así como *ffflupp*, y allí se quedó pegada.

Satisfecho por su éxito, Guille lanzó una cucharada tras otra:

ffflupp
ffflupp
ffflupp
ffflupp
ffflupp

Fue disparada la última cucharada y el plato, con la cuchara dentro, quedó inocentemente vacío delante de Guille. En el techo podía contemplarse, si a alguien se le ocurriera mirar hacia arriba, algo así como el paisaje volcánico de un remoto planeta.

Cuando la señora Remartínez y la señora Tortajada regresaron, Guille estaba sentado en su silla. El plato vacío le pareció suficiente a la señora Remartínez, pero a la señora Tortajada no le gustó la cara de Guille. No era la cara de un niño que, al final, no ha tenido más remedio que comerse la crema de sémola. Sabía que algo raro había pasado. Lo sabía. Pero si la crema no estaba en el estómago de Guille, ¿dónde estaba? Miró hacia las otras mesas. Miró hacia el suelo. Y cuando Guille se levantó para irse, le palpó los bolsillos y la camisa como los detectives que había visto en la televisión registrando a los criminales en busca de armas de fuego. Pero encontró a Guille «limpio» de sémola.

—Muy bien, Guille —dijo la señora Remartínez—. Puedes irte.

Guille se fue.

—Bueno, señora Tortajada —concluyó la directora—. No creo que Guille vuelva a ser nunca un problema.

La señora Tortajada, sola en mitad del comedor, no compartía la confianza de la señora Remartínez. Aquella sémola estaba en algún sitio que no le correspondía. Y, justo

cuando lo estaba pensando, algo asqueroso se chafó sobre su cabeza. Si hubiera estado en la calle, hubiera pensado que un pájaro le había hecho sus cosas encima; pero no estaba en la calle... Y lo que encontró pegado a sus dedos cuando se atrevió a mirárselos era... ¡crema de sémola..!

¡FÚTBOL, fútbol, fútbol! —gritó la mamá de Guille—. Es en lo único que piensas. Deberías tener un balón en lugar de esa cabeza, que la tienes más hueca que un balón de fútbol, eso desde luego... ¿Pero cómo es posible que tengas tan poco seso?

La mamá de Guille se había puesto así porque Guille, en vez de comprar una barra de pan al volver del colegio, se había quedado jugando al fútbol con sus compañeros de clase y se había olvidado de todo lo demás.

—¡Muy bien! Pues por mí ya puedes que-

jarte de que no tienes merienda, si quieres. La culpa es tuya. Y además...

Cuando quería, la madre de Guille podía seguir y seguir y seguir. Lo hacía muchas veces. Una vez, Guille miró al reloj de la repisa de la chimenea y la estuvo cronometrando. Siguió sin parar durante trece minutos. No es que a Guille le divirtiera, pero sí que sintió un cierto orgullo de tener una mamá capaz de hacerlo. Pensó que se merecía figurar en el *Libro Guinness de los Récords*.

Pero esta vez, mientras esperaba a que ella terminara, se estaba imaginando que él era el capitán de la selección nacional y, en el momento en que iba a marcar el gol de la victoria, su madre gritó:

—¡Guille! ¡No has escuchado una sola palabra de lo que te he dicho!

—Claro que sí, mamá —tartamudeó Guille.

—¡A ver! ¿Qué estaba diciendo?

—Es... esto... que... cómo es posible que tenga tan poco seso...

La madre de Guille dio un resoplido como cuando se escapa el vapor de una olla exprés. Parecía a punto de explotar.

—¡Lo que he dicho es que tienes que ir a llevarle su revista al abuelo!

—¡Pero mamá! —protestó Guille—. ¡Va a empezar el fútbol en la tele!

—¡Voy a gritar! —gritó la mamá de Guille—. Voy a gritar... Eso es lo que voy a hacer. ¡Voy a gritar!

Guille reconoció la señal de peligro, así que se apresuró a decir:

—Lo siento, mamá... ¿Dónde está? Voy ahora mismo corriendo a llevársela.

El abuelo de Guille vivía solo. Su casa estaba a unas pocas calles de distancia y, casi todos los días, Guille tenía que ir allí con algún recado. El jueves era el día en que al abuelo había que llevarle su revista. La mamá de Guille la compraba en el quiosco y luego Guille tenía que ir a entregársela. La revista del abuelo se llamaba *Supermúsculos*. Era la que le gustaba porque estaba obsesionado por estar en forma y desarrollar su musculatura.

Cuando Guille llegó a casa de su abuelo, llamó a la puerta.

¡Pam, pam, pam, pam...! ¡Pam! ¡Pam!

Era la llamada especial de Guille. Cuando

Guille llamaba, nadie decía: «¿Quién será?».
Aunque en la casa de su abuelo tenía que llamar dos veces porque el abuelo estaba un poco sordo.

¡Pam, pam, pam, pam...! ¡Pam! ¡Pam!

Se abrió la puerta y allí estaba el abuelo, con su chándal puesto y un tensor en una mano.

—Hola, abuelo —dijo Guille—. Te he traído tu revista.

—¡Ajá! —jadeó el abuelo—. Será mejor que pases.

Guille le siguió a la cocina, al fondo de la casa, que era donde el abuelo solía pasar el tiempo cuando no estaba haciendo ejercicios físicos en su dormitorio. Pegadas a las paredes y a las puertas de la alacena había fotos de hombres con unos músculos como melones.

El abuelo había hecho té y echó un poco en la jarrita conmemorativa del 92 que guardaba para Guille.

—Bien, bien —dijo el abuelo—. ¿Estás en forma?

—¡Estoy bastante en forma, abuelo! —gritó Guille.

—¡Bastante en forma, bastante en forma! —dijo el abuelo—. ¿Qué contestación es ésa? ¿Bastante en forma para qué?

—Tú sabrás, abuelo —dijo Guille.

—Lo que yo sé, jovencito —dijo el abuelo golpeando la portada del *Supermúsculos* de la semana—, lo que yo sé es que éste no ha llegado a ponerse así a base de pasarse la mitad de la noche viendo la televisión y de decir luego que está «bastante en forma».

—¿No, abuelo?

—Desde luego que no. Se ha impuesto a sí mismo un severo plan de entrenamiento y lo ha cumplido a rajatabla todos los días. Lo mismo que hago yo... Voy a cumplir setenta y tres años, y toca esto: unos músculos de auténtico acero.

El abuelo dobló el brazo, y Guille tuvo que tocar el músculo. No era tan grande como un melón; era más bien como una mandarina.

—¿Dónde se te ha ido, abuelo? —preguntó Guille.

—¡Mira, no me calientes! —rugió el abuelo—. ¡No vaya a tener que calentarte yo a ti!

—¡Primero tendrás que pillarme! —se rió Guille.

—¡Ah! —dijo el abuelo—. O sea que te crees un corredor, ¿no? Pues muy bien. Justo ahora iba a salir para mi carrerita de la tarde: cuatro vueltas a la manzana. Ven conmigo y vamos a ver quién es el mejor.

A Guille no le gustaba correr si no tenía un balón en los pies.

—Esta tarde no, abuelo —dijo—. Tengo cosas que hacer.

—¡Excusas, excusas! —se burló el abuelo—. ¿Tienes miedo de que te gane un viejo como tu abuelo?

—No —contestó Guille.

—Pues vamos —dijo el abuelo—. Inténtalo. Gáname y te daré... te daré algo. ¿Qué tal diez pavos?

Guille frunció el ceño.

—¿Veinte? —añadió el abuelo

—Vale. Hecho —dijo Guille.

—Muy bien. Vamos a la salida —dijo el abuelo quitándose el chándal. Debajo llevaba unos calzones cortos de corredor muy pulcros, con una banda roja a cada lado, y una camiseta a juego.

—¡Vamos! —repitió bailoteando para hacer el precalentamiento.

Guille se bebió un trago del té que quedaba y salió al trote detrás de su abuelo.

—¡Y cierra la puerta al salir! —le gritó el abuelo, que ya brincaba en la acera, cada vez sobre un pie, impaciente por echar a correr.

—Venga, ¿estás listo? —dijo—. Diré «preparados, listos, ya», ¿entendido?

Guille asintió con un gesto, el abuelo dijo de carrerilla *preparadoslistosya* y estaba ya lejos antes de que Guille se diera cuenta de que la carrera había empezado. Guille se puso a su altura y siguieron trotando el uno junto al otro.

—¿Viste el partido, abuelo? —preguntó Guille.

—No —jadeó el abuelo—. Muy tarde... (puf, puf)... Acostarse temprano... (puf, puf)... Levantarse temprano... (puf, puf)... Así soy yo.

—Tendrías que haberlo visto, abuelo. ¡El gol de la segunda parte fue fantástico!

—Deja de parlotear —resolló el abuelo—. Te cortará... (puf, puf)... la respiración...

(puf, puf)... Respirar bien... (puf, puf)... es el secreto... (puf, puf)... para correr bien... (puf, puf)... No se puede correr bien si no se sabe respirar.

—No creo que haya muchas cosas que se puedan hacer si no se sabe respirar, abuelo.

El abuelo empezó a decir:

—No seas descarado...

Pero prefirió seguir su propio consejo y guardarse el aliento para continuar corriendo.

El abuelo era un espectáculo habitual en el barrio. Los vecinos estaban acostumbrados a verle trotando por las calles y le gritaban al pasar:

—¡Buenas tardes, Fredo!

—¡Ánimo, muchacho!

—¿Dónde es el fuego, Fredo?

—¿Has perdido los pantalones, colega?

—¡Mucho estilo, Fredo!

El abuelo respondía a las alusiones amistosas moviendo la cabeza. Pero cuando le decían impertinencias, las ignoraba y se concentraba en su propia respiración.

A la cuarta vuelta a la manzana, el abuelo iba cada vez más despacio. Guille hubiera po-

dido adelantarle y dejarle muy atrás. Incluso hubiera podido sentarse en la puerta de la casa del abuelo y esperarle alargando la mano para que le diera los veinte pavos. Pero decidió no hacerlo. Al final, hasta dejó que el abuelo corriera un poco delante de él.

—Bueno —susurró el abuelo—, no está mal teniendo en cuenta que no entrenas... (puf, puf)... Si te entrenaras como es debido, podrías ser realmente bueno... (puf, puf)... También es que yo he ido frenándome... (puf, puf)... No has ganado, pero te daré los veinte pavos de todas formas... (puf, puf)... Vamos dentro y...

El abuelo se detuvo. No porque le siguiera faltando aire. No. Se detuvo porque se había acordado de algo.

—¡La puerta, Guille! ¡Has salido y has cerrado la puerta!

—Pues claro, abuelo —dijo Guille—. Tú me lo has dicho.

—¡Y ahora no podemos entrar, majadero!

—¿Y tu llave?

—En la repisa de la chimenea. Me hubiera acordado de llevármela si tú no hubieras andado con tantas prisas.

Aquello no le pareció muy justo a Guille, pero todo lo que dijo fue:

—¿Y ahora cómo vas a entrar, abuelo?

—Tendrás que ir buscar la copia que tiene tu madre. Y date prisa, que no me gusta nada el aspecto de esas nubes de ahí arriba.

—¡Jo! —gimió Guille—. ¡Otro viaje más!

La verdad es que la cosa era de lo más sencilla. Cinco minutos para llegar a casa y otros cinco para volver. Abrir la puerta del abuelo, y todo solucionado...

Pero con Guille nada era nunca tan sencillo. Lo de ir a casa no fue un problema. El primer tropezón fue la madre de Guille, porque no podía darle la llave sin decirle de paso lo que pensaba de un señor de la edad del abuelo que corría por la calle en calzoncillos, y de los niños como Guille que encima le animaban, y que cómo era posible que los dos tuvieran tan poco seso. Así que, cuando Guille echó a correr de vuelta hacia donde estaba el abuelo, los primeros goterones del chaparrón de otoño empezaban a estrellarse en la acera.

Guille se dio mucha prisa. En primer lugar porque no quería mojarse demasiado; y luego porque pensó en el abuelo, vestido sólo con unos calzones cortos de algodón y una camiseta. Cuando Guille llegó a la calle del abuelo, llovía ya a cántaros, y el abuelo, calado hasta los huesos, trataba de protegerse

arrimándose a la puerta de entrada. Cuando vio a Guille, le llamó con impaciencia.

—¡Espabila, muchacho! ¿Tienes la llave?

—¡Sí! —gritó Guille—. ¡Está aquí, mira!

Sujetó la llave en alto y giró para cruzar la calle. Pero la lluvia había vuelto muy resbaladizas las gastadas suelas de sus zapatillas de tenis. Los pies se le fueron y la llave del abuelo voló de sus manos, hizo un giro en el aire, cayó, se metió por la rejilla de un sumidero y desapareció. Guille, sentado en un charco, miró horrorizado a la alcantarilla por la que, detrás de la llave, se metían en remolino palos

de chupa-chups y envoltorios de caramelo arrastrados por la tormenta.

—¡No te quedes ahí sentado! —le chilló el abuelo—. ¡Haz algo!

Pero ¿qué podía hacer Guille? Pensó profundamente y dijo:

—Si tuviéramos una caña de pescar y un imán, podríamos pescarla.

Como contestación, el abuelo empleó una serie de palabras que los abuelos como deben ser no deberían conocer siquiera.

De pronto, Guille observó que la ventana del dormitorio del abuelo estaba entreabierta.

—¡Eh, abuelo! —dijo—. Si tuviéramos una escalera, podríamos entrar ahí.

—Pero como no tenemos una escalera —dijo el abuelo—, no podemos.

—Hay una escalera de limpiacristales en esta misma calle —dijo Guille—. La he visto al venir. Podríamos pedirla prestada. Voy por ella.

—¡No te olvides de pedirla! —gritó el abuelo tras él.

La carretilla del limpiaventanas, con la escalera encima, estaba junto al bordillo de la acera, delante de un café. Dentro del café, el

cristalero estaba echando un trago mientras esperaba a que escampara. Pero Guille no lo sabía, y decidió que no tenía tiempo para buscar al propietario de la escalera. Así que la sujetó por un extremo y empujó la carretilla hasta la casa del abuelo.

El abuelo y Guille apoyaron la escalera en la pared, debajo de la ventana del dormitorio. Guille se moría de ganas de trepar hasta arriba.

—¡Anda, déjame subir, abuelo! —pidió.

—¡De eso nada! —dijo el abuelo—. Si tuvieras un accidente, estaría toda mi vida oyendo a tu madre.

—Pero es que yo peso menos que tú —razonó Guille.

—No hay peros que valgan —dijo el abuelo—. Tú sujeta la base de la escalera para que no se mueva.

—¡Pero, abuelo!

—No discutas conmigo... ¿Ya la tienes? Bien, voy a subir.

Y, dicho y hecho, el abuelo empezó a trepar. Despacio, entre sacudidas, subió peldaño a peldaño. Por fin llegó arriba y se encaramó al estrecho alféizar de la ventana. Allí se puso

a forcejear para levantar la falleba y abrir la ventana del todo, pero sin éxito.

—No hay forma, Guille —concluyó—. La abertura no es suficiente para pasar.

Y aquél fue el momento en que don Abdón Malasaña apareció por la acera bramando, hecho una furia. El señor Malasaña era el cristalero que, cuando salió del café y vio que su escalera había desaparecido, primero se sorprendió y luego se enfureció. Pero pronto vio adónde habían ido a parar sus pertenencias, y ahora venía a reclamar lo que era suyo.

—¡Eh..! —rugió.

Guille no era un chico especialmente timorato, pero un vistazo al señor Malasaña le bastó para ver que la mano de tortas estaba más cerca a cada rápida zancada que daba el señor Malasaña, de modo que salió corriendo una vez más.

—¡Eh..! ¡Usted! —volvió a rugir el señor Malasaña en dirección al abuelo—. ¿Qué se ha creído que está haciendo ahí?

El abuelo también estaba de mal humor, así que le gritó al de abajo:

—¿Y a usted qué le parece, vamos a ver?

—¡Un mono en la punta de un palo, eso

es lo que me parece! —bufó el señor Malasaña—. ¡Y, por mí, puede usted quedarse ahí arriba!

Y, al decir esto último, agarró su escalera, la puso en la carretilla y se marchó.

—¡Eh, oiga, vuelva! —gritó el abuelo—. ¡No puede dejarme aquí!

—¿Que no? —replicó el señor Malasaña—. ¡Espere y verá!

—¡Vuelva aquí! —se desgañitó el abuelo—. ¡Vuelva aquí! ¡Vuelva aquí! ¡Vuelva aquí!

El señor Malasaña no volvió. Y allí se quedó el abuelo, encaramado en el alféizar de la ventana, sin poder entrar ni bajar.

—¡Y todo por culpa del chico! —rabiaba—. ¡Verá cuando le ponga las manos encima!

Cuando ya no hubo moros en la costa, Guille volvió furtivamente al lugar.

—¡Abuelo! —gritó—. ¡Se ha llevado la escalera!

—¡Ya lo sé! —chilló el abuelo—. ¡Vete a buscar ayuda, deprisa! No puedo pasarme aquí toda la noche.

Era la oportunidad que Guille había estado

esperando toda su vida. Si alguna vez había habido un momento para marcar el teléfono de la policía, era aquél. Salió corriendo, por quinta vez aquella tarde, en busca de la cabina telefónica más próxima.

Diez minutos después, entre tañidos de campanas, aullidos de sirenas y destellos de reflectores, llegaron ambulancias, coches de bomberos y radiopatrullas a la puerta de la casa del abuelo. Un bombero bajó al abuelo echándoselo al hombro como un saco de patatas.

—¿A qué se creía que estaba jugando, abuelo? —le preguntó—. ¡Un hombre de su edad! ¡Debería darle vergüenza!

La mamá de Guille nunca entendió muy bien lo que había pasado. Pero su instinto le dijo que Guille tenía que ver con el asunto.

—Aunque no sé quién es peor —dijo—. ¿Qué se puede pensar de un viejo destarifado jugando en el antepecho de una ventana? ¡A ti te estoy hablando!

Cuando a la escuela de Guille venían profesores nuevos que no se sabían su nombre y querían hablar de él con otro profesor, solían decir:

—Ya sabe... El niño ese de los pantalones...

Los demás niños también llevaban pantalones, claro. Pero si hubierais visto los pantalones de Guille, sabríais exactamente lo que querían decir los profesores.

La madre de Guille estaba empeñada en que fuera «de pantalón corto». Un término poco adecuado para definir la prenda en la que Guille se introducía todas las mañanas.

Para empezar, dentro del pantalón cabían tres chicos del tamaño de Guille, y las perneras le llegaban más abajo de las rodillas, entre las rodillas y los tobillos. Además, aquellos llamados «pantalones cortos» colgaban de un par de viejos tirantes de rayas, de forma que en invierno, cuando hacía frío, Guille podía meter los brazos en las perneras para guardar el calor.

Pero, para Guille, la mayor ventaja de aquellos pantalones eran sus bolsillos. Los pantalones grandes tienen bolsillos grandes. Y aunque no había mucho Guille para meter en semejantes pantalones, Guille tenía una barbaridad de cosas para meter en aquellos bolsillos. Era un milagro que los tirantes, estirados por el cargamento, no se soltaran. La gente que veía los abultados bolsillos de Guille se preguntaba muchas veces qué llevaría en ellos. Hasta que una tarde su clase conoció la respuesta.

El profesor les había estado hablando del dinero y preguntó si alguno sabía cuál era la moneda francesa.

—¡Francos! —contestó alguien.

—Muy bien —dijo el señor Centenera.

Guille levantó la mano.

—Yo tengo uno.

—Estupendo. ¿Puedes enseñárnoslo?

—Sí —dijo Guille sumergiendo la mano en un bolsillo—. Lo tengo aquí.

Escarbó un rato buscándolo hasta que el señor Centenera sugirió que seguramente acabaría antes si sacaba las cosas del bolsillo una por una. Y es lo que hizo Guille.

Empezó por el bolsillo derecho. Y apareció:

un ovillo de bramante,

un destornillador,

un imán,

un cochecito con tres ruedas,

unas esposas (de juguete),

un grifo de latón,

un trozo de plastilina,

una armónica,

un tubo de pegamento,

un tapón de cristal de una vinagrera,

un pañuelo (muy mugriento),

un caramelo a medio chupar (muy pegajoso)

y la *Agenda 1986 del Aficionado a los Peces Tropicales*.

Pero ningún franco francés.

Luego, Guille empezó a vaciar su bolsillo izquierdo. Era como ver a un mago sacando conejos y ristras de banderas de un sombrero vacío. El segundo montón que se formó sobre el pupitre de Guille se componía de:

una castaña muy vieja (y muy arrugada),

un cowboy de plástico (sin caballo),

una pelota de tenis pelada,
un botón del mando de una radio,
un faro de bicicleta,
una lupa,
un interruptor de la luz,
varias clases de gomas,
un cepo para ratones,
un botón plateado,
un reloj de bolsillo sin agujas,
otro pañuelo (realmente muy mugriento),
un muelle de alguna cosa,
una nave espacial-sacapuntas
y, lo último de todo, una toñera de porcelana.

Cuando Guille vio la toñera, sus ojos se iluminaron.

—¡Estaba aquí! —dijo—. Creía que la había perdido.

El señor Centenera se puso algo sarcástico:

—Si algo cae en tus bolsillos —dijo—, es como si se hubiera perdido. ¿Qué hay del franco francés?

—¡Ah, sí! —dijo Guille, que se había olvidado completamente del asunto—. Sé que tenía uno.

—Muy bien —dijo el señor Centenera—. Ahora, si no te importa volver a meter toda esa basura en tus bolsillos, seguiremos con la clase. ¡La verdad es que llevas ahí suficientes trastos para poner una tienda!

Así es que Guille volvió a llenarse los bolsillos con todas sus posesiones. Todas menos la toñera.

Si no sabéis lo que es una toñera de porcelana, una cosa es segura: que no fuisteis a la escuela de Guille el curso pasado... Toñeras... Era de lo único que hablaban todos. Como para ponerle a uno la cabeza como una toñera... Perdón, como un bombo.

Las toñeras son canicas. Canicas grandes. No de las pequeñas; a ésas las llamaban caponeras. Las toñeras de porcelana no son canicas transparentes, de las de cristal; son canicas opacas de colores. Y muy bonitas.

Bueno, pues las canicas se pusieron de moda. Toda la escuela había enloquecido con ellas, los chicos y las chicas. Hasta que la moda pasó como pasan siempre todas las modas: de golpe y porrazo. Un día daba la sensación de que todo el mundo iba a la escuela

con una bolsa de canicas, y al día siguiente a nadie le interesaban en absoluto.

Guille se había guardado su toñera favorita en los bolsillos, con todos sus demás tesoros, y hacía meses que no había vuelto a sacarla a la luz del día. Ahora volvía a contemplarla con cariño, recreándose en sus volutas azules, verdes y rojas que tan claramente recordaba. Y en aquel preciso momento decidió que la toñera tenía que ser su canica de la suerte.

—Me alegro de haberla encontrado —les dijo a sus compañeros—. Eso quiere decir que ahora tendré buena suerte.

—Pero, si ha estado metida en tu bolsillo todo el tiempo —dijeron ellos—, tendrías que haber tenido buena suerte todo el tiempo.

—Supongo que sí —dijo Guille—. Lo que pasa es que, como yo no sabía que aún guardaba la toñera, tampoco sabía que tenía buena suerte.

Algunos chicos intentaron convencerle de que eso era un disparate, pero Guille no los escuchó y la discusión acabó poniéndose fea, como pasa tantas veces con las discusiones.

—¡Venga, pues demuéstralo! —le gritaban—. ¡Demuestra que da buena suerte¡

—¡Vale! —aulló Guille—. ¡Vale! ¡Ya lo veréis!

No parecía que la toñera de porcelana fuera a traerle ninguna suerte a Guille, porque aquella misma tarde se quedó sin ella. La cosa ocurrió así:

Los pupitres de la clase de Guille eran de esos muy viejos que tienen un agujero para un tintero pequeño. Los tinteros de marras no se usaban desde los tiempos de Maricastaña. Pero los agujeros seguían allí y se podía dejar caer por ellos cualquier cosa pequeña dentro del pupitre sin necesidad de levantar la tapa. Y Guille decidió sacarle partido al asunto.

Con libros y reglas, construyó dentro del pupitre un pequeño circuito muy sinuoso. Luego se dedicó a soltar la toñera por el agujero, y la canica rodaba por la pista hasta meterse en una jarrita de esmalte que Guille se había traído para la fiesta de Navidad. Era de lo más divertido, porque podía oírse la toñera rodando entre los libros y las reglas, y

luego el nítido clink cuando se metía en la jarrita.

El circuito de la toñera tenía absorbidos todos los pensamientos de Guille. Así que, en vez de dedicarse a su redacción, se dedicó a soltar la toñera por el agujero, esperar el clink, levantar furtivamente la tapa del pupitre, sacar la toñera y volver a empezar.

El señor Centenera se dio cuenta de que Guille no estaba trabajando y, en el silencio de la clase, también él escucho el tenue y acusador clink. Luego, Guille vio una gran mano extendida delante de sus narices y no hubo necesidad de palabras. Dolorosamente, sacó la toñera del pupitre y la depositó en la palma extendida. Unos dedos de hierro se cerraron sobre ella. El señor Centenera se encaminó lentamente hacia su mesa, abrió el cajón y metió la toñera. La toñera se reunió allí con todos los demás objetos valiosos que habían sido confiscados en la clase. El cajón se cerró de golpe, y Guille supo que no había esperanzas de libertad para su toñera hasta que llegaran las vacaciones.

—¡Así que ésa era tu toñera de la suerte! —se burlaban sus compañeros cuando acabó

la clase—. Ahora nos dirás que la suerte es que no te haya retorcido las orejas...

—¡Callaos ya! —les contestó Guille furioso.

A veces, Guille iba a casa de su abuelo sin que se lo dijeran. Y aquel día, camino de su casa, decidió pasar a verle. El abuelo estaba practicando el ejercicio de los cuarenta ronquidos seguidos en el sillón de la cocina. Hacer flexiones y levantar pesas es un duro trabajo... El aldabonazo de Guille le sacó de su concentración.

¡Pam, pam, pam, pam...! ¡Pam! ¡Pam!

Rápidamente, el abuelo se agarró a sus pesas. Le gustaba que Guille pensara que siempre estaba haciendo ejercicio.

—¿Qué pasa? —preguntó cuando abrió la puerta.

—Sólo he venido a decirte hola, abuelo —dijo Guille.

—Pasa —repitió el abuelo—. Estaba a punto de descansar unos minutos, así que puedes entrar si quieres.

Hizo té para los dos y se sentaron para tomárselo. Todo lo que se oía era el tictac del

viejo reloj del abuelo y el ruido de los sorbetones que daban el abuelo y Guille al beberse el té. A la mamá de Guille no le gustaba el ruido de los sorbetones, y ésa era una de las razones por las que el abuelo no vivía en la casa de Guille. También había otras que la mamá de Guille les contaba susurrando a sus amigas.

—¿Qué...? —dijo el abuelo.

—¿Qué, de qué...? —dijo Guille.

—¿Qué es lo que pasa?

—No... nada.

—Pues vaya cara larga por nada —dijo el abuelo.

—Bueno, que me ha mangado mi toñera... —y Guille le contó lo que había pasado—, y es mi toñera de la suerte, abuelo.

—Un hombre debe buscarse su propia suerte —dijo el abuelo.

—Pero es que sé que da suerte, abuelo. Sé que la da.

—Ya —dijo el abuelo—. ¿Y cómo piensas recuperarla?

—Podría mangársela yo a él.

—Las cosas mangadas dejan de dar suerte

—dijo el abuelo—. Lo más seguro es que te trajera mala suerte.

—No le ha traído mala suerte al Centeno, y él me la ha mangado a mí —protestó Guille.

—Con tenerte a ti en su clase —dijo el abuelo—, ya le ha traído toda la mala suerte que le podía traer.

Guille frunció el entrecejo.

—Está bien; piensa, Guille —razonó el abuelo—. ¿Por qué te has quedado sin ella?

—Porque no he seguido escribiendo mi poesía.

—¡Poesías! —exclamó el abuelo—. ¿Sobre qué?

—Naturaleza —dijo Guille—. Flores y todo eso.

—Ya —dijo el abuelo—. A lo mejor, si hicieras una especialmente para él, te devolvería tu canica.

—¡Pero es que soy muy malo escribiendo poesías! —dijo Guille—. No sé nada de flores y esas cosas.

El abuelo se rascó la cabeza.

—Solíamos tener un libro de poesías —dijo—. Si consigo encontrarlo, podría darte algunas ideas.

Guille se fue de casa de su abuelo con un libro muy viejo que había sido de su abuela. Tenía muchas poesías sobre flores y todas esas cosas.

A la mañana siguiente, en clase, cuando el señor Centenera terminó de pasar lista a los niños para el comedor, Guille sacó un trozo de papel sucio de su bolsillo y se lo ofreció al profesor.

—Lo hice anoche —dijo.

El señor Centenera pinzó el papel entre las puntas de los dedos índice y pulgar de cada mano y lo desdobló. A medida que iba leyendo, se le iban arqueando las cejas.

—¿Lo has escrito tú? —preguntó.

—Sí, claro —dijo Guille.

Al señor Centenera se le veía muy impresionado.

—Lo que es realmente increíble —llegó a decir— es que Antonio Machado escribiera un poema idéntico a éste hace unos cincuenta años.

Guille se sintió como un castillo de arena que se derrumba al subir la marea.

—Así que la has escrito tú mismo, dices
—repitió el señor Centenera.

—Eso es —musitó Guille.

—Ya; si reconozco la letra y la ortografía...
Pero las palabras, Guille...

No había respuesta. Guille bajó la cabeza
mientras la clase entera ahogaba una risotada.

—Muy bien —dijo el señor Centenera—. Creo que lo mejor que puedes hacer para pagar tu deuda con Machado es aprenderte su poema de memoria. Así que, mientras los demás tienen hoy su mañana de deportes, te dedicas a aprendértelo y esta tarde nos lo recitas a todos.

—¿Sigues pensando que es una toñera de la suerte? —se burlaban sus compañeros en el recreo.

Guille casi lloraba. Había sido una faena. Después del recreo, toda la clase salió corriendo a jugar al fútbol o al baloncesto y él tuvo que quedarse en el patio con las clases de los pequeños, aprendiéndose de memoria la poesía. Odió su toñera de la mala suerte con toda su alma.

La hora de la comida llegó y pasó. Sonó el silbato y todas las clases entraron en fila a sus aulas respectivas. Guille se sentó en su sitio esperando a que el señor Centenera le hiciera recitar la poesía. Pero apenas habían acabado

de sentarse todos cuando se abrió la puerta de la clase y entró la señora Remartínez seguida de otra persona a la que ninguno había visto antes jamás. Era una señora mayor, pero una señora mayor a la que le debía de encantar disfrazarse, porque llevaba puesto un abrigo peludo de color rosa y un sombrero lleno de flores y mariposas temblequeantes, enganchadas con alambres. Miró sonriente a los niños, a las paredes, al techo... Miraba sonriente a todo.

La directora pidió disculpas al señor Centenera por la interrupción.

—... Pero es que esta tarde tenemos una visita muy importante y distinguida: la señorita Filomena Albarracín. La señorita Albarracín es una famosa escritora y espero que muchos de vuestros padres hayan leído sus libros. Sin embargo, lo más interesante para nosotros es que la señorita Albarracín fue alumna de nuestra escuela hace..., bueno, hace ya mucho tiempo. Hoy, como está de paso en la ciudad, ha querido venir a visitar su antigua escuela. Y resulta que el aula que mejor recuerda es precisamente ésta...

—¡Oh, sí! —exclamó la señorita Albarracín—. Recuerdo bien las horas felices que pasé aquí. ¡Horas felices! ¡Felices días!... ¿Estáis todos pasando felices horas y días felices también?

Y todos los niños, con los ojos clavados en la señora Remartínez, dijeron a coro:

—Sí, señorita Albarracín.

Todos menos Guille. La única cosa feliz en que podía pensar era que la visita había retrasado su recitación poética. Ahora, con un poco de suerte, a lo mejor al señor Centenera se le olvidaba... ¡Con un poco de suerte..! Se le olvidaba que se le había acabado la suerte.

Entretanto, la señorita Albarracín seguía hablando:

—¡Oh, cuánto amaba nuestras lecciones de poesía! Nos aprendíamos un poema cada semana. ¡Y cómo nos encantaba aquello! ¿Siguen los niños aprendiendo poemas, señor Centenera?

El señor Centenera tosió, carraspeó y dijo con voz algo balbuciente:

—Bien... Tratamos de animar a los chicos

a que expresen las cosas con sus propias palabras, señorita Albarracín, más que a memorizar lo que escribieron otros.

—¡Oh, pero eso es terriblemente triste! —gorjeó la señorita Albarracín—. No llevar las palabras de Juan Ramón Jiménez, de Federico García Lorca o de Antonio Machado cantándonos para siempre en el corazón, es una trágica pérdida. ¿No hay aquí ningún niño maravilloso capaz de recitar un poemita para mí? —y abrió el bolso y sacó de él un billete de mil que chasqueó entre los dedos—. Ésta es una pequeña recompensa para el niño o la niña que me recite sólo unos pocos versos.

El único voluntario fue Guille. Levantó la mano. La señorita Albarracín le miró y vaciló. Guille no parecía la clase de niño que lleva las palabras de nuestro maravilloso Antonio Machado cantándole para siempre en el corazón.

—¿Sí? —dijo nerviosamente.

—Me sé una poesía —dijo Guille.

Puso los ojos en blanco para concentrarse y empezó:

Érase un marinero
que hizo un jardín junto al mar
y se metió a jardinero.
Estaba el jardín en flor
y el jardinero se fue
por esos mares de Dios.

La señorita Albarracín aplaudió y le dio a Guille el billete de mil.

—Señor Centenera —dijo—, debe de estar usted muy orgulloso de este hombrecito. Gracias a él, piense que todo su esfuerzo vale la pena.

—Bueno —dijo Guille al salir al patio—, ¿qué os dije? Era una toñera de la suerte. Porque si no la hubiera tenido, el señor Centenera no me la hubiera quitado. Y si el señor Centenera no me la hubiera quitado, yo no hubiera copiado esa poesía. Y si yo no hubiera copiado esa poesía, el señor Centenera no me hubiera hecho aprendérmela de memoria. Y si no me la hubiera aprendido de memoria, no hubiera podido recitársela a esa mujer. Y si no se la hubiera recitado a esa mujer, no me habría dado las mil.

Y todos tuvieron que aceptarlo.

Pero ése no fue el final. Cuando ya se iban a casa, el señor Centenera llamó a Guille. Abrió su cajón, sacó la toñera de porcelana y se la devolvió.

—Has ganado, Guille —le dijo—. ¡Por esta vez!

GUILLE y Óscar

GUILLE y Óscar eran grandes amigos. Iban juntos a todas partes. Casi siempre iban donde quería Guille, pero a Óscar no parecía importarle.

Se encontraron por primera vez en el huerto del abuelo, y comprendieron inmediatamente que se caían bien. Guille estaba —a su modo— ayudando al abuelo a quitar las malas hierbas. Óscar... Bueno, Óscar acababa de subirse a una hoja de lechuga fresca especialmente apetecible. En realidad, el primero que vio a Óscar fue el abuelo; y dijo:

—¡Peste de caracoles! ¡Ya les enseñaré yo a comerse mis lechugas!

Era evidente que Óscar no necesitaba que

nadie le enseñara a comerse una lechuga, y hasta hubiera podido darle al abuelo dos o tres consejos útiles al respecto. Pero lo que quería decir el abuelo era que iba a tirar a Óscar al suelo y a aplastarlo de un pisotón. Óscar lo tenía francamente mal. Si no hubiera estado allí Guille, hubiera terminado machacado bajo la suela de la bota del abuelo y convirtiéndose en un sabroso piscolabis para cualquier pájaro que pasase.

Pero Guille estaba allí, y lo primero que hizo fue salvarle la vida a Óscar.

Y lo primero que hizo Óscar en cuanto Guille lo rescato fue, como es natural, meterse en su caparazón. Pero enseguida miró tímidamente fuera y se encontró de narices con la amistosa y admirada cara de Guille.

—¡Oye! ¡Eres precioso! —dijo Guille.

Era la primera vez que alguien (además del abuelo) le hablaba a Óscar. Los caracoles, todo hay que decirlo, llevan una vida muy solitaria.

—¡Eres genial! —insistió Guille.

Semejante alabanza conmovió el corazón de Óscar, así que salió completamente de su caparazón y respondió:

—¡Pues yo creo que tú también eres genial!

Óscar viajó a casa de Guille en una caja de hojalata que pertenecía al bolsillo derecho de Guille. Guille hizo varios agujeros de ventilación con un clavo y un martillo, y la recubrió por dentro con parte de la hoja de lechuga que había estado a punto de ser la perdición de Óscar.

Guille no presentó a Óscar a su madre porque intuyó, con acierto, que los sentimientos de ésta hacia los caracoles debían de parecerse

mucho a los del abuelo. Esto suponía que, dentro de la casa, Óscar sólo podía salir de su lata en la zona de seguridad que era el cuarto de Guille. Pero, una vez allí, podía corretear por todas partes a sus anchas... Ah, ya sé lo que estáis pensando: «¡Pero si los caracoles no pueden corretear por ninguna parte!». Pues, a pesar de tener sólo un pie, Óscar era la mar de ligero, sobre todo para ser un caracol. Si se le dejaba en el suelo de linóleo (el cuarto de Guille no tenía más que una alfombra pequeña junto a la cama) frente a una hoja de lechuga a una distancia que pudiera olerla, salía disparado como un caballo de carreras. Podía recorrer un metro en algo menos de un minuto.

Óscar y Guille jugaban juntos durante horas. Su juego favorito era cuando Guille se ponía a Óscar sobre la frente, Óscar resbalaba hacia abajo hasta quedarse colgado de la punta de la nariz de Guille y Guille se ponía bizco intentando verlo. Esto siempre le hacía reír a Óscar de tal forma que Guille se asustaba pensando que su madre pudiera venir corriendo a ver quién estaba haciendo todo aquel ruido.

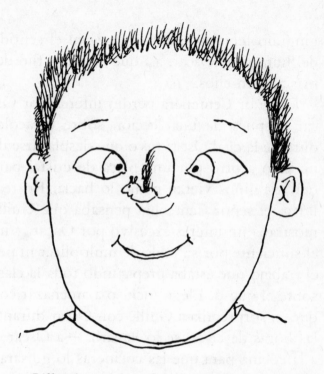

—¡Cállate! —susurraba—. ¿Quieres que mamá te pesque, caracol estúpido?

Pero Óscar seguía riéndose hasta que también Guille empezaba a contener las carcaja-
das con tales espasmos que Óscar tenía que
agarrarse como una lapa para no salir despe-
dido. Naturalmente, fue con Guille a la escuela, y pronto fue un personaje conocido y
popular en el patio de recreo. Algunos chicos
decidieron traerse también sus caracoles, pero

63

ninguno tenía ni la inteligencia ni el sentido del humor de Óscar, así que nadie se fijó demasiado en ellos.

El señor Centenera perdió interés por Óscar después de una lección sobre caracoles durante la cual Óscar tuvo que desplazarse de un lado a otro por una placa de cristal para que los niños vieran cómo lo hacía. En realidad, el señor Centenera pensaba que Guille mostraba un interés excesivo por Óscar, y no el suficiente por su tabla de multiplicar ni por el trabajo que estaba preparando toda la clase sobre el queso. Llegó incluso a amenazar con que, si sorprendía a Guille con Óscar durante las horas de clase, se lo llevaría —a Óscar— a la cocina para que las cocineras lo guisaran con ajo y mantequilla y se lo sirvieran a Guille para comer. Eso, explicó el señor Centenera, era lo que algunas personas hacían con los caracoles. Cuando Óscar oyó semejante cosa, se metió en su caparazón en menos tiempo del que tardó Guille en cerrar la caja.

Desde aquel momento tendrían que andarse con cuidado. Como es lógico, Guille no podía dejar a Óscar encerrado durante una hora de clase. Si él mismo no hubiera podido

resistirlo, no veía por qué tenía que hacerlo Óscar. Así que, de vez en cuando, mientras la atención del señor Centenera estaba ocupada en otra cosa, Guille levantaba la tapa de su pupitre, sacaba la caja, la abría y le dejaba echar a Óscar un rápido vistazo a lo que estaba pasando. Era peligroso, pero a los dos les producía un escalofrío emocionante.

Por la noche, Guille dejaba la caja de Óscar destapada sobre la mesilla de noche. Óscar nunca estaba allí por la mañana, y Guille tenía que seguir la huella plateada que Óscar dejaba tras de sí por donde pasaba. Seguir el rastro de Óscar era de lo más divertido. Guille nunca sabía por dónde se le habría ocurrido meterse. A veces iba por el suelo y Guille tenía que arrastrarse debajo de la cama para alcanzarle. Y a veces la huella de Óscar recorría la pared y cruzaba todo el techo. Óscar tenía esa clase de espíritu que impulsa a los hombres a explorar simas y a escalar montañas.

Guille y Óscar habían sido compañeros inseparables durante casi un mes cuando, una noche, Guille dejó a Óscar en su caja junto a la cama, como siempre. Pero, antes de darle

las buenas noches, le apostó lo que quisiera a que al día siguiente le encontraría antes de que pasaran dos minutos. Como ya sabemos, las apuestas y desafíos pueden llevar a la gente a hacer verdaderas estupideces. Y no se puede desafiar a un caracol como Óscar sin pensar que hará todo lo posible por ganar.

Por eso, cuando Guille se despertó el domingo por la mañana, dijo muy bajito:

—Contaré hasta diez, Óscar. Y luego iré a buscarte y te encontraré. Uno... dos... tres...

Cuando llegó a diez, Guille se sentó y miró a su alrededor. No se veía a Óscar por ninguna parte. Guille buscó el rastro revelador. Allí estaba, subiendo por la pared encima de su cama, girando para meterse detrás del armario ropero y reapareciendo por el otro lado. Luego seguía hasta llegar a la ventana... ¡La ventana abierta! Las noches de verano son calurosas y Guille dormía con la ventana abierta. Óscar había llegado a la abertura y se había deslizado por ella.

Guille sacó la cabeza fuera y exploró con la mirada el muro de ladrillo de arriba abajo, a un lado y a otro. Ni rastro de Óscar. A esas horas ya estaría en el tejado, o por el jardín,

o colándose por otra ventana abierta dos casas más allá. ¿Qué podía hacer Guille? «Para empezar, nada de pánico», pensó. Mientras lo pensaba, no se enteró del porrazo que se dio en la cabeza con el marco de la ventana.

Guille se metió en sus pantalones, se deslizó por la escalera sin hacer ruido y salió al jardín. Volvió a mirar de nuevo las paredes de la casa tratando de descubrir el caparazón de Óscar en aquella superficie jaspeada de colores rojizos y parduscos. De Óscar, nada. Y, por mucho que lo intentó, no pudo descubrir el rastro plateado, que ya había secado el sol de la mañana.

Allí estaba, preguntándose dónde se habría metido su minúsculo amigo, cuando escuchó un leve tintineo, como una especie de golpeteo. Pudo oírlo porque el mundo en general estaba en silencio el domingo por la mañana, a pesar de que algunas personas ya se habían levantado y estaban haciendo cosas. La gente que da las noticias en la radio ya estaba despierta y haciendo su trabajo. Los curas ya estaban de pie y afeitándose a toda prisa antes de salir corriendo para decir la primera misa. Los lecheros ya andaban repar-

tiendo las botellas del domingo por las puertas de las casas. Los repartidores de periódicos estaban ya metiendo con gran pericia las ediciones dominicales en los buzones equivocados. Y los pájaros estaban ya dedicados a extraer lombrices de sus agujeros y a picotear cualquier otro bocado de los que les suelen apetecer para su desayuno pajaril.

El golpeteo continuaba, y al fin Guille supo de dónde venía el sonido. En el fondo del jardín, un tordo llevaba en el pico algo que estaba golpeando contra un ladrillo de los que rodeaban el macizo de lechugas de la mamá de Guille. Luego, Guille lo vio todo. Lo que estaba golpeando el tordo era Óscar. Intentaba romper su caparazón para comerse la jugosa carne que tanto les gusta a los tordos y a algunas personas. Su insaciable hambre de lechuga y su indomable hambre de aventura habían arrastrado a Óscar a su propia destrucción.

Con un grito agudo, Guille se abalanzó sobre el asesino de Óscar. Pero era ya demasiado tarde. Los trocitos de caparazón estaban esparcidos por el suelo y el cuerpo indefenso estaba ya hecho trizas.

Guille no era de esos chicos que lloran. Pero estuvo a punto de hacerlo cuando contempló aquel despojo magullado y escuchó al tordo silbar sus groseros comentarios desde la chimenea de la casa de al lado. Entristecido, se dio la vuelta y se dirigió despacio hacia la casa. Se detuvo en la puerta, con la mano en el pestillo. Y allí, sobre la pared de ladrillo, a la altura de sus ojos, estaba Óscar. Era Óscar sin ninguna duda, con su caparazón brillando al sol y una ancha sonrisa en su cara de caracol.

—¡Hola! —dijo Óscar—. Te la he pegado bien, ¿eh? ¡Apuesto a que creías que era yo!

—¡Óscar! —dijo Guille.

*L*AS dos cosas más importantes —aparte de Óscar— en la vida de Guille eran el fútbol y la tele. Guille se tragaba todos los programas menos los que sólo consistían en gente sentada hablando. Y cuando televisaban un partido, nada podía mover a Guille de su sitio ante la pantalla. Desde allí gritaba, abucheaba y pegaba saltos sin parar durante cada segundo de juego.

—Haces tú más ruido que mil de esos forofos —decía la madre de Guille—. Y siéntate bien, ¿quieres hacer el favor?

Pero Guille ni se enteraba, y continuaba tremolando sobre su cabeza la bufanda de su club mientras aullaba:

—¡Atleti! ¡Atleti!

Aunque penséis que la mamá de Guille exageraba un poco, tendríais que admitir que Guille armaba un jaleo impresionante para ser sólo un niño que nada más tenía una boca y dos pulmones. Con todo, Guille no estaba satisfecho de sus actuaciones y estaba deseando producir un día un estruendo tal que demostrara de verdad lo estupendo que era su equipo y la partida de petardos que eran todos los demás. Había visto que los forofos del fútbol utilizaban distintos aparatos para hacer más ruido: viejas bocinas de coche con grandes perillas negras para apretar, bocinas de mano (parecidas a un espray con trompetilla), y hasta cornetas. Pero por lo que Guille bebía de verdad los vientos era por una carraca pintada con los colores del Atlético que, al hacerla sonar, produjera el ruido de una ametralladora. Además pensaba seguir gritando y animando, claro, porque todo cuenta a la hora de producir un estrépito realmente satisfactorio.

Pero Guille —con gran alivio de su mamá— no tenía carraca. Y, a pesar de todas las indirectas que Guille dejaba caer, su mamá no

tenía la menor intención de comprarle una ni por su cumpleaños, ni por Navidad, ni por nada del mundo.

Fue un tío de Guille, el tío Juancho, quien hizo que su sueño se realizara. El tío Juancho viajaba mucho y no le veían con frecuencia. Pero, cuando aparecía inesperadamente, siempre traía algo para su sobrino. Una vez fue un periscopio con el que se podía ver por detrás de las esquinas y por encima de las tapias; y otra vez le había dado a Guille una caja entera llena de cosas para gastar bromas a la gente, como flores que soltaban un chorro de agua y dulces con pimienta dentro. Al tío Juancho siempre se le ocurrían regalos que a uno le gustaría poder comprarse. Sin embargo, el mejor regalo que jamás le hizo a Guille fue la carraca más grande que hayáis visto en toda vuestra vida. Estaba pintada de rayas rojas y blancas, algo que os dará igual si no sois del Atlético; pero, incluso aunque así sea, tendréis que admitir que, para hacer ruido, no se os podría haber ocurrido nada mejor.

Guille estaba mudo de la emoción. Y la

mamá de Guille también estaba muda... o casi.

—¡De verdad, Juancho, podrías tener un poco más de seso! —le recriminó.

Guille blandió la carraca. Pesaba tanto que tuvo que usar las dos manos. El estruendo ahogó el tiroteo de una película de la televi-

sión, ahogó el pitido de la cafetera, ahogó la música del grupo pop que ensayaba en la casa de al lado, ahogó el ruido de los camiones que pasaban por la calle, ahogó el zumbido del avión que sobrevolaba la casa en aquel momento... y ahogó el grito de la mamá de Guille.

Cuando Guille dejó de agitar la carraca, la habitación se convirtió de pronto en puro silencio.

—¡Qué genial! ¡Es fantástica, tío! —jadeó Guille.

—¡Fantástica! —despotricó la mamá de Guille—. ¡De milagro no se han roto todos los cristales de la casa con el ruido de esa carraca! ¡No vuelvas a usarla nunca, nunca, dentro de casa!

—Pero, mamá...

—Como vuelvas a hacer otra vez ese ruido en casa —dijo la mamá de Guille—, la hago astillas para la lumbre. ¡Por éstas!

En vista de que no podía usarla en casa, Guille le dijo adiós al tío Juancho y se llevó la carraca fuera, donde estuviera a salvo de su mamá y del hacha vengadora. Ya en la

acera, se puso a sacudir la carraca y a aullar después de cada meneo:

—¡Atleeeeti! ¡Atleeeeti!

Al otro lado de la calle, se abrió de golpe la ventana de un piso alto y en el hueco aparecieron los hombros y la cabeza de una señora.

—¿Qué demonios te crees que estás haciendo? ¡Has despertado a mi nene! ¡No se te ocurra seguir armando semejante alboroto! ¿Me has oído?

Y la ventana se cerró de golpe otra vez.

Guille le dirigió una mueca, pero recorrió un buen trecho de calle antes de hacer otra intentona.

—¡Atleeeti! ¡Atleeeti!

Se abrió violentamente la puerta de una casa y un hombre que parecía muy enfadado se plantó en el umbral.

—Estoy intentando telefonear a mi hija de América, no puedo entender nada de lo que me dice y la conferencia me está costando un dineral. ¡Lárgate antes de que te dé una patada en el trasero, aprendiz de gamberro!

Guille se largó otra vez, en esta ocasión a otra calle.

—¡Atleeeti! ¡Atleeeti!

A un lechero que estaba ocupado en su reparto se le cayó una caja de botellas. Las botellas se hicieron añicos y el suelo se llenó de leche y de cristales rotos.

—¡Dios mío! —gritó el lechero—. ¿Quieres que me dé un ataque al corazón? ¡Fuera de aquí! ¿Me oyes? ¡Ábrete! ¡Fuera!

Guille se apresuró a irse, pero la injusticia le reconcomía. ¿De qué sirve tener la carraca más maravillosa del mundo si no le dejan a uno utilizarla? ¿Y por qué no podía toda esa gente mayor disfrutar con ella como las personas normales, en vez de ponerse furiosos?

Guille siguió su camino hasta que dio la vuelta a la esquina. No se veía a nadie por allí, aparte de cuatro chicos mayores sentados en lo alto de la valla de un jardín. Era la oportunidad de lucirse ante un auditorio capaz de valorar una supercarraca de fútbol. Guille la agitó vigorosamente y luego vociferó:

—¡Atleeeti! ¡Atleeeti!

Mientras Guille se limitó a hacer sonar la carraca, comprobó que las caras de los chicos reflejaban aprobación. Fue al gritar «¡Atleeeti!

¡Atleeeti!» cuando cambiaron de expresión, y Guille supo que se habían unido a las filas de mamás con nenes, papás telefoneando y lecheros nerviosos.

—¡Cogedlo! —tronó el chico más alto.

Y echaron a correr hacia Guille rugiendo:

—¡Raaaayo! ¡Raaaayo!

Guille no esperó. Empezó a correr. Corrió tan rápido como sólo un forofo del Atlético es capaz de correr cuando le persiguen cuatro forofos del Rayo dispuestos a aplastarle sobre la acera como si fuera mantequilla sobre una tostada. Corrió hasta la casa de su abuelo y aporreó la puerta.

¡Pam, pam, pam, pam! ¡Pam! ¡Pam!

Sus enemigos se quedaron en la puerta del jardín jadeando como lobos que acabaran de fracasar en su intento de arrancar de su trineo al solitario trampero.

Guille volvió a aporrear la puerta y agitó la carraca, desafiante. Todavía la estaba moviendo cuando la puerta se abrió.

—¿Qué diablos es todo este jaleo?

—Me persiguen —jadeó Guille, colándose rápidamente por detrás de su abuelo en busca de la seguridad del pasillo.

El abuelo se encontraba «haciendo unos largos» en su aparato de remar cuando Guille le interrumpió, y estaba en pantalón corto y camiseta.

—¡Mirad! ¡Es Tarzán! —chillaron los chicos en la calle—. ¡Fijaos qué musculatura de atleta!

El abuelo cerró de un portazo y siguió a Guille a la cocina.

—Abuelo, ¿a que es fantástica? —dijo Guille con orgullo mientras giraba su carraca—. Me la acaba de dar el tío Juancho.

A pesar de su sordera, aquel ruido entre las cuatro paredes de su cocina era demasiado para el abuelo.

—¡Por lo que más quieras, Guille, para ya! —protestó.

—Es para los partidos de fútbol, abuelo —dijo Guille.

—Ya sé para qué es —dijo el abuelo—. No soy lerdo. Pero no vas a usarla dentro de esta casa.

Era el día de la semana en que el abuelo solía ir a la biblioteca a cambiar sus libros. Había terminado de leerse *Buena forma física para pilotos de caza y desarrollo muscular; mi mé-*

todo, por el capitán J. P. Lombardero, y estaba ansioso por averiguar si habían devuelto ya *Halterofilia para la tercera edad*. Le preguntó a Guille si le apetecía ir con él.

—Iremos en autobús y volveremos echando una carrerita —dijo.

A Guille no le entusiasmaba la idea de correr con el abuelo después de lo que había pasado cuando se dejaron la llave dentro, pero siempre le divertía un viaje en autobús al centro. Y además no tenía otra cosa que hacer.

El abuelo se puso el chándal, y se dirigieron a la parada del autobús. El abuelo llevaba sus libros para la biblioteca, y Guille su carraca futbolera. Cada poco trecho, Guille, sintiéndose a salvo junto al abuelo, agitaba la carraca y aullaba:

—¡Atleeeeti! ¡Atleeeeti!

Llegó el autobús y subieron al piso de arriba. El abuelo decía que el ejercicio de subir era sano y que se respiraba mucho aire fresco sentándose delante con las ventanas abiertas. Había otros pasajeros en el piso de arriba, y ninguno de ellos parecía disfrutar con el vendaval que entraba en el autobús ni con la ca-

rraca de Guille. A los dos minutos ya habían bajado a quejarse furiosos al conductor:

—¡Ese ruido! ¡Es espantoso! ¡Haga el favor de hacer algo ahora mismo!

El conductor, al contrario del abuelo de Guille, no pensaba que subir las escaleras fuera para él un ejercicio sano, y además tenía que conducir su autobús. Pero tampoco a él le gustaba el estruendo de la carraca, así que dejó el volante y subió a ver qué estaba pasando.

No obstante, desde que el conductor puso el pie en el peldaño inferior de la escalera hasta que llegó arriba, ocurrió algo que es importante que conozcáis.

Guille, desmadrado con la excitación, al agitar su carraca le había atizado un buen carracazo a su abuelo detrás de la oreja. El golpe le asustó y le dolió al abuelo. Primero, dio un grito de angustia y sorpresa. Segundo, le lanzó a Guille un manotazo fallido. Tercero, le arrancó a Guille la carraca de las manos y empezó a girarla tratando de sacudirle a Guille con ella. Y cuarto, rugió:

—¡Atleeeti, atleeeti! ¡Te voy a dar yo a ti Atleeeti!

Y desde luego que le dio. Pero lo que el conductor vio fue sólo a un caballero de edad vestido con un deslumbrante chándal, agitando una carraca sobre su cabeza y gritando:

—¡Atleeeti! ¡Atleeeti!

Aquello le bastó. Se precipitó al pasillo y agarró al abuelo por el brazo.

—¡Fuera ahora mismo! !Vamos, fuera! ¡Ultras del demonio! ¡Un hombre de sus años! ¡Debería darle vergüenza!

—¿Qué?... ¿Qué? —gritó el abuelo, tratando de colocarse el sonotone en el oído—. ¿Qué?... ¿Qué?

—¡A mí no me venga con qué, qué, colega! ¡Salga de mi autobús antes de que llame a un policía!

Y mientras lo decía, agarró al abuelo por el cuello y el chándal y tiró de él escaleras abajo hasta sacarlo del autobús. Guille recogió los libros de la biblioteca y le siguió. Todos miraban por las ventanillas, y los peatones se paraban a mirar haciendo gestos de desaprobación:

—¡Es vergonzoso!

—¡Un viejo de esa edad!

—¡Algunos son peores que niños!

Cuando el autobús arrancó, el conductor le gritó al abuelo:

—¿Por qué no se busca unos libros, como ese chaval, y se dedica a hacer cosas más propias de su edad?

—Abuelo... —dijo Guille.

—¿Qué?... ¿Qué?... —seguía diciendo el abuelo.

—¿Me puedes devolver mi carraca?

El abuelo aspiró profundamente y dio un paso hacia Guille. Pero Guille no se quedó quieto. Se dio la vuelta y huyó mientras el abuelo, pulverizando su marca personal, corría tras él por la acera a grandes zancadas.

6 GUILLE Y EL REGALO
DE CUMPLEAÑOS

GUILLE sólo había
ido a tres fiestas en su vida. No contaba los
de su prima Rita porque, en primer lugar,
Rita tenía que invitar a Guille, y, en segundo
lugar, porque sólo había chicas: el único chico era él. Los tres cumpleaños habían sido de
chicos de su clase, pero luego no habían vuelto a invitarle. La verdad era que a las madres
de sus compañeros no les gustaba demasiado
Guille. No les gustaban sus pantalones, no les
gustaba que le saliera la camisa por fuera de
los pantalones, no les gustaban sus modales
en la mesa. Todas echaban la culpa a Guille
cuando, en vez de jugar a juegos de los que
se juegan en las fiestas, todos los chicos se

dedicaban a trepar por los muebles y se peleaban por el suelo. No era realmente culpa de Guille, pero la cara de Guille era de esas que hacen que a uno le echen siempre la culpa de todo.

Cuando se acercaba el cumpleaños de alguien y se repartían las invitaciones, Guille casi nunca encontraba una encima de su pupitre. En el fondo de su corazón, aquello le dolía. Primero porque a nadie le gusta ser siempre aquel al que no invitan, y segundo porque Guille lo pasaba muy bien en las fiestas. No en las de su prima Rita, claro. Aunque, si hay que ser sinceros, las meriendas de su prima eran fantásticas: mermelada, helados, pasteles... ¡El completo!

Sin embargo, una mañana, al entrar todos a clase en mogollón después del recreo, había unos sobres de color azul colocados en diez pupitres. Uno de los sobres estaba en el pupitre de Guille y llevaba escrito su nombre. Guille lo abrió y encontró dentro una tarjeta de invitación a la fiesta de cumpleaños de Ricardo Bolaños.

Ricardo era un chico nuevo que sólo lle-

vaba en la escuela una o dos semanas. No
tenía aún muchos amigos, y su madre pensaba que podía ser una buena idea invitar a
algunos compañeros de clase a su merienda
de cumpleaños. Dijo que podía invitar a diez,
a los diez que él quisiera. La madre no sabía
todavía quién era Guille, ni tampoco conocía
a las otras madres que sí lo sabían.

Guille se quedó encantado.

—¡Qué genial! ¡Gracias, Ricardo! —exclamó.

La fiesta era dos semanas después, y Guille inició inmediatamente la cuenta atrás del gran acontecimiento: catorce días para el cumpleaños de Ricardo..., trece días para el cumpleaños de Ricardo..., doce días para el cumpleaños de Ricardo... Cuando faltaban nueve días para el cumpleaños de Ricardo, a Guille le asaltó un pensamiento realmente preocupante: ¿Qué le iba a regalar a Ricardo? Era importante que fuera un buen regalo, porque Guille tenía la sensación de que no le invitaban a demasiados cumpleaños porque sus regalos eran muy poco emocionantes. A fin de cuentas, unos pañuelos, ¿para qué los iba a querer un chico? Y Guille siempre regalaba pañuelos porque su madre trabajaba a tiempo parcial en un taller de pañuelos, y podía conseguirlos baratos.

—Y siempre se usan —decía la madre de Guille.

Guille decidió ver algunos escaparates. Si era capaz de encontrar algo verdaderamente fantástico y no demasiado caro, quizá podría convencer a su madre de comprarlo en lugar de los pañuelos. Guille se pasó tres horas mirando escaparates de jugueterías. Había mon-

tones de cosas fantásticas: un submarino que
podía sumergirse y emerger en la bañera; un
traje de Batman; un equipo de detective completo, con lupa, guantes y polvo para encontrar huellas dactilares; un tanque que se ma-
nejaba con mando a distancia; una máquina
de vapor auténtica... Bueno, una lista inter-
minable de cosas fantásticas si uno tuviera el
dinero. Y Guille no tenía el dinero.

Abordó a su mamá aquella misma noche.

Dijo como de pasada:

—He visto algunas cosas fantásticas que
podría llevarle a Ricardo de regalo de cumpleaños.

—Conseguiré en el trabajo un par de pañuelos bonitos —fue la contestación de su
mamá—. Es un regalo que siempre se usa.

Y pasaron los días: ocho días para el cumpleaños de Ricardo..., siete días para el cumpleaños de Ricardo..., seis días para el cumpleaños de Ricardo... Y cada día que pasaba,
Guille sabía con mayor certeza que su regalo
sería el más aburrido de todos los que ten-
dría Ricardo. Se sentía tan desgraciado que
hubiera preferido que jamás le hubieran in-
vitado.

Llegó el sábado. La fiesta iba a empezar a las cinco y media, así que, después de comer, Guille tuvo que lavarse a fondo y ponerse una camisa limpia y una corbata. Su madre rastrilló con el peine su pelo enmarañado y pelirrojo y le recitó las advertencias de rigor: que si quería alguna cosa, esperara a que se la ofrecieran en vez de abalanzarse sobre ella; que comiera con la boca cerrada; que no soplara por la pajita de la naranjada; que pidiera perdón si se le escapaba un eructo; y que le diera las gracias a la madre de Ricardo por haberle recibido en su casa. Consiguió escaparse a las cinco en punto diciendo que iba a pasarse a saludar un momento al abuelo por el camino.

Por una vez, el abuelo no estaba ocupado con sus aparatos para el desarrollo muscular. Llevaba puestos unos pantalones viejos y un jersey muy, muy viejo, y estaba cubierto de polvo y telarañas.

—¡Estoy ordenando la cueva de Alibabá!

Guille siguió a su abuelo escaleras arriba y, tras subir unos cuantos escalones desvencijados, llegaron al desván. Aquélla era la cueva

de Alibabá del abuelo. Allí, en la oscuridad que protegía el tejado, el abuelo conservaba todos los tesoros que había ido guardando. Tesoros o cachivaches, según se mirara. Había cajones, cajas, baúles, latas, sacos, atestados de cosas hasta que alguien los abriera; periódicos, trapos, cuadros y espejos apoyados en la pared, mesas, sillas y percheros sujetándose amontonados unos contra otros, y toda clase de objetos colgando de las vigas de madera.

Guille había estado allí antes, una vez que el abuelo decidió —al menos eso era lo que había dicho— poner orden. Naturalmente, no puso orden alguno. Se limitó a pasar una tarde estupenda husmeando, rebuscando y recordando todas las cosas que le habían sucedido en sus tiempos. En aquel momento, si no hubiera sido por lo del regalo de Ricardo, Guille se hubiera sentido allí, en la cueva de Alibabá, con su abuelo, más contento que una pulga en el pelo de un perro. Pero ni siquiera la emoción que suponía el montón de trastos del abuelo esperándole en la oscuridad podía hacer que se olvidase del lamentable paquetillo del que era portador.

—A ver, ¿qué pasa contigo? —dijo el abuelo—. ¿Te deben y no te pagan?

—No —dijo Guille.

El abuelo tomó en sus manos un collar de dientes de tiburón y se arrellanó en una vieja butaca.

—Pues esto —dijo— me lo dio el jefe Opon-Opa a cambio de mi vieja pipa y media libra de tabaco de picadura. Aquéllos eran tiempos en los que yo no sabía lo que me hacía, claro está, y por eso fumaba. Fumar es

muy malo para la respiración, Guille. Te la destroza, y no puedes ponerte en forma si no respiras como es debido... A propósito de respirar... ¿Te he hablado alguna vez de los tiempos en que fui pescador de perlas en los arrecifes coralinos de la Gran Barrera Australiana? ¿No? Bien, pues ocurrió lo siguiente... —y el abuelo se enfrascó en una de sus largas historias.

Guille se sentó sobre un caparazón de tortuga gigante y dejó que su mirada se perdiese en la penumbra que reinaba bajo las tejas del desván. Y mientras el abuelo divagaba sobre cómo se había tirado al mar desde una goleta, buceando con un cuchillo entre los dientes, los ojos de Guille se fueron acostumbrando a la tenue luz de la bombilla que el abuelo había subido hasta el desván colgada de un trozo de cordón. Pronto, Guille se dio cuenta de que tenía la vista clavada en una cabeza fea y pequeña. Pensó que debía de ser una de esas cabezas de goma que se compran en las jugueterías. Esas cabezas con expresiones espantosas y grandes pelambreras. Guille estaba fascinado por ella, quizá porque su gesto era el reflejo de cómo se sentía él mismo.

—Abuelo, ¿qué es eso? —dijo Guille.

—¿Qué...? ¿Qué es qué? —preguntó el abuelo, que odiaba que le interrumpieran cuando estaba contando una historia.

—Esa cabeza tan pequeña —dijo Guille, señalándola con el dedo.

—¿Dónde... ? ¡Ah, eso!

El abuelo se levantó trabajosamente de la butaca y desató la cabeza de la cuerda de la que colgaba.

—Aquí la tienes —dijo, dejándola caer en el regazo de Guille—. Bonita, ¿eh?

Guille la levantó en el aire. Era maciza y mucho más pesada de lo que se había imaginado. Guille miró su cara. Bonita, lo que se dice bonita..., no lo era en absoluto. Sus ojillos miraban a Guille con malignidad y tenía la boca torcida en un gesto de ira.

—¿Qué es, abuelo? —volvió a preguntar Guille.

El abuelo rió entre dientes.

—Pregunta en todo caso de quién es... Es la cabeza de un indígena del Amazonas.

—¡Venga ya! —dijo Guille—. ¡No me tomes el pelo, abuelo!

—Hablo en serio —dijo el abuelo—. Ahora no es mayor que mi puño, pero antes era

tan grande como tu cabeza o la mía... ¡Antes de que el salvaje que la rebanó la redujera, quiero decir!

—¡Puaj! —dijo Guille.

—Sí señor —dijo el abuelo, animándose otra vez—. Cazadores de cabezas. Eso es lo que son en las selvas del Amazonas. Cuando matan a un enemigo, le cortan la cabeza, la vacían, la deshuesan y la reducen hasta dejarla de este tamaño. Luego se la cuelgan con las otras alrededor de la cintura. Coleccionan cabezas como si fueran copas o medallas.

Guille palpó cautelosamente la horrenda cabezuela. Era espantosa, pero al mismo tiempo era fantástica. Bueno, cuando les dijera a los otros que su abuelo tenía una cabeza reducida... Se pondrían verdes de envidia. Todos querrían tener una. Darían cualquier cosa por tenerla... Y, de pronto, Guille tuvo una de sus estupendas ideas. ¿Qué pasaría si pudiera darle a Ricardo una cabeza reducida auténtica de regalo de cumpleaños? Sería sensacional... Guille podía hacerles perder el tiempo a sus profesores, pero él nunca lo perdía. Así que se la pidió a su abuelo:

—Abuelo —dijo—, ¿me la podrías dar?

—¿Cómo? —dijo el abuelo, desconcertado—. ¿Quieres decir, darte mi cabeza reducida?

—¡Venga, abuelo! —le apremió Guille—. Sé gene... Te daré un par de pañuelos nuevos por ella.

—Bueno... —dijo el abuelo—. La verdad es que no creo que la disfrute ya por mucho tiempo, y seguro que tu madre tampoco lo hará cuando yo me haya ido. Así que vale, puedes quedártela.

—¡Qué genial! ¡Gracias! —dijo Guille—. Ahora tengo que darme prisa, abuelo. Voy a un cumpleaños.

Cuando Guille llegó a casa de Ricardo, vio que era mucho más elegante que la suya. En vez de una aldaba con la que poder usar su llamada especial, había que apretar un botón que hizo sonar dentro de la casa un carillón con una suave melodía de campanas. Guille nunca había oído un timbre como aquél, de modo que, antes de que la mamá de Ricardo pudiera abrirle, ya había apretado el botón seis veces.

—¡Caramba! —dijo con una ancha sonrisa—. ¡Ya estábamos impacientes!

Un rápido vistazo a la cara de Guille, su pelo, sus pantalones y su camisa la convencieron. Aquél no era, pensó, un compañero adecuado para su Ricardo.

—Bien... Pasa, querido. ¿Cómo te llamas?

En un gran salón estaban todos jugando a ese juego en el que, si llevas prendida en la espalda la palabra *gordo*, tienes que encontrar a alguien que lleve en la suya la palabra *flaco*. Estaban allí los otros chicos de la clase de Guille, unos desconocidos que eran primos de Ricardo, y tres chicas que eran primas o hijas de las amigas íntimas de la madre de Ricardo.

Cuando Guille entró en la habitación, los chicos que le conocían se apiñaron a su alrededor; los demás se quedaron mirándole con curiosidad.

—Llegas tarde —dijo alguien.

—Lo siento —dijo Guille—, pero tenía que ocuparme de algo... de algo importante... ¡Ah, feliz cumpleaños, Ricardo!

Se produjo un incómodo y embarazoso silencio. Aquél era el momento en que se suponía que Guille tenía que darle a Ricardo su

regalo; pero bien a la vista estaba que Guille no tenía nada en las manos. La madre de Ricardo, desconfiando de la repentina calma, permanecía expectante al fondo del salón. Todos los ojos estaban clavados en Guille.

—La verdad —dijo Guille cuando supo que era el centro de la atención general— es que tenía que ir a un sitio especial a buscar tu regalo. Ni siquiera he tenido tiempo de envolverlo en papel de regalo. Lo llevo en el bolsillo.

Los chicos de la escuela de Guille, que sabían lo que significaban sus bolsillos, se preguntaron qué clase de porquería iba a tener la cara de ofrecele a Ricardo.

—¡Y aquí está! —dijo Guille. Y, agarrando el pelo del indígena del Amazonas, empezó a tirar de él sacándolo del bolsillo.

Era un pelo muy largo y muy espeso. Poco a poco, centímetro a centímetro, las greñas lacias y negras fueron derramándose fuera del bolsillo, dándole a todo el mundo la sensación de que el muslo de Guille había reventado y se le estaba saliendo el relleno. Por fin, Guille levantó el brazo, y la cabeza reducida

propiamente dicha emergió y quedó balanceándose, colgada de su propio pelo.

—¡Puaj!

Eso fue lo que dijeron todos a coro. Luego, los chicos se acercaron en masa.

—¿Qué es, Guille? ¿Dónde la has conseguido? —preguntaron ruidosamente.

Ricardo tomó posesión de su regalo y lo observó de cerca. Empezaba a sentirse orgulloso de ser el propietario de un objeto tan extraordinario, pero no estaba seguro de que se pudiera considerar como un verdadero regalo.

La madre de Ricardo, que no podía verlo con claridad, se acercó diciendo:

—Deja que mamá lo vea, Ricardo.

Sujetó la cabeza entre las puntas de los dedos con un gesto de repugnancia.

—¡Puaj! —se estremeció—. ¿Qué es esta cosa, Guille?

—Una cabeza —dijo Guille.

—Eso ya lo veo —dijo la mamá de Ricardo—. Pero ¿quién la ha hecho?

—Bueno, en realidad no las hacían —dijo Guille, deseando poder explicar todo lo maravilloso que era su regalo.

—¿Qué quieres decir con lo de no las... bueno, no la han hecho?

—Pues es que —dijo Guille— es de verdad, ¿sabe? Es una cabeza humana reducida de verdad. Los salvajes del Amazonas las cortan, les quitan los sesos y...

Pero nadie estaba escuchando su explicación. Con nuevos gritos de ¡puaj!, todos se apartaron del repugnante objeto que sujetaba la mamá de Ricardo. Y en cuanto a la mamá de Ricardo... ¡Bueno!... Cuando comprendió del todo el significado de las palabras de Guille, su cara se llenó de asco y espanto.

—¡Oh, Dios mío! —gritó, y arrojó la cabeza lejos como si le hubiera mordido.

Sus gritos continuaron mientras la cabeza volaba por el aire y caía en un gran cuenco de crema y bizcocho en almíbar que estaba en mitad de la atestada mesa. Allí desapareció despacio, igual que los malos que se hunden en los pantanos de las películas de Tarzán. La sustancia pringosa se cerró sobre aquellas facciones pequeñas y perversas, pero las largas greñas parecían brotar de la crema y arrastrarse sobre los pasteles, bollos y mermeladas como una exótica planta trepadora.

Guille había confiado en que su regalo fuera la sensación de la fiesta, pero no había previsto que la sensación resultara tan espectacular.

La merienda, naturalmente, se había echado a perder. A nadie le apetecía realmente comer nada, y menos que nada la crema con bizcocho en almíbar. De hecho, nadie se acercó a la mesa hasta que el papá de Ricardo llegó a casa y pescó la cabeza con unas tenazas. La verdad es que tenía un aspecto aún peor que antes, porque la pasta de papel que el abuelo había usado para hacerla muchos años atrás había empezado a ablandarse y uno de los ojos de cristal se había caído...

Los chicos se echaron a reír y se pusieron a darle a Guille palmadas en la espalda. Todos dijeron que era la mejor broma que habían visto en su vida. Bueno, todos no: la madre de Ricardo no consiguió entender en absoluto qué tenía aquello de divertido...

7 GUILLE Y EL CONCIERTO DE VERANO

HABÍA montones de cosas que Guille era capaz de hacer. Aunque quien escuchara a su madre podría pensar que era una auténtica nulidad, no era cierto. Para empezar, era capaz de silbar con los dedos en la boca mucho más fuerte que ningún otro chico de la escuela. Además, era capaz de eructar siempre que quería, con unos eructos potentes y retumbantes que le salían de lo más profundo del estómago. Lo malo era que los mayores no valoraban tales habilidades. Desde luego, la madre de Guille no las valoraba en absoluto. Y cuando el señor Centenera redactaba los informes escolares de Guille, jamás escribía: «Progresa notablemen-

te en los eructos», o «Sus silbidos son sobresalientes para un chico de su edad». Según el señor Centenera, que siempre trataba de fijarse en las mejores cualidades de sus alumnos, Guille desconocía la ortografía, no sabía utilizar los signos de puntuación, no se había aprendido nunca la tabla de multiplicar, no era capaz de restar llevando las decenas cuando el número de arriba era menor que el de abajo, ignoraba los días que tiene un año bisiesto y jamás llevaba al colegio la ropa de educación física los días que tocaba.

Pero lo que peor hacía Guille era cantar. Era una pena porque, aunque no le interesaba ninguna otra cosa de las que era incapaz de hacer, a Guille le entusiasmaba cantar. Y cantaba muchísimo. Cuando no estaba silbando con los dedos o practicando unos cuantos eructos triples, cantaba.

El canturreo de Guille era parte del ruido de fondo de la clase, pero eso es algo que no entenderéis hasta que os lo explique mejor. Cuando al señor Centenera le nombraron profesor de 3.º D, aquel ruido le preocupó, y al descubrir que el gemido procedía de Guille, se apresuró a preguntarle dónde le dolía.

Eso hubiera podido ofender a Guille si hubiera sido un chico sensible, pero lo único que hizo fue sorprenderle, y en cuanto le explicó que no le dolía nada, siguió con su canturreo. Prefiero decir su canturreo, y no su canción, porque Guille no cantaba ninguna melodía reconocible —con un principio, una parte central y un final—, y además no solía haber letra.

El señor Centenera, que, él sí, era muy sen-

sible y musical, se sentaba detrás de su mesa mirando a Guille con pesadumbre. No sólo, pensaba, tenía en su clase a un niño que no sabía si echar se escribe con una o dos haches, sino que además era un niño que iba a resultar difícil de silenciar.

Para el señor Centenera, ya era terrible que Guille cantara solo; pero cuando se unía a otros para cantar a coro, en las solemnidades o en las clases de música, aquello era un tormento. Por muy vigorosamente que hicieran resonar sus voces el resto de los niños de la escuela o por muy fuerte que marcara la melodía en las teclas del piano la señorita Pradillo, siempre se oía, dominándolo todo, la voz de Guille graznando cualquier nota menos la debida.

Durante mucho tiempo, el señor Centenera consideró la voz de Guille como una de esas cosas por las que le daban cada mes una cantidad de dinero a condición de que la mantuviera —la voz de Guille, se entiende— encerrada con garantías de seguridad dentro de la escuela, de forma que los ciudadanos decentes no pudieran tropezarse con ella. Así que apretaba los dientes de nueve a cuatro y

luego se pasaba veladas enteras escuchando discos y se iba de vacaciones a solitarias casas de campo.

Hasta que llegó el concierto de verano.

Al terminar el curso, antes de las vacaciones de verano, los niños de la escuela de Guille dedicaban un concierto a sus padres. En él se esperaba que cada clase hiciera alguna aportación musical. Pues bien, el caso es que el señor Centenera no sólo amaba la música, sino que incluso intentaba componerla él mismo, así es que había compuesto una canción especial para su clase. Y, lo que es más, pensaba que era bastante buena. Pero... había que contar con Guille. La canción no sobreviviría si Guille cantaba.

¿Y cuál era el problema?, preguntaréis. Pues precisamente decirle a Guille que no cantara.

La cosa no tenía un arreglo demasiado fácil. De entrada porque, en la escuela de Guille, la directora insistía en que cantar era algo en lo que debían participar todos, y no sólo los que lo hacían bien. Y el señor Centenera estaba de acuerdo. No esperaba que todos sus

alumnos tuvieran el don de una voz angélica. Pero todo tenía un límite; o, en cualquier caso, el señor Centenera creía que debía tenerlo. Y Guille estaba leguas y leguas más allá de la raya divisoria. Del lado malo, claro está.

Al mismo tiempo, el señor Centenera tenía también sentido de la justicia. Creía que había que ser justo e intentaba serlo él mismo. Sus alumnos no siempre creían que era justo, pero la justicia era en todo momento el ideal que perseguía. Por eso, en aquella situación no pudo decidirse a agarrar a Guille de la oreja, retorcérsela salvajemente y gruñir: «¡Mantén la boca cerrada o te muelo a palos!». Hubiera sido lo más fácil, y Guille le hubiera entendido inmediatamente. Pero el señor Centenera decidió intentar métodos más sutiles.

Después del primer ensayo, aunque sin muchas esperanzas, dejó caer:

—Supongo que no habrá nadie que no quiera participar...

Por lo que a Guille respectaba, el señor Centenera suponía bien. En cambio, tres de sus mejores chicas levantaron la mano, y tu-

vo que aplastar aquel conato de rebelión diciendo:

—¡Bobadas! ¡Naturalmente que cantaréis!

La canción que había escrito el señor Centenera trataba de indios americanos y tenía un magnífico acompañamiento de tambor durante toda la canción. La mayor parte de los niños, sobre todo los chicos, opinaba que era muy emocionante.

Danzan los indios de la pradera,
porom-pom, porom-pom, porom-pom-pom-pom,
su belicosa danza guerrera;
porom-pom, porom-pom, porom-pom-pom-pom,
gritos, pinturas, hachas de guerra,
porom-pom, porom-pom, porom-pom-pom-pom,
suenan tambores, tiembla la tierra,
porom-pom, porom-pom, porom-pom-pom-pom.

Eran ocho versos.

A Guille le parecieron estupendos, sobre todo los del *porom-pom*. Al señor Centenera no le emocionó que Guille admirase su canción. Aquello hacía que fuera más difícil evitar que Guille intentara cantarla. Les explicó

el problema a sus colegas en el cuarto de profesores.

—Tiene usted que emplear un poco de psicología —le dijo la señora Pedernales.

—¿Qué quiere decir con eso? —dijo el señor Centenera.

—Quiero decir —dijo la señora Pedernales azotando con su bolígrafo rojo una pila de libros de matemáticas—, quiero decir que haga usted que se ocupe de algo que no sea cantar, pero sin que note lo que a usted le preocupa de verdad.

—Pero ¿de qué se va a ocupar? —gimió el señor Centenera.

—¡Por el amor de Dios, hombre! —estalló la señora Pedernales—. No sea usted tan patético. Use su iniciativa.

La señora Pedernales no había sido profesora de Guille todavía. Pero iba a serlo el próximo curso, y al señor Centenera le encantaba la perspectiva.

Aquella sugerencia, no obstante, hizo reflexionar al señor Centenera. Estuvo pensando el resto del día y, cuando llegó la hora del siguiente ensayo, tenía ya una idea. De forma

que, cuando toda la clase estuvo alineada para cantar, el señor Centenera les explicó su plan:

—Para lograr el ambiente ideal —dijo—, quiero que alguien se disfrace de indio, se ponga la pintura de guerra y toque el tam-tam.

Se alzaron inmediatamente cuarenta manos. Sólo había treinta niños en 3.º D, pero algunos chicos levantaron las dos manos para tener más posibilidades. Hubieran levantado tres si las hubieran tenido.

El señor Centenera vaciló. Hizo como si la elección fuera a resultarle difícil. Pero, después de que su mirada perdida planeara sobre Guille unas cuantas veces, acabó por fijarla en él.

—Sí... Me parece —dijo—, me parece que Guille es el hombre indicado para ese papel.

La decisión fue acogida con un suspiro general de desencanto, y el señor Centenera supo que acababa de ganarse veintinueve enemigos. El costo era alto, pero la canción lo valía, pensó.

—Muy bien, Guille —dijo alegremente el señor Centenera—, puedes salir del coro ahora mismo.

Guille parecía perplejo y no se movió.

—Bueno, supongo que no puedes cantar y tocar el tambor al mismo tiempo —dijo el señor Centenera.

—¡Ah! —dijo Guille.

—Claro que —dijo el señor Centenera— si prefieres no ser tú el que...

Volvieron a levantarse unas cuantas manos ansiosas.

—No, no. No se preocupe por eso —dijo Guille—. Pero ¿qué hay de las otras canciones?

—No sabes cuánto lo siento —dijo el señor Centenera—, pero si estás disfrazado con tus plumas y tu pintura de guerra, no puedes quedarte en el coro de ninguna manera. En el mejor de los casos, echarías a perder la sorpresa a los papás y a las mamás.

—Ya —dijo Guille, que entendía que la cosa tenía su fundamento—. Pero sí podría tocar el tambor y cantar, ¿no?

—La verdad es que no —dijo el señor Centenera suave pero firmemente—. No quedaría bien.

—Vale —dijo Guille.

El corazón del señor Centenera le bailaba de alegría en el pecho. Había sido mucho más fácil de lo que jamás se hubiera atrevido a esperar. Y cuando empezó a sentirse culpable por ello, se dijo a sí mismo que Guille iba a hacer algo que todos los demás niños de la clase estaban deseando para sí mismos. En pocas palabras, que le había hecho un favor a Guille.

—Y ahora vamos a empezar de una vez —dijo.

—Por favor...

—¿Sí, Guille?

—¿Dónde está mi tambor?

—Todavía no lo he conseguido.

—¡Ah... ya! ¿Y con qué puedo ensayar ahora?

—Quizá por esta vez lo mejor es que te dediques a escuchar —dijo el señor Centenera—, hasta que el ritmo te entre bien en la cabeza.

—Podría usar la lata grande en la que solemos guardar la plastilina —sugirió Guille.

—Ah, me parece muy bien —dijo el señor Centenera, impaciente por empezar—. Bue-

no, ¿estáis todos listos? Recordad que hay que darle más fuerza al *suenan tambores, tiembla la tierra*. Vamos allá... Un, dos, tres, cuatro.

Toda la clase entró a coro cuando la batuta se movió hacia abajo, y un compás y medio más tarde entró Guille con su lata de plastilina. En aquel mismo momento, el señor Centenera se dio cuenta de que había metido la pata hasta el fondo. Porque si era cierto que Guille cantaba fatal, no había palabras para describir lo horrorosamentemente que golpeaba la lata de plastilina. Por más que le había gustado lo del *porom-pom*, era absolutamente incapaz de producir un *porom-pom* en una lata de plastilina. Transmitía tanto sentido del ritmo como una cabra metida en un baúl de hojalata.

—¡Su padre! ¡Menudo follón!

Eso no fue lo que dijo el señor Centenera. Fue lo que dijeron todos los demás niños. Pero era más o menos lo mismo que pensaba el señor Centenera.

—¡Va a cargárselo todo! —vociferaban los compañeros de Guille—. ¡Lo va a destrozar!

—¡Está bien, está bien! —dijo el señor

114

Centenera—. Sólo es su primer ensayo. Hay que darle otra oportunidad.

Naturalmente, el señor Centenera sabía que daba igual la cantidad de oportunidades que se le dieran a Guille. Cuando acabó el ensayo, se llevó a Guille aparte y le dijo que por fin había decidido que otro niño se encargase del tambor y que él volvería al coro.

«Al menos así», pensó el señor Centenera, «los demás tendrán una posibilidad de que se les oiga».

Las tres semanas de ensayos que siguieron fueron un tormento para el señor Centenera, mientras Guille graznaba, gemía y aullaba a su aire todo el cancionero de 3.º D.

En el último ensayo, Guille estornudó. Un poco de polvo o alguna otra cosa se le había metido en la nariz. El señor Centenera encontró algo a lo que agarrarse —el estornudo de Guille, no su nariz, claro—, y después del ensayo llamó a Guille y le puso ante los ojos un billete de mil que sacó de su billetera.

—Menudo resfriado has pescado, Guille —dijo el señor Centenera—. No me sorprendería nada que luego te doliera la garganta. Y con un resfriado y dolor de garganta no hay manera de que cantes en el concierto de esta noche. Será mejor que te limites a estar en el coro y mover los labios como si cantaras... ¿Me entiendes? Quizá con esto puedas comprarte unos caramelos que te quiten el dolor. ¿Te parece bien?

El billete a la vista hizo que todo le pare-

ciera a Guille perfectamente bien en aquel momento.

—Muchas gracias —dijo, y hasta se las arregló para toser mientras se metía el dinero en el bolsillo.

El señor Centenera se sentía muy culpable. ¡Haber llegado a sobornar a un alumno para que no cantara! ¡Qué vergüenza!

Aquella tarde, a la hora en que 3.° D se reunía ruidosamente en su aula antes de dirigirse al salón de actos, las atareadas fauces de Guille despedían un penetrante aroma de trufas de chocolate y caramelos de menta. Era como atravesar las puertas de una fábrica de dulces. El señor Centenera dirigió una furtiva mirada a Guille, y Guille le correspondió con otra llena de inocencia.

Por fin le llegó el turno a 3.° D. El señor Centenera levantó los brazos y contempló las hileras de rostros impacientes. Se detuvo en Guille, y Guille le dedicó una amplia sonrisa.

«Menos mal», pensó el señor Centenera, «que el chico tiene sentido del humor, ¡bendito sea Dios!».

Con el corazón aliviado, hizo una señal con la cabeza a la señorita Pradillo, sentada al piano, y empezó a dirigir la primera canción de su clase. Y entonces fue cuando la fe del señor Centenera en la bondad de la infancia se extinguió definitivamente, en concreto desde que el primer graznido de Guille chirrió en cada uno de los oídos que se habían dado cita en el salón de actos. Guille estaba cantando. Guille continuaba cantando. Guille siguió cantando y desafinando a su aire en absolutamente todas las canciones.

—Esperaba —dijo el señor Centenera cuando acorraló a Guille más tarde en un rincón—, esperaba que te doliera la garganta esta noche.

—Ya —dijo Guille—. Eso es lo que yo pensaba. Pero esos dulces que me dijo que me comprara creo que me han hecho efecto. Después de las dos bolsas que me he comido, ni me duele la garganta ni nada. Ah... ¿Le apetece uno?

8 GUILLE Y LA HORMA DE SU ZAPATO

A Guille nunca le habían interesado mucho los niños pequeños. Había visto unos cuantos, claro, pero nunca se había parado a fijarse en ninguno. Y sabía —aunque le resultaba muy difícil de creer— que alguna vez había sido él también un niño pequeño.

Por eso, para Guille fue una desagradable sorpresa encontrarse un buen día, sin previo aviso, con que tenía que ocuparse de Carlitos.

Carlitos aún no tenía dos años, y era de una madre y un padre que nunca lo sacaban de casa, unas cuantas casas más allá de la casa de Guille. Carlitos apenas si sabía andar. De momento, le resultaba más rápido y sencillo

gatear. Y no sabía hablar, cosa que no le importaba porque, si gritaba lo bastante fuerte durante el tiempo necesario, siempre acababa consiguiendo lo que quería.

Carlitos era el primero y único niño de su mamá, que lo adoraba y se pasaba el día entero lavando a Carlitos, vistiendo a Carlitos y dando de comer a Carlitos; y luego volviendo a lavar y vestir a Carlitos de arriba abajo otra vez. Con el resultado de que Carlitos estaba siempre inmaculadamente limpio, gordo, y muy aburrido.

Os sorprenderá enteraros de que un chico como Guille llegara a acercarse a Carlitos en algún momento con semejante madre. Y cuanto más penséis en ello, más sorprendente os parecerá. Os contaré cómo ocurrieron las cosas.

Una mañana de vacaciones, llevaron a Carlitos a casa de Guille. La madre de Carlitos tenía que ir al dentista y le pidió a la madre de Guille que se ocupara de Carlitos mientras tanto. A la madre de Guille le encantaban los niños de los demás, y solía estar dispuesta a complacer a la gente. Así que a las diez en punto llegó Carlitos, impecablemente vestido

con un pelele azul pastel en el que cualquier manchita se veía como a través de un cristal de aumento, y con una colección de juguetes esterilizados para que se entretuviera toda la mañana. Después de una letanía de repetidas instrucciones sobre la taza de leche con biscotines que había que darle a Carlitos a las once menos veinticinco, la madre de Carlitos se marchó para no llegar tarde a su cita.

—Bueno, Guille —dijo la madre de Guille después de depositar a Carlitos, rodeado de sus relucientes sonajeros y pelotas de plástico, sobre la alfombra del cuarto de estar—, tú siéntate aquí, en el sofá, a vigilar a Carlitos, mientras yo voy a la cocina a preparar la carne para tu comida.

La mamá de Guille siempre decía tu comida o tu desayuno o tu merienda, como si ella no los probara y Guille se lo comiera todo.

—¡Pero, mamá, es muy aburrido! —protestó Guille—. ¿No puedo salir a la calle y...?

—No, no puedes. Lo que sí puedes es sentarte aquí y leer tus tebeos.

Guille miró a Carlitos con ferocidad; Carlitos, por su parte, se quedó observando aten-

tamente a Guille con aire reflexivo. Ninguno de los dos dijo nada. Guille porque no quería; Carlitos porque, aunque quisiera, no podía.

—¡Qué asco de bebés! —murmuró Guille abriendo su tebeo con tan mal humor que lo rompió—. ¡Qué asco de bebés! —volvió a decir entre dientes; y se sentó a leer con aire sombrío las aventuras del Capitán Trueno mientras Carlitos se dedicaba a investigar en sus juguetes.

Cada diez minutos, más o menos, la mamá de Guille asomaba la cabeza para decir:

—¿Cómo está mi Carlitines? ¡No le quites el ojo de encima, Guille!

Y así es como habría transcurrido, con toda seguridad, la mañana si... si el abuelo no hubiera sido un fanático de la buena forma física. En realidad todo fue culpa del abuelo. Por lo menos, eso es lo que Guille dijo cuando todos le echaron la culpa a él del estado en que se encontraba Carlitos una hora después.

De pronto, alguien empezó a aporrear brutalmente la puerta de la casa y, cuando la mamá de Guille abrió, apareció en el umbral una niña pequeña que dijo casi sin aliento:

—¡Por favor, señora Gálvez!... Que mamá dice que tiene usted que venir ahora mismo... Que su padre ha vuelto a hacerse una avería.

—¡Viejo mentecato! —exclamó la madre de Guille—. ¿Qué ha hecho esta vez? Y encima yo con un bebé que cuidar...

—Mamá dice que debe usted darse prisa —insistió la niña.

—Guille —dijo la mamá de Guille precipitándose a coger su abrigo—, no le quites a Carlitos los ojos de encima mientras yo estoy fuera. Ni un solo momento. ¿Entendido?

Guille lo entendió, pero, antes de poder objetar algo, la puerta de la casa se cerró de un portazo detrás de su madre y... allí se quedó él, solo con Carlitos.

Pues bien, hay gente en este mundo que dice que a los niños pequeños no se les puede echar la culpa de nada, porque no saben lo que hacen y no son capaces de diferenciar lo que está bien de lo que está mal. Guille no está de acuerdo con esa gente. Una hora a solas con Carlitos le convenció de que los niños pequeños son personas taimadas, malévolas y sin compasión.

Tan pronto como se cerró la puerta detrás de la madre de Guille, se produjo en Carlitos un horrible cambio. Quizá alguna vez os hayan dejado estar levantados hasta muy tarde para ver una película de terror. Si es así, sabréis que siempre llega un momento en que una persona perfectamente normal sonríe y se le ven sus colmillos de vampiro. Bueno, pues a Carlitos no se le vieron precisamente unos colmillos de vampiro, pero la mirada que bri-

lló en sus ojos y la mueca malvada que iluminó su gorda cara de bebé le helaron a Guille la sangre en las venas.

Lo primero que hizo Carlitos fue agarrar todos los juguetes con los que había estado jugando y arrojárselos a Guille con una fuerza verdaderamente extraordinaria. Por suerte tenía mala puntería, pero un tentetieso de plástico que alcanzó a Guille en el menisco le hizo dar un aullido de dolor. Esto estimuló claramente el sentido del humor de Carlitos, porque soltó una risita y miró a su alrededor buscando otro proyectil. Como no encontró ninguno, se lanzó al galope hacia la puerta.

—¡Eh tú, basta ya! —dijo Guille plantándose en medio de la ruta de Carlitos.

Carlitos, viendo que no podía sortear a Guille para llegar al pasillo, aposentó en el suelo su trasero cubierto de pañales y gritó. Fue espantoso. Como cuando alguien araña despacio una pizarra, como cuando a un conductor novato le rasca una marcha en el coche, como cuando aúlla la sirena de un coche patrulla americano, todo al mismo tiempo.

—¡Basta ya! —repitió Guille, muy alarmado.

Pero Carlitos redobló su potencia hasta que Guille tuvo que apartarse de su camino. Entonces, como si alguien lo hubiera desconectado, Carlitos dejó de gritar y continuó su excursión fuera del cuarto de estar.

En el estrecho pasillo había una mesa pequeña, y sobre ella una maceta con una planta que la mamá de Guille había ido cuidando desde que era un minúsculo esqueje. Estropear la planta de su madre podía tener bastante más importancia que el valor de la vida de Guille, y Carlitos debía de saberlo, porque inmediatamente se agarró a una pata de la mesita para ponerse de pie. Guille lo vio ve-

nir, pero estaba tan petrificado por el terror que no pudo hacer nada por evitarlo. La mesita osciló y la maceta se estrelló en el suelo. Reventó como una bomba, salpicando tierra oscura y húmeda por toda la alfombra. Guille hubiera podido creer que aún quedaba algo de justicia en el mundo si la maceta le hubiera caído a Carlitos en la cabeza, pero no le cayó, de modo que, con un gorgorito de satisfacción, la criatura se abalanzó sobre el montón de tierra. La probó, se la restregó por la cara, se la echó en el pelo, se revolcó en ella y, a continuación, le tiró a Guille lo que quedaba de la desgraciada planta.

Guille trató una o dos veces de agarrar a Carlitos y tirar de él para sacarlo de la zona catastrófica. Pero sólo con que Guille le tocara, Carlitos se ponía a chillar como si Guille estuviera tratando de asesinarlo. Por fin, cuando Carlitos le hubo sacado a la tierra todo el partido posible, decidió explorar la cocina.

Violeta era la gata de la madre de Guille. Y Violeta vivía a cuerpo de reina. Es decir, que la madre de Guille se gastaba cada semana una pequeña fortuna en latas de la co-

mida para gatos favorita de Violeta. Pues bien, justo antes de salir disparada de casa, la madre de Guille había puesto en el suelo de la cocina un platillo lleno hasta arriba de *Felino Gourmet* para cuando Violeta volviera de tomar el aire en el jardín, como tenía por costumbre todos los domingos de buen tiempo. En el momento en que Carlitos entraba en la cocina, Violeta se deslizó por la abertura de la ventana, que siempre se dejaba sin cerrar del todo para que pudiera entrar y salir, y saltó ágilmente al suelo. Se acercó a su platillo y empezó a olfatear la viscosa mezcla antes de atacarla con gran voracidad.

Carlitos, que se movía más o menos a la misma altura del suelo que Violeta, vio a Violeta y vio el *Felino Gourmet*. Sin vacilar un solo segundo, se lanzó sobre ambos objetivos. En un abrir y cerrar de ojos, Violeta, con un chirriante maullido de alarma, dio un brinco hacia la ventana. Se produjo un frenético torbellino de zarpazos de sus patas traseras cuando luchó alocadamente por volver a colarse a través de la abertura y desapareció, dejando a Carlitos en posesión del platillo de *Felino Gourmet*.

Probar sólo una pizca fue suficiente para Carlitos, que, para demostrar lo que pensaba del *Felino Gourmet*, agarró el platillo y lo vació sobre su propia cabeza. Chorros de nutritiva salsa resbalaron por el rostro de Carlitos y fueron a mezclarse con la tierra que había ya formado una costra sobre su pelele. Por la risa histérica de Carlitos, era evidente que los fabricantes de *Felino Gourmet* podrían triplicar sus ventas si lo anunciaban como el producto ideal para verterlo sobre las cabezas de los bebés.

Durante los cuarenta y cinco minutos siguientes, Carlitos hizo cosas asombrosas con el contenido del cubo de la basura, una botella de detergente líquido de las que se aprietan, medio kilo de tomates y un barreño de ropa de mesa que la mamá de Guille había dejado metida en jabón. Cuarenta y cinco minutos es lo que corrieron las agujas del reloj, pero a Guille le parecieron toda una vida. Y mientras aguardaba con desesperación la vuelta de su mamá, no sabía sí su deseo de que volviera para rescatarlo de Carlitos era más intenso que su temor por el jaleo que iba a armar cuando descubriera el estado en que

estaban Carlitos y su propia casa. Y es que ni por un momento se le ocurrió a Guille que no fueran a echarle la culpa a él.

Por fin se oyeron voces. La madre de Guille se había encontrado con la madre de Carlitos, y estaba intentando explicarle por qué había tenido que dejar a Carlitos en la casa y lo seguro que estaba al cuidado de Guille. Enseguida se oyó el crujido de la llave en la puerta de la calle. Y luego... Bueno, pareció el fin del mundo cuando la madre de Carlitos chilló, la madre de Guille gritó y Carlitos aulló, mientras el pobre Guille trataba de explicar que en realidad no era culpa suya.

Después de aquello, Guille no fue nunca el mismo. Ya no era que no le interesaran los niños pequeños; ahora le producían terror. Si veía que un cochecito de niño se le acercaba por la acera, cruzaba al otro lado de la calle, y era capaz de dar un rodeo a toda la manzana con tal de evitar pasar por delante de la casa de Carlitos.

Un día, en la escuela, el profesor propuso un juego de palabras a la clase de Guille. Le decía a cada uno de los alumnos una palabra y tenían que responderle inmediatamente con

la primera que se les pasara por la cabeza. Cuando le llegó el turno a Guille, le tocó la palabra *monstruo* y su respuesta fue instantánea:

—¡Bebé!

ÍNDICE